DON'T LOOK BACK

JO SPAIN

QUERCUS

First published in Great Britain in 2023 by

QUERCUS

Quercus Editions Ltd
Carmelite House
50 Victoria Embankment
London EC4Y 0DZ

An Hachette UK company

A CIP catalogue record for this book is available
from the British Library

HB ISBN 978 1 52941 917 7
TPB ISBN 978 1 52941 918 4
EBOOK ISBN 978 1 52941 919 1

10 9 8 7 6 5 4 3 2 1

Typeset by CC Book Production

Printed and bound in Great Britain by Clays Ltd, Elcograf S.p.A.

Papers used by Quercus Editions Ltd are from well-managed forests and other responsible sources.

DON'T LOOK BACK

Also by Jo Spain

PART I

Saint-Thérèse
21 September 2022
Present

All is not lost, the unconquerable will.

The words of the epic poem fill Luke's head as he walks on the soft white sand, grimacing as he reminds himself that, today, paradise is lost.

Normality beckons.

The beach is small by the island's standards. He has already covered one length of the cove and is now on the return leg. This is one of the private bays, set aside for a certain kind of tourist. Pristine, idyllic – perfection for a small fortune.

Through the hazy, late morning sun, he can see his and Rose's villa. There are tall palm trees to either side, a burst of blushed pink bougainvillea against its white wooden slats.

He walks close to the water's edge, letting the foam from the gently encroaching waves splash against his feet. In his left hand, he holds a bottle of island-brand beer by the neck. It's too early for alcohol but he's still on holiday. At least for the next few hours.

It's as relaxed as he's felt in . . . ever.

What he wouldn't give for one more day.

Luke thinks of his reaction when Rose sprung this surprise trip on him. She'd collected him from work in a taxi, with a suitcase, his passport and an uncertain smile on her face. Would he be enthused or annoyed?

He'd been taken aback.

He's up to his eyes in his job – the very reason they hadn't had a honeymoon in the first place. There's something about autumn and pensions. People of a certain age start to ask themselves existential questions about the seasons of their own lives.

Do they have enough put away to retire on?

Luke's company gets extremely busy in September.

But how could he complain? This trip is the first time Rose has taken charge, organised something, and when she told him of her plan, he wanted to encourage that in her, not respond negatively.

In any case, he wanted this holiday. He needed it. The sun and the beaches and the restaurants, the cocktails and lazy mornings and strolls hand in hand.

And she must have needed it too, even more so, because as soon as they hit midweek and the date for returning home loomed, he sensed a change in Rose.

He knows why she's being like this.

Rose moved to London for a new start. It was somewhere she could be anonymous. But he knows she still doesn't feel safe. Though she tries to hide it, and tells him regularly she's fine, he sees the signs.

That look in her eye when she thinks she's seen someone she recognises. The little flinch when a bang sounds or somebody accidentally brushes against her.

Maybe they could stay, Luke muses. Leave England behind.

Even though Saint-Thérèse was colonised by the French initially, the locals mainly speak English now.

Luke could get a job. He imagines the market for pension advisors on luxury Caribbean islands is already well served, but perhaps he could turn his hand to something more fun. Learn how to teach scuba-diving or to paint villas.

Rose is a teacher. Her skills are more transferable.

How would Rose react if he suggested it? She'd be sensible and say it wasn't viable. That it was running away – and she knew what that entailed even if he didn't.

Up ahead, he sees Rose emerge from inside the villa to stand on the deck. She's spent the morning sleeping, trying to recover from the killer headache that came on last night. Their last evening on the island, but Luke had been able to tell by her pale face and bloodshot eyes that Rose hadn't been up for anything but an early night.

He watches her now. The wind pulls at the red sarong-type dress she's wearing, and in the sunlight he can see the silhouette of her body, the curve of her hips, the swell of her chest. Her blonde curls lie long against her back as she tilts her face up to the sun.

He can't get enough of her body. The feel of her, the taste of her, the smell of her. No matter how many times they're together, every time he sees her, he wants her.

Long may it last.

He raises his bottle, takes a final sip of beer and turns away from the water to join his wife.

They're mostly packed. While Rose was in bed, Luke had sorted their suitcase.

They have time before they need to order the taxi to the airport.

He'll see how she feels. Perhaps, now rested, she'll be up for a last swim or a glass of wine on the deck.

As he approaches Rose, she switches her gaze from the horizon to him and he sees her face.

He knew she was off-kilter for the last couple of days, but this is new.

Rose looks desolate.

Luke jogs the few steps up to the villa's deck. He puts down the beer bottle and wraps his arms around her waist, concerned.

'Hey,' he says. 'What's wrong?'

'You have the suitcase ready,' she chokes.

Luke frowns.

'I'll get you whatever you need from it,' he says. 'We don't have to order the taxi for another couple of hours. Do you still have a headache? We could try a walk on the beach?'

Rose rests her head against his chest. Her whole body feels like a sigh.

'I know,' he says, softly. 'I don't want to go back either. But, I've been thinking.'

'Luke—'

'Hear me out. What if we went home for a while and planned another trip? A longer one, I mean. A proper adventure. A few months. Six months, even. We could go to Europe. Or Australia. You could take a sabbatical, couldn't you? We should do it before kids come along. Everybody says it's the one thing you don't regret. Why not?'

Luke stops talking. Rose has started to cry.

Something is very, very wrong.

'I'm sorry,' Rose mumbles through tears. 'I can't go back to London.'

Luke squeezes her tighter.

'Sweetheart,' he says. 'What is it? Tell me.'

'Luke.'

Rose pulls away and looks up at him again. She's stopped crying but the expression on her face . . .

It's not one Luke has seen before.

It's terrifying. She's terrified. As if she's too frightened to speak. And then she finds the words.

'I *can't* go back,' she says.

Luke suddenly feels very cold. His conscious brain is thinking, whatever it is, it's fine; we can go home and sort it out. Nothing could have happened that warrants this sort of fear.

But Rose is trembling and Luke knows whatever she's about to tell him is not going to be good.

'He's dead,' she says.

'Who? Who's dead, sweetheart?'

Rose sucks in a breath that sounds like a sob.

'*He* is. I killed him.'

Luke drops his hands from her waist. He stares at his wife, sure that he's misheard her.

'What?' he says. 'Did you say you killed somebody? Killed who? Rose, what are you talking about?'

'The day we left. Before I collected you from work. I killed somebody.'

Luke shakes his head. Rose may as well be speaking in tongues.

'I don't understand,' he says. 'You haven't *killed* anybody. What are you talking about?'

Rose grabs him now, placing both her hands on his arms;

7

Luke only realises how badly he's started trembling when she's holding him steady.

'Luke, listen to me. Listen to what I'm saying. I killed him. *Him*. He's in our apartment. I can't go back. Do you understand? There's a dead body in our apartment.'

London

December 2021

It's an after-work Christmas party that Rose doesn't want to be at.

She likes her colleagues just fine, but she likes them sober. Particularly the men. In school, they're pleasant. Helpful. Good workmates. Full of creative ideas and comradely support. The ones who see teaching as a vocation and not just something that brings in a pay cheque for which a classroom of children must be endured.

Here, six rounds in, they're sloppy. Forward. Sleazy.

Mr Simms (Rose won't call him Julian, no matter how many times he slurs it in her ear) has had his hand on her knee twice already. Vice Principal McGrath has suggested that they – and by 'they', he means Rose and he – go on somewhere afterwards. Alone.

Rose's best friend in the staffroom, Ann-Marie, says it's a rite of passage and the only way to deal with it is to politely decline everybody. With the notable exception of Mr Simms, who requires more than a pleasant refusal: '*He only understands a knee in the balls, that one.*'

Ann-Marie wants to do more shots. They've paid into the kitty all year, like everyone else. There's no way Ann-Marie is letting Rose skulk off early.

Rose is up at the bar when she spots him.

He's tall, with pale skin, smart grey eyes and dark hair flecked with a smattering of silver.

He's with a group, too. They look like a work gang, but employees in a job that remunerates at a rate a few steps further along the career ladder. They look like they're going to go on somewhere more salubrious; like this is their handy after-work drinking spot, but the next stop is a Michelin-starred restaurant.

His group are talking and laughing, but he's somehow apart. Somebody hands him a pint of ale. He takes it, sips from it, and then he looks up and catches Rose staring at him.

She glances away quickly. Her cheeks flush red at being caught.

Movement beside her, a hand on her back.

Rose freezes. She turns. Mr Bloody Simms again.

'I'll get these in, young Rose.'

'Mr Simms—'

'It's Julian. Lovely pub you suggested here, Rosie, a bit nicer than the dive the vice principal brought us to last year. You and Ann-Marie know your bars! Honestly, I'll get the round. You young ones have to watch your pennies.'

'Mr Simms, it's the money from the kitty.' She pauses. He's not going to leave her alone. 'You know what? Here. If you could sort the barwoman out when she comes back? I've got to nip to the loo.'

Rose hands him the fifty-pound note. Mr Simms is delighted. Now she's asked him to do her a favour. She's in hock to him.

Rose is not going to drink any of those shots she's just ordered.

Rose is going to the toilet and then she's going to leave.

She can't do this.

When she emerges from the corridor to the ladies, the guy from the bar has inched closer to her table.

Rose has to pass him to get her coat and bag.

The pub is packed, though, and the path to her table has narrowed.

Rose tries to squeeze through. The pub's front door opens. A cold draught blows in as more customers enter. The crowd swells.

Rose is level with the stranger, stuck in a confined tunnel, facing his chest. There are people blocking the way in every direction.

'Hi,' he says.

Rose looks up.

Those eyes! You could get sucked into those eyes.

'Hi,' she replies.

They are practically touching body parts.

'Come here often?' he asks.

Rose snorts.

'You didn't just say that.'

'I did,' he says. 'I did just say that. I'll cut my tongue out when I get home. I think you're stuck, by the way.'

'I've figured that out. I'm just trying to get to my table.'

'Why don't we try to move together? Strength in numbers.'

'Or it could make it more awkward. Like a three-legged race.'

'Like what now?'

He laughs. She laughs.

They're glued together and Rose can't say she doesn't like the feel of his chest against hers.

And then the crowd shifts and he's able to step back. He gives a little bow. He's well mannered. He could have taken advantage and stayed close to her. He's giving her space.

Rose feels eyes on her. Eyes plural. Ann-Marie is looking up from the table, approvingly. Mr Simms, on approach with a tray of sambuca shots in his hand, not so approvingly.

How quickly, Rose muses, did she go from '*young* Rose' to 'total slut' in dear Julian's eyes?

'I guess we don't have to find rope for our legs now,' the stranger says.

Rose smiles. She doesn't know what to say, or how to act now that the sudden moment of intimacy has passed.

She's about to move off when he touches her arm, lightly.

'I'm Luke,' he says.

'Rose,' she replies.

She wants to say more.

She should say: yes, I feel it too. Isn't it weird? I felt it the moment I saw you and you caught me watching. That connection. But we're in a bar and while I'm not drunk, you might be, and this might be something you do, but it's not something a good girl like me does. I don't pick up guys in bars. I don't go home with guys I meet in bars.

I don't go home with guys, full stop.

It's not safe.

I'm not safe.

You don't want to be around me.

She doesn't say any of those things.

She just shrugs and goes back to her table, feeling him watching her the whole time.

But she hopes she'll meet him again. She really, really does.

Saint-Thérèse

Luke and Rose are still standing on the deck.

His heart is hammering in his chest. She hasn't said anything else. She's looking at him with sheer desperation in her eyes and he knows, he just knows, that she's telling the truth.

'Rose,' he says. 'What did you do?'

Rose hangs her head. She pulls away from him, folds her arms across her body. She stares out at the glasslike sea, then turns and walks inside the villa.

Luke remains where he is because he can't move his legs.

When he unfreezes, he follows her, anger and alarm pulsing through him.

Rose is sitting on the large white couch, one of the plump pillows grasped between her arms.

They'd made love on that couch a couple of nights ago. Luke remembers looking at Rose, just before he climaxed. He'd wanted her to look at him, but her eyes were closed and she . . . he had thought she was feeling pleasure, but had she been grimacing? Was there something else on her mind?

The fact that she'd fucking killed somebody, maybe?

Luke kneels in front of her, afraid to touch her. In the space of a couple of minutes, he's gone from thinking everything is normal to not knowing what to say or how to be.

'Is this for real?' he asks.

She glances up at him.

'Yes,' she says.

Luke takes a deep breath.

'You need to tell me what happened,' he says.

Out of the corner of his eye, he sees their suitcase packed and sitting beside the door. Their flight is in five hours. The cleaners for the villa will be here in two, ready to prepare it for the next couple.

Rose stays mute.

'For God's sake,' Luke snaps. 'Talk to me. What happened?'

'It was an accident,' Rose whispers.

'Who did you kill? How did it happen? Was it really . . . him? Did you say it was in our apartment?'

Luke is running through every possible scenario in his head, hoping he's misunderstood something along the way. Hoping that Rose has got it wrong.

Had she walked in on somebody robbing the apartment and lashed out? Was she having some sort of PTSD moment?

He can come up with alternatives, but in his heart, Luke knows what she's going to say.

'It was Kevin.'

The blood rushes to Luke's ears.

Kevin Davidson. Rose's ex.

'I didn't mean to,' Rose says. 'He was already in the apartment when I got home and I—'

Rose takes a deep breath. It's not deep enough. She's struggling to breathe. Luke can see her replaying in her mind whatever happened and she's beginning to hyperventilate.

'Rose, baby.'

Luke tries to put his arms around her, but she needs space, she needs air. She bats him away.

He jumps up, looks around, desperately trying to spot something that might help. There's a jug filled with water and ice on the breakfast island.

Luke pours a glass and rushes back to Rose.

'Drink it,' he says, trying to sound like he knows what he's doing as he kneels in front of her again. 'Please, Rose. Take a sip.'

She takes a sip. She coughs, splutters, then takes another.

'I'm sorry,' she says. 'I'm so sorry, Luke.'

'You don't have to say you're sorry. Just breathe. And then I need you to calm down and tell me exactly what happened. It's going to be okay. You're not there now, do you understand? You're here with me. You're safe. Listen to me.'

Luke takes the glass of water from her shaking hands and puts it on the floor.

'Listen to me,' he repeats. 'What did he do? How did he find you?'

'I can't do this,' she says.

'You can,' Luke pleads. 'You can.'

Rose looks at him. She takes a deep, shuddering breath. Then she nods, resolutely, spurred on by his support.

'He . . . I don't know. I'd just come home. I thought I heard something when I let myself in but I presumed it was you. That you'd come home early. I'd stopped worrying . . . I'd stopped thinking he'd turn up. I let my guard down.'

He's been nodding and now he shakes his head. No. He's not

going to let her blame herself. He was the very one who'd told her she didn't have to live in fear any more, that she was safe.

'I walked around the apartment, putting stuff away. I'd been down to the market. I'd picked up some flowers and scallops. I was planning to cook that dish you like, the saffron sauce one. And I heard something in our bedroom and I went in. And he was—'

Rose puts her hand over her eyes, trying to block out whatever image has presented itself.

'He was sitting on our bed and he said . . . he said . . .'

Luke bites the inside of his cheeks so hard, he almost draws blood. Rose meets his eye.

'He said, "So this is where he fucks you, is it?" and then I tried to run, but he got up so fast.'

Rose slumps. He can see the effort it's taken for her to tell him even this much.

Luke gets off the floor and sits beside her on the couch. He puts both his arms around her.

'Did he hurt you?' he says. His voice sounds strange to his ears. Weirdly detached. And he realises, in the midst of this surreality, he's less concerned about the idea that Kevin Davidson is lying dead in their apartment in London and more about the thought he might have harmed Rose.

That he might have even laid a finger on her . . .

This is love, Luke thinks, and he almost snorts. Nothing feels real, but that thought has arrived with such clarity, it's like a punch.

'He pushed me,' Rose whispers. 'And he kept pushing me. I was screaming. I knew what he was going to do. But, this time, I fought back. He's not . . . I never used to do that. I don't think he realised I would.'

Good woman, Luke thinks, even as he wants to vomit and smash something simultaneously. His reaction is primitive, he knows that, somewhere deep down. Rose is a strong, independent woman. She doesn't need him; she doesn't need anybody. She's proved that time and again. But all he can think in the most basic, Neanderthal way is – why wasn't I there to protect my wife?

'I was so scared of what he was going to do,' Rose continues. 'I thought, he'll kill me if I don't do what he says. And you know the chest of drawers?'

Luke knows the drawers. The huge, dark lump of furniture that he bought when he moved into the apartment. Rose hates it because she likes pastel colours and soft things but Luke loves the chest of drawers because, well, a man should have some proper furniture to bring balance to his recently redesigned pale-grey and sky-blue life.

They're heavy and solid and the corners of those drawers are like weapons.

'Did he fall against the drawers?' Luke asks.

'He didn't fall,' Rose says. 'I pushed him into them.'

'You pushed him,' Luke repeats.

'I screamed and I . . . well, I lunged at him and he fell backwards. I wanted to hurt him. I wanted to kill him. I heard a crack and—'

Rose stops. She places her hand over her mouth.

Luke feels something harden inside him.

'It's okay,' he says. 'Rose, listen to me, it's okay. What you did – it's self-defence, do you understand? You're allowed to defend yourself. He's not allowed to—'

Luke can't even finish the sentence. He pulls Rose close again, but she only lets him hold her for a moment before she pulls back.

'Luke, don't you get it? It would have been okay. It's not any more.'

'What do you mean?'

Rose is staring at Luke like he's lost all his reason.

'Luke, I left him lying on the floor. I packed a suitcase. I went online in the next room and I looked at flight tickets. I was going to run away. From him. From you. And then I . . . I couldn't leave without you. I packed clothes for you as well and I went back online, and I bought us two tickets to here and then I went to your work and told you we were going on a surprise honeymoon. I lied and lied and lied. Don't you understand what that means?'

Luke is shaking his head but the reality of what she's telling him is starting to sink in.

Rose was attacked. Rose defended herself. Rose accidentally killed somebody.

Then Rose fled the scene. She fled the country.

And he's with her.

Luke looks at Rose.

They are in deep, deep shit.

'We need help,' Luke says.

'Nobody can help us,' Rose says.

'No, we can—'

'Luke, nobody can help us. But you can help yourself. You need to go home.'

'What?'

'You have to go home and go to the apartment and report what you find. Go home without me. I need you to report what I've done to the police. Are you listening to me? Tell them I didn't say anything until the last day. Your workmates will vouch for you being in the office the day we left. The taxi driver will confirm he took us straight to the airport. Tell the truth. You can clear yourself.'

Luke can hear every word. But he's not listening.

He stands up and walks to the window.

Time is running out. The cleaners will be here soon.

Luke needs to think.

He needs to plan.

And he needs help.

London

Present

Neither of them want to go into the apartment.

That's abundantly clear as they sit in the stationary car.

But they're running out of time.

Mickey Sheils turns and looks at the woman in the passenger seat beside her.

Petra Jurgis is staring up out the passenger window, through the rain that's falling in sheets, at her former home. A number of apartments are lit up in the well-to-do building, beacons of warmth on the overcast, rain-sodden day. But Petra's penthouse apartment is in darkness.

'You don't have to come in. You can give me a list. I have some-body—'

'No.' Petra's one word is adamant.

Mickey sighs. The hard way, then. Hard, but often necessary.

'Okay, then,' she says. 'We've got to get a move on.'

She pointedly eyes the old-fashioned clock on the Bentley's dash-board.

Sometimes it hits Mickey how strange it is. To be barely 42 and driving a Bentley. But then, Mickey is in so many strange situations, that's usually the least odd thing in her life.

Plus, it was bought with her husband's money.

Mickey is aware of the contrasting worlds she lives in. Last night, she was sitting in a Michelin-starred restaurant in Covent Garden, eating oysters and drinking Krug.

Today, she's . . . well, today is going to be very different.

Petra nods but doesn't move.

Her red hair covers the worst of the bruises on the side of her face closest to Mickey. But Mickey knows the bruises are there and so are the memories. That's what has Petra frozen.

Mickey's phone rings. She takes it out of her pocket, frowns deeply when she sees who's calling and knocks it off. That's unexpected. But it will have to keep until later. She puts the phone on airplane mode, so it won't go off in the event they need to be quiet once they're inside.

Mickey takes matters into her own hands. She tucks her shoulder-length brown hair inside her coat collar and opens the driver's door.

A few seconds later, Petra follows.

They dash across the sodden street.

Just two women, trying to get inside to stay dry.

The lift in the apartment building is in use. Neither Mickey nor Petra want to hang around, not now they're moving, so they take the stairwell.

The penthouse is eight floors up.

As they reach the final stairwell, Mickey reaches into the pocket of her raincoat. She runs her fingers over the taser.

It's charged and ready.

At the apartment door, Petra fumbles with her keys.

She gets the right one in, but it won't turn.

'What if he's changed the locks?' she asks Mickey, desperation in her voice.

Mickey calmly reaches across Petra and jiggles the key.

The door opens.

Inside, Mickey glances around at the chaos. The apartment is luxurious, but now it bears witness to the last time Petra was here. Smashed crystal, broken furniture, a streak of blood on the solid oak flooring.

'Fast as you can,' Mickey reminds her. 'Just what you need.'

Petra nods. She doesn't look at the detritus that marks her former life. She hurries in the direction of the bedroom to take whatever clothes and personal items have been left intact.

Mickey looks at the time on her phone, trying to quell her anxiety. She feels unusually nervous today. And she's learned to never ignore her gut.

She encourages women to go back and take what's theirs. That's not to say she enjoys doing it with them. But she's found, over the years, that the women who walk out with nothing often regret it when they feel stronger, later. They tell themselves they should have fought to keep something of their own lives. Even if it was only a practical thing, like their passport or driver's licence.

It used to surprise Mickey, how somebody could leave a life with absolutely nothing to show for it. But it happens more often than not. They turn up in Mickey's office with only the clothes on their backs and the willpower that got them there.

When they need an essential item, but can't bring themselves to return to their homes, sometimes Mickey will step in and go with her business partner, Elliot Ibekwe. Even though he's not a hulk of a man, and is actually a big softy, Elliot works out so he doesn't look like a pushover. His presence is usually enough to give most ex-boyfriends and husbands pause for thought.

Petra needs to disappear. And, in this apartment, she has the means to do so. She didn't get the chance to make her escape of her own volition. She ended up in hospital before she could take anything. So, the pile of money she's hidden in the apartment is still hidden.

They both hope.

A few minutes pass. Mickey is getting nervous, checking her watch, checking the hallway outside the apartment.

'Petra, are you nearly ready?'

Petra emerges from the bedroom. She has a suitcase and she's not quite smiling, but she looks satisfied.

'Let's go,' Mickey says.

'One last thing,' Petra replies.

Mickey doesn't want to wait another second. Her bad feeling is growing.

They should have brought Elliot.

She takes a proper look around the apartment. There's money written all over it, from the marble countertops in the open-plan kitchen to the walnut flooring. Plenty of people assume domestic violence goes hand in glove with poverty, with the less well off. Mickey knows better. Behind closed doors . . . vicious men are vicious men. Whether they have money or not.

Mickey watches as Petra walks back into the bedroom. She returns with a football jersey. A Lithuanian league team, Mickey guesses, and she's only able to do that because her husband Nathan loves football almost as much as he loves money.

'FBK Corinthians, his favourite thing in the world,' Petra says, by way of explanation.

Mickey blinks. Petra seems to have got her nerve back.

'Stick it in your bag then and let's go,' Mickey says.

But Petra doesn't stick it in the bag. She places it on the floor.

Then, as Mickey watches, Petra lowers her jeans and pants and squats over the jersey.

The two women maintain eye contact the whole time Petra is emptying her bladder.

As Petra zips up her jeans, Mickey glances at the wet mess on the floor.

'He did that to me once,' Petra says, shrugging, by way of explanation.

Mickey touches her gently on the arm.

'To hell with him,' she says.

In the hallway, Petra raises her hand to summon the lift.

But she drops it just as quickly.

The lift is already moving.

The display over the door says it's on its way to the penthouse.

Petra and Mickey look at each other. It could be cleaners. A delivery man. It doesn't necessarily mean anything.

Petra looks out the window that faces on to the street.

And Mickey can tell from the way her features contort that the lift coming their way isn't coincidence.

The ex's car is outside.

'Quickly,' Mickey says.

She grabs the other end of Petra's suitcase and the two of them slip into the stairwell.

They race down the stairs, trying to be quiet as they do so.

Mickey's heart is in her mouth.

Will he know they've only just left? Will his instinct be to come straight back down and give chase?

Then they're outside the building. Petra wants to look back: Mickey won't let her.

They run to the Bentley. Mickey throws the suitcase in the back as Petra jumps in the passenger side.

Mickey races around to the driver's side. She's still not looking back at the building.

Her hands are shaking as she puts the key in the ignition.

'Mickey!'

Petra's shout is not the shout of a woman who's just revenge-urinated on her ex's favourite possession. It's the cry of a woman in terror.

Mickey looks up and sees all six-foot-four of crazed Lithuanian aggression bearing down on the Bentley from across the street.

The car starts.

Mickey puts her foot down, barely checking to see if she's pulling out into the path of an oncoming car.

Petra's ex lands one slap on the boot and they're out of his reach.

Mickey drives fast, taking turn after turn until she eventually pulls out on to a high street.

Neither woman has spoken.

When they get to a red light, Mickey fumbles in her pocket and takes out her phone. She knocks off airplane mode and places it in the hands-free. In the unlikely event Petra's ex has got into his car and somehow finds them, Mickey will dial the police.

Mickey's about to look at Petra, to make sure she hasn't had a heart attack, when she hears laughter.

She glances sideways.

Petra is chuckling with pure, adrenaline-fuelled relief.

'Fuck,' she says, when she catches Mickey looking at her.

'Fuck,' Mickey replies.

'And you do this regularly?' Petra asks.

Mickey nods. She smiles now, too.

Her phone starts to ring.

It's the same number as before.

Luke Miller, again? He doesn't ring for years and then she hears from him twice in a day. What does he want and why won't he stop ringing this time?

Mickey knocks it off. She turns and smiles again at Petra.

She's still smiling when the SUV comes out of the side street and slams straight into the Bentley.

The sound of breaking glass is the last thing Mickey hears.

Saint-Thérèse

Damn it.

Luke stares at his phone.

Why won't she answer?

Rose is pacing the floor of the villa.

The clock is ticking. Whatever about speaking to Mickey Sheils about what they need to do in London, Luke has to deal with their present situation on Saint-Thérèse.

'Rose, we need to go into town and find a hotel.'

'What?'

'We have to leave the villa.'

'Luke, did any of what I've told you sink in? You've barely spoken for the last half hour. You need to leave. You have to go home to London.'

'I heard you fine, Rose. But if you think I'm heading to the airport and getting on a plane without you, after what you've told me, you're out of your mind.'

Rose stops pacing.

'There's nothing else you can do,' she says. 'I killed a man. I've done a terrible, terrible thing and I've dragged you into it. Aren't you angry at me?'

'Angry at you? Why would I be angry at you?'

Rose stares at him, her expression the definition of gobsmacked.

'Luke, I turned up at your work and tricked you into . . . I don't know, becoming a *fugitive* with me. I may have got you into serious trouble.'

'Rose, I'm incandescent that you didn't tell me straight off. That's what I'm angry about. But I've been in enough odd situations in my life to know that people do weird shit when they're not thinking straight. And when they're scared, especially. Given what happened to you and how you dealt with Kevin before, I can only assume shock made you react in the same way: you ran and you tried to block it out. I'm just grateful that this time you ran with me.'

Rose blinks. Her eyes fill with tears.

'Do you really mean that?' she asks.

'Yes,' Luke exclaims. 'Now, listen. We need to leave the villa. When the taxi comes, we'll go straight to town. We need to check in somewhere, but we're better off not using our own names. Do you have cash? Anywhere high-end will want our passports, so we should get somewhere basic and hope for the best. We can say we've been robbed, our passports are being replaced, something along those lines . . .'

Rose shakes her head.

'Luke, how are you . . . how can you even talk like you know what you're doing? I barely know what I'm doing.'

Luke shakes his head. He doesn't have an answer for her. He looks down at his phone again.

He'll keep trying Mickey.

Because, as in control as he sounds, he knows he's flying blind.

He'd really like a grown-up to help.

London

Mickey is groggy when she wakes.

How much wine did she have last night?

She tries to remember. God, she hasn't had a hangover this bad in . . . actually, she can't remember ever having a hangover like this.

Is Nathan beside her? She's going to beg him to get her water and Nurofen. No, morphine. This calls for something extreme. Where can you get morphine these days? Will they give you that in a pharmacy?

Mickey opens her eyes. She's immediately blinded by the bright white light of the room. She closes her eyes again.

Wait.

Has she died?

Surely, death would feel better?

'Michaela, you're back with us. It's okay. You're okay.'

Mickey's eyes flicker open again.

There's a shape leaning over her and it's morphing into Nathan, her husband. He's wearing the suit she saw him put on when he left the house this morning. But he doesn't look his usual self. Composed. Professional. He looks absolutely panicked.

'You're in hospital,' he says. 'But you're fine. Nothing broken.'

JO SPAIN

'What?' Mickey's voice comes out as a croak.

'I know it feels bad. You have a lot of bruising. But it will heal.'

'Mickey, do you remember what happened?'

A new voice. Familiar.

Mickey turns her head to the left. The light is becoming more bearable now. She opens her eyes fully. It's Elliot. He came here from the gym. Probably ran all the way. She can tell by his T-shirt and sweats and the damp glistening on his dark skin. She can imagine him getting a call at the weights section and literally running out the door.

'Petra?' she says.

'Petra's . . .'

Mickey sees the look Elliot and Nathan give each other.

She knows what it means and she suspects what's coming next.

'We can talk about her later,' Elliot says.

'No. Petra. She was in the passenger—'

Mickey winces as the memory returns.

'She's alive, Mickey,' Elliot says. 'That's all that matters. You should have taken me.'

'You can stop a speeding car, eh?'

Mickey winces as Elliot snorts. She knows, as far as these two men are concerned, that if she's cracking jokes she's on the mend.

She *should* have taken Elliot. He's strong and clever and she hired him because he's the exact partner she needs. But Petra is so scared of men.

Petra.

She's alive.

Mickey breathes a painful sigh of relief.

But then, she thinks, is that all that matters?

30

She's met women who've had the absolute worst things done to them by their exes. She knows that when people tell them they were lucky they got out alive, that's not what's going through their minds.

Some things scar worse than death.

Mickey feels her eyes growing heavy. She's struggling to stay awake. She doesn't know if that's her body's response to trauma or if there are drugs in her system. If they have given her something, it seems to be doing sweet FA for the pain.

'It's okay,' Elliot says. 'You rest. Don't worry, Mickey. He's got his just deserts.'

'What?' Mickey says, her eyes snapping open again.

'Petra's boyfriend. The one who drove into you. He's dead.'

Elliot pats her hand. He's never usually this gentle and affectionate. Their relationship leans more into banter and ribbing than deep and meaningful.

He must have been worried.

Mickey tries to nod her head, even though it hurts. Good. She's glad.

'Sorry 'bout the Bentley, love,' she says.

Nathan murmurs some reassurance.

From somewhere, she hears her phone ringing.

Answer that, she thinks, before she drifts off again.

When Mickey next wakes, it's late at night. A kindly young Irish nurse with the whitest teeth Mickey has ever seen tells her Nathan had to step out to take a work call. *Quelle surprise*, Mickey thinks, then feels guilty because she can only imagine what had gone through her husband's head when he got the call from the hospital.

She feels more alert now. Whatever they gave her has worn off. She takes in her surrounds. A private hospital, her own room. Two huge bunches of sweet-smelling flowers already in vases on the windowsill.

She imagines she came in through a regular A&E but Nathan would have wasted no time getting her transferred. And, she suspects, he will have taken care of Petra, too.

'Nurse,' she says. 'The other woman from my car accident, how is she?'

The nurse's features form a tight, no-nonsense expression, the one worn so commonly by medical staff.

'She'll pull through. I'm afraid I'm not allowed to say anything more if you're not family.'

'She's my friend,' Mickey says, plaintively.

The nurse hesitates.

'Are you Irish?' she asks Mickey.

'Born and bred. Here fifteen years, though. Yourself?'

'Came over three years ago. Better pay, you know. I'm from Galway, originally. You're a Dubliner. You haven't lost the accent.'

'Nice to keep a touch of home. I still miss it.'

The nurse looks at Mickey, her expression softening.

They're friends now. Connected by the love of a land lost to them.

'The guy who drove into you did a number on that car. Shattered her pelvis. She will walk again but it'll take a long time. And there might be other issues. You know . . .'

Mickey flinches. She does know.

'She'll have a lot of scars on her face, as well,' the nurse adds. 'But she's very beautiful, and plastic surgery these days . . .'

Mickey releases a heartbroken sigh. Even dead, Petra's boyfriend has left his mark.

'Thank you,' she says.

The nurse nods.

'Somebody is trying to get hold of you,' she says, nodding at the bedside locker.

Mickey looks over. Her phone is buzzing.

She picks it up as the nurse is leaving.

Luke Miller again.

What on earth could be so important? she thinks.

And that's followed by . . . somebody's dead.

'Luke?'

Mickey answers it quickly.

'Mickey. Thank God you picked up.'

'Well, you keep ringing. I presume it's bad news. Who is it?'

Mickey braces herself as she runs through the very few remaining shared contacts they have. It will be somebody who means more to Luke, otherwise Mickey would already know.

'Oh,' he says.

She can hear his hesitation.

'No. It's not like that.'

Mickey frowns.

'Then, listen, Luke, I'm actually in the middle of something—'

'Mickey, I need your help. It's serious. Really serious.'

Mickey props herself up.

She knows Luke so well, even if it's been years.

And she's never heard him sound so frightened.

'What is it?' she asks.

Saint-Thérèse

Luke moves to a corner of the small hotel lobby, the phone still to his ear. He has left Rose sitting at the café outside, a strong coffee in front of her. On the off-chance this hotel gets picky about the passport issue, he doesn't want the receptionist remembering it was a couple that came to the desk.

He wants the least attention possible. In case the police start tracking their movements.

Luke can't even believe he's thinking like this.

'Mickey, I need to ask you a legal question for a hypothetical situation.'

'Luke, I haven't practised in ages. I haven't practised in England, ever.'

'I just need general legal advice and I've nobody else I can go to with this.'

'Fine. Everything except murder is fixable.'

Luke pinches the bridge of his nose with his fingers. Mickey sounds different. Tired. Though, the last time he'd spoken to her, she'd been yelling at him, telling him to piss off out of her life if he wasn't going to be honest.

Not a good reference point.

He takes a deep breath and remembers why he phoned Mickey.
He knows he can trust her. And he needs help.

'If somebody had . . . accidentally killed somebody, but they
didn't stay at the scene – how much trouble would they be in?'

He hears a sharp intake of breath down the line. It sounds like
Mickey is wincing.

'They'd be in a lot of trouble, Luke.'

Luke exhales.

'But there are degrees,' Mickey adds.

'Like?'

'What sort of hypothetical scenario are we discussing? It isn't . . .
is it a hit-and-run?'

Mickey sounds even stranger now. Luke shakes his head. He
doesn't know what's going on with her and why should he? They
haven't actually talked properly in years. But right now, he can only
think about his own situation.

'Because a hit-and-run can be explained,' Mickey continues. 'It happens. It's wrong but it happens. The driver is in shock, they don't want
to get out of the car, they drive home hoping they'll wake up and it
will have been a dream, then they hear the news report and it registers
that the nightmare is real. If they come forward, it's taken into account.'

'Not a hit-and-run. Self-defence.'

There's a beat.

'Self-defence is very defendable,' Mickey says.

'But if you . . . if a person killed somebody in self-defence and
then fled the scene . . .'

'Still defendable. Especially if we're talking domestic abuse.
Luke, is this why you rang me? Do you know somebody—'

'And if they got on a plane and flew somewhere—'

35

Another beat.

'For how long?'

'A week.'

Mickey sighs.

'It's becoming more problematic. What's going on?'

'I . . . I can't say. It's just hypothetical.'

'Sure. And jail is just a place.'

Luke listens as Mickey sighs again and this time he hears it: she's not sighing in exasperation. She's in pain.

Luke pauses his frantic train of thought.

'Mickey, are you okay?'

'Honestly? No. But let's get into that another time. Why would somebody kill someone and then . . . you know what, forget it. Luke, manslaughter, even self-defence manslaughter, is really serious. Leaving the scene, claiming shock, it's all normal. Getting on a plane, flying somewhere, that's a whole other scenario. Any prosecutor is going to claim premeditation.'

'Even if the flights were booked minutes after the person died?'

Luke realises how it sounds even as he says it.

'Is there something you have to tell me, Luke?'

Luke silently shakes his head. He takes the phone from his ear and rests it against his forehead.

'Hold on,' Mickey says.

He puts the phone back to his ear.

He waits.

He hears movement, like Mickey is adjusting herself, and now she's doing something, tapping a screen. Her phone screen.

'Okay,' she says. 'There's nothing on the news saying the police have just found a week-old body.'

'I said it was hypothetical.'

'You did and I'm not an idiot. You know what's crucial here? Go to the police. As quickly and as honestly as possible. I know I said a week is bad and flights out of the country are bad but . . . longer is worse. Do you understand me?'

'Yes.'

'And there's nothing you want to tell me, right now?'

'No.'

'I know plenty of good barristers. I can get you advice—'

'Mickey? Will you delete this call from your phone?'

'You don't know much about the police and IT skills, do you, Luke?'

'I'm sorry, Mickey.'

Luke hangs up.

He takes another deep breath and approaches the hotel lobby desk.

The young, black receptionist wears a permanently bored expression. He seems more interested in the football on his phone than the fact Luke has been hovering yards away from him for the last ten minutes, and Luke is glad to see it. This guy would never be able to describe Luke to the cops.

Luke coughs to announce his presence.

'Yeah?' The guy barely looks up. Luke can see the screen of the reception computer now and realises it's open on a gambling site.

'Eh, hi. Good afternoon. I wonder if you can help. My wife and I, we were the victims of a robbery—'

'Room is forty dollars a night.'

'No. I mean, yes, we can pay. We have money. But our passports were stolen.'

The guy drags his eyes from his phone and looks up at Luke.

'You have other ID?'

'No. Sorry. Not on us. We didn't bring driving licences. Look, my wife is coming from the police station now. We're tourists and we've had an upsetting experience and we just need somewhere to rest while we get it sorted. The police just told us to check in somewhere local. I can pay up front for the room.'

'The police told you to check in somewhere local?'

'Yes.'

'Without passports? Why didn't they ring ahead? Why is your wife still there?'

Brilliant, Luke thinks. A fucking detective.

'I don't know why they didn't ring ahead,' he says. 'They seemed busy. I left my wife there to speak with one of the female officers. She was distressed. The guy who robbed us . . .'

Luke bows his head. He rubs his forehead. This isn't going to work.

'Hey, sorry, man,' the receptionist says. 'I didn't mean to upset you. Guess I'm having a bad day, too. Listen, as long as you can pay for the room, you can have one. I, eh, hope your wife is okay.'

Luke looks up, surprised.

He could almost kiss the guy.

'Thank you,' he chokes out.

It doesn't matter that this receptionist is looking at him with nothing but pity. It doesn't matter that he thinks Luke is the sort of bloke who can't defend his wife from a random mugger.

Luke is the sort of bloke who can't defend his wife from any man, it would seem.

But he's going to bloody well defend her now.

After the transaction is complete, Luke walks out of the hotel and a few yards up the street to the near-empty café where he'd left Rose.

She's staring into the distance, her coffee untouched.

A memory surfaces. An afternoon during the week when they'd walked the town's streets after Luke said he wanted to buy Rose some jewellery. They'd stopped to give their legs a rest, at a café not unlike this one. Luke had ordered coffee and some pastries and had never tasted a better chocolate tart. It had felt like bliss. Then he'd looked across to see Rose staring into the distance, completely distracted.

All week, she's kept this thing from him.

If she could keep this from him for that long, without him even guessing . . .

What else could she keep from him?

Luke blinks rapidly.

He won't let his head go there.

He knows Rose. He loves her. She panicked and did something incredibly stupid and then she tried to pretend it hadn't happened.

And hadn't she warned him? She'd told him, her exact words . . .

I don't trust any man. I don't know if I'll ever trust you.

He thought he'd changed her mind.

Luke's chest feels sore.

He's broken-hearted.

But they'll fix this. He'll fix it. And when he does, she'll trust him, then.

London

December 2021

It's Christmas Eve and Rose absolutely hates Christmas Eve.

She also hates Christmas Day. She hates St Stephen's Day, or Boxing Day as everybody here calls it. New Year's Eve. In fact, the whole bloody season.

She used to love it. Many years ago, before she lived in London on her own, before she came to England – before everything, really.

She's conscious of being a Scrooge, and the one thing she is careful about is that she doesn't ruin the fun for others. When friends ask her what her plans are for Christmas lunch, she gives vague replies about travelling to be with family, or catching up with friends she hasn't mentioned before. People often assume, because she's from Donegal, that she goes home. She's fine with that. She doesn't want the people in her life feeling like they need to invite her over, or worrying that she's sitting alone in her flat, with no decorations, no turkey, no festivities.

Which is exactly what she has planned for tomorrow.

Rose stands in front of the deli section in Waitrose and tries to identify the least holiday-specific option available. Sushi. Will sushi keep in the fridge overnight?

She lifts up a pack, checks the price – well, that's outrageous – puts it back and selects a smaller carton. She adds a cheesecake slice and starts in the direction of the alcohol aisle. No bubbles, no wine, nothing that resembles festive cheer. She's going straight for the hard stuff. A bottle of vodka to go with the orange juice she already has chilling in the fridge.

She's trying to get past a group of lads, stacking cases of beer in their trolley like an alcoholic's game of Jenga, when her phone rings.

Seeing there's no way through to the spirits, Rose puts her basket down and takes the phone out of the handbag slung across her body.

It's a mobile number she doesn't recognise.

'Hello?' she says.

'Eh. Hi. Hello.'

Rose waits. Do they make marketing calls on Christmas Eve? If so, the poor sod is having a worse time than her, so she'll give him a minute.

It's not like she's busy.

'Is this Rose?'

'Yep.'

'Eh, you might not remember me, Rose. I don't normally do this. I, well, eh, Ann-Marie Dowling gave me your number.'

'Okay?'

Rose starts to feel a heat on the back of her neck. She recognises the voice.

'I met you in the bar at your work Christmas party? When I say met . . . I'm Luke. You probably don't even remember me. I'm sorry, I feel a bit mental doing this but, I've had a few Christmas drinks in the office. I mean . . . I'm not a big drinker. What I mean is – fuck – what do I mean? I'm not calling because I'm pissed. But I am feeling brave. When you left the bar – are you still there?'

'Yes.'

'I, um, well, I got speaking to your friend. Ann-Marie.'

Rose tenses. She'd told Ann-Marie that she fancied the good-looking guy she'd bumped into. God, that woman could be so predictable. To just hand over her number like that!

'And I, eh, I told her you were the most beautiful woman I'd ever seen. I'm sorry. This was a stupid idea. You must think I'm crazy. But I just wanted to call and tell *you* that you are the most beautiful woman I've ever seen. That's all. And also, that teacher who works with you? Simms? I don't think he's a good guy. In fact, I'm pretty sure I saw him take an upskirt pic.'

Rose laughs before she can stop herself.

'Oh, no. Now you're laughing at me. This is going worse than I planned.'

Rose looks around her. The group of lads have moved on, pushing their delicately balanced trolley with the sort of care and diligence you'd expect from a new father bringing his wife and baby home from the hospital.

The aisle is only populated now by couples, smiling and holding hands. It's like central casting sent out a call: tomorrow is Christmas Day. Let's remind the lonely people that it's the one day of the year when you're supposed to have somebody, anybody, in your life.

'I'm not laughing at you,' she says. 'I'm laughing with you. Simms is a dirty old sod.'

'Thank Christ for that. You laughing with me, I mean. Not for him being a dirty sod.'

'I remember you.'

'You do?'

'Sure. We had quite an intimate moment.'

She can almost hear him blush.

'I think I felt your phone in your pocket,' she adds.

There's silence. She wonders if she's gone too far. Maybe he thought she was the shy, retiring type. And now, here she is, cracking crude jokes.

The irony being, she normally is the shy, retiring type.

But this feels safe, somehow. Talking on a phone with this . . . well, he's technically a stranger but she feels like she knows him.

'It's a very old phone,' he says, eventually. 'Huge. One of those brick-types from the nineties.'

Now Rose blushes.

'You don't think I'm a crazy stalker for getting your number, do you?' he asks.

Rose has started walking and now she's in front of the vodka.

Grey Goose, Smirnoff, Absolut, Ketel One, Belvedere.

Rose reaches out and grabs the Smirnoff, the one in her price range. She's not buying it for taste; it doesn't matter if it's the cheapest.

'I don't think you're a crazy stalker,' she says. 'I think you're brave. And I'm flattered.'

'You can't see me, but I'm smiling,' he says.

'You're welcome. And I hope you can't see me. Because that *would* be stalking.'

He laughs.

'So, could I ask you something?'

'I thought you only wanted my number so you could call me and tell me I'm the most beautiful woman in the world?'

'I'm a pathological liar.'

'Is your name even Luke?'

'What do you want it to be?'

Rose is enjoying this. The banter. He's clever. And also hot as fuck. That was what she thought when she first saw him. *God, he is good-looking*.

But none of it matters.

She's not going to let herself have feelings for this guy.

'Can we meet for a drink?'

His voice is so filled with hope.

Rose's grip tightens on the neck of the vodka bottle.

This is it.

'I, um . . . I don't know,' she says.

'I'm sorry. You're probably not even single.'

'I'm single.'

'Is it me? Did my breath smell really bad in the pub? I did have a packet of cheese and onion earlier that night. I'm a complete amateur in the picking-up-women-in-pubs department. I swear, if you meet me for a drink, I'll eat nothing all day and chew gum for a half hour beforehand. I'm not a serial killer. I promise. I know that's exactly the sort of thing a serial killer would say. But I can give you my full name and you can check all my socials. You can ring my boss, if you like. You could even bring a friend. I could bring a friend. Not a good-looking one, though. I'd only get jealous if you liked him . . .'

'I'm just . . . I'm not in a good place, right now,' Rose says.

He falls silent. Rose feels a pang of guilt.

'I'd be willing to wait,' he says, after a few moments.

Rose's chest constricts. Ann-Marie had told her once that the playing-hard-to-get routine only made Rose more desirable to men.

It's not a routine, Rose had pointed out.

She looks down at the bottle of vodka in her basket. The sushi and cheesecake for one.

'What are you doing the day after tomorrow?' she says.

There's a beat of silence.

'I'm taking you for a drink,' he answers.

Rose smiles.

'Are you sure?' she says, checking. 'You don't have a family thing planned? It is Boxing Day . . .'

'I'm sure,' he says. 'I hate Christmas, if I'm honest. Shit. Why did I say that? Now you think I'm Ebenezer. I think I'll just stop talking now.'

'You don't have to stop talking. I'm not judging you.'

'Can I ask – what changed your mind?'

Rose shrugs to herself.

'I guess . . . Christmas,' she says.

He's silent, then he laughs.

'Ho ho ho,' he says.

'Text me the details.'

She hangs up.

She looks at the blank phone screen.

She wants to call him back. Tell him to run. To keep running. To stay clear of her. She's nothing but trouble.

But she can't.

She's going to be selfish for once. She's going to do this for her.

Saint-Thérèse

Luke makes two G&Ts while Rose sits on the bed.

It's not the sort of hotel that has minibars in the rooms. He found the alcohol and tonic in a tiny supermarket down a side street. He bought bread and cheese, and fresh fruit and water, so they don't need to go out for a little while.

They need the time to strategise.

What do you do when your wife has accidentally killed a man and his body is lying in your apartment in a different country?

Luke gives Rose the drink. He's amazed at how steady his hand is, how in control he appears. He doesn't feel it. He feels sick and panicky and he's sure his blood pressure has risen since this morning.

'I'm not sure I should,' Rose says. 'I need to keep a clear head.'

'If you don't drink it, I'll have them both,' Luke replies.

They eye each other over the glasses and then Rose lifts it to her lips and takes a gulp.

Luke does the same.

'Look,' Rose says. 'I know what you're thinking. And I appreciate it. I can't even tell you how much. I'm relieved you're not angry with me. Surprised, but relieved. But Luke, you don't have to do this. You love me, I get it. And maybe you can, I don't know, visit me in jail.' She laughs, despairingly. 'If they catch me. But I've already asked too much of you. You've got to leave me. I have to do this on my own.'

'Is that your plan, then? You want to go on the run?'

Rose stares down at the tired bed sheets, once white but now an off-grey colour thanks to a few hundred spins in an industrial washing machine. It's a far cry from the luxurious villa, Luke thinks.

'I can't go to jail,' she says. 'I'm not tough enough.'

'Rose, where you go, I'm going.'

'For God's sake!'

Rose stands up. She walks away from the bed and slams her glass back on the dressing table, liquid splashing over the sides.

'We only met nine months ago, Luke. All of this . . . it's too quick. It's too much. I don't expect you to stand by me. We— We shouldn't have got married.'

'Didn't we go through this already?' Luke says.

They had. When he'd asked her to marry him, three months ago.

We've only known each other six months, she'd said. *It doesn't matter,* he'd replied. *We both know where this is going. I know what I want. I want you.*

What had she said? *I'm worried you want to protect me. That you've mistaken that for love.*

No, he'd replied. *I love you* and *I want to protect you.*

Months, years, it wouldn't have made any difference to how he felt.

'You've done so much for me,' Rose says, staring up at the ceiling. 'I can't stop thinking about that. You were . . . not what I expected. Please, take this chance. Leave me and don't come back.'

'I'll go on the run with you.'

Rose lets out a gasp, somewhere between exasperated and furious.

'I don't want you to!'

'We made vows. In good times and bad.'

'Jesus, Luke. Nobody takes vows this seriously—'

'I do.'

Rose falls quiet. They look at each other.

There's a tiny part of Luke's brain asking a question.

He meant forever. He meant through thick and thin. What did Rose's vows mean to her?

But he reminds himself of what she's been through. Not right now, but in life. What was done to her. And why she might be less willing to promise to stay with somebody, no matter what.

He'd made her go further than she'd wanted, hadn't he? He'd pushed her to love him as much as he loved her, to agree to marry him when they barely knew each other.

He'd been the more certain of the two.

Rose looks at her hand, like she's just realised the G&T is no longer there.

Luke gives her his.

Over their heads, the room's fluorescent light starts to buzz. The window is open; the air conditioning is not up to much and, too late, Luke realises that the buzzing is an insect, not a bulb.

He stands up and shuts the window while Rose slam-dunks his G&T.

There's a plan forming in the back of Luke's brain.

If he's honest, it's been there a while, he's just been too shocked to articulate it.

Why should they go on the run? Why should Rose's life be turned upside down, again, by Kevin Davidson?

This isn't her fault. None of it. Not how she reacted and not how she defended herself.

It's all his fault. Davidson's.

'I think I know what to do,' Luke says. He's still got his back to Rose. He's looking down at the street, at the tourists starting to emerge for evening meals and convivial drinks. Men, normally stiff in city suits and ties, now let loose in linen trousers and pastel polo shirts; women wearing light floral dresses and strappy sandals. All of them thinking their newly acquired pink-skinned tans make them look as exotic as the locals when, really, they're more reminiscent of a parade of well-dressed lobsters.

'What?' Rose says.

'I'm going to go back.'

She says nothing. Luke turns and looks at her. Her shoulders are slumped. She looks relieved. And defeated.

She thinks he agrees with her; that she has to do this on her own. And she's glad but she's devastated.

'Not like that,' he says, quickly. 'I'm not suggesting we go with your plan.'

'Then what are you suggesting?'

'That I go back and I . . . I hide the body. Dispose of it.'

Rose's eyes widen.

'Oh my God,' she says. 'Why would you even think that? You would do that for me?'

'Of course I would.'

His mind is made up.

He's not going to let her suffer for this.

'We can book you in here for a week or so,' he says. 'I'll fly over and tell people you fell ill when we arrived. I've come back to sort out some work and will rejoin you while you're recuperating. The school will give you more time off. Meanwhile I'll—'

'Stop.'

'– figure out a way to move him.'

'Stop.'

'I don't know how I'll do it but I'll figure it out. Probably best I don't google *How to get rid of a dead body*—'

'Stop!'

Luke does stop. Rose is seething.

'Stop being so bloody stupid!' she cries. 'You are not the sort of person who disposes of a fucking dead body. Listen to yourself! You sound like a crazy person!'

And suddenly, it's happening. All the anger and fear and panic he's been trying to contain surges through him. That surreal feeling he's had all day, like he's been walking through a dream, is suddenly shattered and he realises the cold, hard reality of the situation they're in. Of the situation she's put him in.

'Listen to me?' he says, his voice low and angry. 'Listen to *you*. You left a dead man on the floor of our apartment. You booked us tickets to a Caribbean island. You waited until the day, almost the hour, we were going home to tell me all this. And you think I sound crazy? I'm the only one who's not acting nuts right now. The *only* one!'

Rose starts to cry, and Luke, to his horror, realises that he is crying as well.

And perhaps it's the fact that his tears are coming thicker and faster than hers which makes Rose stop and take both his hands in hers, her expression calmer than it has been all day.

'Luke, I'm sorry. I'm sorry I shouted at you. I just can't believe you'd do that.'

She can't meet his eyes. She looks ashamed, Luke thinks, like this is her fault.

It is but it isn't.

'I can't leave you to deal with it alone,' he replies. 'I won't.'

'I'm begging you to walk away from me.'

Luke squeezes her hands.

'I won't,' he says. 'If you won't let me do this, we'll do it another way. I'm coming with you. It could be weeks before he's discovered. Nobody has a key, there's no reason for anybody to go to my apartment. I can send an email to work. We have time. We can plan this. We can go on the run.'

'You've lost your mind.'

'I haven't. I'm your husband. You're not on your own.'

He thinks it's the last sentence that gets her. She collapses into him, her head buried in his chest. He can feel his heart thumping loudly and he knows she can hear it.

He takes a few deep breaths.

'There's just one thing,' he says.

She tenses, waiting.

'I need something from the apartment.'

'Luke.' She groans his name.

'I have to get it,' he says.

'What? What could you possibly need? If we do this . . . We have credit cards, we can empty our accounts from here, we could just run. Forget everything from before, just leave it all behind . . .'

'It's in my safe.'

'What? What is so important in the safe that you'd be willing to risk everything?'

Luke grimaces.

Does he tell her now?

Does he tell her the secret he's been keeping from her?

London

Mickey has to hand it to Nathan, he's gone all out for her.

He collected her from the hospital this morning – he didn't even send a driver. He kept asking her if she was okay the whole way home. As soon as they arrived, he got straight to plumping up the pillows in their bed, settling her in and downloading a selection of her favourite movies with Sky On Demand. He'd bought in the freshest pastries and squeezed orange juice and a pile of what he imagines are fluff magazines she'd like to read while laid up.

There's only one issue.

Mickey doesn't plan to be laid up.

Once the doctors told her the sheer agony she was experiencing was basically down to bruising, Mickey decided it was mind over matter, and she's not the sort to stay in bed because of a little bruising. She has work to do.

Though, who knew bruising could hurt this bad?

Mickey gives herself an internal head-shake. Mind over matter.

Mickey knows that Petra's ex allowed her access to a bank account, set up in his name, so she had money to buy the clothes he wanted her to wear, to pay for make-up, beauty treatments and so on. The things he expected her to do so she would look good for him.

It always amazes Mickey how much effort some men can put into moulding women into a certain image while simultaneously destroying their self-esteem.

Mickey wants to make sure the account is not shut down by the ex's very wealthy family or legal team before she gets its contents transferred into a bank account in Petra's name.

It's not exactly legal. Well, it's not legal at all. But one of the positives of working as a solicitor all those years ago (and sometimes Mickey struggles to remember the positives) is that she's met a lot of useful people in her life.

She'd stopped practising when she moved to England. It hadn't been her plan. She'd originally intended to secure the relevant qualifications she'd need to operate in a different jurisdiction. But even before she left Dublin, she'd already fallen out of love with the law. She'd realised, after one horrendously painful case in particular, how utterly useless the system was to secure justice for the marginalised and vulnerable.

While she'd been trying to decide what she wanted to do with her life, she'd gotten involved in a project aimed at helping rehabilitated former prisoners return to normal life. They needed some simple legal advice, and she had just enough knowledge to explain the English system in an informal, useful way. That's where she'd met Elliot Ibekwe. He was teaching computer skills to the former prisoners. He walked her home one evening and when she asked him how he'd started working with the group, he told her it had been at his sister, Nana's, request. Mickey had asked why his sister was so eager to see ex-prisoners rehabilitated and Elliot explained that Nana had barely escaped from a violent marriage, and her former husband had ended up in jail after his last attack on her.

Mickey was still confused. Why did Nana care so much for prisoners? She was the exact sort of person who'd fall into the category of demanding people be locked up for life. The fact her ex had apparently only been imprisoned for eighteen months only compounded Mickey's puzzlement.

Elliot told Mickey then that Nana had two wishes. One, that her ex would go on to live a better life and never harm a woman again, and two, that her brother Elliot would keep himself busy and not go find the ex and beat him to death.

It wasn't that Elliot had gotten Mickey interested in helping abused women.

It was that she'd needed the reminder that that was the work she really wanted to do.

And Elliot wanted to work with her. But he didn't want to do it in a conventional way. He, like Mickey, didn't have a huge amount of faith in the system, despite it eventually bringing justice for his sister.

Elliot gathered useful people to him. He spent half his day on computers for work and the other half on computers for pleasure. There was nothing and nobody the man couldn't find via the web. Sometimes his contacts operated on the fringes of illegality, sometimes they were just well-positioned.

Mickey knew exactly what was and wasn't achievable in legal terms and she too had a bit of a network. More importantly, she had money.

They were a dream team.

Mickey knows Elliot can help in Petra's situation. He'll know a guy who knows a guy who's good at forging signatures and Petra's ex's money will be in an untouchable account for Petra before the bank even realises the account holder is dead.

Mickey sits up against the freshly propped pillows on the bed and lets Nathan fuss a little more, knowing he'll need to go to work any moment now . . .

'You sure you have everything?' he asks.

'Absolutely.'

'And you'll take it easy today?'

'Absolutely.'

'You'll sleep?'

'Yep.'

'You're going to try to help that woman who was in the car, aren't you?'

'In between taking it easy and sleeping.'

Nathan leans down and kisses Mickey on her cheek. They're rarely this close any more. His hair is receding, she thinks. He's nearing fifty, after all. Not that she can comment. Her own has started to turn grey. And not just at the roots. Whole hairs. And it's thinning. She keeps finding strands on her pillow and clothes. Forty-two, but her body is changing and she can feel it. She's ageing quicker. Starting with her knees clicking when she gets out of the bed in the morning and now her hair. And the sides of her eyes, where fine lines keep appearing. And her eyelids, which are looking droopier every time she applies eyeshadow. Not to mention her neck, which seems to have creases in it that she'd never noticed.

Cheesy nachos, as Elliot would say. Stop.

Mickey chastises herself. She's never been a vain woman. Never had cause to be. She's not classically beautiful but she's not ugly and it doesn't matter either way because looks have never mattered to her. She's always placed more emphasis on brains.

'Is everything okay?' Nathan says.

'What do you mean?'

He sits down on the side of the bed. He's uncharacteristically still. Nathan is normally on the go, always rushing to this meeting or that meeting. Hedge fund managers don't exactly have time to stop and smell the roses. They're too busy shitting all over the world.

She doesn't judge that either, his career choice. His money allows her to do what she wants.

'You just seem a little on edge,' Nathan says. 'That guy driving into you . . . I know you're a tough cookie, but I don't take it for granted. It shook me. For a moment I thought . . .'

'I know,' Mickey says. 'I hate that you had that scare. It can't have been easy getting that call.'

'Forget about me. The second I found out you were fine, I was fine.'

Mickey hesitates.

'I am a little shaken,' she says. 'But I'll get over it.'

'And I'll get over the Bentley being totalled. Next time, I'm buying you an armoured tank.'

She smiles.

It's not the crash that's on her mind.

Sure, the whole experience was disturbing. But she's dealt with violence from abusive partners before. Not this extreme, perhaps, but certainly frightening situations.

She's upset for Petra, too, but she squeezed more information out of another doctor this morning and Petra will walk again, eventually. They also haven't entirely ruled out her ability to carry children in the future. Plus, the greatest threat to her has removed himself, so, in the long run, Petra will probably accept the horrifying crash as the last sting of a very dangerous wasp and thank her lucky stars it wasn't worse.

It's that call from Luke Miller that's left Mickey on edge.

She knows Luke.

Well, she used to think she did. Things changed between them, things that left her thinking she didn't know him at all.

But she can still tell when something is wrong, and when something is really, really wrong.

You never stop caring for somebody who's been that important in your life.

He hasn't rung again and Mickey is afraid to phone him, but she feels in her bones that whatever is going on, she's going to be involved. She already is.

Nathan is watching her, studying her.

He's good at reading people. Almost as good as he is at reading numbers.

'You'd tell me if it was anything more, wouldn't you?' he says.

'Yes,' Mickey reassures him.

She's lying.

She knows it and he knows it. But he won't say anything. The success of their marriage is based on what they do and don't tell each other.

It works for them.

Nathan stands up, pecks her cheek again and leaves.

Mickey sighs.

Luke Miller.

Even in the midst of yesterday's trauma, just one phone call with him has upended her.

And there's more to come. She can feel it in her bruised bones.

Saint-Thérèse

The hotel is not a long-term solution. Despite it being low-budget, with people keeping to themselves and no shared bar or restaurant area, there are still too many common areas where Luke and Rose will be noticed. Remembered.

So Luke has embarked on the next stage of his gut-reaction plan.

He rests the rented moped against a palm tree and opens his phone to check the Google Maps location the villa's manager has sent.

He probably shouldn't be using his phone. Will they be able to pinpoint his location, when they come looking for him? He doesn't know how sophisticated current investigative technology is, as pointed out by Mickey.

Still. They just need this place to lie low at for a few days. When he gets what he needs, they can move on. They can become invisible.

He's close, less than one hundred metres away, but the villa is off-road and he has to walk. He can't take the moped. Which is no bad thing. Out of sight . . . out of sight.

Luke starts towards the sea, following a man-made path through the white sand. There's lush green grass to either side and sea purslane, with its dainty purple flowers, creeps out among the blades.

The villa is expensive but with the money comes privacy. It's run by an agency and all they wanted was Luke's credit card details to ascertain proof of funds. He promised to forward on a scan of his passport but he thinks he'll get a few days' grace before the office contacts him again. It's all he needs. Names are one thing, photos are another. If somebody received his picture at the same time the police released a wanted image . . . well, his goal is to slow the process just a little.

Luke grimaces. The way he's thinking, the thoughts flitting through his head. He can't even take a breath or he'll start to analyse it all and realise how insane this is.

He's planning to uproot his whole life. To go on the run.

With a woman he's known only nine months.

But what was his life before he met Rose? Work. Making money. Superficial relationships. The gym. The pub. He has no immediate family left. He's had nobody close, properly close, for years. He thinks that's what drew him and Rose together so swiftly and so intensely. Both are only children, both have no parents. In Rose's case, because they've both passed away; in Luke's, because his mother is sadly deceased and his father is sadly still bloody living.

And it's not like he hasn't done insane, spontaneous things in the past.

Lost in thought, he doesn't notice the path widen until suddenly he can see the ocean, and there, to his right, stands his and Rose's temporary new home.

It's not unlike the place they've been staying for the last week. White paint; plantation shutters across the windows and doors to keep out the morning sun and evening's insects; a low sloping roof and a roped deck decorated with rattan furnishings and a swing seat. Caribbean lilies and hibiscus grow in the grass planted around the villa and the leaves of coconut palm trees sway against its sides.

But, whereas the resort villa was one of several dotted along a strip of beach, this place is alone in its small cove.

It's perfect.

It feels like somewhere you'd escape to.

Somewhere you could hide.

Luke has left Rose in town picking up a few bits. They'll need more personal items if they're staying. Rose had packed in a panic in London. He realised that as the week went on, when he ran out of underwear on day four and had no deodorant or razors to speak of. He'd mocked her about her organisation skills; she'd laughed it off. He'd had no idea she'd been flinging stuff in a bag while stepping over a dead man on the floor.

She hadn't planned to return to London but she'd left her jewellery, her birth cert, everything important, back in the apartment.

He still can't figure out how she managed to keep going all week without breaking down. The only thing he can imagine is that she very successfully blocked it out. She blanked the whole episode from her memory as best she could and was only forced to relive it when the prospect of returning to the apartment became a reality.

Luke finds the lockbox for the villa's keys and inputs the number the agency provided.

It's cool inside and smells faintly of neroli. The housekeeping staff – staff which Luke has told the agency he won't need again for the duration of his stay – have already been in to give the place a once-over and they've left the air conditioning on. A welcome basket of exotic fruit sits on the counter beside a bottle of Veuve Clicquot. The fridge will be stocked, too, and the bathroom equipped with tiny bottles of branded beauty products. All included in the exorbitant price.

Luke sits on the couch and takes out his phone. The call he's about to make will be one of the hardest of his life.

What choice does he have?

The thing that is going to help him and Rose escape from this mess is sitting in the very place he can't get to.

He hasn't told Rose what he plans. She was right, last night, when she told him he was mad to think of returning to London. She had a point.

How could he dispose of a body? He's not a bloody professional. How do you even do these things? Acid in a bath? Roll him up in a mat and dump it in a river?

Rose must have thought he'd lost his mind.

But there are some things she's not right about.

He has the means to help them do this.

Just not on him, and there's only one way to get it.

With a heavy heart, Luke dials Mickey's number again.

She picks up after a single ring.

'I knew you'd call,' she says.

'Because I've always been so predictable?'

'Ha.'

They both let that hang in the air for a few moments.

Luke looks up at the overhead fan, spinning noiselessly.

'Nobody makes a call like that without a follow-up,' Mickey says.

'You sound better,' Luke replies. He's playing for time. Delaying the inevitable. 'What had you so stressed yesterday?'

'Aside from the hypothetical scenario you presented me with? I was in a car accident. Not so much an accident as somebody driving into me deliberately.'

'Mickey! What?'

'Indeed.'

'Are you all right?'

'Well, when you rang I was in the hospital, but I'm home now. Bad bruising. My passenger took the worst of it. She'll be okay. Eventually. You should have seen the other guy.'

'Glad to hear it.'

Luke scrunches his eyes closed. He imagines Mickey lying in bed, battered and sore yet sitting up to take his call. So many years have passed since he last saw her. She'd been crying, that last time, but she was still beautiful. Mickey never did anything without looking beautiful, and the fact she didn't care what she looked like made her even more so.

Luke never thought he'd meet another woman like Mickey. And when he did, that woman was Rose.

He's still fond of Mickey. It pains him to know he's about to request that she do something for him that he has no right to ask of her. Especially now he knows she's not at her best.

'Mickey, I know I've no right—'

'Just ask it,' Mickey says.

Luke laughs, nervously.

'How can you read me so well when I'm on a phone in another country and you can't even see my face?' he says.

'Where are you, actually?' she asks.

Luke sighs.

'It's better I don't say. I'm in a spot of bother.'

'No shit.'

'I wouldn't involve you but I can only go to—'

'Someone you trust.'

'Exactly.'

'Is this to do with the dead body and the fleeing-the-scene scenario?'

Luke runs his tongue around his teeth. His mouth is suddenly very dry.

He stands and walks to the fridge, listening to Mickey's quiet breathing as he does.

He grabs a bottle of chilled mineral water and pops the cap, his phone resting between his ear and his shoulder

'There's something in my apartment and I need it.'

'Okay.'

'There's also something else in my apartment.'

Silence.

Followed by:

'Oh, Luke. I can't—'

'Just hear me out. I don't want you to cover up for me. I want you to report me to the police.'

'What?'

'All I'm asking is that you get this thing from my safe, first. You can hide it on your person, it's small. And then you can phone the police and tell them what you've found.'

'And what will I have found?'

Mickey's breathing is a little louder now, the only indication she's panicking.

'A dead man, on my bedroom floor.'

'Can I ask why he's there?'

'Mickey—'

'Luke, if you are asking this of me, I get to make demands in return.'

Luke closes his eyes again. That low-lying headache that's been there since Rose's revelation keeps threatening to peak.

'Yes,' he says. 'You're right. Of course. This man tried to hurt somebody I love.'

'In your apartment?'

'Yes.'

'So, it was self-defence.'

'Yes.'

'Why didn't you just report it?'

'Panic, Mickey. Who knows how they'll react to killing a person until they've actually killed a person?'

'Right. So – this man was hurting somebody you loved and what . . . You happened in on it?'

'Something like that.'

He knew she'd do this. Mickey is no fool. She can sniff out a lie from a million miles away. She's impossible to be around.

'Mickey, I can't tell you any more. But look, we both know I'm in a lot of trouble. And . . . I've phoned you twice now so there'll be a record of it.'

Mickey falls silent again.

'You utter bastard, Luke.'

Luke hangs his head.

They both understand what he means. Mickey can either do what he's suggesting, and clear herself in the process, or she'll have to explain to the police at a later date why Luke Miller didn't ring for years but rang her twice in a week after he killed a man in his apartment.

'Maybe,' she says, her voice low and angry, 'I should just call the police now and save myself the bother.'

'You could do that,' he says.

He waits. Listens to her mind running the calculations. Totting up the balance sheet between the pair of them. Knowing how little sits on his side of the page.

A minute passes. Maybe more. The silence feels endless.

'What do you need from the apartment?'

'Mickey—'

'Just tell me.'

'There's a safe in my sitting room. Under the bookshelves. I'll give you the code. And I'll give you an address where you can send the item. It has to be sent absolutely securely, do you understand? Secure and fast.'

'If it's that important, are you sure I should be posting it? Shouldn't it be brought in person? Nothing is absolutely secure, Luke.'

'If it's lost it can be replaced, but I'd rather not have to deal with the bother.'

'Fine. So, I get this thing and then what? Do I stuff it up my fanny or something? And then I phone the police and tell them I wandered into your bedroom and made a gruesome discovery? Why am I there, Luke? What sends me to your apartment and how do I get in?'

'It's a keypad entry. You know the code. We're old friends and we were meant to meet for dinner before I left London. I didn't show. You grew concerned. I rang you twice, I made some excuses, but I sounded off on the phone. You decided to come to the apartment to check up on me. I didn't answer. You thought you . . . smelled something funny. You let yourself in.'

'Jesus Christ.'

He can hear Mickey take a deep breath.

'If I can smell this thing outside your apartment, won't your neighbours have picked up on it?' she asks.

'There's only two apartments on our floor and the other one is empty until November. A professor. He's teaching in France. I've been watering his plants.'

'How very convenient.'

'I was due some luck.'

Mickey sighs heavily.

'What's in the safe that you're so desperate to get your hands on?'

'You'll know it when you see it.'

'Luke . . . I know you think this is the only way, but I swear to you, if you come back—'

'I can't, Mickey. If I thought I could, I would.'

Neither of them says anything for a few seconds.

'Because it's not about you,' Mickey says. 'It's about her.'

Luke presses his hand against his forehead.

'I hope she's worth it,' Mickey says. 'I've got a pen. Give me what I'll need.'

Luke sends a silent prayer of thanks to a God who has no reason to be on his side.

Within hours he'll be a wanted man.

He knows Rose is worth it.

London

December 2021

Luke had offered to pick her up at her place but Rose told him she'd prefer to meet in the bar.

He probably thinks her reaction is normal. Isn't it safer for women to meet in a public place and not give out their address first thing to a complete stranger?

It's more than that with Rose, though.

It's not strangers that she fears.

She stops outside the bar. The street is quiet. It's starting to freeze; the pavements glisten with early evening frost and the lure of the Boxing Day sales has waned now it's past four and growing darker by the second.

Soft light pours out from the window of the pub he's chosen. It looks warm and welcoming. Rose peers inside. The optics behind the bar are illuminated with a mirror of backlights; the candles on the tables reflect against wine glasses; the clientele are men in suits and well-dressed women, toasting themselves for getting through Christmas.

He's arrived early. She can see him perched on a high stool at one of those thick oak tables erected on an old barrel. She hates high stools. She has an irrational fear of falling backwards.

He's wearing jeans and a shirt and has a glass of what looks like sparkling water in front of him. He's checking his phone and the door, anxiously. He can't see her looking in the window, she's just out of his eyeline.

She's impressed that he's drinking water. It shows thoughtfulness and confidence. He doesn't need Dutch courage for when she arrives. Given their first meeting was in a pub and their second conversation was with him, as he put it, having had a few drinks, she could be forgiven for assuming he needs alcohol to make small talk.

Rose steels herself.

She can do this.

Before she can move, she hears her phone beep in her handbag. She takes it out, her fingers trembling in the cold.

She reads the message.

Her heart beats faster.

It's an unknown number. All it says is, *Thinking of you.*

It's probably just a wrong number. Rose frowns and puts her phone back in her bag.

Luke stands when he sees her. A gentleman.

'Hi,' he says. 'You came.'

Rose's chest tightens. His face is filled with a hopeful sort of happiness.

And she's only here to tell him she made a mistake. She doesn't know what she was thinking on Christmas Eve. It must have been the day itself, all her memories and her loneliness. Whatever it was, there was no excuse for letting her guard down.

She can't bring this man into her fucked-up life, she'll tell him that. She'll be honest.

She'll say that she wouldn't stand up anyone, that's the only reason she's here. Explain that she's not at a place in her life where she's ready to date people, that he's better off not knowing her. But before she can get a word out, he starts talking. He's nervous, she realises. Desperate to ensure there are no awkward silences.

'Can I get you a drink?' he says. 'I didn't know what to order or I'd have had one in for you. I figured it was too early for shots but that's all I saw you drinking in the pub that night.'

Rose blushes.

He holds out the stool for her as he speaks, but just as she's about to sit, he stops her.

'Oh, wait, look. Here's one with a back.'

He crosses to a recently vacated table and takes that stool instead.

'Sometimes I get vertigo at these tables,' he says. 'And I'm tall enough to be able to touch the floor when I sit.'

Rose's stomach flips. He's considerate. It's only making this harder.

'Thank you,' she tells him. She hadn't intended to stay but now she's taking off her coat and sitting down. He helps her nudge the stool in. He's strong, he can almost lift the stool with her on it.

'You look beautiful,' he says.

Rose glances down at herself. She's wearing a cream wool sweater over jeans and has barely a lick of make-up on. Passable, is how she'd describe herself.

'Luke, I—'

He's back in his own seat, now, facing her.

'Don't say it,' he says.

'What?'

He looks crestfallen.

'You're about to say you didn't want to stand me up but you're regretting agreeing to meet.'

She frowns.

'I could see it on your face when you walked in,' he says. 'Look, I don't know you very well. Scratch that. I don't know you at all. Maybe you want to concentrate on your career. Or maybe you like living alone. Maybe your last boyfriend was a complete dickhead and now you think all men are dickheads and—'

'I don't think all men are dickheads.'

'Well, great, but I guess you still don't want to see anybody and I get—'

'My last boyfriend left me for dead.'

Rose takes a sharp breath as soon as the words have left her mouth. Luke's eyes, those deep grey eyes, widen. His jaw falls slack. He stares at her.

There's not much point in dancing around it, Rose thinks. Why string it out, letting him think he has a hope with her when what she is will never alter?

Rose is never going to feel anything for Luke Miller.

'It's true,' she says. 'My ex is a psychopath. There's not much more I can say. I know you like me. I could go on a few dates with you, I could smile and be friendly and try to hide how fucked up I am, but what would it achieve? Eventually, you'd know. You'd realise I'm scared of my own shadow. That I can't bear to be around you. Around most men. I'd push you away. You'd be hurt. It would be a waste of time for both of us. I'm sorry. You were right. I did come to tell you that I shouldn't have made plans. It would have been better to just stand you up and leave you thinking I'm a bitch. That's on me. I don't want you to pity me. I just want you to understand.'

Rose starts to lower herself from the stool. Luke looks like he's in shock.

'Wait,' he says.

Rose doesn't want to meet his eye.

'Please,' he says. 'Just . . . just give me five minutes to process this. You don't owe me anything. But, I'm begging you, if you'll just—'

'Why?' Rose says, hopelessly. 'I am as damaged and broken as you have probably already guessed. Luke, you're right, we don't know each other, but you seem to be a nice chap and you're handsome and funny and I'm sure you don't go short of girlfriends—'

'My father used to hit my mother.'

It's Rose's turn to be shocked. She sits back on to the stool. Luke's face – he looks appalled at what he's just spat out, like he wishes he could suck it back in.

Rose stares at him.

'I'm sorry to hear that,' she says. 'But I'm . . . I'm not looking for a saviour.'

'I'm not offering to be one. I'm just saying, I understand. No. That's wrong. I don't know your life or what happened to you. But I can appreciate why you might not want to see anyone. I won't make any judgements about your choices or try to convince you I'm not that sort of man. Can I just ask for one thing, though?'

Rose sighs. She nods, barely.

'Can we have a drink? I feel like we could both do with one and I know I'm going to order one whether you're here or not.

71

I'd hazard a guess you might want something stiff, too, so why drink alone?'

Rose hesitates. The right thing to do is leave. She knows that. Every fibre of her being is telling her to walk away from this table, from the bar, from this man and how all of this will play out.

And yet . . .

'White wine,' she says.

Luke wins the attention of a passing waiter, who pauses long enough to hear the order.

'White wine for the lady and a whisky, straight, please.'

'Pinot Grigio or Chardonnay or—'

'Sauvignon,' Rose says, cutting the waiter off. He departs, instinctively knowing this isn't a table to run through the list of Sauvignons they have behind the bar.

'You don't beat around the bush, anyway,' he says.

'Yes. I'm sorry. I just . . . I've been here before. I don't mean here, here.'

'I know what you mean. On awkward dates. Do you, um, usually tell them what happened to you?'

'No. But I'm tired of skirting around it. I'm tired of pretending to be normal.'

'I'm glad you decided to be up front with me.'

'Sure. I bet you're thrilled this is how your Boxing Day is going. Sitting in a bar with a crazy woman who sounds like she's applying for a slot on a daytime shock reality show.'

'I've had less interesting Boxing Days, it's true.'

Rose looks at him. There's a hint of a smile behind his eyes. Why is he not running for the hills?

'I'm sorry about your mam,' she says.

'My what?'

'Your mum. Sorry. We say mam where I'm from. You ever hear of a place called Donegal?'

Rose watches him blink a few times as the county name registers. He narrows his eyes and seems to think for a few seconds.

'I know Donegal,' he says.

'Most English people only know Dublin and Belfast.'

'You'd be surprised. I know people from all over Ireland.'

Luke frowns, like he's remembering something unpleasant. Rose watches him, wondering what's going on in his head.

'If you're going to ask if I know them too, the answer is probably no,' she says. 'Ireland is a lot bigger than people think, but everybody assumes we all know each other.'

'I get that. Though I'm surprised there's anybody left over there. You all seem to live here.'

'Well, you lot spent a fair amount of time over in ours,' she says.

He smiles and she half smiles in return.

'We emigrate a lot. I think more people leave Donegal than any other county in Ireland, proportionally speaking. It's the isolation. You know it's the last place in Europe before Nova Scotia? But I've gone off-topic. Your mum?'

He blinks, like he's dismissed something else he was thinking about, and meets her eye.

'It's not something I like to dwell on,' he says. 'It wasn't . . . It only happened a few times. When my dad had drink on him. He stopped drinking, eventually. Just as well. I got old enough to land punches of my own. He . . . he wasn't a good role model.'

'Is he still alive?'

'Yeah. But I have nothing to do with him. Not since Mum died.'

Rose says nothing. Luke's eyes glaze with what she imagines aren't happy memories but then he shakes his head and gives her his full attention again.

'This isn't about me, though,' he says. 'And I hate when people do that. You tell them something that's happened to you and they say, I get it, it happened to me. It didn't happen to me. But I understand it a little and I'm sorry for what you went through.'

She shrugs.

'Me too.'

'But, you got away.'

This time, she stares at the table.

How much should she tell him? Does she give him the rehearsed story or tell him the truth? Spin it like a heroine who survived or reveal the coward she really is?

In for a penny, in for a pound, Rose decides.

'Look, Luke,' she says. 'I didn't get away. Not in that way, anyway. I didn't stand up to my ex. I didn't have him arrested or charged or any of that. I ran.'

'What do you mean?'

He's confused. He's already reassessing, she thinks. This isn't like his folks, with his dad lashing out while blasted. This is more serious than anything he can get his head around.

'I mean, I came to London to get away from him and he doesn't know where I am.'

'Jesus.'

'Yes.'

'Is Rose your—'

'Real name? It is now. Rose Gillespie.'

He seems to mull on this.

'I don't know what to say.'

'You don't need to say anything. You just need to know that I'm not straightforward. I've more baggage than a flight back from the States after the Thanksgiving sales.'

Luke snorts.

'What?' she says.

'I can't believe you can be so self-deprecating when you're speaking about this.'

'What else can I do?' she says. She swallows; there's a hard lump in her throat. Just in time, the waiter arrives back with the drinks. He places three napkin coasters on the table and puts down the wine, Luke's whisky and a small glass of water.

Luke thanks him and Rose picks up the wine and takes a large sip.

'I left my home and my job and people I knew,' she says. 'I gave up everything. All I took with me was my sense of humour.'

She looks at him, watching her, listening to every word. He still doesn't look alarmed. Why? Why isn't this alarming him?

'I don't know why I'm telling you all this,' she says.

'Maybe you need to,' he says. 'I'm a stranger. It sounds like you've a lot on your chest and I'm guessing you think you'll never see me again.'

'I won't,' Rose says.

Luke shakes his head at her. It's gentle, but determined.

'You will,' he says. 'I hope. I don't want to pressure you. I wouldn't have, anyway, but if you think what you've told me will scare me away . . . it doesn't.'

'Why? Why doesn't it? I've just told you I'm on the run from a violent, nasty man. It's not a game.'

'I don't imagine it is. But it sounds like you've already done the hard yards. You've just told me what you've had to give up. Are you supposed to live on your own now, not make friends, never see people?'

'He's dangerous, Luke. If he ever found me . . . If I was with somebody . . . Do you understand? It would be worse if I was with somebody. He would see that man as a target and he'd punish me twice as much.'

Luke says nothing. *Now*, she thinks. Now he's starting to realise what she means. He'll hardly keep pushing, not after that.

He picks up his whisky and sips it.

'There are a lot of dangerous people in the world,' he says, when he's placed the glass back down. 'Do you really think he's looking for you?'

'I know he is.'

'Where does he live?'

'He still lives in Donegal.'

'And he doesn't know you're in London?'

'I hope not. I get paranoid. For all I know, you could be working for him.'

'I can assure you, I'm not.'

She snorts.

'Well, you would say that.'

'I suppose I would,' he says. 'But, did you ever see *Sleeping with the Enemy*?'

'Oh my God.' Rose almost laughs. 'I'm not Julia Roberts. This isn't a film. My life is not a movie.'

'I'm not saying it is. I'm saying, you remember her neighbour? The nice bloke with the beard?'

Rose arches her eyebrows.

'I'm the nice guy,' Luke says.

'You're the gorgeous actor from that Hollywood movie who swoops in and saves Julia Roberts. Ego, much? Shall I ask the waiter can he stick on *"Brown Eyed Girl"*?'

Luke smiles, softly.

'I never said I wasn't a fucking idiot,' he says.

He meets her eye.

'I realise you might not want to spend time with me for other reasons,' he says. 'I understand if that's the case. And I don't know everything that happened to you. I'm happy if you want to tell me, but you don't have to. I can see you've been hurt. But if you'd let me, I'd like to be your friend. Can we start with that?'

Rose's eyes start to prickle.

She wasn't expecting that.

Luke Miller is not what she expected.

But he doesn't know what he's getting into.

Even as she thinks it, she hears her phone beep again in her handbag.

It's probably nothing, she tells herself again.

Nobody is watching me.

She almost believes it.

London

Elliot drops Mickey on the corner of the street where Luke lives.

It's the same apartment he's lived in for the last eight years. She wonders about that, why he and Rose decided to live there, and not in hers. Or buy somewhere completely different.

But then, she doesn't know anything about Rose. Luke sent her an invite to the wedding. Mickey said she couldn't make it and sent champagne. They have tried, over the last decade, to talk. She and Luke. It was always going to be difficult to go from their sort of closeness to absolute absence, and for a while, Mickey thought they could stay friends. They'd managed a stiff sort of accord for a while. But then, one night, a few drinks were taken. Mickey lost her temper with him and she knew, then, they couldn't be friends. That's not what they were.

'You want me to come in?' Elliot asks. His Nigerian accent has become mixed with East London over the years and now it's a hybrid, melodic sound. It suits him, makes him even more unusual. Because nothing about Elliot is usual. He's a contradiction in terms. He's handsome, and he has a physical strength that sometimes Mickey is grateful for. But he doesn't exploit that strength. Elliot would never start an argument with anybody. Finish one, if it was necessary, but Elliot is not the violent kind. He prefers computer screens to people. He likes films and old music and he tries not to swear because his church-going mother finds it uncouth. Mickey's never known anybody to take care of his family so well. Elliot lives with his sister Nana and her two kids now and he has dinner with his parents every week. He works his backside off to make sure his family has a wonderful life.

'No, there's nothing dangerous here,' Mickey lies. 'You don't need to hang around, either. In fact, it's best you don't.'

Elliot studies her, sees she's not going to tell him more and nods. They have an easy shorthand between them.

Mickey steps out on to the pavement. The rain of two days ago is but a distant memory. An Indian summer has made itself known and even the ground feels warm beneath her sandals.

She winces a little as she turns to wave goodbye to Elliot. It's a waste of time; he's already driving off and he doesn't look back.

Nathan isn't happy about her returning to work today – which is what she's told him she's doing. He doesn't have a leg to stand on, though. She's seen him for approximately thirty minutes since he brought her home from the hospital because, once he realised she was doing okay, he went back to work and stopped checking on her.

It was never an option for Mickey to spend a second day in bed. The doctor had told her rest would speed up recovery. But Mickey is only getting sorer and stiffer.

And she doesn't plan to do too much today, anyway.

Just report a murder.

Mickey sighs, heavily.

She lets herself into the sleek, modern apartment building.

She winces in the lobby as she waits for the lift. The events of forty-eight hours ago are still fresh in her head. Petra's apartment and everything that happened afterwards.

Inside the lift, Mickey is forced to see herself reflected in the mirrors on every wall. She looks pale and tired; the bruises on her forehead and cheekbone are still dark but nothing compared to those on her ribs and back, which are making her hunch slightly.

She looks like a battered woman.

She's going to have to think of a reason why she decided to check on her friend Luke, given she's the one who looks like she should be in bed. The police will ask. Two days after an accident? You were so consumed with worry about this man that you dragged yourself from your sick bed and went to his apartment?

Mickey has a sort of plan in place. She'll phone an old friend of Nathan's first. Met detective Des White. It's natural that's who she'll call when she's in shock. And he'll tell his colleagues what she's like. Oh, that Mickey one. She can't sit still for five minutes. She's the exact sort of person to keep going two days after somebody drove into her.

Des should act as a mitigator for some of the more suspicious minds.

Outside Luke's door, Mickey notes that there is, indeed, only one other apartment on the floor. She hasn't actually been in this apartment; she just knows it's where Luke moved after his flat in Camden. She remembers that flat and, hell, it wasn't a patch on this one.

That's another question she's hoping the cops don't ask.

How friendly are you with Luke Miller and his wife, Rose? How well do you know them? How often do you see them?

Never. That's the honest answer.

They spoke about this on the phone, Mickey and Luke. She understood why it was her he came to, but for her to be concerned about him, they'd have to be in frequent contact. And the truth is, they're not. Two phone calls in the last few days and before that – nothing.

They've added detail to their fabricated story. They fell out of touch for a few years. Both caught up in their careers, their lives. But in the last few months, they met up again, an accidental meeting in a bar . . . nostalgic memories, drinks, all the old friendship flooding back. They were meant to meet before he travelled, but he cancelled. He rang a couple of times; he sounded strange on both occasions. He'd assured her they'd meet when he returned from holidays but when she tried to pin him to a date, he was evasive. She had tried to call him a few times (and Mickey had, with Luke letting the phone ring out, just so that part of the story could be backed up). But he didn't answer his phone.

So Mickey became very worried and very curious. And she has his apartment code because he gave it to her years ago, so she could take care of the place for him the odd time.

But equally, given how busy they've both been, she doesn't know a lot about his life in recent years so no, she doesn't know how he could do this or where he is now.

Mickey's fingers hover over the keypad.

Once she does this, there's no going back.

She types the passcode.

The door opens with a soft click.

Mickey lets herself in. She braces herself; she's expecting her senses to be assaulted by the smell of decomposition.

There's nothing, and Mickey realises, her fingers still on the thick, solid front door, that the quality of the apartment build might be playing its part.

If Luke's internal doors have a similar density to this one, they're stopping any smell from travelling.

She'll need to open the bedroom door to let the stench into the apartment. Otherwise, the part of her narrative that sends her into Luke's apartment – it was the smell, Officer, that's when I knew something was very wrong – is all off.

But she has a job to do first. She closes the front door.

Mickey looks around. The apartment is tasteful in a clinical, faux 'New England seaside'-type way. Soft colours, a light grey couch covered with white scatter cushions, carefully selected paintings of boats in blue and white hues. There's a lot of money in this apartment. But it's the complete opposite of her and Nathan's house. Mickey leaves most of the styling in her home to her husband, not having any inclination, time or great desire to put her stamp on things. Their house is mainly dark wood and low lighting and expensive designer pieces.

Everything in here speaks to Rose's taste, not Luke's, unless Luke has had a personality transplant.

Mickey shakes her head. When she first met Luke, one of his favourite things to do on a Saturday afternoon was visit antique furniture stores looking for bargains. Mickey used to joke that his future house would have to be the square footage of Versailles, he wanted to buy so much.

She often thought Luke would love her house. Him and Nathan, they could live there together and be perfectly happy surrounded by all the dark oak and manly furniture.

Mickey walks to the mounted bookshelves.

Just as Luke said, on the floor beneath is a small safe.

Even though she knows there's nobody there – nobody living at least – Mickey feels spooked.

She glances over her shoulder before putting on her gloves, the gloves she brought specifically so her fingerprints wouldn't be on the safe, and dials in the six digits.

The safe opens.

Mickey ignores the small amount of money and documents. Instead, she takes out the wallet-type box. She opens it and sees a small, square metal chip inside. In shape, it resembles a casino token.

Mickey knows what it is. It's a crypto card, designed to transfer digital amounts of money. Mickey can't fathom why Luke has one or how much is on it.

But they're questions for another day.

Mickey puts the chip inside her bra. She puts the wallet back in the safe. It means nothing without its contents and the cops will notice it, but if they know what it is, they'll most likely assume Luke took the chip out.

She closes the safe.

It's time.

She can't put it off any longer.

Mickey walks towards the hall she imagines leads to the bedrooms.

She's guessed correctly.

The first door she opens is to what looks like a guest bedroom.

On the wall as she passes, there's a framed photograph of Luke and Rose on their wedding day. Rose, even in a simple dress, with her blonde hair in a French knot, looks exquisite.

Luke looks the same as ever.

They appear to be very much in love.

Mickey swallows. She walks on. Her heart is beating too fast and her mouth feels dry as she approaches the next door on the corridor.

When she lifts her hand to open it, she realises she is shaking.

Mickey has seen a lot of awful things in her life but never this. Not a body that's been in situ for, what is it now, nine days?

She turns the handle.

The first thing she sees is blood.

There's a lot of blood.

The next thing she sees makes her legs buckle.

Saint-Thérèse

When they've put away the items that Rose bought in town, Luke convinces her to go for a swim. She's been edgy ever since she got to the villa and he wants to distract her.

Rose stares at him.

'Swimming?' she says. 'Right now?'

'Right now,' he says. 'What else are we doing?'

'Going on the run.'

'Fair enough, but is there a schedule we're meant to follow?'

Rose looks at him unhappily. She thinks the fact he's making jokes means something more than it is. That he's not processing what's happened or that he is in shock.

It's neither of those things. Luke knows his brain can only handle so much at any given moment and he needs to give himself time out from the madness so he can keep going. He wants to swim in the sea and stare up at the sky, just for a few minutes, so he can feel normal. He needs it. And she needs it, too.

They walk hand in hand into the water, cold at first against the heat of the day, but as they submerge themselves, their bodies adjust and Luke throws himself back so he's floating. Rose looks at him for a moment, then does the same.

When he hears her flip over and start to swim, Luke also turns and takes a few strokes. He catches up with her quickly, his arms longer and stronger, and tugs at her calf. She starts and spins around to him, surprised.

They're a little out of their depth now and they bob in the water as Luke holds Rose, feeling her skin next to his. With her hair wet and her face free of make-up, she looks so much younger and more vulnerable.

He places his forehead against hers.

He loves this woman.

'This is mental,' Rose says.

'More or less mental than everything else we've been through in the last twenty-four hours?'

He's broken through. She smiles. She hasn't smiled since she told him.

'Arguably more, in context,' she replies.

'Where do you want to go?' Luke asks. 'When we leave here?'

She shrugs.

'I haven't thought that far ahead. Somewhere I can work, so it has to be either English- or French-speaking. My French is good.'

'I have some Italian.'

'I don't think asking for wine in a sing-song accent counts towards fluency.'

'*Mamma mia.*'

She smiles again.

'I need to be able to earn,' she says.

'You won't have to worry about that.'

'Of course I have to worry about it, Luke. What are you going to do, anyway? It's not easy, you know, to start up a new life. You have to find somebody to help you create a name, a back story, qualifications. Teaching is an easy one. Managing pension portfolios is a little more boutique. Are you going to be happy getting a job in a bar or on a building site so you don't stand out?'

'Not with these soft hands. I'll stand out like . . . somebody who goes for manicures.'

'Luke, be serious.'

Luke cups her head in his hand. His legs are already tired. The irony of that is not lost on him. Rose is better at treading water than he is.

'I am being serious. We don't need to worry about money. I have enough.'

'Not enough to live off forever, though,' she says.

Luke doesn't answer. She looks worried again, and he wants to take that away, but he can't. Not yet. Not until everything is in place.

'Tell me about last time,' he says. 'Tell me about how you planned it.'

He tugs at her hand, leading her back to a depth he can reach with his feet.

She paddles with him. When they're on firmer ground, he stands upright while she turns on her back again and floats, looking up at the sky.

'I told you before,' she says.

'Not in detail. You told me you ran but you didn't tell me how you did it. The steps involved to get away.'

She's quiet for a few moments. Then she speaks.

'I met a man in a bar, in Derry. It was a work conference, teaching across borders. The man wasn't with our group. He was older and, I don't know, we got chatting. And I think he saw something in me. That I was somebody who needed kindness. He told me his life story. He'd been to jail. And when he'd got out, he wanted to start again but it was impossible because he had all this baggage and, well, Ireland is a small place. So I asked him whether he had considered moving.'

Luke nods to show he's listening, even if Rose is not looking at him. She's still looking up at the sky. Some clouds have rolled in, blocking out the harsh sun, and he can see how pale her face is, the tiredness and angst of the last week taking its toll.

'He asked me then where I thought he could go. He couldn't travel to lots of places because of his record. The United States and Australia were completely out. He could go south in Ireland, or over to England, but his convictions would follow him. He had no languages, he didn't want to try to settle on the continent, but even then, he'd struggle to get work. I told him I thought it was awful that he couldn't have a second chance and then he said he could have if he really wanted to. That he knew somebody who could create a whole new identity for him, but that would mean leaving everybody he knew. His family, his friends. He'd never be able to come home properly.'

'A forged ID?' Luke asks.

'Exactly that. But if he moved to the States with a fake ID, he couldn't risk going back and forward to Derry. We talked some more and we exchanged numbers and that night got me thinking.'

'How long did you think about it? I mean, how long did it take to plan and organise?'

Rose comes out of her floating position and now she's facing Luke, as he holds her by her waist.

'A lot longer than deciding in the course of one afternoon, or one week,' she says. 'Everything about this is messed up, Luke. It takes ages to create a new life, to be able to hide. And look what happened to me. I'm still running. If you think I know what I'm doing here, you're wrong. I'm going to ask you again—'

'Don't,' Luke says. 'Because the answer will be the same. And things are different now.'

'Yes. They're worse.'

'They're different because you have me.'

They stare at each other, in silence. Rose looks like she's trying to read him; Luke is trying to convince her that, with sheer willpower, everything is going to be okay.

'There must have been things you regretted leaving,' Luke says. 'I know your parents are gone and you weren't close with your family, but, other things.'

'I've told you all this before, Luke.'

'I know. But I suppose I was just listening to it with a sympathetic ear. Now, I want to learn from it.'

'He isolated me so much, it didn't matter. I didn't have friends I was worried about never seeing again. I wasn't going to see them again, regardless. You have friends. You have family.'

'Distant. And my friends are . . .'

He trails off. It's not the same for Luke. He loves his friends. Sure, he's not the most sociable of people. But his mother died when Luke was 21 and Luke broke off all contact with his father after that, so he's tried to plug that gap with people he's met over the years. People he's given a lot of his time to and who he knows he can call on when he needs them. His best friend, Xander, the rest of the guys from the footie team, some of his work colleagues.

But none of them have ever really known him. They've never realised what he's capable of. The last person Luke really let in was Mickey and that ended disastrously.

Luke has never feared properly losing somebody. Not until now.

Until Rose.

'They're not as important as you,' he says.

Luke has made his choice, he thinks. He will have this one person. He can allow himself that. Everything else — work, friends, his past — none of it is important. All that matters is this woman. His wife.

Rose is staring at him.

'If you're really serious about this, then I've been thinking,' she says.

'About?'

'If there's stuff you need from the apartment, maybe you should go back. Get our things and come back. If you can stomach it. I can't go back, Luke, but you could take whatever you need.'

Luke doesn't know what to say. Rose has no idea he's already put events in train.

In the silence, he thinks he can hear a phone ringing.

It's his, in his shorts pocket, back on the beach.

He realises what time it must be.

Mickey will have been to the apartment.

And now it begins.

London

January 2022

Rose makes her way through the cemetery grounds, picking up the pace as she gets closer to her destination.

The light is fading from the day and Highgate closes at four in winter.

She'd only stumbled on the grave by accident, a year ago. She'd been strolling through the cemetery after Ann-Marie had offered it up as a suggestion. Rose had mentioned she liked old graveyards and Ann-Marie said this was the best.

It had been summer and Rose was enjoying reading the names and dates on the headstones when she spotted it.

His name.

This find had felt serendipitous.

She arrives and stands at the foot of the grave for a few minutes. She looks at the name and summons memories of happier times, of a life before it all went wrong.

Then she places the small bunch of winter tulips against the headstone. She offers up a Hail Mary and turns for the gates.

She's going to Luke's this evening and she wants to get changed first.

It's too early to be meeting people in his life, Rose thinks, but Luke has insisted. Not aggressively. Just in that gentle way he has of convincing her that this is the best decision she can make at this time.

Like the way she met him for that drink on Boxing Day. And then a few days later, when they went for that meal. And letting him ring her on New Year's Eve, when he talked to her through the clock turning midnight and they celebrated the start of 2022 together, even if it was only on the phone.

And then they started going for walks in the evenings.

All of it a persistent persuasion that he should be in her life and she in his.

Rose feels almost happy to be led. He's pursuing her, she knows this, but so far it has been at a pace she can handle. He's been to her door, but not inside her flat. His hand has brushed hers, but he hasn't tried to touch her.

But now he wants her to come to his apartment. It's not an intimate occasion. It's a friend's birthday and the guy doesn't like surprises so, of course, Luke and his other friends have organised a surprise party, with Luke's apartment as the venue. The friend, Xander, thinks he's going to be hanging out at Luke's to watch a match and order pizza.

'There'll be loads of people there,' Luke has told Rose. 'You won't be the centre of attention, that will be Xander, and he'll hate the lot of us for it. But you should meet the people in my life. So you know I'm normal. Ish. I mean, we're a bunch of idiots, but idiots you'll like.'

So, Rose finds herself in the lift of Luke's apartment building at 7 p.m. that Friday night – a building she can't ever imagine being able to afford to live in – asking herself what the hell she's doing. Who is she at this surprise party? She's not one of his friends. It's too soon to be his girlfriend. How will he describe her when he introduces her? This is Rose. I met her a few weeks ago. She's a bit weird. We've already spent a lot of time together but she won't even let me hold her hand.

Rose shakes her head. She doesn't know why she's doing this.

Meeting the friends, that's normal dating behaviour. Nothing about this is normal.

The guy who lets her into Luke's apartment doesn't ask who she is. He's friendly as he introduces himself as Jack, welcomes her and takes her coat. Inside the apartment, there's an open-plan living and dining area, and through a small crowd, Rose sees Luke making cocktails at a large quartz breakfast island. He lifts his hand in greeting and signals he'll be with her in a tick. Somebody else approaches her, a woman who says her name is Ellen as she hands Rose a mojito.

Ellen ushers Rose towards another group, who all smile and introduce themselves.

It takes a full five minutes before Rose realises not one person has asked her name and every single person in this apartment knows who she is.

Luke has primed them.

When he comes over, he gives her a chaste hug.

He smells of limes and aftershave and it lands with a jolt that she likes how he smells.

'You got here okay,' he says. 'Xander will be here in a few. Kick-off is at 7.45. The little shit will be predictably late because he follows Liverpool.'

'I don't know what that means.'

'It means he has no interest in whether the teams playing tonight win, lose or draw because his team is already at the top of the league. So he's not rushing to arrive on time.'

'Why is he coming at all?'

'It's football. Why wouldn't he? What did you get up to this afternoon? I tried calling but your phone was off.'

'Nothing,' Rose lies. 'I just had a bath. The battery died.'

Luke smiles.

Rose looks around the room. The people here, they seem . . . nice. Luke has told her he works in pension investments and Rose imagined something more . . . laddish, she supposes. The city-boy types who hang out in the high-class bars in London, flaunting their cash with expensive suits and eye-watering drinks orders. Nothing about Luke has indicated he's like that yet and his friends certainly seem normal. But the apartment is incongruous. It looks like the home of somebody who earns a healthy six figures a year.

'Rose, are you hungry?' It's Jack, the guy who took her coat. 'We have pizzas coming in an hour but there are plenty of snacks.'

Rose eyes Luke. The way everybody is speaking to her, like she's already part of the gang.

'I'm fine, thank you,' she says.

'What?' Luke says, when Jack moves away.

'What have you told them?'

'Me? Nothing.'

'So, how come I haven't had to introduce myself to anybody?'

'They all work in very intuitive jobs.'

'I thought you were investors. Not psychics and psychiatrists.'

'This lot aren't investors.'

'No?'

'Fuck no. I don't just socialise with workmates. Unless it's a work do, obviously. Everybody here has a normal job. Xander's one of

94

my best mates and he and Jack are on my footie team. Ellen is Jack's sister. That gang over there are half football team, half girlfriends. The two guys in the kitchen work in my local pub.'

'Some of your best friends are barmen?'

'Isn't that a life goal?'

Rose laughs.

'So you made them all part of this plan to make me feel comfortable when I arrived? Do people always do what you say?'

'No,' Luke says. He touches her cheek, ever so gently, and looks at her with mock sadness.

The doorbell rings.

Luke smiles.

'That's him!'

While he's distracted, she touches her cheek where his fingers had brushed. Her skin feels on fire.

The crowd fall into surprise-mode unprompted, people giggling as they crouch behind pieces of furniture, the breakfast island, down a corridor that probably leads to the bedrooms.

Rose looks around, wondering where she should stand, what she should do. The apartment, cleared of all the bodies, looks so much larger and she feels like a sore thumb, even though Luke is still with her. She also realises, now she can see it properly, that the furniture in this place didn't come cheap. She looks at the back of Luke's head, wondering just how wealthy he is and how he manages to come across so normal.

'What are you crazy bastards doing?' Luke laughs. 'I'll just knock off the lights.'

'And how are you going to explain not having any lights on?' a bodiless voice replies.

'We only have to get him inside from the hall, I don't plan on keeping him in the dark for the next hour,' Luke retorts.

'Play along, for fuck's sake.'

Jack pops up from behind the breakfast island and walks towards the little hall that leads to the apartment's front door. Luke grins at him and then he takes Rose's hand and leads her to the corner of the living room area. They crouch down behind an armchair.

They listen as the doorbell rings again and then Jack opens the door. Muffled voices in the hallway into the apartment.

Then the door to where they're all hiding opens and everybody jumps up, yelling 'Surprise!'

Rose stands too, feeling embarrassed and awkward because she doesn't know Xander, she doesn't know these people. This is their night and she's an interloper, no matter how welcome they are determined to make her feel.

The newly arrived ginger-haired guy, Xander, looks caught between shock, pleasure and absolute disgust. His friends are smug and elated to have pulled off the surprise.

Rose turns to look at Luke, imagining his face too will be full of one-upmanship. But he's not looking at Xander. He's looking at her.

While everybody around them laughs and cheers and Xander's voice rises over the melee to call them all a shower of dickheads, Luke stares at Rose and she at him.

She can't take her eyes off him.

No, Rose thinks. No, no, no.

But that's just in her head.

Her body . . . that's saying yes.

Saint-Thérèse

Luke has three missed calls from Mickey.

Rose stands across from him, drying her hair with a towel as he dials Mickey's number, a look of puzzlement on her face.

Mickey answers after one ring.

'Luke, thank God. Why didn't you answer?'

'I was away from the phone.'

Luke frowns. She sounds panicked. He can't understand why she's ringing him. The police will be watching her now. He's expecting the cops to be calling him, chasing him, not Mickey.

'What's going on?' he asks. 'Did you do what we said?'

'I did what we said.'

'Where are you now?'

A deep breath on her end of the call.

'I'm in your apartment.'

The colour drains from Luke's face. What the hell is she playing at?

'Are the police there?'

'There's nobody here.'

'Jesus, Mickey – the police—'

Rose stops what she's doing and stands completely still.

'I haven't called them.'

'Mickey, we had a plan. What's going on? Are you able to talk?'

'There's nobody here.'

'You said! Why haven't you called the police? This wasn't part of the plan.'

He's growing more confused by the second.

'Luke, there is *no body* here.' This time she places the emphasis on separating the *no* and *body*. Luke grips the phone tight in his fingers.

'There's blood,' she adds. 'But there is no dead body in your apartment.'

'What the fuck?'

Luke looks at Rose, who, he sees now, has turned deathly pale.

'Has he been moved?' Luke asks, the only thing he can think of. 'Did somebody . . . has somebody been there already?'

'I don't think so. It looks like your shower was used and some towels. I mean, there's blood on the towels like somebody cleaned up, and I can see blood on the door handle in the bedroom and the bathroom, so I assume—'

'What is it?' Rose asks. She's standing beside him now. 'Who's that on the phone?'

'It's Mickey,' Luke tells her.

'Who? What have you done? Luke, what's going on?'

'Is that Rose?' Mickey asks.

Luke is looking at his wife and listening to Mickey and trying to process what's going on.

'He's not in the apartment,' Luke says.

Rose grabs his arm.

'What do you mean, it's Mickey?'

Luke tries to concentrate on Mickey for a moment.

'Are you sure? Mickey, did you look—'

'Jesus, I'm sure, Luke. If you're going to ask me if I somehow missed a dead body because I didn't look under the bed—'

'Okay. I need a moment. Can I phone you back? Will you stay there?'

'Don't be long.'

Mickey hangs up.

Rose pounces.

'Luke, what did you do?'

Luke puts his phone down on the countertop. He feels dazed.

'He's not there,' he says to Rose. 'Kevin Davidson is not in our apartment.'

'What are you talking about? What has Mickey Sheils got to do with all this?'

'There was something in the apartment I needed. I asked her to get it.'

Rose covers her mouth with her hand. She looks like she might pass out.

She's shocked that he put something into action without telling her.

The important point hasn't registered for her yet.

'Do you know what this means?' he says. 'Rose, you didn't kill him. Kevin Davidson is not dead. He got up and left that apartment.'

'No,' she says, shaking her head. She turns away from him. 'No. I can't believe you would do that. That you would go behind my back—'

'Rose, aren't you listening? You didn't kill Kevin.'

She's still looking away from him. When she speaks, her voice sounds different, clipped. She's in shock. She's not processing what he's saying.

'Why her? Why would you involve somebody else in our business?'

'Rose!'

He's exasperated now.

And this time, she turns and looks at him, but she's shaking her head.

'I killed him,' she says, her voice cold. 'I left him there. This is all wrong. Somebody has moved him.'

'Nobody has moved him,' Luke replies. 'Think this through. Why would they do that? If he was killed in our apartment, it's obvious you or I did it. Nobody would move and hide a dead body they hadn't murdered. They'd let the police find it. They'd let us be punished. Mickey said there was blood on the door handles, that the shower was used, there were towels . . .'

Rose looks like she's about to faint. Luke shepherds her towards the couch. He, on the other hand, is starting to come back to life. Kevin is not dead. Rose must have left him unconscious, but Kevin left that apartment alive. They're not on the run. They're not wanted for fleeing a crime.

He almost laughs. He's only starting to understand the weight he's been carrying since yesterday, now that it's lifting.

Rose is crying and Luke imagines it's with relief.

'Rose, we're in the clear,' he says. 'We can deal with what comes next.'

'Are you stupid?'

Rose's words come at him like a punch. She's not even looking at him.

'Rose, he's not dead!'

'I know!' She yells this but it comes with a sob. Luke is confused. Did she want Kevin's body to be found? Had she come to terms with the idea that the man was dead, that she'd murdered him?

'Have you any idea what this means?' Rose says. 'He's going to come after me and he's going to kill me. He found me before and he'll find me again.'

Luke listens to all this, his jaw slack. He has never seen Rose like this. She's trembling. Everything he thought he knew about her, all the strength he'd attributed to her, he sees now it was all a front. He is looking at a woman who is terrified to her core.

His idea of Kevin Davidson, the brutality Luke had assigned him in his head, it wasn't enough. It couldn't have been, not if she is this afraid.

'This is not a relief,' Rose says. 'It's not a get-out-of-jail card. I was glad he was dead. I was glad! Because Kevin Davidson alive is Kevin Davidson coming after me.'

Rose pushes Luke's hands away and stands up. She looks around the villa. Luke doesn't know what for, but it's almost like she thinks Kevin Davidson is already here and she needs to find an escape.

'You can't be around me,' she says. 'I can't be around you. I need to be on my own. I need to think. I need to work out what to do next. You . . . you should have told me what you were doing. I trusted you. I . . . I need space.'

She doesn't get very far.

Rose takes two steps and faints.

London

Mickey is sitting on Luke's sofa when the doorbell rings. Luke still hasn't phoned back but Mickey is already in planning mode. And there's nobody better to help than Elliot.

She lets him in to the apartment; he lets out a low whistle.

'Nice. Money.'

'Yes, I think Luke must be doing very well for himself,' she says.

'Your plans changed?'

'Let's just say I came expecting to find something and it wasn't here.'

'You want me to help you look for something?'

'Not exactly. I want you to help me cover something up. Then I need you to do some of your IT magic.'

Elliot frowns.

He follows her into Luke's bedroom.

'Cheesy nachos,' Elliot groans.

'Oh, I think the Lord's name in vain is okay at a time like this,' Mickey says.

She wasn't lying. There's a lot of blood on the floor.

She doesn't know who this Kevin guy Luke mentioned is — somebody connected to Rose, Mickey suspects — but whoever he is, he isn't here now. The whole apartment, though, screams *crime scene*.

And Mickey is going to clean it up in case Kevin decides to call the cops.

The fact the 'dead' guy obviously walked out of the place and didn't immediately phone the police means Mickey isn't worried about them arriving imminently.

But you can never be sure.

'There's in here and a bit of a mess in the bathroom, too,' she tells Elliot.

'Seriously, Mickey. Are we like that guy from *Pulp Fiction* now?'

'Who?'

'The guy who cleans up after a murder.'

'There hasn't been a murder,' Mickey says.

'Not for want of trying.'

Mickey flinches. Somebody tried to kill somebody in here. And if that person survived, well, they must be pretty angry.

When they've cleaned up the bedroom and bathroom to an acceptable standard – Mickey is sure a police team would still find plenty of trace blood with a luminol light but, to the naked eye, everything looks good – Mickey leads Elliot to the computer on a desk in the corner of the living area.

'Can you hack into that?' she asks.

Elliot gives Mickey that look that always makes her feel like a child. He can hack into anything.

But when he touches a button on the keyboard, the screen comes to life.

Elliot snorts.

'Pretty easy to hack when there's no password,' he says. 'And these people have no consideration for the environment. Man, how long has this thing been plugged in?'

'They left in a hurry,' Mickey says. 'And that's one of the strangest observations I've ever heard you make.'

Elliot shrugs.

'I'm trying to be a good person,' he says. 'Even cut out meat two days a week.'

'What? What has that got to do with anything?'

'Methane? The cows' farts are killing the atmosphere. My niece told me.'

Mickey stares at the back of Elliot's head as he focuses on the computer screen, wondering if she'll ever be able to figure out what goes on inside it.

He makes himself comfortable, taking the seat in front of the desktop.

'What am I looking for?' he asks.

'Whatever was done last on the computer.'

'Why?'

'Because I have a friend in trouble and I need to know where he is.'

'You think he's stupid enough to have left a trail on his home computer?'

Mickey arches her eyebrows.

'There's no password for the computer,' she says.

'Fair point.'

'There's no way you're cutting out meat to save the planet,' she says.

'I am.'

He hesitates.

'And there's a lady working in the phone shop on my corner who's a vegetarian.'

'Mm-hm.'

That makes more sense.

Elliot hits a few keys. While he's busy, Mickey walks around the apartment again, looking at Luke's books and furnishings. She opens cupboards in the kitchen and sees jars and spices she would never have paired with Luke, who, in her memory, used to live off pizza and burgers.

To be fair, nothing about the apartment screams Luke, bar the huge chest of drawers in the bedroom. It's the sort of furniture she knows he loves.

Rose hasn't been in his life very long but she's left her mark.

And Mickey grudgingly admits it's probably good for Luke. She likes that he's found a woman who is taking care of him and making him eat, what is that, tahini?

What she doesn't like is that the woman comes with baggage in the form of a possible dead body and a lot of spilled blood.

'Hey, partner?'

Elliot calls her just as her phone rings.

Mickey prioritises the call. It's Luke.

'I'm still here,' she says. 'I've done a bit of a clean-up but I took pictures first and I'm going to send them through. But like I said: blood, but no body.'

There's a pause while Luke considers again what she's just said.

'I . . . thank you,' he says. 'You didn't need to do that, but thank you.'

'So, what do you want to do?' Mickey asks.

'We're still discussing that,' Luke says.

Mickey bites her lip.

'Luke, fill me in a bit. The guy you thought was dead. You said self-defence before. Who was he?'

Another moment of hesitation. Then a sigh.

'Rose's ex. A very violent one.'

Mickey grimaces. Okay. Now it's starting to make sense why he called her. Luke knows what she does. He knows how she feels about abused women and more importantly . . . abusive men.

'You need to come home,' she tells Luke. 'Come home and I can help. He's not here, Luke. So, he's not dead, but—'

'We know what the but means,' Luke interrupts. 'That's what we're discussing. That chip, can you send it out to me anyway?'

'Do you need me to? Honestly, Luke, I think you should come back here.'

'We should stay out of the country for now. We're better off here.'

Elliot is signalling urgently to Mickey. She walks to the computer and looks over his shoulder to what he's pointing at. Her stomach drops.

'I don't think you are,' Mickey says.

'Why would you say that?'

'I don't know which one of you booked the tickets but you did it on your home computer. You're on the island of Saint-Thérèse. If I can see this . . .'

Mickey listens as Luke's breath catches. She can hear him move the phone to his chin and say *'You were right'* to somebody. She presumes Rose.

'Is she worried he's coming after her?' Mickey asks.

'Yes.'

'How violent is violent? How bad was he when she was with

him? Has he just snapped—'

'This isn't the first time she's run from him.'

Mickey considers this. If Rose was hiding in London and this Kevin guy still found her . . .

'She's right to be scared,' Mickey says.

'I don't know what to do, Mickey.'

Mickey nudges Elliot's fingers off the keyboard and types in the name of the island. She scans the key facts: geography, population centres – it's a decent size for a Caribbean island but not big enough to hide on indefinitely.

'It's important you don't panic,' Mickey says. 'Are you staying somewhere touristy?'

'No. I found a private villa.'

Mickey thinks for a few moments.

'Okay. Good. Stay there. Don't go into town too much. He might be watching the airport. It's important now you do everything carefully. Give me a few hours.'

'What are you going to do in a few hours?'

'I'm going to find out where Kevin Davidson is.'

Muffled voices over the phone again. Mickey waits until Luke has relayed the information to Rose.

'Okay,' he says, when he's back. 'We'll hunker down. Mickey . . .'

'Yes,' Mickey says. 'I can help make her safe.'

'I don't deserve your help.'

'You mightn't. But she does. Send me everything you know about this bloke.'

Mickey cuts him off and hangs up. She looks at Elliot, who's waiting, expectantly.

'Back to what we're used to, partner,' she says. 'Find me everything you can on Kevin Davidson. I'll get Luke to send more details.'

'Bit common, that name,' Elliot says.

'Sadly, yes. Maybe we can pin it down once we find his home-town.'

'Where are you going?' Elliot asks as Mickey picks up her bag.

She hesitates before answering him. She's deliberating whether or not to place the money chip back in its wallet in the safe.

Fuck it, she decides. It's better off on her person where she can keep an eye on it.

'The airport,' she tells Elliot.

'You flying somewhere?'

'Nope. I'm trying to find out if somebody else has.'

Mickey doesn't do it very often but she was struggling to get a cab and Nathan's drivers always arrive promptly.

She's only in the car five minutes when she remembers why she doesn't use Nathan's drivers.

'No, sorry,' she says, leaning forward in the back. 'Darren, isn't it? I said Heathrow.'

'Yes, ma'am, but Mr Sheils has requested you join him at the office.'

Mickey sits back, frustrated, just as her phone starts to ring. This is so bloody Nathan.

'Nathan, what are you playing at?'

Mickey stares out the car window at the traffic backed up on Southwark Bridge.

'What am I playing at?' He sounds confused. 'Isn't this why you wanted the car?'

'Wanted the car for what? You've lost me.'

'I presumed you were coming in.'

Mickey screams inwardly.

'Coming in for what?' she asks, through gritted teeth.

'Richard's retirement party.'

'Oh, Christ.'

Mickey places her palm against her forehead. It had gone clean out of her head.

If it had been anybody else.

But Richard is Nathan's mentor, the boss who guided him through his career, the man who introduced Mickey and Nathan.

'I assumed you wouldn't feel up to it, but then Darren said you'd ordered the car. What are you doing in Whitechapel, anyway?'

'Just some follow-up work on a case,' Mickey lies. 'I'll be there shortly.'

Mickey left the house this morning in cut-off jeans and a silk blouse. She's not dressed for a leaving do, especially not with this crowd.

A quick drink, she thinks. Show my face. Then she can go to Heathrow and speak to her contact. Getting information on passenger manifests is not his speciality. He's the guy she uses when she wants to get somebody on a flight quickly and quietly. But she's hoping he'll be able to do this for her. She's praying he can.

Nathan's office building is premium real estate looking out over the Thames, and Richard's retirement party is on the roof terrace. Mickey has been here hundreds of times before, usually squeezed into an evening gown and wearing ridiculous heels. The firm's social events are always OTT. The finest wines, the most expensive catering.

She's barely out of the lift before trays are being floated under her nose – delicate canapés, their aromas mouth-watering, sparkling glasses filled with wines that cost more than most people's weekly wage.

Mickey takes a glass of champagne, conscious of the fact she hasn't had a painkiller in six hours and hoping the alcohol numbs the rising pain she can feel in every aching bone of her body. Then she grabs a caviar-topped blini, hoping that stops her from aggravating an old ulcer. Alcohol on an empty stomach. She's fairly certain that's a no-no.

The second Richard sees her, he's on the approach. He's unmissable, with his shock of grey hair, tight goatee and dapper, if two decades out of fashion, pinstripe suit from Savile Row. Sixty-nine and easily passes for mid-fifties.

He stops short of grabbing her in his usual bear hug.

'My poor, broken girl,' he says. 'What is to be done with you?'

'I'm not broken and I'm not a girl, you old codger,' Mickey says.

'God damn it, Mickey. It's my retirement party. Play nicely. You know, I'm giving myself a delightfully large exit package. What say you dump that sad sack of shit you married and you and I flee to the Bahamas and live out our days drinking pina coladas? You in a tiny bathing suit, me, as naked as the day I was born. Can you think of anything better?'

Mickey flinches, both at the reminder of people fleeing to Caribbean islands and at the idea of Richard naked.

'I'm very happy with that sad sack of shit and you were best man at our wedding,' Mickey says.

'I was hoping you'd change your mind last minute, and I planned to be on hand as a stand-in. *Palma non sine pulvere*. You know what that means, eh? No reward without effort. Hmm. I bet if I told you I'm happy to let you spend my lump sum on your little caged birds, you'd be interested.'

Mickey cocks her head and takes a sip of her champagne. That's the other reason she's fond of Richard. He's a swine in many respects – nobody manages hedge funds while standing in line for sainthood – but Richard has been quietly donating towards Mickey's work for years. She doesn't know the motivation for his generosity, whether his dad used to beat his mother or if he has just decided helping women in abusive relationships is his little piece of atonement for being a womaniser himself.

She doesn't care. She's just grateful. And he's given enough for her to let him flirt outrageously with her every time he sees her.

'A large lump sum, you say,' Mickey says. '*Parvus pendetur fur, magnus abire videtur.*'

'Ouch. *The petty thief is hanged, the big thief walks free.* You are such a cynic, Mickey. What's so wrong with making money?'

'Nothing. But you guys make and break people, too.'

'No politics at the dinner table!'

Richard smiles and toasts Mickey's glass.

'All right then,' he says. 'I suppose I'll learn to live without you. Your husband is over there, doing business while pretending to be at a party.'

Mickey looks behind Richard and sees Nathan in a corner talking to two grey-hued men and an absolutely stunning blonde woman in a tight red dress. Mickey frowns. She's seen that woman before, at another party in Nathan's office. And once, when she was in the city, she spotted Nathan leaving the restaurant at the Connaught with her.

Mickey has wondered about Nathan's affairs.

She knows he has them.

She knows she doesn't have a leg to stand on, were it to come to challenging him on them. He's never challenged her, after all.

He sees her and raises his hand in a wave, a broad smile on his face.

Mickey waves and turns back to Richard, who's studying her closely.

'You've drunk half that glass already,' Richard says. 'And, though you'd look stunning in a sack, I know even you wouldn't choose to wear denim to a party with this gang. You weren't planning to come here, were you? You're bound for somewhere else.'

'I'm sorry, Richard,' Mickey says. 'I'd completely forgotten.'

'Of course you had. You were in a bloody car crash two days ago. You shouldn't even be out of bed.'

Richard arches his eyebrows and studies her some more.

'The fact you are out of bed tells me you are in the middle of something. One of your cases. And it's . . . urgent? Yes, it's urgent. Your jaw is twitching. Where were you headed before you were rerouted here?'

'Heathrow.'

'Good God, don't tell me you're trying to get some poor girl on a flight and you've had to stop off here to toast me with the rest of these old bastards!'

'No, it's not that,' Mickey says. She smiles. Even with a lot on her mind, she can appreciate how shrewd Richard is.

Shrewd and, she reminds herself, very well connected.

Mickey's smile grows wider. Maybe this diversion was meant to happen. God works in mysterious ways.

Richard sees the change in her demeanour and smiles back.

'Ah,' he says. 'You need my expertise.'

'You know everybody, Richard.'

'This is going to cost you, my pretty bird.'

'A kiss on the cheek and a hug,' Mickey says. 'And if you try to drop the hand, I swear to fuck, you'll lose a finger.'

'Your lips on my cheek will be like nectar from the gods. Ask away.'

Darren doesn't ask why Mickey is back in the car not fifteen minutes after he dropped her off, and luckily Nathan was too distracted to notice that his recently arrived wife was already departing.

At Heathrow, Mickey has Darren drop her off at the entrance to Terminal 3. Inside, she texts the number Richard has given her and stands beside a sunglasses kiosk while she waits.

Five minutes later, a petite, attractive blonde woman swamped in a black and yellow security jacket finds her.

'Mickey?' she asks in a thick East London accent.

Mickey nods.

'Rachel?'

'That's me. Come on.'

Rachel leads Mickey through the terminal to a discreet staff elevator and uses her employee pass to operate the door and floor buttons.

'How do you know Richard?' Rachel asks, as they wait for the lift to ascend.

Mickey isn't being paranoid; Rachel looks her up and down as she asks.

'He's my husband's boss.'

'Ah. He seems to be everybody's boss. Have you been in an accident? You look pretty banged up.'

'Yep. Car crash. How do *you* know Richard?'

'Met him in another life.'

Mickey struggles to imagine what life Rachel and Richard's paths could have crossed in. Then it clicks. Rachel is hardly earning a ton of money in airport security. But that's a Versace watch on her arm. And Richard enjoys the company of a beautiful woman.

She says nothing. It's not her place to judge how this young woman gets to where she needs to go. And given that Mickey lives off her husband's money and relies on the kindness of strangers to help her work . . .

The lift opens and Rachel leads Mickey down a bland corridor to another bland corridor. She's short, but Rachel walks at a pace that Mickey struggles to match with her current pain levels.

This isn't lost on her guide. Rachel looks around, checks Mickey's face, then slows down.

'Sorry. The place is so big, you get used to practically jogging around. You must be in agony if those bruises are in more places than your face.'

'I'm okay,' Mickey says, nearly crying with relief.

'You don't look it. You poor lamb. It's just in here, anyway.'

Rachel opens a door to an office filled with computer screens. There are three other security guards in situ, all men. The room has an odour of sweat and bodily functions. Mickey glances at Rachel again and thinks she'd probably shag Richard too if it offered an escape from this.

The men glance up at the new arrival, but if any of them are surprised to see Rachel escorting Mickey in, none of them say anything. Mickey realises within moments why.

'So, *Officer*,' Rachel says.

Mickey stifles a smile. She's the most casually dressed policewoman to ever call into this office, she imagines, not to mention one who looks like she's been through the wars.

'We ran the name you sent through the passenger manifests for the airline that flies to Saint-Thérèse,' Rachel says. 'We got a hit.'

Mickey opens and closes her mouth. She's lost the ability to form words. Rachel looks at her, concerned, then offers Mickey a chair. Mickey takes it gratefully.

She steadies herself.

'You got a hit for a Kevin Davidson?' she repeats. '*Kevin Davidson?* You're sure?'

Mickey can't understand why she's so shocked. This is the reason she's here, to confirm Kevin Davidson flew out after Luke and Rose, but actually hearing it almost takes Mickey's breath away.

She'd expected to have to wait longer for confirmation. Maybe to have to harangue this woman to help her. But she'd forgotten how useful Richard can be, and the knack he has of getting people to do things for him, quickly and efficiently. And this room, she realises, is where all the information for the airport can be accessed.

Rachel might just be the most interesting contact Mickey has ever made.

Rachel is staring at Mickey, her confusion evident.

'Yes,' she says. 'Isn't that what you were expecting? Richard said you were pretty confident he'd be on a flight list.'

'I was. I'm just, eh, I didn't expect you to find out so fast.'

'We have to be able to respond to passenger information requests at speed for security reasons,' Rachel says, shrugging. 'But, it is a common name so I've pulled up footage from passengers going to the gate for that flight. You have a photo for him? We can make sure it's the same guy then.'

Mickey opens her phone. Luke doesn't have any photos of Kevin Davidson to send her, and the last message he sent Mickey said he was dealing with a crisis with Rose. So they can't get her on the phone to tell them where to find an image of her ex, or what he looks like.

Elliot has been compiling a list of possible candidates based on what they know about him and tapping into social media public profiles. It's an inexact science and while Mickey has eight photos sitting on her phone right now, she can't be sure any of them is their man, though one seems to fit the criteria.

Still, she stares at all their faces, memorising them, then nods to Rachel.

Rachel turns on the camera footage.

'There were 200 passengers on the plane and I can't tell you which one of them is Kevin Davidson. The airline doesn't have cameras on the check-in desks, just at the gate. If you want to match the time his ticket and passport were checked at the desk and try to catch him at the gate, you'll need the airline to supply that data. I can only show you our camera footage and tell you he was on that flight.'

'That's fine,' Mickey says.

She watches as the passengers for Flight 649 Caribbean Air stream through.

She studies the face of every man that passes but none of them match the faces on her phone. Which means not a jot because one could still be Kevin Davidson – and she just doesn't have a photo-graph of him.

Mickey is losing heart when she sees a recognisable profile.

Rachel senses the shift in Mickey's posture and freezes the screen. 'Him?' she asks.

Mickey stares at the man on screen. Then she looks back down at her phone. Kevin Davidson. She opens the link to what she'd believed was the most promising Facebook profile. The only public information says that he's 35 and from Donegal.

Rose's ex is from Donegal and is 35.

That's the Kevin Davidson who is walking through the gate to board a flight to the same island as Luke and Rose.

It can't be coincidence; when Luke gets in touch again, Mickey can have Rose confirm that this Kevin Davidson from Donegal is the same one she's running from.

'When was this?' Mickey says. 'What's the date?'

Rachel points at the screen. The date and time code is captured on the bottom right corner.

Mickey's stomach flips. Eight days ago. Kevin Davidson flew out to the island the day after Rose and Luke left.

She has to tell Luke.

Davidson may have been watching them all week. If he was, nowhere is safe. Not even the villa Luke has moved them to.

'I'll rewind it so you can look again,' Rachel says.

Mickey nods, distractedly. Rachel turns the footage back on but it plays for a few seconds before she can rewind it.

Mickey looks at the screen and at Kevin Davidson.

And then, as she's watching, Kevin turns and looks up at the camera recording the footage.

Mickey's heart palpates.

He doesn't care if anybody sees him, she thinks.

He doesn't care if he's caught.

And that's very bloody scary.

Saint-Thérèse

Rose was only unconscious for a few minutes but Luke has made her go to bed to get some rest, so he's alone when the call comes in from Mickey.

He answers and asks her to wait a moment, then steps out of the villa. Luke doesn't want Rose overhearing the conversation.

'What is it?' Luke asks.

He can hear Mickey suck in a deep breath.

'Luke, a Kevin Davidson flew out to Saint-Thérèse the day after you. I'll send you through a Facebook photo of him for Rose to confirm it's the same guy, but this man is 35 and from Donegal, like you said. It's too much of a coincidence. He's been there all week . . .'

Luke stares out at the calm, blue sea, white sand beneath his feet, the sun strong overhead. Paradise, he remembers. That's how he'd thought of this place.

What the hell do I do now? he thinks. His stomach knots.

He's scared.

Properly scared.

'Jesus, Mickey,' he says.

'I know. Luke, how dangerous is this guy? What's his background? Is he a lone wolf? Is he involved in anything?'

'I don't know,' Luke says, honestly. 'She ran away from him because he nearly killed her. She's terrified of him. I thought, when we met, it was just an abusive relationship, but she's hinted, over the months, that he was . . . I don't know. Psychotic. I don't think his family are the most law-abiding in the world and Rose says even they tried to warn her off him.'

'Doesn't he have a job? Anybody he'd be willing to avoid prison for?'

'I don't know, Mickey. Does it matter about before? He was meant to be dead. You said there was a lot of blood. He got up from that, tracked our movements and booked a flight to follow us. Who does that? Who . . .'

Luke trails off. He can't even process what's happening.

'Rose said he'd find her and kill her,' he tells Mickey. 'She passed out when I said he wasn't dead. She would have preferred that. Think about that. She'd rather be on the run from a murder charge than for him to still be alive. She's beyond frightened and I'm starting to understand why.'

'Luke, listen to me. You have options. You can go to the police.'

She says it so weakly that Luke almost scoffs.

'And tell them that a man who should be dead is now on the island and trying to kill my wife and possibly me?' he says.

Mickey says nothing for a moment. Then: 'It was Rose who defended herself, wasn't it? You didn't happen in on them. It was Rose who fought back. You were trying to take the blame for it.'

Luke hesitates. There's no point pretending in this conversation.

'Yes,' he says.

'Then it's her word against his that she tried to kill him. He broke into your apartment and attacked her. She defended herself

119

and fled. That's the truth of it. I've cleaned up that apartment. It doesn't look like anything bad happened there.'

'It's too complicated, Mickey. And Rose doesn't trust the cops. I think she tried to get help before. You told us to lie low. What if he's waiting for us to raise our heads? He could be watching the police station, watching the airport, like you said . . .'

Mickey falls silent. Luke kicks at the sand on the deck. He wants her to tell him what to do. He needs to know what to do.

'Okay,' she says, after a few moments. 'You said you're in a private villa and it's somewhere out of reach?'

'Yes.'

'You booked it discreetly?'

'Yes.'

'And you're absolutely sure you weren't followed on the way there?'

Luke hesitates. He wasn't when he arrived, he's sure of that. But Rose went to town to get them provisions and he went back in to get her. When they came out the second time, was he checking over his shoulder the whole time? He wasn't. He hadn't expected anybody to be following them. He was waiting for the police to be an issue, not Kevin Davidson.

'I don't think so,' he says, uncertainly. 'But I don't know.'

'Okay,' Mickey replies. 'We need a day or two to plan this. It's best to get you home. Once you're here, I can organise something.'

'Should we go to the police in London?'

Mickey sighs, heavily.

'Luke, my whole life these days is spent helping women get away from men because the police are utterly useless.'

'What do we do back in London?'

'We try to stay ahead of him and we get you two moved. Without leaving a trail this time. I can operate from here, I can't from there. That's presuming this is what you want? To leave your job, your friends, your family? I'm assuming that was your plan anyway, if this chip inside my bra is anything to go by.'

Luke almost smiles. Because of what she's said or because of the irony of the situation, he isn't sure. He didn't have a plan. He isn't happy to be leaving everything he knows. He's just reacted. He's been reacting since Rose dropped the bombshell.

'I want to be with her,' he says. 'She's my wife. I have the means to start somewhere else.'

'It's a big decision,' Mickey says. 'Luke, you haven't known her that long.'

'But I love her.'

'And you'd do anything for somebody you love? Even this?'

Luke feels a horrible pang in the pit of his stomach. Mickey doesn't know him these days. She doesn't know how much he needs to make this work. How lonely he's been.

How much Rose has changed him.

'Okay,' she says, into his silence. 'Look, leave it with me tonight. I think it's best if I fly out. I'll bring somebody and we'll take care of you both on the way home.'

'I can take care of her.'

'Luke, you'll have to start trusting me. I know what Kevin Davidson is. Rose knows what he is. You don't. We'll speak later.'

Mickey hangs up.

Luke continues to stare out at the sea.

He doesn't know what Kevin Davidson is. But he's going to find out.

★

Luke wakes Rose with a cup of coffee he's made using the space-age coffee machine in their temporary new kitchen.

She sits up, the white sheets bundled around her, uneasy sleep leaving her face. It's replaced by the worried expression that's become a familiar sight.

'How long was I out?' she asks.

'Not long,' he says.

He reaches across and brushes a curl of hair from her cheek, before cupping her face with his hand. He doesn't want to tell her what he's just discovered but he has to. He can't protect her from the knowledge that Davidson followed them out. He can only try to protect her from what might happen next.

'Rose, can I ask you about him?' Luke says, as she takes a sip of the coffee.

She swallows quickly and looks at him.

'Ask what?' she says.

Luke waits.

'I don't like talking about him, Luke.'

'I know. But we're past that now. I need to know what I'm up against.'

Rose flinches.

'*You're* not up against anything,' she says. 'It's me he's after.'

'If he's after you, he's up against me,' Luke says. 'Rose, I can only say this so many times. Stop trying to deal with this on your own. This is our problem. Not yours. Ours.'

'If it's our problem, why did you involve somebody else?'

'Because I had to. She can help.'

Rose looks into her coffee. He can see she's on the verge of tears again so he takes the cup from her and embraces her, trying to instil in that one hug how much he is there for her. He can feel tension in her whole body. She's a ball of stress.

Rose pulls away.

'What's his family like?' Luke asks. 'Isn't there anybody there to, I don't know, keep a muzzle on him?'

'His family aren't . . . normal,' she says.

'How?' Luke presses. 'Are they a rough bunch? What's wrong with them?'

'They live in a tiny fishing village.'

Luke frowns, still clueless.

'And they run a fishing business there. They run the whole village, to be fair.'

'So?'

'It's not only fish they bring in on the boats,' Rose says. 'At least, that's what the rumours are. Kevin liked to take cocaine. He always had a lot of it. But the family, they keep to themselves. If you're not in their world, it's nothing to worry about. Kevin, though – his sister once told me there was no controlling him. She visited me in hospital. After . . . after he put me there. She gave me a bunch of grapes, a couple of magazines and some advice: go to the police and I was on my own. Keep my mouth shut and they'd try to look after me. That's how they operate. So, no, I wouldn't say he has a lot of *stable* influence in his life.'

Luke shakes his head, incredulous.

'How did you end up in this, Rose? How did you end up knowing a man from a family like that? I know you didn't have much family yourself . . .'

'That's exactly how,' she answers. 'Mam and Dad were always busy. They came from nothing; they didn't want our family to live like that so they worked themselves to the bone. And after they died, I had nobody there to guide me. To keep me straight. I was . . . untethered, and I fell in with Kevin. He didn't present himself as a lunatic when I started seeing him, Luke. He was charming and funny and smart and he had all this money. He came from a big, important family. They literally live in the biggest house in Donegal. It's a mansion. He had lots of siblings, loads of nieces and nephews. I wanted a family. They used to throw parties in the main part of the house – it was all chandeliers and champagne and oysters. He brought me out on a yacht, once. I was seduced. By him, by the life. I fell in love with him. With it.'

'But, how long did it take before you realised?'

Rose looks into the distance.

'Too long. Everybody around him seemed fun and I knew they were a little dangerous, but not in a way I needed to worry about. I didn't realise until I was in deep that he was the most dangerous one of all.'

Luke stands up from the bed as Rose kicks her legs out from under the sheet. She's annoyed with him. He knows she doesn't want to rake over the past, even if the past has caught up with her.

He walks to the window and looks through the venetian blinds. The bedroom is in the back of the villa and all he can see from here are the surrounding palm trees.

Are they safe here? Would they be better off in a hotel in town? The letting company he used presented themselves as small, boutique. Used to dealing with wealthy clients and protecting their privacy. Would Davidson even know to contact them?

Unless he doesn't need to contact them. Because he's been

following the couple all week. Which, Luke guesses, is what Mickey Sheils has already considered.

Luke tries to shake the thought from his head. Why would Davidson do that? Why not make his move earlier, if he already knew where they were?

Because he's insane, a voice in Luke's head pipes up.

Why come at you straight away when he can toy with you?

Get you somewhere private, isolated.

Luke shudders. Suddenly the villa doesn't feel hidden and secure. It feels remote. Too far from other people.

'What is it?' Rose says. 'You're shaking.'

Luke turns to face her. She's sitting on the edge of the bed.

'I need you to look at something for me,' he says.

Rose nods, slowly.

Luke approaches her with his phone out. The image Mickey has sent over is on the screen; Kevin Davidson's Facebook profile picture.

'Is that him?' Luke asks.

Rose stares at the picture. Then she looks away.

'Yes,' she says.

'You were right,' Luke says.

'About what?'

Her voice tells him she already knows what he's going to say.

'About him coming after us. He's on the island. He flew out the day after we did.'

He doesn't know how he expects Rose to react. Maybe to faint again or cry or go into denial.

She doesn't do any of those things.

She nods her head again.

'I knew it,' she says. 'I told you. And it makes sense, now.'

'What makes sense?'

Rose averts her eyes.

'I thought I saw him.'

Luke's mouth is suddenly dry.

'What? When?'

'In town. When I was buying us things. But I didn't think any-thing of it because I've spent my whole life imagining I can see him following me; but this time, I thought he was fucking dead.'

Luke's palms are sweating now.

'Jesus,' he says. 'Jesus. Do you think he followed us here? Rose?'

Luke looks out the window again. He's panicking, expecting Davidson to show up at any second.

'No.'

'How can you be sure?'

'I can't. But there was nobody on the road when we arrived. We'd have heard another vehicle.'

She sounds so calm. Luke doesn't understand it. She's the one who's been terrified and now she sounds . . . in control. He turns and stares at her.

And he realises – she might sound calm but she doesn't look it. There's a sheen of sweat on her face and a red rash climbing her neck.

Luke tries to take back control. They can't go down this route, wondering how and where and when. It will paralyse them from taking action.

'I've spoken to Mickey,' he says. 'We have a plan—'

'We need to be ready.'

'What?'

Luke is surprised. Rose might be petrified but her voice is like steel. The terror she must be feeling has manifested itself as something else now.

He looks at her, sees how resolute she is and thinks – this is the woman she had to be before, when she ran from him. This is the woman who got away.

'He's going to come for us,' Rose continues. 'I'm not letting him catch me off guard this time. We have to imagine he might know where we are or, if he doesn't, it's only a matter of time. Are you still sure you want to be here?'

'Absolutely. Rose, if I'd gone back to the apartment myself and realised he'd come here, you know what I'd have done, right?'

She stares at him.

'You'd have got on a plane and come right back out.'

He nods.

'I know,' she says. 'I know what you would have done. I know what I mean to you, Luke. And I know what you're willing to do for me if this goes where we think it might. But we're going to take care of each other, okay?'

Luke nods again.

All this time he's been telling Rose she's not on her own, that she has him. But he's had in his head that he, in fact, is the one who's on his own. That he has to protect her, to deal with this guy alone.

Luke lets the feeling of relief wash over him.

They're in this together.

London

February 2022

Rose puts the finishing touches to the beef bourguignon, ladling the mushrooms fried in garlic and butter into the pot before replacing the lid. She's followed the Julia Child recipe step by step, and realised roughly halfway through that it would have been a million times easier to order take-out or just roast a chicken. Anything that would have required, oh, maybe twenty fewer hours.

She leaves the galley kitchen and walks back into the living/dining area of her apartment. She's tried to tart the place up by hanging fairy lights on her bookshelves and lighting candles on the coffee table. It's not a bad apartment but she can't hide the fact it's bloody tiny compared to Luke's and in a part of London that can best be described as 'up and coming'.

With the up yet to come.

She's nervous. Really, really nervous. This is the first time she's had a man back to this apartment. That's why she's making all this ridiculous effort, she tells herself.

She catches sight of herself in the mirror near the door. She knows she looks good especially in this low light. She smells nice.

She likes what she's wearing. She likes what she's wearing underneath what she's wearing.

What the hell is she doing, she asks herself. Where does she think this night is going to go?

Her underwear is matching, for fuck's sake. Everybody knows what that means.

Her laptop is still open on the couch. A flash catches her eye.

The emails are still coming in. One after the other.

From the same email address.

Rose crosses to it and closes the cover, a little too hard. She winces.

That's enough of that, she thinks. How can she concentrate on anything when she's being so paranoid.

It's just spam. That's all.

She goes back into the kitchen and stirs the stew, even though the recipe has not told her to do that, and pours herself a glass of Bordeaux. She has white wine in the fridge, too. And beer. What if he drinks something else? Should she have bought more beer?

'Jesus!' Rose says out loud, then laughs, a little release. She's losing her mind. She doesn't have long to think about it, though, because there's a knock on the door and she knows, even though she hasn't buzzed him up, that it's Luke.

Still, she doesn't answer the door without checking the peephole. He's on the landing, holding a bunch of flowers too big for any of her vases and a bottle of Pol Roger champagne.

'Hi,' she says, when she opens the door.

'Hi.'

He beams at her, holding out his offerings.

'This is too much,' she says.

He enters the apartment and she smells his aftershave as he passes. He's done himself up, she thinks. The shirt looks new, and the suit is definitely not off the rail. And he's had a haircut.

Her stomach fills with butterflies.

'Sorry,' he says, looking worried. 'I didn't know what to bring. Flowers or drink. It seems a bit stingy to not bring a bottle and I didn't want to not give you flowers. It was Valentine's last week.'

'Yeah, but we're not . . .' Rose doesn't know how to finish that sentence, so she lets it drop.

'I know,' he says. They stand facing each other for a few moments, an awkwardness creeping in that hasn't been there before.

'Sorry, I'll take them,' Rose says, holding out her hands for the flowers. Thank Christ they're in some sort of bucket thing that appears to have water in it. Otherwise she'd have had to plonk them in the sink.

She turns to place them on a small table beside the door.

'Do you want to put that in the fridge?' she asks.

'Sure. Your apartment is lovely. You look gorgeous. And what is that smell?'

Nerves, Rose thinks.

'Dinner,' she says.

'Wish I hadn't eaten now,' he says.

She whips her head around.

'You haven't?' she says. She's spent hours on this meal. Hours!

'Well, I didn't want to risk it; what if you were a terrible cook?' A smile tugs at the sides of his lips.

'Bastard,' she says, smiling.

'I am bloody starving,' he says.

'Well, good, because I made enough for ten people. If you don't get stuck in, I'll have to invite some of my other boyfriends over after you've gone.'

As soon as she's said it, Rose regrets making the joke. She doesn't want him thinking she's so relaxed she can make those sort of jokes. It just came out. She's not that sort of girl.

Luke smiles.

'I can eat for nine,' he says.

He's true to his word. Rose has forgotten the size of the apartment and what he must think of it by the time he's on his third helping and they've talked non-stop for almost two hours. She knows the champagne and wine are helping her to feel more confident, but it's more than that. It's him. He's easy to be around. He makes her feel comfortable. Dangerously so.

'So what exactly do you do?' she asks him, as he takes a break from inhaling her food. 'I know it's pensions but what does that mean? Are you advising people to take them out or what?'

'I really want to blow your mind with how fascinating my job is,' he replies. 'But it would all be lies. I work in investment. It's safe and it's dull.'

'Okay. But what does investment mean? I don't understand how pensions work.'

'Please tell me you're not going to be relying on the state pension?'

Rose shrugs.

'I'm in my thirties. I don't really think about pensions.'

Luke groans.

'That's the problem,' he says. 'Most people don't. But those who do, they're the ones living comfortably in their old age and going on all the nice holidays. People on state pensions are hand to mouth. If that.'

'So you invest the pension pots?'

'Yes and no. It's not like the stock market, or not as you imagine it. The investments tend to be reliable. Steady. You don't gamble with somebody's pension. There are risky funds out there but the client has to want to take the chance. Most of my investment port-folios have a low rate of interest but protect the lump sum. You're slipping into a coma, aren't you?'

'Just a little,' Rose says, smiling.

'Does my job make teaching sound like *Mission Impossible*?'

'You wouldn't make a joke about that if you'd ever had to shep-herd thirty 7-year-olds on a field trip.'

Luke laughs.

'Have you ever lost somebody's pension?' Rose asks.

'Sure, but when I check the back of the couch, it's usually down there.'

She cocks her head. He smiles.

'No,' he says. 'Not completely. I've had a few portfolios take a dip. Normally, because it's such a long-term investment, you can recover the gains. But if it happens near the exit package, a pension can be hit badly. During the big recession, a fair few people got a shock when it came to withdrawals. Banks used to be the safe bet. Until, it turned out, they weren't. I was still junior, then, though. I've never had to deal with a proper pension loss.'

He gazes down at his food. Rose watches him. He looks like he's remembering something awful and she wonders if he's thinking of telling her, but then he looks up at her and smiles and the moment is gone.

'So, I should start a pension,' Rose says, thoughtfully. 'Can I trust you with my money?'

'God, no,' he says. 'Haven't you figured it out yet? This is what I do. Go around attempting to seduce primary school teachers so I can have access to their state-funded pot of gold.'

It's Rose's turn to laugh. He's right. How can she save for a pension when she's barely existing as it is? She only has this apartment because she managed to leave Donegal with an unexpected pile of cash, thanks to somebody who saw her predicament and helped her out.

'Would you feel bad if you lost my money?' she asks.

'Sure,' he says. He doesn't add anything more, and again, Rose thinks, he's holding something back.

'I think I'm beaten,' he says, putting his fork down. 'Does this mean I have to leave so you can invite somebody else in?'

'Lucky for you, it's too late now,' she says. 'I guess you can stay a while.'

They move from the two-seater kitchen table to the two-seater couch. Rose glances at her laptop on the floor, wondering if the emails are still coming and what they say.

She shakes her head to clear the thought.

Rose has never been more aware of how tight that couch is until now.

Luke is not awkward in the space. He's already physically at ease in her company and he angles himself so he's facing her. She doesn't know how to sit. She doesn't want to be face on with him so she sits with her back ramrod straight against the back of the couch and looks into the room. Which immediately becomes uncomfortable because she has to turn her head to see him. Sitting across from him at the table was fine. This is . . . too intimate.

Rose takes a deep breath. She can do this. She can be normal.

She turns her body a little so she's facing him, but not before taking another large gulp of wine.

'I have an idea,' he says, and he gets up. Before she can ask what he's doing, he's pulled the foot pouffe closer to the couch and then he's sitting on it, facing her.

It can't be comfortable. He's too tall for it and his legs are at an awkward angle between the pouffe and the couch.

'What are you doing?' she asks.

'Facing you,' he says. 'And giving you space. I can tell you're nervous sitting so close to me.'

Rose closes her eyes. How does he always know what to say?

'I'm sorry,' she says.

'You have nothing to apologise for. Will we put on some music?'

'Sure. I have a speaker.'

He already has his phone in his hand.

'I'm connecting to it,' he says. 'Any preferences or guest's choice?'

'Guest's choice.'

She wonders what sort of music he listens to. Whether he's a classic rock kind of man, or a white boy who doesn't listen to anything but rap because he's hyper cool.

He surprises her by putting on Frank Ocean.

She smiles wryly as 'Thinkin Bout You' starts to play.

'Are you making a point?' she asks.

'I have no idea what you mean. Unless you're implying I listen to the lyrics of songs, in which case, you are sadly wrong. Until recently I thought Dire Straits were singing through the bars of Orion.'

'What?' She laughs. 'Oh! "Romeo and Juliet". Bars of a rhyme.'

'I think my lyrics are better.'

'You might be right.'

He smiles.

'I just like melodies,' he says.

'Mm-hm. And really romantic songs sung by Frank Ocean.'

'I had a poster of him on my wall when I was a teenager,' Luke says, with a completely straight face. 'Just something else you should know about me.'

'I'd already guessed.'

They grin at each other.

She's warming to him, more and more. His musical taste. His manners. How aware he is of his size and physicality and of how she must feel around him.

This is going to be nothing but trouble.

'Did Xander have a go at you over the surprise party?' she asks. She's desperate to try to get back to small talk. Anything that's not personal, that isn't leading to where they both know this is leading.

'Yes, he fucking did. If you'd stayed longer, you'd have heard him drunkenly lambasting us all at the end of the night.'

'Sorry. Essay marking. It doesn't let us take weekends off.'

'You said. And I'm sure the fact I forced all my friends on you had no effect on you at all.'

He reaches over to the bottle of red and tops up her glass.

'Are you trying to get me drunk?'

'The amount of wine in that stew, I'm pretty sure it's the other way round.'

'Julia Child says two bottles. Or one. I can't remember. I used three to be on the safe side.'

He laughs.

'Do I need to get you drunk?' he asks, putting the bottle back down.

She doesn't answer, just looks at him over the rim of her glass.

God, it's unbearable.

Her body is doing things she doesn't want it to do.

He senses it. He reaches over, takes her glass and puts it down beside his own. Then he places his hand on her cheek. She tries to make the wince unnoticeable but he senses that, too.

'I'll go slow,' he says, then he leans in and gently kisses her on the lips.

She lets him. He draws back and looks at her, checking for her reaction. She knows there's fear on her face but she knows there's longing, too.

He's not convinced, though. He starts to sit back. She doesn't want him to. She wants him to kiss her again. She needs him to.

Rose leans forward. She has her mouth on his before he knows it's coming and this time, the kiss is longer, deeper, and when his tongue probes between her lips, she doesn't pull back. She doesn't try to resist.

It's just kissing, she tells herself. She's done it before; she will do it again.

They stand in unison, their mouths still locked. She starts to walk backwards towards the bedroom. She knows the way; he takes her lead.

They stumble into the room and then she's lying back on the bed and she can't help it: she's enjoying herself as he kisses her face and neck. His hands move across her body with the experience of somebody who knows what he's doing.

I want this, she tells herself.

She's determined to want it. To enjoy it.

And as soon as she says that in her head, she starts to think about what's happening, and it's like a bucket of ice water.

He picks up on it almost immediately.

His mouth is coming up to hers when he stops, looks down at her and starts to remove his hand from inside her top.

'Too fast?' he asks.

She can't even nod. She can't speak, she can't move. She's paralysed with fear.

'I'm sorry,' he says, getting up.

He sits beside her on the bed.

'I'm so sorry. That was me. I went too fast and I promised I wouldn't.'

He turns to look at her, offering her his hand so she can sit up. She takes it.

'It's not for you to apologise,' she says. 'It's my fault.'

'It has nothing to do with fault. You're not ready and you've told me that. I just got carried away. If you're angry at me and don't want to see me again, I'll understand. But . . . please, don't want to not see me again.'

Rose's mouth is dry. She should have had some water to temper the wine.

That's the problem. She does want to see him again.

She has to see him again.

She feels tears welling in her eyes.

'Oh, fuck. Rose. I'm sorry. Please forgive me.'

Luke puts his arms around her.

'I'm an idiot,' he says. 'I didn't mean to do that. I just want you, so badly. I forgot myself.'

'It's okay,' she says. 'You didn't do anything wrong. I wanted you to kiss me. I wanted—'

She can't finish the sentence with anything but a sob. He must think she's crazy. He can't be expected to understand what's going on in her head, how frightened she is of falling for this man.

'You don't have to say anything else,' he says. 'I'm not going anywhere. I'll be here until you're ready, and if you're never ready, then I'll still be here. I'm just happy to have you in my life. I'm so glad I met you.'

Rose buries her head in his chest.

He's making this so very hard.

'You say that,' she says. 'But Luke, I really don't know if I will ever be ready.'

'Because of your ex?'

She says nothing. He squeezes her tighter.

'He's not here,' Luke says. 'I'm here.'

Rose sighs.

Luke's here. And it doesn't sound like he's going to leave her.

Rose thinks about the emails on her laptop.

The text messages.

She's putting Luke in danger.

He just doesn't know it yet.

Saint-Thérèse

Luke hasn't told Rose what he's about to do. He's left her in the villa, under the impression he's going for a walk to clear his head. She'd started asking again why he'd brought Mickey into this. She knows of Mickey, he's mentioned her in the past, and they sent an invite to the wedding which, thankfully, Mickey turned down. But she doesn't know about Mickey. She doesn't know the whole story.

'She's an old friend,' Luke had told Rose. 'But what she does now, it's useful. There's nobody else I could have asked.'

'What does she do now?' Rose asked. 'You said she used to be a barrister?'

'Yes, but she left that line of work. She works with people leaving abusive situations.'

He'd watched as Rose absorbed that.

'What did you need from the apartment that you trusted her to get?' she'd probed.

Luke had obfuscated on that one. Documents, he told her.

In any case, Rose had seemed less concerned about that and more about whether he had told Mickey what Kevin had done to her.

'I had to,' Luke had said. 'And she's the best person to tell. She understands the situation. She works with women—'

'I'm not a situation,' Rose had barked. 'She doesn't know my life or my story.'

He emerges into the clearing near the road and looks left and right. The two mopeds, his and Rose's, are parked up behind trees. If she was upset about him contacting Mickey, she'd lose it if she knew what he was going to do now. As would Mickey.

But Luke is not willing to just sit around. He can't. So far, everything he's done has been a reaction to what's happened to Rose. Now, he needs to be proactive.

The young guy at the hotel's reception presumes he's back to book a room again.

'No, it's not a room I need this time,' Luke says. 'Sorry, I didn't get your name when we stayed.'

'James,' the guy says.

'James. I was wondering if you could help me with something.'

James is trying to look disinterested even while he's interested. Luke is taking a big risk doing this. But he's hoping he's made the right call.

'Yeah?' James says.

'When I came in first, I told you my wife and I were victims of a robbery.'

James nods, suspicious about where Luke is going with this.

'That was true,' Luke says. 'But there was more I didn't say. My wife wasn't just mugged. She was . . . she was attacked.'

Luke lets that register.

James' eyes widen. His shock quickly turns to pity.

'Sorry, man, that's rough. The cops get the guy?'

'No,' Luke says. 'Thing is, something like this happened to my wife before and now she's absolutely terrified. I need to get my hands on something to calm her down.'

James' big brown eyes look alert now and about ready to go on the defensive.

'Listen, friend—' he starts to say.

'I hope you're not offended, and I assure you, I'm not implying anything about you or this hotel,' Luke says. 'I'm just far from home, I don't know anybody here, and I thought – I hoped – that as a local and somebody who deals with the public, you might have some knowledge at least of where to point me. If you don't, fair enough, I'll walk back out that door and I apologise for having bothered you. But if you can help at all, well, I'll make it worth your while.'

Luke watches as James' jaw twitches. He tries to disguise it but his eyes flick to the reception computer screen. The gambling site is not open on it but Luke imagines it's on the guy's mind.

That's why he took this risk. Money talks, but it practically screams at somebody with a gambling problem. If he's watching a betting site at work, that could be James.

Luke hopes.

A few more uncomfortable seconds pass.

Then:

'What do you need?' James asks.

Luke smiles.

The house that James sends Luke to is on the outskirts of the town. This isn't a neighbourhood tourists ever see. This is where those who serve the tourists live.

It's pleasant, not impoverished by any stretch. Most of the homes are single-storey, white wood, surrounded by basic fences, a little bit of lush garden sprouting up here and there through the sand that's a constant on Saint-Thérèse.

It's not as green as the resorts are kept but neither is it parched. Tropical storms at this time of year deliver enough water to feed the island's foliage and the sun does the rest.

Luke pulls up outside a house with a number half on, half off the gate. James told him he'd recognise it by the tall white gates and walls, and the fact it's the only two-storey building on the road.

He presses a buzzer on a small box beside the gate and waits patiently until he hears a thickly accented voice say, 'Who is it?'

'My name is Xander,' Luke says. 'James from the hotel called ahead.'

There's no reply. Luke waits. After what seems like an impossibly long time, the wooden gates open. They look simple but they're attached to an electronic mechanism that swings them apart, and when Luke drives his moped into the landscaped grounds, he realises there's more money in this house than on the rest of the road put together.

He parks up, his nostrils assaulted by the smell of frangipani growing in flower beds.

There's a compound feel to the property, which fits right in with the two muscular men sitting under the royal poinciana tree in the garden, drinking the ubiquitous island-brand beer while looking vaguely security-like.

Luke ignores them and goes straight to the front of the house. Nobody answers his knock, but the shutter-style door swings open to his touch. Luke walks in and looks around him. He's in a cool hallway, a staircase at its centre, rooms off to either side. The house is old, plantation-era in colour and design. Large indoor ferns are dotted around the hall in huge gold pots and the wallpaper has a monied look to it.

In the room to his left, Luke catches a brief glimpse of several people around a large table, passing items to each other in an assembly-like fashion. The door is closed quickly but not before Luke puts two and two together.

They're packaging product.

He takes a deep breath. This holiday has been full of unusual firsts.

A small black man appears in front of Luke. His skin is as smooth as porcelain. He could pass for in his twenties. But his hair is entirely white, as is his beard. It's weirdly disconcerting.

'Xander,' the man says.

'Yes. I'm sorry, James didn't tell me your name.'

'You don't need to know my name. The colour of your dollars is sufficient introduction.'

Luke winces. He's pretty sure this guy is a proper gangster, not just playing at one, but Jesus, he could try for a more original line.

'Follow me,' the guy says, and he leads Luke to the rear of the house. As they walk, Luke notices a framed movie still on the wall.

Al Pacino in *Scarface*.

He almost laughs. Everything about this scenario would be funny if it wasn't so terrifying.

'For what you want to procure, I will need some sort of security,' the man says.

Luke frowns.

'I told James I would pay the asking price up front.'

'I'm not talking about the money.'

143

The man opens the door to a room at the end of the corridor. It's a sitting room, decked out like something conceived by the art department of *Dynasty*. Wooden panelling on the walls, giant white couch, open fire, fur rug, chandelier, the lot.

Luke thinks of the dusty road he took to get here and all the tiny houses.

Where the hell am I? he wonders.

The man turns and faces him.

'Your name is not Xander,' he says.

Luke baulks.

'I do not care that you lied,' the man continues. 'But for this transaction, I will need to see identification. Actual identification. You have money, sure. But you are not known to me and I have invited you into my home. You are not police. This I know. I also know that you and your wife were not mugged or, if you were, you have not reported it. I have friends in the police station. You have not been inside it.'

Luke feels weak at the knees. He's starting to question what he was thinking coming here. He was expecting some back-alley exchange, a lot of money for a very necessary item. Instead, he's being given the third degree in the living room of what appears to be the Caribbean's biggest gangster, and this man could give the head of the CIA a run for his money.

'I do not know why you need this item,' he continues. 'Perhaps you have discovered your wife is cheating and want to teach her a lesson. Perhaps it is somebody else you want to punish. But whatever happens, I do not want you leading anybody back to me. So I want to know your real name. Once I know your name, I will know everything about you. And you will not think, even once, to mention me to the police if they ask you where you got this item. Because you will know that, knowing everything about you, I have the ability to destroy everything in your life. This way, our transaction is fair, no?'

Luke takes a deep breath. The man is still staring at him, and Luke doesn't know if he has blinked since he started talking, but he knows that this is a man who sees everything.

Fair, perhaps. Fucking intimidating, absolutely.

'So,' the man says. 'Do you want to do some business or would you like to leave? I am a busy man. I have much to do today.'

He shrugs.

Luke swallows.

What are his options?

'My real name is Luke Miller,' he says.

Rose is cooking. Luke can smell frying meat as he approaches the villa. Steaks.

It's too hot to eat steak, and after the afternoon he's had, he's not sure he has any appetite anyhow.

And yet, as he climbs the steps to the deck, his mouth starts to salivate and he can feel pangs of hunger in his stomach. What has he eaten today? He can't remember. Did he grab some fruit this morning?

Rose is a great cook. It was one of the things that made him start to fall in love with her, God forgive him for the cliché. The first time she cooked for him, she made beef bourguignon and he couldn't get enough of it. He'd been so nervous going to her flat that night he didn't think he'd be able to swallow a bite and he'd ended up having several helpings.

He doesn't go straight into the villa. Instead, he checks his phone to see if there are any updates from Mickey. Nothing. He wishes she'd call or text. Anything, something to tell him she has everything in hand, that she's coming and it will all be fine.

He looks out at the calm sea. It's too calm, a stillness to it that feels unnatural. The breeze has dropped, too. It hasn't rained since they arrived on the island and Luke had been thanking their lucky stars. It feels like that rain might be due now. The agency brochure at their last villa had informed them that tropical storms are spectacular. They bring torrential downpours, hurricane-like winds and yet, when they clear, there is absolute peace and everything is dry within hours.

He hopes it doesn't rain tonight. Rain is loud. Rain disguises tracks and noise.

He kept looking over his shoulder the whole way home.

He can't shake the feeling something is coming and he needs to be able to hear it when it does.

Luke shivers.

Inside, Rose is preparing a feast. The expression on her face is pure focus and he knows she's making an effort to distract herself. She does this at home, too. Cooks or cleans or paints walls. When she needs to switch off, she has to throw herself into something with vigour.

There are salads on the breakfast island, crusty rolls; the steak has been seasoned with something that smells divine and she's opened a red wine.

'Honey, I'm home,' he says.

She glares at him.

'Where were you? You've been gone ages.'

'I had to get something.'

'From where?'

'From town.'

The wet dishcloth hits him before he realises she's thrown it. He should probably be thankful a wet dishcloth is all she has to hand.

'Why are you being so fucking stupid?' she cries.

'Rose, I'm not—'

'Sending Mickey to the apartment and now going into town—'

'All necessary,' Luke says, defensively.

'You can't keep doing things without telling me,' Rose exclaims. 'We're meant to be a team.'

Luke doesn't reply. He just looks at her. Rose lowers her eyes.

'It's not the same,' she says. 'What I did was . . . spur of the moment. We should be talking this through, now. Working out a plan together.'

'Really? That's what we do now? Decide everything together? Like when you were telling me to go home and leave you to deal with this on your own? Help me out here, Rose, because I don't know if I'm coming or going. You tell me a psychopath is coming for you, and by proxy, me. You get me to the point where I'm feeling completely paranoid and terrified and then you tell me I should just pop off home. I can't run everything past you. *You're* not making any sense.'

Rose opens and closes her mouth. She has no response for him.

Luke immediately feels contrite. He doesn't want to fight with her. He's just fed up with being attacked for trying to do the right thing.

'I didn't tell you about Mickey because I wanted to sort something on my own,' he says. 'What she got from the apartment, it's necessary—'

'So we can go on the run,' Rose finishes his sentence. 'I know. I've figured that out. I just haven't figured out why you won't tell me what it is. Did you have a hundred grand stashed in your safe or something? I know you're not short of cash, Luke. I just assumed it was all in your bank account.'

'It's something along those lines, but I need to explain it before I tell you what it is and I can't do that right now.'

'Why?'

'Because . . . just because we're in the middle of all this.'

'Fine.' Rose sighs.

'Okay,' he says.

'So, why did you go into town today without telling me what you were doing?' she asks. 'Why keep me in the dark?'

'Because you would have told me not to do what I did.'

'What did you do?'

'You're worried he's coming for you,' Luke says.

'I know he's coming for me,' Rose answers. 'Which leaves me wondering why you thought it was a good idea to leave me here alone for the afternoon.'

'I didn't want to.'

Luke crosses to the breakfast island.

He's about to hug her but his nose distracts him.

'The steak,' he says.

Rose turns her head, distracted, towards the cooker.

'Damn it.'

She grabs the pan from the ring but it's too late.

The steak has burned in the butter.

'Don't worry about it,' Luke says.

'I am worried about it! We need to eat. We have to have our wits about us, Luke.'

'I agree.'

She tosses the pan, steak and all, into the sink and glares at him.

'*What* did you go into town for?' she asks.

Luke reaches into the side pocket of his khaki shorts and takes out the small plastic bag. He removes the handkerchief-wrapped object inside and places it on the countertop.

Rose stares at it. Luke peels back the handkerchief.

Rose gasps and looks up at him.

'What the hell?' she says.

Luke picks up the gun he's bought.

'What is that for?' Rose says.

'It's to defend ourselves,' Luke answers.

'Oh my God.' Rose starts to laugh. 'Oh my God! Have you lost your mind? A gun? Do you even know how to shoot?'

Luke nods.

'Yes, actually,' he says. 'It's the only thing my father ever taught me that was possibly useful. He brought me to a shooting range a few times.'

'You can't shoot people, Luke. Jesus, you can't just . . .'

'I don't have to kill him,' Luke says. 'I want to, but I've no intention of sending us back to where we thought we were yesterday. I know how to shoot, Rose. If he comes at us, I'll incapacitate him and then we'll have him arrested and charged. We are allowed to defend ourselves. And he'll think twice about coming at you again when I blow his kneecap out.'

Rose looks panicked. Then she shakes her head, incredulous.

'How else can I defend you?' Luke asks. 'Davidson is dangerous. You keep saying it. If he comes here, what am I supposed to do?'

'You're strong, Luke, you don't need a gun—'

'Sure, but I don't know what he's bringing to the fight.'

Rose hesitates. Then she reaches into the drawer on her side of the breakfast island. When she takes her hand out, she's holding a large carving knife.

'It was the sharpest I could find,' she says. 'I spent the afternoon going around the villa wondering what I could use if he turned up. I planned to sleep with this by my side.'

'And if he has a gun?' Luke says.

'Why would he have a gun? Why do you keep going on about guns?'

'Why wouldn't he? Just because he used his hands on you doesn't mean he wouldn't think twice about targeting me with something more dangerous.'

Luke puts his arms around her.

'Everything about this, absolutely everything about this, is nuts,' he says. 'Including me buying a weapon from a guy I hope I never have to meet again. But Rose, I meant everything I said. This is my problem now, too. I won't let him harm a hair on your head. I'll deal with him. It won't be you who's done anything, it will be me. And yes, I've thought about what to say to the police about the gun and I've thought about all the various ways this could go. I have this, okay? I've got this.'

In his arms, he feels Rose's whole body sag.

For the first time since she told him what happened, he thinks Rose is feeling some relief.

'I've always said I'll take care of you, haven't I?' Luke murmurs.

He feels Rose nod into his chest.

Outside, the first crack of thunder sounds.

London

March 2022

Rose has never stood on the sideline of a football match in her life, and she doesn't think it's an episode she'll want to repeat. The bitter March wind is cutting through her woollen winter coat and she's forgotten her gloves, so her hands feel like small blocks of ice. She's hopping from one foot to another in an effort to keep her circulation going and all she can think about is how she'd prefer to be in her thickest pyjamas, in her warm apartment, watching Netflix.

Who does this voluntarily on a Saturday?

She does, she reminds herself.

Luke's team is decent; they're all fit men in their thirties who've played soccer since they were kids. Some of them have been friends since they were kids, too. And today, they're playing brilliantly, thanks to the opposing team, which is so poor it makes Luke's team look Premier League.

Luke's friend Xander scores the third goal of his hat-trick and the small group around Rose cheer wildly. The team is winning 6–0 but their supporters never lose their enthusiasm for each new goal.

Rose catches Luke checking on her as Xander celebrates by

pulling his jersey over his head – he'll catch his death, Rose thinks – while the referee chastises him for unsportsmanlike behaviour. She smiles at Luke through chattering teeth. It's important to him that she's here, so she's here. But she's only doing it because he has been the perfect . . . can she call him boyfriend? It feels odd using that term when you're in your thirties, even in normal circumstances, but they have barely kissed, let alone anything else.

And yet, he's hung in there. Texting her good morning and goodnight every day when they don't see each other. Going on long walks where they seem to be able to talk about anything, with one exception. Rose doesn't want to talk too much about herself and neither, it's starting to seem, does Luke. Bar the admission about his father, he's told her that his life has generally been boring. He has no great secrets. A few broken love affairs, a steady career, no money issues.

Rose knows there's something he's holding back.

But he's kind to her. He brings her to nice restaurants for dinner, and always insists on paying, which simultaneously impresses her and drives her crazy. So she insists on buying lunches, but it isn't lost on her that he keeps picking sandwich bars and pubs for midday meals. Nowhere fancy.

They've been to the museums that Rose likes, they've watched movies together – she even managed to get through a whole ninety minutes with his arm around her shoulder, despite thinking she wouldn't be able to bear being touched for that long.

He is earning her trust minute by minute and the least she can do is be here for him in this Arctic weather to cheer him on as he runs around a field chasing a ball.

Afterwards, she waits in his car for him to emerge from the

changing rooms. They're going on for lunch in a pub in South London, owned by Xander's uncle.

She sits on her hands, hoping her thighs will warm them, but her thighs have no heat in them either.

She just wants to go home.

Luke emerges with Xander and another guy in tow. Rose recognises him from Xander's surprise party but she doesn't recall his name.

The men pile into the car and Rose can't help it; she suddenly feels boxed in, even though she's sitting in the passenger seat.

'Nice to meet you properly, Rose,' Xander says, clamping his hand on the back of her chair and making Rose jump. The other guy mock-salutes her. 'Luke is always going on about you, you know. Haven't seen him this happy in a long time.'

Luke looks across at Rose, who's distinctly uncomfortable, then at Xander's hand.

'Seat belts,' he says, and Xander sits back and straps himself in.

Rose mouths a *thank you* to Luke.

'I'm going to whack the heating on high here, lads,' Luke says. 'Rose hasn't been running around like us. You must be freezing.'

'I'm fine,' Rose says.

Luke smiles at her.

'Your lips are blue.'

'You weren't doing much running, Luke, you lazy bollocks,' Xander jokes. 'Stop using your missus as an excuse because you're not a hot-blooded male like the rest of us.'

Luke laughs.

Rose blushes from her head to her toes.

Now, she's starting to feel warm.

The men talk about something and nothing on the drive and Rose is conscious she's being quiet, but outside of answering their questions about what she does for a living and where her flat is, she doesn't have anything to talk to them about.

She's worried Luke will be embarrassed by her reticence but when they pull up in the car park behind the pub, he squeezes her hand and smiles at her before they get out.

The pub is glorious inside. All olde London, with large open fires and low ceilings, comfortable snugs and plenty of ales on tap. Rose begins to relax as soon as she sits down and further loosens up after she's had her first G&T.

The guy with them is called Harry and Rose finds she likes him. He's quiet compared to Xander but he's friendly and funny. By the second drink, Rose has realised that Harry doesn't say a lot, but when he does, it's always witty. She laughs out loud at one of his jokes and catches Luke looking at her. He seems pleased and astonished in equal measure. Rose wants to tell him that she finds Harry non-threatening, that's why she's more relaxed in his company. But she'll have to wait until they're alone.

She drinks too much before they eat and when the pies and chips arrive on the table, Rose is feeling tipsy and too full to eat. She knows she ought to slow down but part of her wants to keep drinking. She's been thinking for a while that she can't keep holding Luke at bay. And it's not just about what he might want or need from her. If she's honest with herself, she knows that she, too, is starting to want something from him, no matter how out of character that might be.

But she's going to need some Dutch courage to get her there.

She's all in for more drink when Xander goes to the bar for

another round, but this time, he returns almost immediately to tell Luke that Tottenham are hammering Chelsea live on the TV. Luke, an avid Chelsea supporter, is out of his seat before Xander can finish his sentence.

Rose and Harry are left to talk.

'You're not into Chelsea or Tottenham?' Rose asks.

'I'm not even into football, really,' Harry says. 'It's just something to keep me fit so I don't have to be down the gym with all those musclemen looking like the skinny, wiry bastard that I am.'

'Fair enough,' Rose says, laughing.

'I can fake a good football chat like the next bloke,' he says. 'It's just a matter of saying things like "*That ref is fucking blind*" and "*How much did they pay for that useless sod?*"'

Rose laughs again.

'I've heard Luke watching the football,' she says. 'He says stuff like that to himself. He becomes a very angry man when he watches it. I think he's done with his love affair with some guy called Roman Abramovich. Whoever he is.'

Harry grins.

'You're easy to talk to,' he says.

'Thank you. So are you.'

'So, what about you and Luke, then?'

Rose blinks, surprised. She's startled at the bluntness of the question.

'Yeah, it's great,' she says.

'Really? You don't seem overly enamoured with him. Are you just not the touchy-feely type?'

'I'm sorry?'

Rose frowns. She's about to ask him what he means. She also

realises, with sudden clarity, that he's not as drunk as she is. But before she can process that fully, he has his hand on her knee.

She's so shocked, she doesn't react at first. She's still thinking, this guy is a nice guy, he's been making me laugh, when he slides it up further, under her skirt. Rose doesn't move. She can't. It's happening so fast and she feels paralysed. All she can do is sit there thinking she's never been so grateful to be wearing wool tights.

'I don't think you're interested in him at all, Rose,' Harry says, as his hand climbs further. 'But you and me seem to be getting along just fine.'

His thumb brushes the inside of her thigh.

It's all she needs to finally react.

Rose shoots up out of her seat.

She grabs her coat and bag and is out the pub door and standing on the street in seconds.

She tries to catch her breath. The cold air hasn't sobered her up. If anything, it's made her feel more drunk.

What just happened? she asks herself. She replays it in her mind, interrogating the perfectly vivid memory. He was so nice and funny and friendly. What did she do wrong? Was she flirting with him too much?

Did she leave herself open to that?

Is it her fault?

She's standing there, trying to figure out if she should hail a cab or start walking, when Luke appears beside her.

'What happened?' he asks, his face grave and full of concern.

Rose bites her lip. Harry is his friend, she reminds herself. And now she's starting to feel sober. Luke and Harry have probably known each other forever. He's only known her for a few months.

They were all talking and sitting together for hours and the guy did nothing untoward. Is Luke going to believe her if she tells him the second they were alone, Harry tried it on with her? Or will he put it down to her paranoia and mistrust because of her past?

'I . . . nothing,' she says. 'I just needed some air.'

Luke looks at her coat and her bag. She watches as his face transforms into an expression that she hasn't seen before.

He looks furious and it alters all his features.

'Did he fucking touch you? Did that fucker . . . did he . . . ?'

Luke can't even finish the sentence. He starts to march back towards the pub.

Rose practically runs after him.

'Luke, no. Please.'

She grabs his arm. He starts to shake her off but then he stops and looks at her.

'It was nothing,' she says. 'An overreaction on my part.'

'I'm going to kill him.'

Rose flinches. She looks down at the ground.

Luke hesitates then. He looks completely torn.

'Tell me what to do,' he says to her, and now his voice is gentle. 'I'm sorry if I've scared you. I'm not violent, Rose. But I know what you've been through. This is the wrong reaction. I understand. I'm making it about me and this is about you. If you tell me to go in there and beat Harry to a pulp, I will. If you want me to have a word with him, I will. If you want me to walk away, I'll do it. Even if it kills me.'

Rose looks up at Luke, astonished. She wasn't expecting this. She wasn't expecting maturity and reflection and self-awareness.

'He's your friend,' she says.

'Not any more,' he answers.

Rose opens and closes her mouth. She's taken aback.

'I – I'd just like to go home,' she says.

'Then we'll go home. I had two pints before lunch and a coffee after. I'm fine to drive if you're okay to let me.'

'Yes.'

'Come on, then. How about we drop the car at mine and walk to yours? We can get you some chips on the way. You barely ate.'

Rose nods.

Luke walks her around to the car, his hand on her lower back. He opens the passenger door for her and when she gets in, he helps her with the seat belt. Rose has never felt so . . . she's never felt so cared for.

She wants to cry.

When they arrive back at his apartment, they go up so Luke can drop off his car keys and Rose can go to the loo.

When she comes out of the toilet, he's in the living area, waiting for her. He's pacing, his face full of concern.

He's worried this reflects badly on him, Rose realises. He thinks that I'll blame him for having somebody like that dickhead in his life.

She swallows.

Dickheads are everywhere, she wants to tell him.

But nobody has ever protected me from them before.

He sees her and is moving towards the hall door when Rose grabs his hand. He turns, surprised. She moves in closer and looks up at him.

They don't say anything to each other, but he begins to understand what she wants, and his eyes ask if she's sure.

She nods, then tilts her head up to kiss him.

He's gentle with her but it's been a long time coming and by the time they're on the rug on the floor, he can't help himself.

Rose lets him, burying her head between his neck and shoulder and closing her eyes when he lifts himself up and tries to meet her eye because he wants to look at her when he's inside her.

And after, as he lies behind her, stroking her hair and nuzzling her neck and telling her he's utterly in love with her, she tells herself that she's a slut and a whore and a stupid dumb bitch.

Because that's what Kevin would call her.

And he'd be right.

London

Mickey's office is not an office but a table in the back of a classy bar that could have traded as a speakeasy in the 1920s. The bar, which is all dark wood and dimly lit optics, is off-street, behind an anonymous door and down a set of steps. It's owned by a woman who could give Mama Morton in *Chicago* a run for her money. Hence her nickname – Mama.

The reasons Mickey likes using the bar instead of a traditional office are manifold. Firstly, Mama, whose real name is Muriel Turner, runs an exclusive establishment. There are two bouncers just inside the front door and if you don't fit a type, you aren't coming in.

Secondly, Mama won the bar from her husband in a court battle after he threw her out of their house and banned her from seeing her kids. He'd gaslighted her for years, then met someone new and decided his first wife was surplus to requirements.

Mama – or Muriel, as she was then – had been a mousy thing who'd let her ex control her as she slaved behind his bar for his profits. Something in her snapped when he tried to stop her from seeing her children and she decided to make him pay in every possible way. She knew the pub was bankrupt and she also knew her husband had been diddling the books. She used that to convince him to hand it over to her as part of the settlement (she also got her kids back). Her legal team couldn't understand why she wanted it.

Mama wanted to rebuild the business in front of her husband's eyes, just to rub it in.

Also, Mickey knows that if she had a public office, it would draw attention to the women who come to visit her and ask for help. Success in her job relies on word of mouth and absolute secrecy. If a husband is following his wife or having her followed, the tail will see the woman go through a plain door that will transpire to be the entrance to a bar.

The woman will order a drink and go to the toilets.

Mickey's desk is in a room just off the corridor past the toilets.

Today, Mickey is sitting at the bar counter itself. She's not expecting any clients.

Elliot is beside her. His sister, Nana, is on her other side.

Mickey has a whiskey sour in front of her, as does Nana, but Elliot is not drinking.

He and Mickey both have their laptops open, much to Mama's chagrin.

'Not exactly helping the ambience, Mickey,' she snaps.

Mickey looks up at the tiny red-haired woman – she might act like Mama Morton, but she certainly doesn't resemble her. Then Mickey looks pointedly around the empty bar.

'Ruining the ambience for who?' Mickey asks.

'Maybe people are ducking their heads in, seeing you two and leaving. *He's* not even drinking.'

Mama nods at Elliot. Elliot looks up, takes a metal water bottle out of the inside of his jacket and shows it to Mama, like that will help.

'I booked a babysitter for this,' Nana adds.

'I told you, if you gave me an hour, I'd bring you somewhere nice,' Elliot retorts.

'I got my nails done. I'm going on Tinder.'

'Do not go on Tinder. Only psychos go on Tinder.'

Elliot tries to take his sister's phone.

'Give her a break,' Mickey intervenes. 'You're not exactly a fun date. Plus, you're her brother. Mama, another two whiskey sours, a sparkling water for cheapskate here, and I'll have a plate of whatever your special is.'

'I don't serve food.'

'There you go, you're missing a trick,' Mickey says. 'I was willing to hand over good money for a hot meal.'

'I'll go microwave some crisps for you.'

Mama heads down the other end of the bar. She's trying to look irritated but in reality, Mickey knows she's glad of the company on a quiet day.

'No flights out tonight,' Elliot says. 'Storm heading to the island.'

'How bad?' Mickey asks. 'It's not a hurricane, is it?'

'Nope.'

Mickey sends up a silent prayer. The last thing Luke and Rose need is to be evacuated into a tiny town hall, along with the man who's pursuing them.

'Elliot, I'm going to phone the sitter and when I come back, I'm downing this next drink and you can get your ass in gear,' Nana says. 'Always work, Mickey. Do you two ever take time off? He wouldn't even let me give him a haircut today. You need a haircut, bro.'

Nana runs her hand over her brother's head.

'I'll schedule a haircut for him tomorrow, Nana,' Mickey says. Nana nods her approval.

She leaves her stool and heads for the stairs to the street. Mickey watches her go.

'She seems in good form these days,' Mickey says.

'Yeah. Desperate for a bloke, though. Don't know why. She has me.'

'She's allowed to have another relationship. It's not going to happen again. You should be glad she's got the confidence.'

'She doesn't, though. She goes on dates, even with nice guys, then backs off.'

Mickey glances over at the stairs.

'She'll get there,' she tells Elliot. 'Anyhow, to the tosser at hand. You discover much about him?'

'He's Irish, Mickey. Not my forte. More yours, I'd have thought.'

Mickey frowns. She should have thought of that. Elliot's reach is impressive within Britain. He always knows a guy who knows a guy. But off the island . . .

'There are probably people I could ask,' she tells him.

'Even with you being from Dublin?'

'Ireland is very small, Elliot.'

'Dunno about that. I couldn't find out much.'

'Because you're not Irish. What *did* you find out?'

Mickey knows Elliot always has something. Even when he says he doesn't.

'He's from a very wealthy family. They run a fishing business, but it's a business in a tiny village in Donegal and they're loaded. So I think they're fishing more than fish, if you catch my drift.'

'Are they on the police's radar?'

'That's the thing. They couldn't not be, right? Small place like that. But there are no prosecutions, nobody has ever been arrested. They hire half the village, I've heard. They might just be one of those families. Above the law.'

Mickey mulls on this. If Rose got involved with this guy in a town like that, she can understand why the woman ended up running. In rural Ireland, with the police turning a blind eye to your boyfriend's family business, you'd have no chance if you turned up at a station door battered and bruised.

She wonders about Rose and how strong she must have been to make her escape. She also knows Rose probably doesn't consider herself strong for running. But Mickey has told plenty of women over many years that that's usually the bravest, best thing they can do.

'That sounds like a good bit to be going on with,' Mickey says. 'This family, they're tight-knit, then?'

Elliot nods.

'I'd guess,' he says. 'Like I said, I didn't get much, bar the gist that they're powerful and have a lot of money. A lot.'

Mickey picks up her phone as Mama places a packet of ready salted crisps and a fresh whiskey sour in front of her.

'By the way, what happened to your face?' Mama asks.

'Car crash,' Mickey answers.

'Jesus, Mickey. That's on the house.'

'You're an angel.'

Mickey has a missed text message from Nathan.

Eating out with Richard. Home late.

She frowns. Before she left Richard's retirement party, Richard told her he was flying out to Paris.

She shakes her head. She doesn't want to dwell on who Nathan might be dining with. Or on.

She scrolls through her contacts and finds a number. The last time she'd spoken to Stephen Cleary was only a couple of months ago, so he won't be surprised to see her phoning.

He answers after a couple of rings.

'Mrs Sheils,' he answers, in his Cork brogue, because he knows the *Mrs* winds her right up. 'How are you keeping?'

'Terrific, Stephen. My husband said I could use five minutes of my phone allowance and I decided to call you.'

'That was good of him. Well, any news? Your girl is fine, by the way. I check in every now and again.'

Mickey had helped a woman move to Ireland earlier in the year, which was when she last spoke to Stephen.

They'd gone to college together, Stephen and Mickey, but rather than stay practising law, Stephen decided to become a guard. He thought he'd be fighting crime at the coalface. Instead, he's been based in a tiny rural village in County Monaghan for the last six years. The village to which Mickey's client moved because, sometimes, small is where people look out for each other and strangers stand out.

'Thanks for that,' Mickey says. 'I figured that would be the last place on earth he'd go looking for her.'

'Nobody looking for anybody round here,' Stephen agrees. 'You're not planning moving another one here, are you? Because I have to say, much and all as I like being on the alert for visiting English headcases, I'm not sure this village is ready to be the destination hotspot for women on the run.'

'What a shame,' Mickey says, smiling. She knows he's not

being serious and she also knows that her request to help the young woman was the most excitement Stephen had had in some time.

'I'm ringing for something else,' she says. 'Some intel.'

She can sense Stephen puffing his chest in delight.

'Shoot,' he says.

'There's a family in Donegal. Davidson.'

'Okay?'

'One of them is called Kevin. He's giving my client a bit of bother. I'd like to find out what I can about him. From what we've gathered so far, he doesn't have a criminal record and nor does anybody in his family. But they have a lot of money. So if he's done anything in the past, it might have been . . . let's say, brushed under the carpet.'

'What are you worried about? That he might kill her?'

'That's always the risk,' Mickey says. 'What I want to know is, has he done this before? How far has he gone? Because he's going pretty far, this time. He's tracked her down in London and he's followed her on from here, too. That's extreme, even for the people I've dealt with.'

'Understood,' Stephen says. 'Leave it with me and I'll ask around. They're a breed apart up there.'

'Donegal people or Donegal cops?'

'Sad to say, I mean our lot, Mickey. The honourable force. It's outlaw land.'

'I leave it in your capable hands,' she says. 'I owe you a drink when I'm home.'

'Mickey, you're never home and you owe me more than one.'

Mickey smiles and hangs up. Of course she's never home. If she went home, she's worried she'd never return to London. Like all emigrants, she's perfectly happy as long as she doesn't think about her homeland too much.

She looks back at her laptop. She has a page open for the airline that flies to Saint-Thérèse. Flights are suspended for the next twenty-four hours.

Mickey books a ticket to fly out tomorrow night. She needs to get the lay of the land on the island. She has to connect with somebody in the local police and find a contact who will help. Until then, she's operating in the dark.

If Luke and Rose can just hunker down and do nothing stupid for the next day or two, everything should be fine.

She hopes.

Saint-Thérèse

Abandoning the burned steaks, their hunger assuaged by adrenaline, Luke and Rose pick at some salad and then sit on the villa's deck drinking beers.

It's started to rain, but they're sheltered by the roof that juts out over the deck. It's designed to allay the worst of the day's sun but, for now, it's coping.

They watch as the storm moves in across the sea. It's stunning. The sky has turned a burnt orange and sheets of rain pound the ocean. The wind is already whipped up enough to make the leaves on the palm trees around them swish and crackle.

Even though they're both afraid, Luke feels strangely calm. It's something about Rose having that knife to hand – he knows now that they're on the same page about how they will deal with Kevin Davidson if he turns up.

Rose cracks open another two beers and hands him one. They're light in alcohol. Just enough to leave them feeling relaxed, not enough to dull their senses if needed.

'All of this, it's my shit,' Rose says. 'And I'm embarrassed by it.'

Luke frowns.

'What do you mean, embarrassed?'

'It's so much baggage. You don't have any baggage.'

Luke is silent. He can feel Rose looking at him, willing him to say something to reassure her, to tell her that he's not as great as she thinks he is. So she can feel less worried that she's the drag on their relationship.

'I'm not perfect,' he says.

She's studying him, waiting.

He doesn't say any more.

He hears her sigh.

'But you've nothing like this in your past,' she says. 'None of us are perfect but at least you've no shameful secrets.'

Luke swallows.

'This isn't shameful, Rose,' he says. 'You can't help what happened with Kevin and you were up front with me from the start. You should be proud of yourself. Not embarrassed.'

He's deflecting back on to her. He can't talk about himself and his many flaws. His many secrets. Not tonight. Not with everything she's going through. There'll be a time when he will let Rose know he's not the dream man he's presented himself as. When this crisis is done, they'll be stronger for it and he can be more honest.

He turns to look at her. He can't read her expression but he senses something different in her. It's almost like . . . like she's lonely. Like she wants him to be a little bit damaged so she doesn't feel on her own.

Luke sighs, inwardly.

If only she knew.

He sips his beer.

Rose does the same then looks out at the sea again.

They're quiet for a while, both lost in thought.

'I know I've told you I can handle this,' Rose says. 'But I can't. Not on my own. I need you to take care of me tonight.'

'Of course I will,' Luke says.

'No, I mean, I really need you to take care of me.'

Luke turns his head to look at her. Rose's face is set in the same expression he saw earlier. She's resigned to what's coming.

'I remember the last storm I was in with Kevin,' Rose says.

Luke straightens up. She doesn't like to talk about specifics. He's heard vague references to what Kevin would do, hints at injuries Rose sustained. But not full stories. Not detailed memories. And he knows one is coming.

'Irish storms aren't like this,' Rose continues. 'Not humid and impressive and fleeting. Especially not in Donegal. They're long and loud, and dirty and cold. And they leave a fuckload of muck and crap.'

Luke nods gently, encouragingly.

'We were driving home from Derry. He'd brought me to this exclusive hotel. All marble columns and tasting menus and a wine cellar worth more than a small country's GDP. We had a couple's massage. I was supposed to be grateful for that. He liked spending money on me. Showing me he could.'

She takes a breath.

'We were coming back through Inishowen. It was a stressful drive anyway, the sort where your window wipers just won't go fast enough. It was tense in the car. And then one of the main roads through Inishowen was backed up with traffic, so Kevin decided to take a minor road. I didn't want him to. Driving in Donegal at night in any weather is tough but in that . . . It was stupid to go the back roads.'

Rose shrugs. Luke watches her, recalling conversations they've had in his car when he's been driving.

Would you like me to take this road or that road?

I don't mind. Whatever you want.

Because she was afraid to have an opinion, he realises now.

'Off we went, and thirty minutes later, the car was stalled in a lake in the middle of the road. Normally, I'd have been terrified. That's the sort of thing that would set him off. Me telling him not to do something and him doing it and being proved wrong. But I'd been so stressed for so many hours – it was a nerves thing – I started laughing.'

Luke tenses.

'And then, he laughed, too. You never knew with Kevin how it would go. When his temper would flare properly. Sometimes absolutely nothing caused it. Other times, you could be certain he was going to snap but then he'd just let it go and be completely normal. That was the worst. Never knowing.'

'You spent your life walking on eggshells,' Luke says.

Rose nods.

'Always with him. So, he's laughing and I'm laughing and we were both stuck in this ludicrous situation and I guess I felt relieved and I turned around to kiss him on the cheek and—'

Rose inhales sharply.

'He smashed my head into the passenger window.'

Luke's stomach tightens.

'I remember, even though I was in a daze, not being surprised. Actually, I just felt annoyed at myself. Like, you had that coming, Rose. You didn't see that, no? And at least it was short and sharp. My head hurt, my forehead was bleeding – do you know your head can bleed an incredible amount even if you don't have a serious injury? – but it was over. I thought, he'll drive us home in silence, not talk to me for an hour or so, then beg forgiveness. Then he'll get defensive because I made him do it because I was laughing at him and then I'll have to console him. I'll go to bed swearing I'll leave him and then I won't. Because I don't know how. Same old.'

Luke takes Rose's hand. It's clenched into a fist and he holds it in his, aware of how small it is. She's staring out at the incoming storm. There's a burst of lightning on the horizon, followed by another clap of thunder. The flash illuminates the darkening sky, adding vivid shapes to the rain-laden clouds.

'So, while I'm thinking that, he gets out of the car,' she continues. 'I had no idea what he was doing. Going to look at the water on the road to see if he could go through it or reverse out of it or something. Then my door opened.'

Rose tightens her fist. She's so still, otherwise. Retelling this story like she's just saying words, like it happened to somebody else, not to her.

'He reached in, undid my seat belt and I was still so used to the way things used to go that I thought he was taking me out of the car to hug me and say sorry. So, I got out of the car. He dragged me over to the water on the road and I started to pull back then, because this wasn't typical. But he was stronger and he forced me on to my knees. He held my head under the water. I don't know for how long. I couldn't breathe. He brought me back up, then he held me under again. I thought, I *believed*, I was going to die. I think, that night, he could have killed me. But he didn't. He pulled me up and he just sort of sneered and said, *That's that washed for you.* Then he got in the car, reversed it and drove off.'

'Without you?' Luke asks, aghast, and then he wonders how he could possibly find that the most shocking part of the story.

Rose nods.

'It was two hours before a passing car picked me up. Donegal people, they're friendly, they wouldn't see you stuck out on a night like that. But most people would be indoors on a night like that. It was just me, walking in the rain, my head throbbing.'

Luke inhales sharply.

'I'm so sorry,' he says.

'You don't need to say sorry. I'm telling you this because I think you think you know how dangerous Kevin is. And I guess, in getting that gun, you're starting to really figure it out. But whatever you think, double it. Triple it. People like Kevin . . . they're not human. There's something wrong with them. They need . . . they need to be put down.'

Luke feels his blood run cold.

The couple look at each other.

'I'm tired of living like this,' Rose says. 'With so much anger and fear and hate. I need it to end. I want you to make it stop.'

Rose's eyes are filled with desperation. Luke can't bear how sad she looks.

He doesn't care what he has to do. He will not let that man hurt her again.

They turn their faces back to the sea and sip more beer.

The rain is getting worse.

You'd hear nothing over that rain, Luke thinks.

London
March 2022

Luke had told Rose that the party was on a boat – some of the people he worked with, a charity event. He had a few tickets and he was bringing two of his cousins, Rayna and Chris. Rose would be very welcome.

Even though Rose thought it was too early to be meeting Luke's family, she agreed to go. He was so casual about it and it was only his cousins, in any case.

So, here she is, standing on the deck of one of the largest boats she's ever seen. Rose sips from her glass of white wine and wonders if this is technically a yacht. Do yachts drop anchor in the Thames?

The strains of the string quartet on the upper deck drift through the air. She's surrounded by people who've been to Cambridge and Oxford and see more in their monthly salaries than she does in a year. Her wine is so crisp, Rose thinks she could knock the whole glass back and not feel drunk.

Rose does not fit in with these people.

With the exception of Rayna and Chris, who feel entirely normal.

They're dressed in their best, like Rose, but she knows they too feel like fish out of water. Rayna's dress is from Zara and her red hair colour from Boots. Chris has a buzz cut and the starch in his shirt collar appears to be giving him neck hives. They are, as Ann-Marie would say, gussied up for the occasion.

Luke, though, moves among his better-dressed colleagues with ease. Rose is amazed how he can be one thing with her – accessible, friendly, one of the gang – and with this group, an investor, a finance man, part of the machine. He's spending as much time as he can with Rose and his cousins, but he has to mingle, too.

Rose doesn't mind. Rayna and Chris have been really kind to her. They've probed a little bit as to her relationship with Luke but nothing too intrusive. It's all gentle fun.

When Chris goes to find the gents (promising Rayna he'll tell her if there are toiletries worth slipping into her handbag), Rayna and Rose get talking properly.

'I am so far out of my comfort zone, I'm almost in a parallel universe,' Rayna whispers.

They watch a woman walk by, shoulder blades like weapons in a sleek, backless designer dress.

'I bet that dress could fund our school's breakfast club for a year,' Rose responds.

'I always come when Luke invites us to these things, though,' Rayna says. 'Free booze, fancy food. If the trade-off is smiling and not getting too lairy, I see that as fair enough.'

Rose laughs.

'Luke is so natural at all this,' she says. 'I know he wasn't born into money but was there wealth in the family?'

'God, no. If anything, Luke's parents were probably the poorest of our whole gang. No, he pulled himself up.'

'Good on him,' Rose says.

Rayna smiles, but for the first time, Rose notices a little discomfort in her demeanour.

'So, teaching,' Rayna says, moving the conversation on. 'I always wanted to be a teacher. But somebody told me the pay was rubbish.'

'It is,' Rose agrees. 'What did you end up doing?'

'I'm a carer,' Rayna says, pulling a face. 'I know. Might as well have chosen busking. I probably wasn't clever enough to teach, anyway.'

'You'd be surprised,' Rose says.

A waiter passes and Rayna catches his attention. She and Rose top up with duckling canapés and he pours them more white wine. They thank him profusely, which seems to be something he hadn't expected, and he promises to watch their glasses all evening.

'So, how long have you known Luke?' Rayna asks, when they're alone again.

'We met before Christmas.'

Rayna frowns, and Rose catches it.

'What?' she asks.

'Nothing. I thought it was longer.'

'Why would you think that?'

'It just doesn't seem like a long time but I suppose that doesn't matter.'

'A long time for what?'

'Well,' Rayna hesitates. 'He's head over heels for you.'

Rose doesn't respond. She sips more wine and eyes the crowd. She can see Luke, shaking the hand of a besuited man who's clearly delighted with their exchange.

'Sorry, I hope I haven't scared you off by telling you Luke is mad about you,' Rayna says. 'My brother always says if my mouth was any bigger they could use it as a trade canal.'

'It's fine. Why would that scare me off, anyway?'

Rayna shrugs.

'Some girls like guys to play it cool. You seem cool yourself. I don't mean with him. I just mean, in general. You're laid-back.'

Rose mulls on this.

'Maybe I am,' she says. 'But not inside. I'm like one of those swans. Gliding on top, pedalling like fuck beneath. I'm a worrier.'

'You're cool. I can tell.'

Rayna hesitates again and Rose can sense she wants to tell her something but isn't sure.

'Look, you're a nice girl,' Rayna says.

Rose narrows her eyes. Where's this going?

'And Luke is family and I love him, but, you know, men are men. We girls need to stick together.' A pause. 'You should take care with him.'

'Take care how?'

Their friendly waiter passes again and this time, Rose covers her glass. She doesn't want to get too drunk. Not on this yacht, not around these people. Rayna allows hers to be topped up. She's a little apprehensive now, like she knows she's stumbled down a road of conversation she should have avoided.

Rose waits for her to continue.

'Luke hasn't had a girlfriend in about ten years.' Rayna sighs. 'He was besotted with his last one. Then he dropped her. And he doesn't seem to be able to make any of them stick ever since.'

'Did something happen between them?'

Rayna's frown deepens.

'I don't know. But . . . well, I guess what I'm saying is Luke always looks out for number one. He's done well for himself. But has he helped his dad? Not so much.'

Rayna stops talking just as Chris reappears.

'You were gone ages,' she says.

'This place is a maze,' he retorts. 'A maze with gold and marble walls instead of hedges. What are you two talking about?'

'Nothing,' Rayna says, smiling.

Rose smiles, too. Chris shrugs and grabs a drink from a passing tray.

Rose looks through the crowd. Luke sees her looking and their eyes meet. He holds up his hand to indicate they can leave soon.

Rose nods.

They get a taxi to his but the road is blocked with traffic works, so they get out and walk towards his apartment. Rose is silent, still thinking about the evening.

'Is everything okay?' Luke asks her. 'You've been a bit quiet. You're not having second thoughts about me now you've seen how boring I am at work things?'

Rose shakes her head but doesn't say anything.

They're just at the door to his building when she realises she can't keep going like this. She can feel the concern coming off him in waves and she doesn't have it in her to lie to him.

'Luke,' she says, turning to him. 'I think I might go home tonight.'

He looks at her, trying to read her face.

'Okay,' he says. 'Can I ask why?'

She considers fobbing him off but decides to confront it instead.

'You know when I met you, I told you the worst thing that had happened to me. My deepest secrets.'

'Yes.'

'Is there anything you want to tell me?'

'Like what?'

His voice is calm but she sees the tiny quiver in his jaw.

'Luke, you haven't . . . you're a good person, aren't you? You wouldn't deliberately hurt somebody?'

He blinks. He seems to be thinking about his answer.

'I'm not an angel, Rose,' he says. 'I've made mistakes in my life. I've never been violent – I've told you that already – but I've let a few people down. I'm not a bad person, though.'

She looks up at him, trying to read his expression.

His face is full of honesty.

'Did Rayna or Chris say something to you?' he asks.

'Nothing terrible,' she says. 'Just that . . . you aren't great at having relationships.'

Luke shrugs.

'I wasn't,' he says. 'Because I hadn't met you.'

'And that you don't help your dad. But you've told me what he did to your mam so I understand that.'

His jaw twitches again.

'That's the thing with family,' he says. 'Everybody expects me to look after that prick, no matter how rubbish he was at looking after me or Mum. Like I should take the moral high ground. You know what, though? Sometimes the high ground is overrated.'

'I don't disagree.'

'And it's not entirely true. I've sent him money in the past. He told me to go fuck myself, that he didn't want my charity. Made a big song and dance about it. Ranted at me down the phone. And actually, he did take the money, but that's not the point.'

Rose touches his arm. When he talks about his father, she can see how vulnerable he is.

'You met some of my family tonight, Rose, and like all relatives, they have opinions on who and what I should be. I got out. I did well. And even though I haven't changed, they think I have. All I ask is that you judge me on who I am now. I'm a good person. I promise. And I'm not lying to you about anything. I'm in love with you. Nobody else mattered until you.'

Rose lets that sink in.

She watches him, trying to see if there's *any* deceit there.

He looks back, his face completely earnest.

Rose sighs.

She has to believe him.

She lets him kiss her and they go inside.

But the whole time she's thinking . . .

I can't trust you.

London

Mickey lets herself into the house. It's in darkness; Nathan isn't home yet.

She wonders why she doesn't feel more annoyed that he's probably in a hotel room with that blonde.

They love each other, she and Nathan. That's not in doubt. And he would never leave her. But they're not in love. Or lust. Whatever way you want to phrase it.

They have sex the odd time. Mickey is human, after all. And she loves him enough when she's in the mood and the stars align.

But they don't have the fairy-tale marriage that people assume you have to have, or else it's a failure. Mickey thinks that's why so many relationships disintegrate. When people believe it's all or nothing. Constant love and lust and sex and monogamy. She used to think that, too. She used to judge people if they had affairs or one-night stands. She once confronted a friend of hers who was having an affair with a married man, and told her bluntly that men couldn't have affairs if women weren't complicit. What sort of a feminist are you, she'd said, accusingly.

That friendship ended badly.

God, she'd been naïve.

She's happy with Nathan. And she's grateful because she broke him first and he stayed.

She walks through the beautiful home they've built for themselves. Through the oak-floored sitting room to the dining area with the Italian chandeliers and into the modern kitchen in the large extension at the back of the house. The kitchen opens through French double doors into a garden made exquisite by expert gardeners.

Mickey pauses at the breakfast island to make a peppermint tea to settle her stomach after the whiskey sours. Her body is aching still, but the alcohol has numbed the worst of the bruising pain. She realises she's barely thought about the car crash today. It's been hard to focus on anything bar Luke and his crisis.

Out in the garden, she pulls a blanket around her shoulders and sits on the swing seat. She sips the tea and enjoys the smell of her midnight-blooming jasmine in the dying hours of the Indian summer evening.

Her phone rings. It's Stephen, her guard friend.

'Stephen,' she answers.

The line breaks momentarily. Stephen is calling from his mobile phone and it sounds like he's driving.

'Sorry,' he says, when they get a working signal. 'I'm on my way home from Donegal. Just went through a patchy bit there.'

'You drove up from Monaghan?' Mickey asks.

'Aye. Felt like the best way to get some info.'

'Very efficient. Are you looking to get on my payroll?'

'Sure I am. You know what they pay guards in Ireland, Mickey?'

She smiles.

'Did you find out anything?' she asks.

'A little. Your Kevin Davidson, he's been on the missing list for a while.'

Mickey is well aware.

'He's been gone a couple of years,' Stephen says.

'What?' Mickey says, straightening up. 'Did you say years?'

'Yep.'

'You're positive?'

'I said, didn't I?'

'Okay,' Mickey says, trying to process this new information. 'Does anybody know where he's gone?'

'Let me start at the beginning.'

Mickey makes herself more comfortable. Stephen likes to tell a story. She could be here for a while.

'So,' he says. 'I told you our lot in Donegal are a bit Wild West. True, that. But there's a young lad after starting in Letterkenny and his dad was my training sergeant in Templemore. He asked me to have a few words with the son when he got the Donegal posting because, you know, rural postings are rough on a young lad expecting to be sent to a big city.'

'You told him all about the badlands of Monaghan to help ease him in.'

'Hey, we've got a bit of fuel smuggling going on again since Brexit,' Stephen retorts. 'Not to mention a fugitive from London holed up here.'

Mickey arches her eyebrows.

'Go on,' she says.

'Stop interrupting me, then. Anyway, the young fella hasn't been fully subsumed into the culture up there yet so I brought him for a pint.'

'Jesus, you're not drunk-driving home on country roads, are you?' Mickey says. 'You know that's an automatic loss of your licence, unless you're a cop, in which case you can probably kill four sheep and a farmer and get away with three points.'

'Har de har. You want me to hang up and concentrate on driving?'

'Please forgive my honesty and continue.'

'Hm. So, my contact told me our lot have always had a complicated relationship with the Davidsons.'

'"On the payroll" complicated?'

'Not that he knows, but there's definitely a divide about how the family are perceived. Some suspect they're making all that money not quite legally and it should be explored. Others would be of the opinion they're creating a lot of employment in the local economy and as long as there's nothing too overt, a blind eye is best.'

'Community policing. I love it.'

'Small towns, Mickey.'

'What does any of this have to do with Kevin Davidson?' Mickey says.

'Not a whole lot, except some people wonder if him being on the missing list is tied into whatever his family may or may not be doing. He could be just living abroad, doing work for the family somewhere. But there's a bit of gossip about him, just rumour like, saying that he did something to piss off the family, because they are awful quiet about him. Maybe he ran somewhere or maybe he was sent somewhere. They're a private lot, the Davidsons, so it's hard to get information.'

Mickey sits up.

'So, he's been gone a while but his family aren't looking for him?' she asks.

'Not that I know of.'

'You said he might have done something to piss them off. Like what?'

'By all accounts, he got into quite a few scrapes. Not good for a family that likes to operate below the radar. But he doesn't have a record. So – and I'm only speculating here – there might have been a scenario where he was hauled in by our lot for something and given a choice to face a sentence or start talking about his family. We're good at scaring the bejesus out of people. Does any of this help you at all?'

'I don't know,' Mickey says, truthfully. 'I wanted to know what his family is like and if anybody is looking for him. It sounds like nobody cares where he is. Which is good.'

'Glad to help.'

'Thanks, Stephen.'

'Stick it on my growing bar tab.'

'Will do. Listen, you drive safe. Text me when you're home.'

Stephen bids her goodnight and hangs up.

She ponders what he's told her.

This has to be good news for Luke and Rose, she thinks. It means that, while they might have Kevin to contend with, he's a lone wolf. Although that brings its own worries. If the Davidsons are a crime family and even Kevin is too rogue for them . . . what does that say about Kevin?

A couple of years missing, Stephen said. From what Luke has told her, Rose moved to London a couple of years ago.

Stephen thinks Kevin's disappearance might have something to do with his family but what if it doesn't? What if it's all about Rose?

What if Kevin went looking for her as soon as she left?

Mickey shudders. Two years is a long time to stalk somebody.

After a few minutes, she hears movement inside the house. She looks over her shoulder. Nathan is in the kitchen, pouring himself a glass of water from the bottle in the fridge.

He looks out at her and smiles. Mickey smiles back.

She's oddly relieved to see him home.

Maybe it's thinking about Luke Miller all the time, and worrying about his marriage. It's making her feel marginally better about her own.

She puts her phone on her lap.

Enough work for today.

She can worry about Luke and Rose tomorrow.

Saint-Thérèse

The storm rages all evening.

There's not a hope of Luke sleeping, even though he and Rose are in bed. He's been up three times, checking the access points in the villa are locked up. He's been to the toilet. He's stared at the back of Rose's head, knowing she's not asleep, either, but they're both pretending they are so the other will.

Luke can't shake the feeling of uneasiness that's come over him.

It's the stories Rose told him as they sat on the deck. How vicious Kevin could be. The things he'd done to her.

It's the last couple of days in general. He's completely on edge.

Luke is starting to question coming out to this villa. At the last one, sure, they were alone inside but there were other people nearby. And the hotel was one room, with a door he could watch.

Here feels far from everything and everyone, and while that seemed like a good thing when they were on the run, now he's afraid that somebody is coming after them, it just feels exposed.

The hours pass. Luke, despite himself, starts to feel tiredness creep in. He wants to stay awake; he thinks it makes more sense to sleep during the day. The day feels less dangerous. But then his brain starts to tell him the weather is shocking outside, who's going to find the villa in this? And his eyes grow heavy and heavier; soon, his thoughts are replaced with no thoughts and he's dozing.

He wakes to a scream.

Luke bolts upright in the bed.

Rose is standing at the French doors of the bedroom, looking through the wooden venetian blinds, her whole body shaking.

'What is it?' he says.

'I went to the toilet and I thought I saw somebody.'

Luke's heart hammers in his chest.

'It's just the shadows,' he says. 'You're half asleep. Come back into bed.'

Rose is still trembling.

'No, Luke. I can't sleep. And when I do, I only have nightmares. I have to stay awake.'

'Rose, you're no use to me if you're exhausted. Come to bed.'

She doesn't move.

Luke sighs.

He presses his phone screen. 3.00 a.m. The witching hour.

'How about you go to bed and I'll get up. I'll look around the villa, okay?'

He reckons if he can get her into bed, she'll fall asleep. He can check everything is locked and when he's satisfied she's asleep, go to bed himself. He's stopped being worried; now he's just bloody tired.

Rose considers this and seems to accept it.

She gets back into bed but before he gets out of it, she grabs his hand. Her skin is clammy.

His wife is actually sweating with fear.

In that moment, Luke stops feeling afraid.

He feels rage coursing through him.

How dare Kevin Davidson do this to her? To both of them. How dare he make them live in such terror?

And all he can think of now is how it must have felt for her that day in the apartment; walking into a place where she felt safe, and being attacked. How Kevin had stolen her peace of mind in her own home.

That's his MO, Luke thinks. Creep up on you when you should be safe.

He takes the gun off the bedside locker.

Rose's hand tightens on his.

'Luke, I don't think—'

'I'll only use it if I have to,' Luke says.

Rose looks like she wants to say more but Luke doesn't let her. He kisses her forehead then gets up.

He looks out the French doors first. The palm tree leaves are still dancing in the wind. He can understand why she thought she saw somebody. He can't see anybody now. Not that that means anything.

He goes into the living area. He checks behind the window curtains as he goes. He doesn't care if it's nuts. Kevin Davidson is nuts.

Luke will check in every cupboard if he has to.

He walks towards the doors to the deck. Everything so far has been fine, so when he lifts his hand to check the deck door, he's not expecting anything else.

It opens.

The door is unlocked.

For a few seconds, his brain tries to find the logical answer.

They forgot to lock the door.

They didn't forget to lock the door. He's checked it three times.

The last time he checked, he accidentally unlocked it.

He didn't unlock it.

Luke is frozen to the spot. He's afraid to look over his shoulder. Should he lock it now?

What if somebody is inside?

Lights. Luke must turn on the lights. What do they always do wrong in horror films? They plod around in the dark.

His hand reaches for the light switch.

He hesitates.

If he turns on the lights, he becomes visible, too.

Fuck.

Luke spins on his heel. He hadn't realised he wasn't breathing until he sees nobody is behind him.

He's walked through the whole villa. There's nobody here.

But the door is open.

What if he's on the deck?

Luke steels himself.

He has a gun in his hand, for God's sake. He knows how to use it.

He opens the door to the deck and practically leaps outside.

There's nobody there.

Luke scans the beach. There's nothing to see except sand and falling rain and an uneasy sea. He looks down at the gun. He can't keep his hand steady. The way he's quivering right now, he could end up shooting himself.

He takes a deep breath. Tries to slow his pulse to something less than heart attack territory. This is no use. He's paralysed with fear. He's worked himself up to a frenzy at just the thought of this man appearing.

He'd be less scared of the real Kevin Davidson than he is of the thought of Kevin Davidson.

He needs to get it together.

Tomorrow, they're going back into town. They're going to book into that hotel again and wait there until Mickey arrives. And then they're going home and he'll do whatever Mickey says – but at this precise moment, he's leaning towards finding the first cop he can and spilling his guts.

Luke is stepping back into the villa when he hears Rose scream again.

This time, her scream is guttural. It's panicked, urgent.

He doesn't hesitate.

He races up the corridor and into the bedroom.

Rose is out of bed, and in the half-light, Luke sees she's not alone.

There's a man standing in their bedroom. One of the French doors is open behind him.

Luke notices three things at once: Kevin's skin is pale in the moonlight, he's grown a beard, and he's really tall and muscular, way more so than his Facebook photo implied.

Luke enters just as Rose tries to push Kevin away, but he grabs her wrists and holds her like she's a doll.

Luke sees the look of abject terror on her face.

'Get the fuck off her,' he roars.

Luke raises the gun.

Kevin tosses Rose aside.

Luke doesn't even have a moment to react.

The gun, the thing he thought would save them, is knocked from his hand as Kevin rushes him.

Luke hears the metal hit the parquet floor and slide towards the bed but he's too winded to reach for it.

Luke falls to the floor and within seconds, Kevin is on top of him.

He's heavy and he raises his fist and lands a punch.

Luke feels his nose break on impact. Blood enters his mouth and catches in the back of his throat.

He barely has time to think before Kevin lifts his fist again.

In the split second before the fist comes down, Luke thinks, if this lands, he'll knock me out. I'll be out cold and he'll kill Rose.

The punch comes down and Luke turns his head.

Kevin's fist hits the oak floor.

The pain must be fierce because it gives Luke the seconds he needs to throw Kevin off his body and reach under the bed. He sweeps the floor and there's the gun, back in his hand.

But now Kevin is back on top of him. He's roaring and Rose is screaming and Luke is trying to turn his body so he's facing his attacker.

He brings his elbow back and feels it connect with Kevin's neck.

Kevin's weight is gone and Luke twists himself around and sees the other man sprawled on the floor behind him.

He hears Rose scream, '*Don't shoot him.*'

But in his mind, all Luke can think is: shoot him.

He fires the gun.

The chamber is empty.

Kevin reaches out to grab the gun just as Luke fires again.

This time, there's a bullet.

Luke isn't even aiming properly. He thinks the bullet has entered Kevin's shoulder.

The man falls mid-air and lands at Luke's feet.

Blood is pumping from his chest.

Rose is screaming and sobbing: '*Don't shoot him, don't shoot him.*'

Luke watches as she runs from the bedroom.

It's like a dream.

He can't move. All he can do is stare at the man bleeding to death at his feet as he listens to Rose yelling in the kitchen outside. She's on the phone and she's calling the police, the emergency services, whatever.

They're too late, Luke thinks, in shock.

They're too late.

I've killed him.

He drops the gun.

When the police arrive, Luke is still on the floor in the bedroom. He's covered in Kevin Davidson's blood as well as his own.

He'd tried to revive the man, even though he knew it was hopeless.

Even though he wasn't sure Kevin should get the chance to live.

The paramedics check Luke over and when it's established that there's nothing wrong with him bar a broken nose and some bruises, a black policeman comes to sit with him.

He's not much older than Luke and he's wearing a sharp suit. He has a comforting presence. Kind. Friendly.

In the next room, he can hear Rose sobbing and speaking to another policeman.

Kevin is still lying on the floor, as Luke sits on the bed.

'I did it,' Rose is saying, over and over. 'It was me. I shot him.'

The detective looks at Luke.

'My name is Inspector Alleyne,' the policeman says.

'Luke Miller,' Luke replies.

'Mr Miller, you want to tell me your version of what happened here tonight? We've heard your wife's.'

'That man broke in. He was attacking my wife. He came for me and I – I shot him.'

'Your wife is insisting that she shot him.'

Inspector Alleyne looks down at the gun on the floor. Luke looks at it, too, and snorts.

'My wife didn't shoot him,' he says.

'She wants to protect you.'

'I know. I was trying to protect her.'

'Do you know this man?'

'Yes. His name is Kevin Davidson. He's my wife's ex. He was violent to her before and he followed us here.'

Luke looks at the dead man. In the overhead lights of the villa's bedroom, he looks so harmless. Dark hair, a little younger than Luke, a weathered face. His features are contorted in death but Luke can still see he was attractive, once.

Inspector Alleyne frowns.

'Mr Miller, where did you get the gun? You are not licensed, as a foreign citizen, to carry a weapon on our island and you certainly did not bring it through the airport.'

'I can't say where I got the gun.'

The policeman cocks his head.

'You will, eventually,' he says. 'But the more pressing matter is that you have a gun. You procured one, while on Saint-Thérèse. For what reason?'

Luke stares at Kevin's body.

'To protect us. I didn't know I would have to use it. I didn't want to.'

Inspector Alleyne sighs.

'You killed him with one shot. Unlucky, or did you know what you were doing?'

'I know how to handle a gun but I wasn't aiming to kill him. We were fighting. I just fired. The first chamber was empty and I panicked. I didn't even realise I hadn't loaded it properly. But I was anxious all evening. We knew Davidson had come to the island. I was terrified he'd turn up.'

'I do not know what the law is in Britain,' Inspector Alleyne says. 'You may not know what the law is regarding this sort of incident either. You are probably familiar with the law in the US, because you have seen it on television. In America, you're allowed to protect yourself on your property. Even fatally, if it comes to that.'

Luke nods. He's watched enough TV series and films.

'That is not the case on Saint-Thérèse,' Inspector Alleyne says. 'On Saint-Thérèse you are not allowed to use lethal force, even in a defensive situation.'

Luke nods again. He hadn't meant to use lethal force.

You bought a gun.

From the next room, he hears:

'Don't listen to him, I did it, he's just trying to cover for me.'

Stop, Rose, Luke thinks. Just stop.

'I understand,' he says.

'I must arrest you,' Inspector Alleyne says.

'Yes.'

'We will help you find a lawyer.'

'I have one.'

'Here on the island?' Inspector Alleyne sounds surprised.

'No. She has to come over from Britain.'

He doesn't even know if Mickey can practise law any more, let alone assert herself in another territory.

Inspector Alleyne is looking at him with concern.

He stands, pats Luke on the shoulder, then walks over to a policewoman in the doorway. They talk in hushed tones as they look back at Luke.

He knows they're saying that he's in shock, that they might need to get a medic in with him again.

He can't take his eyes off Kevin's corpse.

At least this part of it is over, he thinks, as he listens to Rose's heartbroken sobs.

PART II

Saint-Thérèse

The heat on the island is stifling. Mickey has two wet patches under her arms within minutes of leaving the airport and is sweating buckets by the time the taxi has brought her into the city centre. Her driver is either saving money on air conditioning or this weather doesn't faze him. Which makes her wonder – what does actual heat on this island feel like?

Mickey looks out the window of the Toyota for the whole drive, pondering what the hell she's doing.

She had explained to Luke she has no authority to practise. Not here, not even in London. But he begged her to come over.

She conceded. Not to represent him. She's arrived to give him and Rose support and to help Luke find somebody to present his case. She'll meet the cop in charge and try to get a feel for how the island works.

Richard has offered to fund whatever she needs. She couldn't not tell Nathan what she was doing, but nor could she tap their bank account for funds.

Not to help Luke.

Elliot is taking care of any clients who come in. Nana has promised to join him for a couple of days so any woman who enters the bar sees a woman at Mickey's desk first, and then Nana and Mama will explain to her that Elliot is one of the good guys and Mickey will be back soon.

The island is charming. It's exactly as she imagined a Caribbean island might look. She's never been on one. She and Nathan tend to holiday in Europe because he's afraid of flying, so the nearer the better.

The drive from the airport is along a stretch of road that can only be described as the opening salvo to perfection. Palm trees sway in the sun and the green verges surrounding them look like they have been manicured by hand with nail scissors. The island's tourist authorities knew what they were doing when they designed this incoming road.

The city centre, if that's what Mickey could call it, is full of low-lying buildings, well maintained. Each street is dotted with restaurants and bars and tasteful shops. Most have views of the harbour or the sea.

Nice for a holiday, Mickey thinks. If she wasn't still covered in bruises and here to try to get Luke Miller out of a jail cell, she'd quite enjoy it.

Outside her hotel, Mickey asks the driver to wait for her while she checks in and leaves her bag.

He tells her he will. She expects him to leave the meter running but he gets out of the car with her and says he's off to get a coffee. He might not have any interest in keeping her cool but he's certainly not out to exploit her.

It's a Hilton, but not as she knows Hiltons to be. This is part of a luxurious resort, a mere two storeys high but sprawling out to the rear. Three pools, the website proclaimed, and a private beach. Mickey doesn't imagine she'll see any of it.

The receptionist gives Mickey a quick, discreetly appraising glance. Mickey has done her best with make-up to hide her injuries but they're still obvious.

She knows what she looks like. A battered woman on the run.

The irony.

A porter takes her bag to the room, then Mickey is outside again, away from the cool air conditioning of the Hilton and back in the metal sweatbox that has become her temporary carriage.

'You want to go to a bar?' the driver asks her, sipping his steaming hot coffee.

I need to go to a bar, Mickey thinks, but instead she asks him to bring her to the police station.

The driver evidently considers this odd for a tourist, judging by his expression, but he does his duty.

Inside the modern-built, white-painted police station, a plugged-in swivel fan is operating at full blast. Mickey stands at the counter, grateful every time it rotates her way.

A young man in uniform approaches the desk with a laconic slowness that Mickey imagines comes from dealing with a level of crime that ranges from stolen handbags to the odd accidental death. She's checked the crime statistics on Saint-Thérèse. It's more renowned for its tax shelters than any serious incidents.

'Mickey Sheils to see Inspector Alleyne,' she says.

The young guy doesn't even respond. He just slopes off from whence he came.

A few seconds later, a man she guesses is Inspector Alleyne emerges from a door behind the reception desk.

Mickey is taken aback.

Inspector Alleyne is a god among men. Early forties, maybe, a suit so sharp you could cut diamonds on it, his black skin smooth as a baby's, dimples on a face that looks like its default mode is smiling.

Mickey closes her mouth. Luke had said the cop in charge was nice.

Course, it would have been weird if he'd described him as gorgeous.

He does a double take when he sees her not-so-pretty face but he covers quickly.

'Miss Sheils,' Inspector Alleyne says. 'Would you care to follow me?'

'Thank you,' she says, stepping through the flip-top section of the reception desk he's opened for her.

She follows him to his office where, thankfully, two fans are working hard to circulate the air.

She sits down.

'Coffee?' he asks. 'Tea, water?' He stands and walks to a small filing cabinet, on top of which sits a makeshift refreshment area. In between the coffee machine and cups, there's a bottle of Cuban rum.

'Something stronger?' he asks, following her eyes.

'Just water, please,' she says. She's yet to determine if Inspector Alleyne is friend or foe and she can't go by Luke's reaction. From what she's gathered, Luke has spilled his guts to Alleyne about everything, except for the fact Rose almost killed Kevin Davidson back in London.

He hands her an ice-cold bottle of water and Mickey holds it to her forehead before opening and drinking from it, gratefully.

'You need any pain relief?' he asks.

'I'm fine,' she says. 'Car accident.'

She's getting tired of explaining her face.

'Arnica,' he says. 'It'll bring the swelling down.'

'Thanks.'

'So,' he says, when she's recapped the bottle. 'We're in a bit of a pickle.'

Mickey wants to smile. It's such a quaint expression to come out of this man's mouth.

'Your friend is facing a murder charge.'

'Hopefully manslaughter,' Mickey clarifies.

'Yes, perhaps. You appreciate I should be having this conversation with his lawyer?'

'Of course. I'm aware I can't represent him. I will be seeking to find him a suitable lawyer.'

'I'm glad to hear it. He's been quite stubborn about seeing only you.'

Mickey cocks her head. She suspects Luke is in a state of shock. The Luke she knew was no angel but he wasn't capable of this. Nothing even remotely like this. She's still trying to get her head around what he was thinking when he went and bought the gun.

'I'm thankful you're taking the time to tell me anything,' Mickey says, with emphasis on the *anything*.

Inspector Alleyne nods. She's starting to see why Luke likes him. There's nothing defensive or offensive in the policeman's body language. He's laid-back. Non-judgemental. His carefully affected relaxed demeanour – if it is an affectation – encourages trust.

'I like Mr Miller,' Inspector Alleyne says. 'He seems like a decent man and I think he has been through something traumatic. After watching him and speaking to him, I do not think he intended to kill anybody. His wife's statement aligns with that. But the justice system will go on facts, not feelings. Mr Miller procured a deadly weapon. He's refusing to tell us where he got that weapon from.

But wherever he bought it, he did so with the intention of using it, if necessary. He did not come to the police, he didn't report any threat, he took the law into his own hands. It will be difficult for his legal team to argue against the prosecution's accusation of premeditation.'

'But Davidson broke into their villa,' Mickey says. 'Luke didn't seek him out. He was scared the man was coming after them and he prepared himself. His actions are the actions of a terrified man, not someone planning to commit a crime. You have two witnesses stating that Davidson attacked Rose and Luke, and he only shot him as a last resort.'

'Mr Miller had a broken nose and a few bruises. The victim had a few bruises and – this is very important – no weapon. As last resorts go, the shooting was arrived at very quickly.'

'Did you say Davidson had no weapon?'

Mickey is stuck on that one. How did he intend to get past Luke to Rose? With his bare hands, or using something from the villa? But then, why break in through the French doors if he needed access to the kitchen? The inspector had said the deck door to the villa was also unlocked.

Perhaps Davidson had planned to come in that way but was disturbed by Luke, so he went around the back and ended up entering via the bedroom.

Inspector Alleyne rests his elbows on his desk and leans forward.

'He had no weapon,' he says. 'And then there's the other, crucial matter.'

Mickey braces herself.

She doesn't know what's coming next, but she can tell from Inspector Alleyne's face it isn't going to be good.

★

The jail where Luke is being held is clean and small and, from what Mickey can see, comfortable.

She's glad of that, at least. After her conversation with Inspector Alleyne, she's anxious about how long Luke could be staying here.

The prison guard brings her into a small room, freshly painted in a pale yellow colour. It's more like a clinic than a prison, Mickey thinks. She sits at the metal table, secured to the floor by bolts, and drums her fingers on its top.

After a few minutes, a door on the far side of the room opens and Luke is brought in.

He's wearing a drab grey tracksuit that looks like standard prison issue.

He's not handcuffed or shackled in any physical way, but that doesn't matter. Already assimilated, Mickey thinks.

It's not just the uniform. Luke's face is grey. His whole body is slumped.

He's defeated.

He lights up a little when he sees her and she sees a glint of the old Luke in his grey eyes. And then he notices her injuries and frowns.

She stands to embrace him but a curt shake of the head from the guard tells her that's forbidden.

They sit across from each other instead, their hands not touching but close enough.

Mickey is in turmoil. It's been years since she's been in such close physical proximity to Luke and every feeling she ever had about this man is flooding back. Sure, his face is a little more lined and his hair isn't as dark. But he looks the same. He's still Luke.

'Christ, Mickey,' he says. 'I didn't realise you were so banged up. I'm sorry . . . for all this.'

'I'm fine,' she replies. 'It looks worse than it is.'

She had to take two painkillers outside. It's as bad as it looks.

'I'm so glad you're here,' he says.

'I'm glad, too,' Mickey replies. 'God, how did this happen?'

He shrugs.

'I don't know,' he says. 'I honestly don't know.'

Mickey takes a deep breath.

'Luke, I'm just here for support. Our first job—'

'Is to get me a legal team. I know. Have you seen Rose?'

'I'm going there next. They're bringing her round.'

'Bringing her round? What does that mean?'

'They've had her heavily sedated. Apparently she became very distressed when they removed the dead body from the villa.'

Luke puts his head in his hands.

'We need to take care of her, Mickey. She's traumatised and she's terrified. I know his family aren't exactly model citizens. I think she's worried they'll come after her now, too.'

Mickey shakes her head.

'I know what you said on the phone,' he says, before she can speak, 'that he hasn't lived there for years, but what if that's okay, as long as it's their decision? What if they're not happy with somebody else causing him harm—'

'Luke. Stop.'

Luke looks up at Mickey. He's on the tipping point of breaking, she realises. And she's worried that what she's about to tell him will send him over the edge.

'Sorry,' he says. 'All I can do in here is think. All I've done since all this started is imagine every worst-case scenario. You know what I realised this morning?' He snorts. 'This is why I'm so good at my job. I have an excellent talent for conceiving of the worst possible investments and taking the safe route.'

Mickey nods.

This is the worst possible investment, she thinks.

'Did you take care of the thing I asked you to?' he says.

Mickey grasps the raft of prevarication he's offered her.

'I'm afraid to let it out of my sight,' she says. 'I'm guessing there's a lot of money on it. How much?'

Mickey thinks of the chip that's taped inside the top band of her knickers at this very moment.

'Twenty million pounds,' Luke says.

Mickey's mouth forms an O.

'Well, we don't need to worry about how you're paying for your legal team,' she says. 'What on earth, Luke? How long have you had that amount of money? You weren't that wealthy when I knew you, surely?'

Luke purses his lips and Mickey can't read his expression. Fucking hell, she thinks. He had twenty million when he knew her and he was driving a Ford Escort. They drank in dingy pubs. Mainly because they didn't want to be seen anywhere together, but still.

'Luke, are you going to tell me how a pensions investment advisor ended up with that amount of money?' she asks.

Luke colours and it makes his face look almost normal again.

'I will,' he says. 'One day. But first I have to tell Rose. I've been keeping it from her.'

'Your wife doesn't know you have twenty million to your name?'

'She knows I'm wealthy. She doesn't know I'm that wealthy.'

'So, she didn't marry you for your money.'

Luke looks at Mickey sharply.

'What?' Mickey says. 'You've known her what? Nine, ten months? It's not unheard of.'

'I know,' Luke says. 'But I did all the pursuing here, Mickey. She didn't want anything to do with me.'

'That she let you think.'

Luke shakes his head.

'You're wrong,' he says. 'I'm already well off. Just from what I do now. She was aware of that. She's a teacher on shit money. She knew from the start I'd give her a lovely lifestyle. She knew from the first night she was in my apartment, and she still didn't want anything to do with me. I had to talk her round.'

Mickey knows she still looks unconvinced. All she can think is that Rose appearing in Luke's life and them getting married six months later suddenly makes sense.

But then her thoughts come full circle. She had no idea Luke had this sort of money and she thought she knew everything about him.

If Mickey had had no idea, how could Rose?

'So, what do you think of my chances?' Luke says. 'I know what the police are saying but it *was* self-defence, Mickey. Davidson came there to harm us. He was in our bedroom—'

'Luke, listen to me.'

Luke stops talking. She guesses he can tell by her tone she has something serious to tell him.

'Am I screwed?' he asks her.

She looks at him. He sounds like a little boy. Absolutely terrified and no idea what he's facing into.

Time to rip off the plaster.

'Luke, the man you killed wasn't Kevin Davidson.'

London
April 2022

April showers, they call them. Which implies they start and stop.

Rose reminds herself of this as she walks home from work, soaked to the skin and getting wetter, because it's been raining solid for an hour.

When she finished up and was contemplating aloud whether to get the bus or walk home, Ann-Marie had told her it was only a shower and she'd be glad she plumped for the walk when she didn't have to go out later to exercise.

Good choice, Rose thinks to herself, sarcastically. Now she's getting a walk and a swim in before tea.

Her phone, in her handbag but close enough to her body that she feels it, buzzes again.

That's the fourth time he's texted her since yesterday.

Before that it was calls. All weekend. And voicemails. His last one: *I don't want to come across like a stalker, I just want to know what I did wrong.*

You did nothing wrong, Luke, she thinks. Other than you being who you are and me being who I am.

Rose sighs. Out loud, she can say it's the warning that his cousin Rayna gave her. She can say it was visiting the grave in Highgate at the weekend, the feeling that seeing the old familiar name always gives her.

But she knows her real reason for breaking it off with Luke stems from the first time they slept together. That was the night that tore it. She knew she was falling for him and she couldn't let herself.

They've had sex a few times since but each time she's shut herself down; let him do what he wanted while she pretended to be there, but really, her mind was elsewhere. He knew it and he tried, gently, to probe for the right way to do things. But he was so goddamn nice about it. He just stopped approaching her, happy to wait until she was ready.

Luke Miller is perfect, Rose thinks.

And she can't be with him. She just can't.

The other calls have stopped. And the texts and the emails. She's blocked all the numbers, all the possible contacts.

Nobody can touch her here, she tells herself.

There's nobody out there.

Nobody is watching.

She can get on with her life.

She waits at the pedestrian crossing by the park. If she cuts through, she'll be home in five. If she walks around it, it will take her fifteen.

Rose crosses the road – then decides to walk around the park.

There have been too many stories over the last couple of years involving women taking shortcuts through empty parks and it all ending badly. It's not quite dark yet but the day is dull and the rain has driven everybody sensible from the streets. She doesn't know who she might bump into in that park. That's just sensible thinking. It has nothing to do with before.

She passes the bus stop near her house, watching as the number 13 pulls up, the bus that would have gone past her school. Lots of warm, dry people hop off.

At least she's nearly home.

She's at the now empty bus stop when he steps out in front of her. Rose almost jumps out of her skin.

Luke is as wet as she is, and he looks as miserable as she feels.

He's blocking the path and she's forced to stop.

'Rose, please?' he says, his voice plaintive. He's wearing a too thin hoodie and he's shivering – the cold comes across in his voice.

He's pitiable.

And it just makes Rose angry. He doesn't want to be a stalker, but what is this? And even as she thinks it, she knows she's being unfair because she just cut him out of her life with no real explanation other than she wasn't ready for a relationship.

But she can't be gentle with him. Not if she wants him to leave her alone.

'This isn't on,' she says. 'You said you understood me after Kevin and that you'd take things at my pace. But I said I was done and you won't respect that.'

'I do respect it! I just don't understand it.'

'You're not respecting it. Turning up here, ringing and texting me all the time, that's not respecting or accepting it. I don't need to make you understand it. I'm just telling you to stay away from me.'

'You don't *need* to make me understand but I'm asking you to. Rose, I get it. I get that you didn't want a relationship and I was trying not to push. I know that sleeping with me changed things.

We can go back. You don't have to be with me. But can't we even be friends?'

Rose wants to scream with frustration. Why won't he give up?

'No,' she says, shaking her head adamantly. 'We can't. I want you to leave me alone. It's for your own good.'

Something in Luke's face changes. It hardens. He's angry at her but he's trying to keep a lid on it.

'You don't get to say that,' he says. 'You don't get to tell me what's good for me. Come on, Rose. The only reason we can't be friends is because you don't trust yourself to be my friend. Because you're in love with me. And while you might be shit-scared of that, I am even more scared of losing you.'

Rose stares at the wet ground. Even in the middle of this excruciating exchange, it crosses her mind that anybody looking at this from the outside would see a couple, in the rain, one of them declaring his undying love and the other resisting, and think it romantic.

Not knowing how absolutely and utterly fucked up the woman was in the scene.

'You barely know me,' she says. 'We met four months ago, Luke.'

'And I have never, ever felt about anybody the way I feel about you.'

Rose shakes her head, but it's a weak gesture.

'You can deny it and you can push me away, but I won't stop feeling it. You will always be the woman I should have ended up with, Rose. I knew it the second I saw you in the bar that night. I knew it the moment we spoke. I will walk away from you right now if you tell me you aren't able for this and you don't think you ever will be. But if there's even the slightest hope that one day you'll feel comfortable enough to be with somebody, will you please, please, let me go inside with you and we can talk this through? Even if it means taking a break for a while, or cooling right off. I'll do whatever it takes. Rose?'

Rose can't look at him.

It's just better this way.

Even if she's letting somebody down.

She shakes her head.

She doesn't want to look up at him, but she forces herself. She shakes her head again.

Luke looks completely heartbroken. He studies her face, and, seeing nothing changing, he shrugs. He has the look of a man who's given everything.

Luke hangs his head, turns and starts to walk away, shoulders slumped. Rose knows that he's crying.

She watches him go a few steps, her own heart breaking.

She can't.

She shouldn't.

She won't.

She's only going to hurt him in the end.

But, God, she loves him. She *loves* him.

Despite who she is, despite who he is.

'Luke,' she calls out.

When he turns and looks at her, sad and yet hopeful, she knows there's only one way this can go.

And still, she can't help herself.

Saint-Thérèse

The medical facility Rose Miller is in reminds Mickey of a luxury spa in London she used to visit with a friend who was obsessed with being hairless. Mickey would indulge in a Swedish massage while her friend was waxed to within an inch of her life. Mickey never understood it. Grown women have hair, she used to tell her friend. They'd leave that spa together, Mickey relaxed and rejuvenated, her friend in pain and looking like a pin-up for paedophiles.

Mickey could do with a massage now, she thinks, as she walks along the clean white corridor, every other windowsill adorned with vases of tropical lilies.

She's disturbed.

Not as disturbed as Luke is, though. He's still trying to absorb the information that the man he killed was not Kevin Davidson.

She stops at the room named the Orchid Suite.

It's just a room, really, but she supposes they justify the prices in this place by telling you that you stayed in a suite.

Rose is sitting on the edge of the bed, facing the window. Her blonde hair is long and thick. She's wearing a white vest and loose white linen trousers and she looks practically ethereal in the hazy sunlight.

She turns her head and Mickey's breath catches. Rose looks utterly wounded and Mickey can tell this isn't just from the last couple of days. This is a woman whose very countenance makes you want to take care of her. She's stunning, of course. But her appeal for many men, no doubt, lies in how fragile she looks.

'Rose,' Mickey says. 'I'm—'

'I know,' Rose says. 'I've seen pictures of you.' She frowns. 'Are you okay?'

She's staring at Mickey's bruises.

Mickey almost laughs. The incongruity of it, this woman asking Mickey if she's all right, when Rose has been sedated since the shooting.

'I'm fine,' Mickey says. 'Car accident. It's fine.'

'Oh,' Rose says. 'I'm glad you're okay.'

Rose's voice is thick and sleepy. Inspector Alleyne said they'd taken her off the heavy medication but Mickey wonders if Rose is still on some form of sedative.

She walks into the room proper and sits on the chair across from the bed.

'I've just been in with Luke.'

'How is he?' Rose winces when she asks.

'He's . . . he's well. But he's in shock. Especially now . . .'

Tears fill Rose's eyes.

'I tried to tell him. When I realised, I shouted at Luke not to shoot.'

'So,' Mickey says, carefully. 'You knew it wasn't Kevin.'

'Only when he moved away from the window and I saw him in the moonlight. I was so scared that night, I'd worked myself up, and when I saw him come into the room, I just assumed. He was tall, like Kevin, and he had dark hair. It's my fault. All of this.'

Mickey purses her lips.

'Luke doesn't want you thinking that. He's the one who fired the gun.'

Mickey studies Rose for a few moments.

'The police told me you tried to take the blame.'

'I *am* to blame. Luke was scared and he wouldn't have been if I hadn't lost it. Neither of us were in our right mind.'

'The police told you who the man was?'

'They told me a name. They didn't explain. Or they might have, but the doctor gave me something and I . . .'

Rose's voice drifts. She looks around her, like she's just seeing the bed and the room for the first time.

Yep. Definitely still drugged, Mickey thinks.

'His name was Jeremiah Williams,' she says. 'He was a petty criminal. Moved here from England a few years ago. He wanted to run a boat business but apparently preferred robbing people. They think he followed Luke from a location Luke visited earlier that day. Somewhere outside of town. Luke won't tell the police where he got the gun, but wherever he went, they reckon this guy was aware of Luke and his money and followed him back to the villa. He waited for the storm to kick off. The police think Williams supposed the noise would mask his movements.'

'Maybe it would have, but neither of us could sleep a wink,' Rose says. 'I got up a few times and I kept thinking I could hear things outside the villa.'

Mickey nods.

'The problem is,' she says, 'the fact he wasn't Kevin Davidson makes Luke's defence more difficult. The law here doesn't permit lethal force defence, even in your own home. If Luke's team made a compelling case that he feared for his life and then Kevin Davidson broke in, it would have ameliorated the sentence. But not with a total stranger.'

'Yes, but don't they see what happened?' Rose says.

'What do you mean?'

'It's too coincidental. Isn't it obvious?'

Mickey frowns. Rose stares at her like she has ten heads.

'Kevin sent him,' Rose says. 'Kevin set this up.'

'Rose, I don't think—'

'Don't say it. Don't say you think that's crazy or that's not something that could have happened. I know Kevin. I know what he's capable of. If we can prove the man was sent to hurt us, can that help Luke?'

'The man wasn't there to hurt you, Rose,' Mickey says. 'He had no weapon.'

Rose's eyes widen.

'He'd no weapon?'

'No. He was a thief. He wasn't intending to use any force—'

'But . . . but he was always going to scare the hell out of us,' Rose protests. 'It's the sort of thing Kevin does.'

'What do you mean?'

'He . . .' Rose hesitates.

Mickey waits but it looks like Rose is struggling to articulate whatever it is she wants to say.

'Rose, it's fine. I've heard plenty of stories about abusive men, believe me. I'm not going to judge you for anything you tell me.'

'I know. I just find it hard to talk about this stuff. I've buried a lot of it.'

'Well, if you think it's going to help, we're going to have to revisit some of it.'

Rose nods. She takes a deep breath.

'When Kevin and I were together, the first time he hit me, I threatened to leave him,' she says. 'This was when I thought I still could, when I thought that was a choice I could make. I didn't think I could be one of those women. If I ever heard of some woman being smacked by her partner, my go-to thought was always, why doesn't she just leave?'

Mickey doesn't say anything. It's a tale she's heard a thousand times. *I didn't think it could happen to me. I couldn't understand women who stayed.*

'So,' Rose says, 'I told him that night that we were over, that I wouldn't stand for that shit. And I was driving into work the next day and this guy pulled out in front of me as I was reversing out of the drive and I nearly crashed into him.'

Mickey winces. What the fuck is it about these men and cars, she wonders, her bruises stinging even as she thinks it.

'When I got out of the car to check he was okay, he rolled down the window. And he said, *Kevin says hi.* That was all. Kevin says hi. You know what that did to me, Mickey? It made me wet myself. The thought that he could get somebody to do that and not even have to do it himself. A man who didn't even know me was happy to scare me to death. And that night, Kevin pulled out the incentives. Because he always knew how to play me. Good and bad. Threats in the morning, roses and champagne that night. So, yes, hiring somebody to break in and steal our stuff and terrify us? This is exactly what Kevin Davidson would do.'

Mickey cocks her head.

This is not a type of story she's unfamiliar with. But for Luke to try to use something like this as a defence . . .

It's off the charts. No cop or court is going to buy a conspiracy theory as a defence case.

Unless it can be proven.

'How could he have done it?' Mickey says.

'You said he was on the island, right? He followed us here?'

'Yes.'

'So, he's here, somewhere. How did Luke get a gun? It's a small island. Maybe Kevin asked around for somebody who'd be willing to do something dodgy for some cash. We just need to convince the police that Kevin was behind this, and then they'll understand why Luke did what he did. Even if we can't find Kevin. Luke can't go to prison for murder. It's not right. We have to fix this.'

Mickey notes the 'we'. She looks at the broken woman in front of her and knows that there's no 'we'.

There's just Mickey, and it sounds like her first job on the island is to chase down a ghost, to try to connect him to another ghost. She has to get Luke Miller off a murder charge by making an impossible link and proving an insane set-up.

Mickey, funnily enough, has faced more difficult challenges.

'Luke wants me to take care of you while he's in custody,' Mickey says.

'I don't need you to take care of me.'

'Whatever. He also wants you to go and see him when he's ready. He has something he needs to discuss with you.'

Rose frowns.

'What?'

'That's for him to tell you.'

'I'll go now.'

Rose gets up off the bed.

Mickey jumps up and grabs Rose by the elbow, just in time to stop the other woman from falling.

'My legs feel wobbly,' Rose says.

'Yep. Best you take it easy until whatever you're on wears off.'

Rose nods obediently and sits back on the bed.

'Maybe you should sleep for an hour,' Mickey says.

Rose nods again and starts to lie back.

'I've never had sedatives before,' she tells Mickey, as Mickey rearranges the pillows beneath Rose's head. 'They offered me them once, when I was in hospital. After he attacked me. I didn't want them. I didn't want to be out of it.'

The woman's eyes are already closing. Mickey watches her, seeing how much more peaceful and beautiful she looks when she's not worried.

Rose from Donegal.

Did the fact she was Irish mean anything for Luke? Mickey wonders.

She shakes her head. She's being stupid.

Just because Mickey is Irish.

If Mickey had meant anything to Luke, they'd have worked things out.

She hadn't been enough for Luke to try.

She'd certainly never been enough for Luke to kill for.

London

Rachel Gray is used to working in all-male environments.

When she finished school, she got a job in a betting shop, where her co-worker was a man, as was virtually every customer, bar the occasional woman on the slot machines.

She'd realised early that betting-shop wages – not to mention weekend working and late hours – were not conducive to bringing up a young son on her own.

It was only when she bumped into a school friend of hers in a bar, Lucy Nesbitt, that Rachel began to think there were options.

Lucy, unlike Rachel, hadn't gotten pregnant at 18. She'd never had to fend for herself. But Lucy still wanted to make money and she'd made a smarter decision than Rachel.

No shop work for Lucy.

That night in the bar, Lucy had been dressed to the nines and on the arm of a man who looked 60 at least.

Rachel hadn't intended to go for a drink; she'd stepped into the bar because she was walking home from work and realised that one of the betting-shop punters, a creepy guy who had a whole foot advantage over Rachel in height, was walking behind her. He was good-looking but still gave off weird vibes and he'd been chancing his arm for a while. She'd politely but firmly declined his offer of a drink on several occasions. Following her home was new and it had frightened Rachel.

She'd ordered a vodka and tonic at the counter and prayed that he'd think she was meeting somebody. Why else call in somewhere this fancy, unless for a date?

She'd taken her first sip and was texting her mother to ask her to put Charlie to bed when Lucy grabbed her arm and shrieked in recognition.

'Rachel Gray, you look fabulous!'

Rachel did not look fabulous. She was wearing her work skirt and blouse under a high-street coat, but Lucy had always been a kind girl.

They'd started talking. With Charlie already asleep, Rachel didn't feel as inclined to get home quickly. She couldn't bear another night sitting in with her mother watching some shit on TV, in a sitting room that hadn't been decorated since 1992. All there was on offer at home was tea and biscuits and a whole heap of judgement.

Rachel found Lucy's date seedy as hell but he was buying all the drinks, and when he went to the toilet ('He does that a lot; ageing prostate,' Lucy explained), Lucy told Rachel that she was in escorting services these days.

She said it like a person would say, *Oh, I'm in hairdressing these days*.

Noticing Rachel's not-so-hidden appalled look (Rachel couldn't do blank face; she'd inherited all of her mother's condemnatory genes), Lucy went on to tell Rachel what she could earn for a night out with a client.

'You don't even need to have sex with them, unless you want

to,' she'd said. 'They're paying to have you on their arm, to show
you off. They buy everything, even your clothes. He had a work
thing earlier so he likes to have some company. Remind everyone
he can buy whatever he wants.'

'But you're still out with him,' Rachel had pointed out.

'Oh, yeah, I'll sleep with him tonight. It's three hundred for an
evening but a grand to stay the night. I'm looking to buy a new car
so . . . Don't look so shocked, Rachel. Literally, it'll be all of five
minutes before he passes out.'

Rachel's eyes had nearly fallen out of her head.

'Honestly, sweetheart,' Lucy had said. 'You should give it a go.
You're gorgeous. I could get him to introduce you to a couple of
his colleagues. You'll be in here ordering champagne in about two
weeks. Wait and see.'

At 22 and with no escape from the humdrum in sight, Rachel
had grabbed the opportunity with both hands.

At first, she just dated the men and went home.

But then she met Richard Cosgrove.

He was old, a good forty years older than Rachel, but he wasn't
bad-looking and he was generous as well as funny and entertaining.

He certainly went for more than five minutes at a time in the
bedroom but, actually, he was quite good at sex and, once Rachel
got over being weirded out by his body and the age gap, she found
he could give her pleasure. It was a shock to the system.

Rachel knew that what she'd done was technically prostitute
herself – even if it was with the same man every time – but then,
half the girls she knew were looking to marry somebody who'd
take care of them. Wasn't that the same thing? And at least she got
to live her own life while also getting to enjoy Richard's money.

But she had also known it couldn't last forever; at a certain point Richard became a friend and offered to help her find a proper job, if she wanted one.

Rachel had always wanted to work on planes and see the world.

Richard could do a lot, but even he couldn't get her hired as an air hostess who got to go home every evening. He could, however, get her a job at the airport.

Which is how Rachel ended up working in security, surrounded by men who farted and belched and smelled like a bloody brewery on a Monday morning.

It was hilarious that she worked in security. Rachel could lose a fight with her 7-year-old, she was so tiny. She could never deal with actual security threats. But she did have an eye for detail, so they'd put her on the monitors.

Rachel's job, 9–5, was to watch for anything suspicious in the airport terminals and call it in.

Everything was working out okay for her. She'd earned enough through Richard to buy a little flat and now she was earning enough to pay for childcare for Charlie after school.

More than that, Rachel had realised she enjoyed observing the airport passengers. One of the lads in her now not-so-glamorous job had suggested that she think of becoming a cop, so enthused was she about spotting suspicious-looking people.

And that is exactly what Rachel plans to do. She's already applied and wakes up every day waiting to see if she's been accepted on to the training course.

She's not thinking about that this morning, though.

She's arrived into work with a bee in her bonnet.

Ever since that friend of Richard's called in, Mickey Sheils,

Rachel hasn't been able to shake the feeling that there's something she's missing. Something that might be able to help the woman.

Mickey had been looking to track the movements of a bloke called Kevin Davidson and seemed, if not happy, at least satisfied, when Rachel had found the footage of him.

But something has been niggling at Rachel. She wasn't able to put her finger on it until this morning when she woke up and thought . . . Wait, I remember.

Rachel is sitting at her desk now, and when the two blokes in the office with her are distracted, she pulls up the old footage on the monitor and begins to look through it.

It takes her a while and she contemplates giving up and getting back to her actual job, but then she gets her break.

Rachel rewinds the screen and watches the clip again.

She knew she'd seen something important; she just hadn't realised what.

Mickey left her number but she'd also texted yesterday and said she was flying out of the country and might be out of reach for a while. She'd asked Rachel to keep an eye out for the passenger Kevin Davidson returning through the airport, and also to watch for any other Davidsons travelling from Ireland via Heathrow to Saint-Thérèse.

In her absence, Mickey had left Rachel a number for a guy called Elliot and told Rachel she could trust him.

Rachel picks up her phone to check she still has the text from Mickey with Elliot's number and it's at this point she gets a shock.

She scrolls through her phone frantically.

Where the fuck is the text?

Then she remembers. Last night, when she was getting her roots done in the kitchen, Charlie had started acting up because his tablet was out of battery and there was nothing on the TV. Her pal Mel had been applying the peroxide to Rachel's scalp at the time and Rachel, in a moment of desperation, had given Charlie her phone to play with.

She looks in her text folder again – yep, the last text in there is two weeks old. He has deleted all her most recent messages.

If Mickey thought seeing Kevin Davidson that day was important, what will she think of what Rachel has found now?

And how the hell is Rachel supposed to contact this Elliot guy?

Saint-Thérèse

Luke hates the idea of Rose seeing him like this. He'd hoped he'd be out on bail by now but Inspector Alleyne has told him that's going to take a while, legal representation or not.

When the guard walks him into the little room that serves for both visits and interviews, Luke almost does a double take.

Rose is at the table, but she barely resembles his wife. She has dark bags under her eyes, her hair is lank and her skin is pale.

He wants to take her hands, to hold her, anything, but the guard gives him the look, so instead he sits across from her, filled with more anguish than he's ever felt.

'Luke, I'm so sorry,' she says.

His head whips back.

'What are you sorry for? You didn't do anything.'

'Of course I did. This is all my fault. If it hadn't been for me, you wouldn't have got that gun, you wouldn't have been so scared that night. You wouldn't have done what you did. A man is dead because of me. I have to live with that.'

Luke furiously shakes his head.

'Rose, don't be stupid. I'm the one who escalated everything.

227

I bought a gun. I shot him. You were shouting at me to not shoot and I did it anyway.'

'I didn't realise you could shoot like that,' Rose says, shaking her head. 'I know you said you'd gone on the firing range as a kid but when you showed me the gun, I was more worried you'd shoot yourself. You said you were going to shoot him in the leg or something.'

'I wasn't exactly thinking straight,' Luke says.

Rose puts her head in her hands. Luke wants to hold her, to comfort her. And he needs to be comforted, too.

'This is a mess,' he says, despairing. 'What are we going to do?'

'I'll help you,' Rose says, her voice small. 'However I can. I'll tell them all at the trial what happened and then they'll know it was an accident. Even if they find you guilty of manslaughter, it won't come with a long sentence, will it? If they find you guilty at all . . .'

Luke sighs.

'I don't know,' he says. 'But, Rose, I have something to ask of you.'

Rose looks up.

'I want you to leave the island.'

'What?'

'Kevin Davidson is still here. That much we know.'

'I know. I told Mickey. I—'

She looks at him, her eyes full of emotion.

'He sent that man in to scare us, to scare you. He knew you'd react. He knew you'd do something. Not what you did. He couldn't have known you'd buy a gun. But I know he's behind this.'

'I think he is, too,' Luke says. 'And you're right. If I hadn't had a gun, I'd have armed myself with something. I was always going to inflict damage on that man. Kevin set me up and there's only one reason he would have done that. I've thought about it.'

'What reason?' Rose asks.

'To get me out of the way so you'd be on your own. If that guy had beaten me up, I'd have been in hospital. If I'd beaten him up, I'd have been brought into the station. Even if I wasn't arrested, I'd have had to answer the police's questions. You'd have been on your own.'

'But I'm not on my own,' Rose says. 'Isn't that why you asked Mickey to come over?'

'Yes. That and for another reason.'

Rose frowns.

'Just let me get this out because I need to say it,' he says. 'You know the way you were asking if there is anything in my past you need to know about?'

She nods, eyes wide.

'I – I have a lot of money,' he says.

'I know.'

'No, you don't.'

'I've seen your bank account statements, Luke.'

'I don't keep it there. I keep it digitally. It's on a thing called a crypto chip.'

Rose frowns.

'Why?'

'Because it's the sort of money you don't leave sitting in a regular bank. Or at least not for long enough to draw attention.'

'Why a chip? I don't understand.'

Luke sighs. He wouldn't have to explain this to anybody who worked in the financial world but he knows this is all foreign to Rose.

'It's pretty much the same as a bank card,' he says. 'You present it in certain financial institutions, with the right ID and passcode, and they will open an account for you with that amount in it. '

'And where is the chip?'

'When you picked me up from work that day, I'd no time to go back to the apartment. I keep it in the safe. I would never leave it in an empty apartment for that long, but I didn't know you were taking me on a surprise holiday.'

'How much is on it?' Rose asks.

'Twenty million pounds.'

The colour leaves Rose's face. She stares at Luke.

'Did you just say . . . ?'

'Yes. And I'm going to transfer it to you. Once it's in your name and you've the passcode, you just need to go to any of the banks I'll refer you to, bring your ID, and they'll open the account and give you whatever you need from it. Mickey has the chip now and she'll help you. Go wherever she tells you after that, once you have the money.'

Rose is still staring at him.

'No.'

She shakes her head with the word.

'Rose, are you listening to me? You need to leave Saint-Thérèse.'

'No. I'm not taking that money and I'm not leaving you to deal with this on your own.'

'I'm not asking you, I'm telling you.'

'I don't want it! I don't want that money! This was never about money!'

Luke flinches as she shouts.

She's still shaking her head.

'It's so you can be safe,' he says, quietly. 'I need you to be safe.'

'I will be safe. But there is no way I'm taking that money.'

They stare at each other. Luke doesn't know what to say.

'Where did you get it?' Rose asks, after a few moments.

Luke takes a deep breath. This is what he didn't want to tell her. This is the part of himself he'd been hoping to hide.

'I didn't always work in pensions,' he says. 'I started off in the same job as Mickey's husband. I was a hedge-fund manager.'

Rose scrunches up her features.

'So, that's how you know Mickey?'

'Yeah.'

'Is that the sort of money you make in hedge-fund management?'

'Not usually, no. Or at least not at the level I was working. I got lucky.'

Rose's face is blank. She has no idea what he's talking about, he realises.

'The ins and outs of it aren't important,' Luke says. 'I just want you to know, I didn't do anything illegal.'

'That sounds like something somebody would say if they'd done something that was on the cusp of being illegal.'

Luke can feel a rash breaking out on his neck.

'You can always read me,' he says.

'Clearly not. I'd no idea there was twenty fucking million in a safe in our sitting room. Wait . . .'

He watches her as she thinks.

'Do your friends know you have this money? Is that why they were so off with me?'

'When were they off with you?'

Rose purses her lips.

'Come on, Luke. They think you proposed too soon. They think I'm a gold digger.'

'They don't think that. And they don't know I have this money.'

'But they know you do well for yourself. Do you seriously think I can take that chip from you? Imagine what they would think then. I can't, Luke. I have to stay and fight this with you. This is my fault.'

Luke sighs.

It's both what he does and doesn't want to hear.

He's never thought for one second that Rose was interested in his money. And he knows for a fact that very few people know how he got that twenty million.

Only three, in fact.

It would be easier if Rose was a gold digger. Then he could get her to take the bloody cash and get away to safety. Buy herself a new life somewhere. God knows she deserves it. To have got caught up with Kevin Davidson and now to be married to Luke.

If ever a woman needed a break.

But she's looking at him with nothing but trust and love and support on her face and it's almost breaking Luke.

He doesn't deserve her. But he wants her to stay. He's grateful she's going to.

Mickey takes Rose to lunch after she's visited with Luke.

The woman seems completely distracted after the half hour with her husband and Mickey reckons that as well as fattening up, Rose needs something strong to settle her nerves.

They go to the bar in Mickey's hotel. Mickey takes charge, ordering two large glasses of white wine and two chicken salads.

When the drink arrives, Rose knocks back a large gulp before she's even thanked the waitress.

'I prefer that to the sedatives,' she says.

Mickey arches her eyebrows.

'Evidently. How did it go? You've barely said a word.'

Worry fills Rose's features.

'Have you ever known somebody who can seem so open, and yet, they're keeping something absolutely huge to themselves?'

'He told you about the money?'

'Yes,' Rose says, nodding. 'What the fuck? I mean, what the fuck?'

Mickey nods in agreement.

'I know what you think,' Rose says. She grabs Mickey's hand, startling her. 'I didn't marry him for money. You need to believe me. I don't want it. You can throw that chip away, for all I care. I won't be taking it from you.'

Mickey glances down at Rose's hand on hers. The woman's nails are bitten to the quick. Her pale blue nail varnish is faded and chipped. Rose is living on her last nerve and Mickey is starting to question her previous assumption.

How can she think this woman is a gold digger if she's refusing to take Luke's money when it's being offered to her?

Unless it's all part of a longer plan.

Keep saying no, no, no, until eventually she says yes.

God, you're cynical, Mickey says to herself.

'Well, let's not throw it away,' she says. 'This legal defence could cost a bit. And I think we're going to need to buy a lot of wine before this nightmare is done.'

Rose stares at Mickey and then laughs without mirth. She picks up her wine, drinks some more, then laughs again; this time, it's filled with despair.

'I suppose I should be grateful,' Rose says. 'You're right. He's going to need that money. It could be a while before either of us get back to work.'

Mickey nods.

Their food arrives. Mickey eats; her appetite is fine. Rose picks at hers.

'So, we need a plan,' Mickey says.

'For his case?'

'For you. We have to track down Kevin Davidson.'

'I don't want to think about him. I'm done.'

Mickey looks up sharply.

Rose's face is a mask.

She's shutting down, Mickey realises. She's seen it before. Pretend the problem isn't there and it will go away. Except, in Davidson's case, it won't.

'How long have you and Luke known one another?' Rose asks.

The question is unexpected and throws Mickey. She's assumed that Luke will have told Rose that the two of them are old friends, but Rose is looking at her now like there's something on her mind.

'Luke told me he worked in hedge-fund management when he made that money,' she says. 'Did you get to know him when he started working there or before?'

'When he started.'

'Was he friends with your husband?'

Mickey meets Rose's eye.

She's only just met this woman but she can already tell that there's no point in trying to bullshit her.

Rose wasn't born yesterday.

'They weren't friends,' Mickey says. 'In fact, Nathan never liked Luke.'

Rose looks surprised.

'I know,' Mickey says. 'He's easy to like, right?'

'I'd have said so.'

'But he has other sides to him,' Mickey says. 'He's always been ambitious. Maybe not so much any more. I was amused when I heard he'd gone into pension investment. It seems so . . . dull. In comparison to what he was doing, I mean. When I met Luke, he wanted to make money and he wanted to do well for himself.'

'He was competitive?' Rose suggests.

'Absolutely. Nathan is older and more senior. He was on track to become a partner when Luke was just starting. But Luke rose up the ranks fast and that really rankled Nathan.'

'And?' Rose says. 'I can tell from your face there's more.'

Mickey sighs.

'And,' Mickey says, dragging out the admission, 'Luke was sleeping with Nathan's wife.'

Rose closes her eyes.

She opens them and Mickey can tell she's trying not to look judgemental but . . . Rose is judging her.

'You had an affair,' she says.

Mickey nods. It's astonishing, how quickly and how sharply the shame can return. All these years later and she still feels like an absolute slut admitting it.

She remembers the first time they met. It was a party organised by Richard. A celebration of the year's profits. It was August, a warm evening on a beautiful hotel terrace. Mickey had worn a new dress, a sleeveless blue slip that had made her feel attractive. But Nathan had been too busy working the crowd to notice, even though everyone was getting drunk and enjoying themselves. Mickey had been left on her own, for the most part. And then Luke had approached with two glasses of champagne. He said he'd noticed she was alone and a woman as mesmerising as her shouldn't be alone.

He was a few years younger and gorgeous and she was flattered. That should have been all, but he was funny and smart and he had a look in his eye. Hunger. He was hungry for things. He was hungry for her.

Mickey hadn't realised she was hungry, too, not until she met him.

'For long?' Rose asks.

'Two years.'

'I see.'

Rose looks down at her food.

'He sent you an invite to our wedding.'

'He was just being polite. He knew I wouldn't come. But . . . we were friends. As well as everything else, we were friends. We tried to keep that up afterwards but it didn't work.'

'Did you love him?'

'Desperately. I've never loved anybody the way I loved him. That's the truth.'

Rose looks up. She shakes her head.

'I don't understand. Why an affair? Why not leave your husband for him? Two years. That seems like . . . it was serious.'

'Yes, but I didn't realise at the start that it would become like that. I didn't want to walk out on my marriage. And Luke . . . there was always something a little distant with him. But it didn't stop me falling in love.'

Rose is watching her with shrewd eyes.

'You wanted to leave your husband,' Rose says. 'In the end.'

Mickey takes a deep breath.

'Yes.'

'What happened?'

'I told him I was in love with another man and I was ending our marriage to be with him. It was awful but there were no children and . . . it was what it was.'

Rose waits for the rest of it. Mickey can feel the lump forming in her throat. The pain is still raw, even now.

'And then Luke disappeared.'

Rose flinches.

'I don't mean he ran away or vanished off the face of the planet. I mean, I was sitting at home, with my bags packed, and he stopped taking my calls. He wasn't in his apartment. I didn't know what to do. Nathan had left me to get on with it. To get my stuff and go, so I had to go. I went to a hotel and I stayed in bed for three days, crying, hoping Luke would turn up. He didn't. But eventually Nathan did. He asked me if I'd come home. He suggested couples counselling. I'm ashamed to admit I was grateful he'd have me back. Nathan wasn't a bad person and I didn't want to be alone. I know that makes me sound weak, but that's the truth. I'm a flawed, fucked-up, weak person.'

Mickey picks up her glass and drains it.

She's never talked about this. Not even to the woman Nathan advised her to see on her own.

The humiliation is as fresh as it was at the time.

Rose's face is filled with both sympathy and disbelief. Mickey can barely look at her.

'What was it like with your husband, after?' Rose asks.

Mickey grimaces.

'Hard. For a long time. He would look at me and . . . and then the anger just wasn't there any more. I can't put my finger on a particular moment or conversation. I just realised at a certain point that we were getting on with things.'

They are silent for a few moments.

'I don't understand,' Rose says. 'Why would you even take Luke's call after what he did to you?'

Mickey shrugs.

'We talked about it, afterwards. He kept phoning and sending letters of apology. We met eventually and he said he'd decided he couldn't live with himself if I left my marriage for him.'

'Did you believe him?'

Mickey hesitates before she answers.

'No,' she says, honestly. 'I think it was something else. Something he couldn't tell me about. It seemed cowardly, what he did. And that wasn't like him. When I first said I'd leave Nathan, he offered to come and tell him with me. But, I had no choice other than to accept what he said. Not to forgive him but . . . accept it. To believe he'd had a crisis of conscience. Rose—'

Mickey summons every ounce of willpower and goodness in her.

'Luke is not a bad man. And it wasn't all his fault. He didn't start our affair. I did. And I kept it going. I knew he loved me but I probably pushed it. I should have left Nathan earlier, before I met Luke. My husband has always been lacking in affection, always distracted and busy elsewhere. I shouldn't have married him at all, to be fair, but I was young and stupid. I mistook silence for sexiness. I thought Nathan was playing hard to get. He wasn't. He's just like that. I was using Luke, at the start. I wanted something for myself. And yes, he hurt me badly but there were no innocents in the situation. I never hated Luke. I never could.'

Mickey says all this because she's looking at Rose and she realises that what she's told the woman has devastated her. The perfect image she had of Luke in her head is just that. An image.

That's what you get when you marry somebody you've only known six months, Mickey thinks, a little meanly.

'Do you know how he got all that money?' Rose asks.

Mickey shakes her head.

'I don't,' she says. 'I assume he was investing for himself. He was always good at it. Nathan's boss Richard used to say Luke was dynamite.'

Rose cocks her head.

'So, you don't think he did anything wrong to get it?'

Mickey considers this.

'What these hedge fund guys do,' she says, 'it's never morally good. They bet on things failing and they can make them fail just by the weight of betting against them. But it's not illegal. Luke wasn't fired and as far as I know, he was still making good money for Richard's firm when he left.'

Rose exhales.

'You were worrying about that,' Mickey says.

'Yes. I wondered why he'd kept it from me if he hadn't done anything wrong.'

'Don't get offended, but you haven't known each other very long.'

'Long enough for him to propose and tell me he wanted to spend the rest of his life with me.'

'Fair point.'

Both women pick up their glasses. Mickey takes a sip, her mind shifting back to Kevin Davidson.

'Right,' she says, decisively. 'Enough about the past. We need to focus on the present. Let's figure out where the hell Kevin Davidson might be staying. We also need to get a legal team sorted for Luke. Inspector Alleyne has given me some names. I think he feels sorry for Luke.'

'How do you plan to look for Kevin?' Rose asks.

'I'm still figuring that one out. But while I am, it's safer for you to stay close. I'll book you a room here. You need a shower and fresh clothes and then a little bit of sun.'

Rose still looks unhappy but she nods.

'Okay,' she says. 'Let's find him.'

Mickey nods.

She likes this woman's determination. She doesn't want to like her at all, but she does.

Rose is growing on her.

London

June 2022

The restaurant Luke has chosen for this evening will be the fanciest Rose has ever been to.

When he sent her the link, she immediately went into a tailspin about what she was supposed to wear. She'd never heard of the place and the restaurant's website was intimidating – just its name on a black background, with a sample seasonal menu. No prices.

Expensive, Rose thought, immediately.

And she didn't have anything decent enough for that sort of place. She'd phoned Luke in a panic.

'I've nothing to wear for somewhere like this.'

'Wear what you always wear. You'll be beautiful.'

God. Men could be so infuriating when it came to this sort of thing.

Which is why Ann-Marie is in Rose's flat right this minute, necking wine while Rose parades up and down her living room in Ann-Marie's dresses.

'I have heard rumours about this place,' Ann-Marie says. 'The actual royals have eaten there.'

'Fuck off,' Rose says.

'I will not. I'm telling you. This place is fancy.'

'If it's that fancy, how do you know about it?'

'I heard from a friend of a friend.'

Rose stands in front of the mirror looking at the blue dress she's just tried on. It matches Ann-Marie's eyes but it's doing nothing for Rose.

'Wear the red,' Ann-Marie says.

'I'm not wearing slut red.'

'It's getting serious with you two. Wear the red.'

Rose shakes her head. She crosses to the couch and picks up the black one she tried on first.

'Black,' she says. 'With some nice jewellery. How in God's name did you end up with a Chanel dress in your wardrobe, Ann-Marie?'

'Haven't you ever heard of TK Maxx?'

'I have never seen a Chanel dress in TK Maxx.'

'You need to be in early and you need to be vigilant. Bat those posh bitches away from the good stuff.'

Rose laughs. Tonight, she'll look beautiful. And she'll enjoy herself. She promises herself she will.

When Luke picks her up, he lets out a low whistle.

'Thought you didn't have anything nice enough?'

'I don't. Luckily, my friends do.'

Luke frowns.

'I wish you'd let me buy you things.'

'You're buying dinner!' Rose exclaims. 'There are no prices on the menu, which means I can't afford the tap water. What possessed you to pick somewhere like this?'

'It's a lovely evening,' Luke says, smiling. 'We need a lovely place to dine.'

It is a lovely evening. They get a cab to the top of a pedestrianised street and as they stroll towards the restaurant, Rose feels nothing but contentment. The sun is still giving off heat, nice food and candle wax scent the air, and Luke is holding her hand like she's the most important thing in the world.

At the anonymous door that serves as the restaurant's entrance, Luke pauses and tips her chin so she's looking up at him and he down at her.

'You look truly beautiful tonight,' he says.

'So do you,' Rose replies.

He smiles.

Inside, the waiting staff click into the most efficient assembly line Rose has ever seen. Somebody takes their coats; somebody else brings them down a flight of stairs. Rose doesn't realise, until they emerge, that the back of the restaurant faces on to the river, each table looking out over the water.

They're seated where they can take in the view. A waiter lights a candle, another gives them menus, another brings a bottle of champagne to the table and pops the cork.

Rose is thrilled at the amount of planning Luke's put into this evening, even as she's panicking at what all of this is going to cost. She hates that she can't contribute to nights like this.

When she's selected what she hopes are the least expensive things on the menu – a simple salad to start and a pasta dish for her main ('I don't want to be too full,' she tells Luke) – she takes a sip of her drink and starts to relax.

The weather is balmy, the flowers and hanging baskets in the restaurant smell divine and everything about the evening is perfect.

She should have seen it coming but she doesn't, right up to the moment Luke gets down on one knee, tiny box in hand.

Rose clamps her hand over her mouth.

'Rose, I know we've only been seeing each other six months,' Luke says. 'Less, to be fair. But I've always said, I knew from the day I met you that I was going to be with you. I don't know how, I just did.'

Rose is too shell-shocked to speak. She can tell, from the way Luke's voice sounds, that he's filled with nerves. But he has prepared this speech and he's going to deliver it.

In the face of his anxiety, Rose feels herself start to unwind.

He's terrified she's going to say no.

She knows she's going to say yes. She's known since that day at the bus stop when she called his name and he turned around. She knew the path this would take.

'We don't have to get married quickly,' he says. 'If you want to have a long engagement so you can figure out if I'm a closet nutjob, I don't mind. But I think about you almost every minute of every day and there is nothing I want more than to have you in my life for the rest of it. So, please, will you marry me?'

Rose can't speak, the lump in her throat is so big.

She nods and Luke's face lights up.

'Is that a yes?'

'Yes,' Rose whispers.

'You've made me the happiest man alive,' he says, and kisses her. There are tears in Rose's eyes.

Later, when they're walking back towards his apartment, or floating as Luke quips, Rose tries to bury the butterflies that won't stop fluttering in her stomach.

She looks down at the diamond engagement ring on her finger and tells herself she deserves this. Luke deserves it. The past has been horrible, but the future can be better.

But when she looks up at Luke, strolling along, not a care in the world, the biggest smile on his face, she wonders . . .

Is it worth it, what's about to happen?

Is it worth the danger she's put them both in?

Saint-Thérèse

Inspector Alleyne is waiting for Mickey when she arrives at the police station.

She left Rose in her hotel room, under strict instructions not to open the door to anybody. Rose reminded Mickey that she was a grown woman, but said she'd stay in if it made Mickey feel better.

They spent the day going from hotel to hotel on the island, showing receptionists the photo of Kevin Davidson.

It was a fruitless search. Even Mickey acknowledged it was unlikely that Davidson would check in anywhere that would make it easy to be found. According to Rose, the man always had plenty of money at his disposal, so he could have easily done what she and Luke had – hired a private villa.

Mickey knows that footwork alone won't get them anywhere. She's also worried that they're making themselves noticeable by asking for Davidson. If he hasn't already found where Rose has moved to on the island, it's only a matter of time before he does.

She isn't sure if she buys into Rose and Luke's theory that Davidson set them up. Not because she doesn't believe that an abusive ex is capable of that sort of thing – she has seen husbands and boyfriends go to extremes to get back at former partners, including the most implausible, mind-boggling tactics. Two years ago, a client of hers was arrested for stealing from her job. It transpired her ex had taken all her passwords from her computer when they were together, including her online work ones. He'd tapped into the system and transferred money from the company using his former wife's email and entry codes. It was only through the diligent work of a police IT officer that Mickey's client was cleared.

Mickey knows that people can and will go to any lengths for revenge.

But Inspector Alleyne showed her the dead man's police record in the station this morning and it was petty burglary after burglary, all targeted at private villas and all committed long before Luke and Rose ever arrived on Saint-Thérèse.

And then there's the fact Davidson couldn't have known Luke would kill Williams. Defend himself, sure, but to actually take a life and end up facing a murder charge that could see him jailed for years? There's no way Davidson could have planned that.

But it's here Mickey comes unstuck.

As Rose had speculated, while they were looking for Kevin, what if that wasn't part of the plan? What if Davidson only needed Luke to be taken out of the equation, to be brought into a police station for a while so Davidson would have access to Rose on her own . . .

Mickey mulls on that one. It still seems extreme but then, this man did follow his ex-girlfriend halfway around the globe.

Whatever happened, whether he was behind it or not, Mickey knows Davidson is still a threat to Rose and they have to find him.

She doesn't know what Inspector Alleyne wants her for now, but it might be to lecture her about traipsing around the island playing amateur sleuth.

Mickey pays the taxi driver and approaches the inspector, who's standing beside the station door, his jacket slung over one shoulder and a foot propped against the wall. He could be posing for a photo shoot. Effortlessly casual.

'Shall we walk?' he asks her.

'Oh. Okay.'

He glances down at her shoes, satisfies himself that she's not wearing heels, and they begin their stroll.

'Are we going somewhere in particular?' Mickey asks.

'Yes.'

They walk in silence. A man of few words, Mickey thinks. It doesn't bother her. Elliot was the same when they started working together. More interested in spouting the odd fact about Assassin's Creed than having an actual conversation. Nowadays, he's practically verbose.

After a few minutes, she feels his eyes on her. She glances at him and sees he's got the hint of a smile at the corner of his lips.

'You are not one of these people who feels the need to make small talk,' he says.

'Not if you don't,' she answers.

He shrugs.

They're walking towards what appears to be the harbour. Mickey can see boats and small yachts bobbing. It's dark now and the many restaurants along the seafront cast a yellow glow out on to the inky water. There's a smell of grilled seafood in the air and Mickey realises she's hungry. She hasn't eaten since her salad at lunch. Maybe Inspector Alleyne is bringing her for dinner, Mickey speculates, and allows herself a smile.

'You're an island native?' she asks. She's fine with them being quiet but she's also interested in the man in step beside her.

'Yes. And where are you from? You're not English. Ireland, maybe?'

'Yes. You really recognise my accent?'

'I've been to Ireland. It's much nicer than London. What brought you there?'

'What brings most people from a small country situated beside a large one? Jobs. Opportunity.'

'Anonymity.'

Mickey glances sharply at Alleyne.

'That too,' she agrees. 'But not in my case. I wasn't running from anything.'

'Unlike your friend.'

'I don't know Rose's story. I know Luke, from many years ago. But yes, Rose wouldn't be the first to come to London to get away from somebody or something back home.'

'Kevin Davidson.'

'Yes.'

'You and she have been asking around for him. Going hotel to hotel. Do you think that is wise if he really is as dangerous as you say?'

'Christ, this really is a small island.'

'A bit like Ireland.'

'Indeed. You're right, of course. It may not be wise but it's all we can do. I don't have a network of people here like I have at home. I have to do the legwork myself. And we can either try to find him or wait until he finds us, but either way, he has to be found. Otherwise, this conspiracy theory of Rose's can never be proved.'

'Ah, yes. The conspiracy theory. Mr Miller has advocated it, too.'

'You think it's nonsense?'

Inspector Alleyne doesn't reply for a few moments. When he does, his answer surprises Mickey.

'No,' he says. 'I have worked too long in my job to dismiss anything as nonsense. I think if I was going to launch a campaign of intimidation against somebody, if I wanted them to do something extreme, I could be very creative.'

'I hope I'm never on the wrong side of you,' Mickey says.

'Me too,' he replies, with such sincerity that Mickey believes him.

'But that is not my style,' he adds. 'And I think that conspiracy theories are also very difficult to prove.'

They pause for a moment while Alleyne helps Mickey over a little railing near the harbour's entrance. They're moving away from the restaurants, she sees. So much for a surprise and highly unusual dinner date.

'You said you've been to Ireland,' Mickey says, changing the subject. 'What brought you there? It certainly wasn't the weather.'

It's 9 p.m. now and Mickey is wearing a thin cardigan over a vest top and she's still warm. She can only imagine that Alleyne was freezing from the moment he got off the plane at Dublin Airport.

'I wanted to tour Europe. Dublin was the first stop. I was meant to be there for a one-night stopover and then somebody brought me on the literary pub crawl.'

'Oh, dear. I'm surprised you ever made it home.'

He smiles.

'It was a wrench to leave. Paris had plenty of culture and plenty of wine but none of the, what do you call it? The craic.'

'The craic is indeed mighty in Dublin.'

They're at the dock now. Up close, Mickey sees that the harbour is filled with as many yachts as small fishing boats. Tourists and locals, cheek by jowl.

'Inspector, you're not trying to deport me via sea, are you?' Mickey asks.

'We have not reached that point. Yet.'

Mickey half smiles. She likes to curate friends in the police. Wherever that police force may be. But sometimes, the nature of her job means she also falls out with the police. When they act to the letter of the law and not the spirit, and Mickey is willing to bend the law to protect someone, then conflict will ensue.

She's not sure yet how Alleyne will turn out.

'I looked you up,' Alleyne says.

'I hope you didn't find anything too scandalous.'

'You don't practise law any more.'

'No.'

'Is there a reason?'

Mickey juts out her lower lip. She doesn't know this man. She owes him neither the truth nor the gloss version. But she's getting too old to not answer straight questions with straight answers.

'When I came to England, I fell in love with a rich man at the same time as I was falling out of love with the legal system. I specialised in family law and I saw too many people fucked over by the guards – they're our police force – and the courts. I planned to train up in the English system in London but I met my future husband and he asked me one night what I really wanted to do. I thought about it and realised I'd be more effective helping women and children escape from abusive partners than trying to get them protection orders and justice via the courts.'

Inspector Alleyne slows his steady stride and Mickey brings her steps into sync with his.

'It sounds like you're leaving something out,' he says.

Mickey looks straight ahead.

'I am. I won a protection order for a woman back in Ireland. It was one of my last cases there. Her ex-husband had been particularly violent and kept showing up at the family home, even after she'd divorced him. Her solicitor brought her in and told me in advance that the woman was reticent about getting the order because she feared it would antagonise her ex, but she was at her wits' end. I gave her some advice. And the thing is, when most people hear advice from a barrister, they take it, because you're important and professional and you know what you're doing.

'I told her to get the protection order because, that way, if he showed up she could report him and, if he did it enough times, the police would pick him up. I also intimated that I knew a couple of guards who'd give him a good talking-to. It wasn't a lie. I knew how scared these women got and sometimes they needed to hear somebody tell them – *I will make sure you're taken care of.*'

Mickey swallows the lump in her throat.

'I was out in a pub that night. The one beside the courts. It had been a long day and I was drinking with some barrister friends of mine, celebrating our successes, when the call came in. Her husband had broken the order the same day it had been awarded. He murdered her. Beat her until her body couldn't take it.'

Inspector Alleyne stops walking. Mickey is still going; she gets a couple of steps, lost in thought, before she realises he's fallen behind.

She turns back and looks at him.

'I am sorry,' he says.

'Me too.' She sighs.

'You know that the blame for what happened lies with him?'

'Yes. Of course. But it affected me. The law was so . . . useless for her. Anyway. We should keep going.'

'No need. We are here.'

Mickey looks at the small fishing boat anchored beside the dock. It looks like it's seen better days.

'This is where Jeremiah Williams lived.'

'Right,' Mickey says. 'I thought he lived out in Peterstown?'

Alleyne shakes his head.

'No. That's where he was seen last. That is where, I believe, Luke Miller bought the weapon. I have a little problem out there.'

'A little weapons-dealing problem?'

'A little everything-dealing problem. Williams was hanging around out there at the time and I'm pretty sure he followed Miller back to the villa. It would not have gone unnoticed. An Englishman calling out there with a lot of money in hand.'

'Okay,' Mickey says. 'So far, we're up to what you've already told me.'

'Five days ago, Williams was here, sunning himself on this deck. One of his neighbours, the owner of that little boat down there, saw a stranger approach.'

Mickey frowns.

'From the description I've received, it sounds like that stranger was Kevin Davidson. Or at least what he looks like in that photograph you have sent me.'

Mickey stares at Alleyne.

'Are you saying . . . ?'

'I don't know what I'm saying,' Alleyne says. 'Like I said, conspiracy theories are hard to prove.'

He looks troubled, Mickey realises. This new information does not fit with the simple account he'd originally established for Luke's case.

'How would Davidson have known about Jeremiah Williams?' Mickey asks. 'He landed on this island a day after Rose and Luke.'

Alleyne shrugs.

'Like you said. This island is small. There is no anonymity here. Jeremiah had a reputation. I have had him in and out of jail many times. You ask anybody on the island: who is renowned for selling drugs? Who is renowned for stealing? Who is violent? No local will volunteer that information to a stranger, but if somebody was willing to pay for it . . . It would not be difficult to ascertain that an Englishman who lives by the harbour is known for being a burglar.'

'So,' Mickey hesitates, 'Rose and Luke are correct? Davidson sent Williams as part of an intimidation strategy?'

Alleyne shakes his head, softly.

'That I do not know. I had no robbery reports that fit Williams' MO in the last few months. I do not think he had turned over a new leaf. I believe he'd got other work. Perhaps as a bit of a heavy for that problematic dealer I was telling you about. So, he could handle himself. He could have been told Mr Miller was alone in the villa. I don't believe Williams was the sort who hurt women. He may have been sent to rough him up or to provoke Mr Miller into a physical fight. I doubt he was expecting Mr Miller to have a gun.'

'But if he saw him in Peterstown—'

'He probably assumed he was buying drugs. In any case, I find myself now wanting to find our Mr Davidson and ask him some questions.'

Mickey frowns.

On the one hand, the inspector's intervention is good news.

On the other, she's starting to worry about how devious Kevin Davidson is.

Mickey feels a sudden urge to return to Rose. She doesn't like the idea of her being alone, even in the hotel.

'Let's get you back,' the inspector says, reading her mind.

Rose has done what Mickey asked – she's sat in her room while Mickey was out – but as soon as Mickey arrives back to the hotel, she can see that Rose is not happy.

'I'm not going to stay in hiding,' Rose says, adamantly. 'This isn't going to work.'

'Fine,' Mickey says. 'Let's go downstairs and see if they'll give us a late dinner. I need food.'

'I mean it, Mickey. I'm not going to run away again. I want to find him. He can't do this to us. I know you don't believe me, but I'm telling you, he's behind this. All of it.'

'Rose. Can we talk about this downstairs? I need a drink.'

Something in Mickey's tone must have worked because Rose stops talking and follows Mickey from the room.

The hotel restaurant staff are happy to accommodate the two women, though it's late. They order food and a bottle of wine and Mickey plays with her napkin nervously while they wait.

'You're unusually quiet,' Rose says.

'I found out something,' Mickey tells her. 'Inspector Alleyne did, actually. Your theory about Kevin being behind the guy breaking into your villa . . . I think you're right. We think you're right. A man matching Kevin's description was seen talking to Jeremiah

Williams earlier in the week. And now Inspector Alleyne is looking for Kevin, too.'

Rose pales.

'Are you serious?'

'You say that like you don't believe me. You're the one who said that's what happened.'

'I . . . I suppose I was hoping I was wrong.'

Mickey shakes her head.

'I don't think you are,' she says. 'Listen, Rose, this changes things. I understand what you're saying about not wanting to leave. And I know why you feel like that.'

'I don't think anybody could understand what's going on in my head.'

'I do.'

Mickey looks at the woman across from her. Rose is wearing a crocheted off-the-shoulder sweater, her bare shoulders and arms visible at the top. She's thin and getting thinner. She looks like a strong gust could carry her away. And yet, Mickey knows that Rose is made of iron.

'When it was just you, when it was your hometown, it made sense to run,' Mickey says. 'And it was, if not easy, easier, because I'm guessing you didn't have a whole lot of people to leave behind.'

'I did have family and friends,' Rose says. 'But . . . he'd isolated me. I'd let him. I cut myself off from people. My head wasn't – well, it wasn't in a good space.'

'I get that. But now Luke is involved. There's a reason you brought him here with you when you ran from London. You don't want to be without him. And now, Kevin hasn't just attacked you.

He's attacked Luke. And all of us are strangely capable of being more protective towards other people than ourselves.'

Rose shrugs.

'I guess all of that is true,' she says. 'But I think I'm also just tired of running, Mickey.'

'I know. But Rose, what this man is doing has surpassed even the most violent offenders I've met. It's clever and devious and sinister. If you could take him on, one-to-one, okay. But you can't. He's coming at you from angles you can't even see. He's coming at you from angles that I find hard to get my head around. He wants to fuck up your life. Yours and Luke's. You two have played right into his hands.'

Rose pushes the food around on her plate.

'What do I do?' she asks.

'Luke wants you safe. Take his money. I can set you up with somewhere to go and only I will know how to contact you. I'll pay for Luke's defence. And when he's out, he'll come to you.'

Rose shakes her head.

'Mickey, I can't.'

'Why not?'

'If this policeman can find witnesses who confirm that Kevin Davidson is on the island and he organised for Jeremiah Williams to break into our villa to scare me – who do you think is the most important witness for the defence? It's me. Don't you get that, as somebody who knows the law? The court is going to need to hear how terrified I am of Kevin. I will have to tell them what he did to me, why I ran from him the first time, how I came to be on the island after he found me the second time. They will need to be made to understand how scared we were the night of the storm.

Why Luke reacted the way he did. Sure, he can tell them my story second-hand, but do you think that will have the same effect as it will coming from me? I *have* to stay. I have to help him. This wouldn't have happened to him if it wasn't for me.'

Mickey stares at Rose.

She's right. God, she's right. Mickey hadn't been thinking with her law cap on. She'd been thinking as somebody who works with abused women. Her head is filled with ways to get Rose to safety. She's forgotten how important Rose is to Luke's case.

'I think that's the bravest thing I've ever heard anybody say,' Mickey says.

'I have no choice,' Rose says, her voice low and sad. 'I have to try to make this right.'

'But you know he's still out there.'

Rose shrugs.

Mickey observes the determination, the courage on her face. She sees now why Luke fell so hard and so fast for this woman.

They eat in silence for a while. Mickey thought she was hungry but actually, her appetite is now almost non-existent.

'I need to go to the bathroom,' Rose says, when she's finished pushing her own food around her plate.

Mickey sips her drink as Rose walks towards the far end of the restaurant. She's afraid to take her eyes off the other woman, paranoid that the moment she's out of sight, Davidson will jump out and grab her.

A waiter passes and Mickey asks him to bring two coffees.

He's just left when her phone rings.

She's surprised to see it's Richard Cosgrove.

Mickey answers.

'Mickey, darling, how are—'

The line breaks.

'Can you hear me, Richard?' Mickey says. 'Hold on a moment.'

She stands and walks to the restaurant's windows, but when she looks at her phone, she sees she has full signal bars.

'I'm in Paris, Mickey.'

'Glad to hear it,' she answers. 'Can you hear me okay?'

'Fine. But I'm—'

Mickey strains her ears as Richard's volume dips.

'Sorry, on the underground.'

'Why don't you ring me later?'

'. . . journey.'

'What? Richard, I can't hear you. Phone me later.'

'Number. Sidekick.'

'You want a number for Elliot?'

'Bloody h— I'll text you.'

He hangs up. A few seconds later she gets a text. *Yes. Send me a number for Elliot.*

Mickey sends on a business card, wondering what Richard could want with Elliot's number.

She sees movement in the quiet restaurant and looks across at her table, expecting to see Rose sitting back down. But it's a waiter walking away. Rose is coming back into the restaurant from the opposite direction.

Mickey heads back.

When she sits down, there are no coffees but before she can grab the waiter again, Rose joins her.

'Did you see that guy who was at our table when we were both away from it?' Mickey asks.

'The waiter?' Rose says, puzzled.

'I thought he was but I don't know. He didn't look familiar to you?'

Rose shakes her head.

'I'm starting to see phantoms,' Mickey says.

'I see Kevin everywhere,' Rose says. 'It's nothing new for me.'

Mickey drinks more wine. Something is troubling her.

She knows to never ignore that feeling. She doesn't imagine things. Mickey can sense when something bad is going to happen. She doesn't know how. Her grandmother used to say the 'sight' ran in their family. Mickey doesn't go in for such nonsense. If she had the sight, she'd have used it to avoid lots of bad situations in her own life.

But she thinks there's merit in listening to her gut. It's perfectly plausible that her body might respond to situations instinctively before her brain catches up.

'Rose, you should sleep in my room tonight,' Mickey says.

Rose frowns.

'Is that necessary?' she says. 'I'll lock the door. I'm not going to let anybody in. Even if they say room service. I'm not stupid.'

'I know. But I'd feel better if we were together. In fact, I might talk to this inspector tomorrow and see if he has the resources to start giving us a little protection.'

Rose looks around her, suddenly worried.

'Why are you saying this now? Do you know something?'

'No. It's just . . . a feeling.'

Rose looks back at Mickey. She studies her face. Then she picks up her wine and drinks it. Mickey does the same. The two women meet each other's eye.

Mickey is spooked. And the expression on Rose's face tells Mickey she's right to be.

London

July 2022

The wedding is small. It was never going to be anything other. Once Rose said yes, she told Luke she didn't want a big affair and she didn't need to wait. She was happy to go away, the two of them, find a registrar and do the deed. And Luke had said, well, if it's just a small wedding, why not do it this summer?

So, between the short time to organise it and the lack of significant relatives in both their lives – Rose certainly couldn't contact any of her extended family and Luke's list was slim enough – they plumped for a short visit to the registry office and an evening do in the restaurant where Luke had proposed.

Several of Luke's family and friends are there and a handful of Rose's friends. Ann-Marie is her bridesmaid; Xander is Luke's best man. Luke is in his best suit; Rose wears a pretty, knee-length cream dress she bought in Oasis. The food is beautiful, candle flames dance in the twilight, champagne flows.

It's an intimate, relaxed, beautiful night with love in the air, which makes it all the worse when Rose overhears Xander and another of Luke's friends, John, in conversation outside the ladies' toilets.

She's gone to the loo because she needs a break. Ann-Marie wanted to accompany her, pointing out the bride is not meant to do anything on her own and Rose might need help with her dress. Rose pointed out that Ann-Marie's dress was harder to adjust than Rose's simple thing and, also, there's nothing traditional or usual about this wedding.

Rose needs some alone time. She always gets overwhelmed at events where there are more than two people, and even though there are only twenty guests at their table, she's struggling to maintain appearances.

She's run cold water on her wrists to try to calm herself and is just about to go back outside when she hears the two men in the corridor.

Rose doesn't mean to listen but Xander and John have had a few and are drunkenly trying to make themselves heard over the restaurant's music, which is louder in the corridor.

'I'm just saying, it's ridiculously quick,' John says.

'The man is smitten,' Xander replies. 'You haven't seen them together as much as I have. I knew he'd propose.'

'Look, propose, fair enough. Though, even then, six months is not a long time to know somebody before you're dropping on to one knee. I've had footie injuries longer than that. But to be married less than eight weeks later? That's fucking nuts.'

'I talked to him. I did. He knows what he wants.'

'It'll end in disaster. Is she pregnant?'

'Apparently not.'

'Then I presume she's after his money?'

'She doesn't seem the type,' Xander says. 'Not from what I've seen. But you never know. She's only a teacher.'

'Course she's after his fucking money. Nice little honeymoon period, pop out a sprog, dump Luke when she's fed up with him, get half his worth. He's an idiot. He's thinking with his dick.'

'That's not exactly progressive of you, mate.'

'Listen, mate, I buy my girlfriend sanitary towels. I'm as woke as the next bloke. I'll tell you what, though, her mate is hot. The bridesmaid.'

'Didn't you just say you have a girlfriend, John?'

'She's not here and it's a wedding.'

'You're a bad man. Maybe you're right about the new wife, though. It does feel indecently quick.'

'You should have tied him to a pole on his stag. Stopped him making the mistake.'

The men's voices drift off as they go into the toilets.

Rose stands at the door of the ladies. She'd thought Xander liked her. It stings more, thinking that even he's not sure about her.

She's always said she's not after Luke's money. She's never wanted it.

The hurt is replaced with anger as she starts to resent the accusation.

This was too soon. Luke pushed for it and she went along, but she should have held out longer. Because what if he too starts to think she's after his money?

Rose leaves the ladies but instead of going back to their table, she heads upstairs and out on to the street. She needs some air, somewhere she can breathe properly.

She's standing on the pavement when something catches her eye.

She turns her head and looks towards some pedestrians further along the path.

Her heart stops.

Is that him? Is it Kevin?

But as soon as the thought forms, she dismisses it.

She's seeing things, paranoid because of the day that's in it.

Kevin wouldn't be stupid enough to show up somewhere this public.

Rose steels herself and goes back inside, back to her wedding and her new husband.

She doesn't see the man further up the road step back out of the shop doorway and walk to her end of the street.

He pauses outside the restaurant door, looks at it.

Then Kevin walks on.

Saint-Thérèse

The jail on Saint-Thérèse is, in Luke's opinion, never going to feature in a 'world's worst prisons' documentary.

He can't even begin to think what being held in a prison in London would be like. Here, he's in a cell on his own, he's brought his meals, he's escorted out for exercise. He's had no interaction with any other prisoners and the guards are curt but professional.

Luke suspects this isn't the regular custody experience. If he was a local, he guesses everything would be a little rougher and he'd be in with the general prison population. He figures that, being a tourist – and a wealthy English one at that – means he's being given the special treatment. Just in case this blows up in the international press and the island's tourism industry is threatened by the scandal of the mistreatment of a foreign national. He knows the story's only being buried at the moment because Inspector Alleyne runs a tight ship and Luke and Rose haven't alerted anybody to their situation.

But no matter how softly, softly everyone is being, Luke is still unhappy. He doesn't want to be incarcerated. He wants to be out, taking care of his wife.

Luke trusts Mickey to look out for Rose. He's never met anybody stronger or more capable.

Mickey isn't aware, but for a long time after Luke betrayed her, he kept an eye on what she was doing.

So many times he had to stop himself from telling her why he'd left her in the lurch the way he did. When he finally did sit down with her, he'd glossed over it. Told her he couldn't live with breaking up her marriage and some other such nonsense.

Luke hadn't cared about Mickey's marriage. He'd cared about her and he'd cared about himself. He'd wanted her.

But he'd wanted something else more.

Luke turns his head on the hard pillow and looks up at the shaft of moonlight coming in the narrow window above him.

He can't sleep. If he's not thinking about Rose and Mickey, he's thinking about Jeremiah Williams.

Luke killed an innocent man.

Okay, not entirely innocent. The bloke was breaking into their bedroom. But he hadn't deserved to lose his life.

Luke plays the moment over and over in his head.

He hears Rose scream, 'Don't shoot', again and again.

What had he thought in that moment?

He'd thought, she doesn't want me to kill him. She doesn't want me to shoot Kevin Davidson. She still loves him. Somewhere in the back of his head, he'd thought that.

She loves him.

He'd pulled the trigger and when he did, it had been with anger. He'd done it thinking: you're my wife and this man doesn't get to touch you.

So, how is he any better than Kevin Davidson?

If he could kill somebody in cold blood, how can Luke be a good man?

Luke closes his eyes and desperately prays for sleep. He can't bear the thoughts in his head.

They're too raw, these early-hour thoughts. Too real.

Luke knows he's no better than Davidson.

He's always known.

There are two double beds in Mickey's room and Mickey is in the one nearest the door. She wants Rose as far inside the room as she can be. If somebody comes in that hotel door, they'll have to get past Mickey first.

Mickey thinks it will take her a while to fall asleep. She feels anxious, nervy – not the usual adrenaline she gets when she knows there may be danger close. This is altogether different. She doesn't feel like herself, not one bit. Her heart is beating out of time and a sheen of sweat covers her whole body.

The hotel room is on the second storey and the gardens are just below. Not being on the ground floor is reassuring, but the fact there's a fire escape leading to the gardens from their window, is not.

Mickey has turned the air conditioning on low and ensured the windows are shuttered tight. The glass isn't the thickest, though, and she can still hear the sounds of the night outside, cicadas in the courtyard and the rumble of the occasional passing car. Still, if anybody breaks that glass, she'll hear it. Davidson was clever enough to hire Williams the first time – a professional burglar who could access Luke and Rose's villa noiselessly. Davidson won't have the same skills.

When she starts to hear Rose's breathing grow deeper, Mickey struggles to fight sleep herself. She'd closed her eyes on the plane during the flight, so she doesn't think jet lag is catching up with her. She's just exhausted.

She drifts off.

Mickey's sleep is filled with nightmares. She sees Luke's face but he morphs into Nathan and he's asking her what she's doing on Saint-Thérèse. She sees Rose, begging Mickey to help her find Kevin Davidson because she's seen him in the hotel.

And then there's Kevin Davidson. She can feel him, watching them, Mickey and Rose and Luke and Nathan. He's everywhere and then Mickey is talking to him, normally, asking him why he's chasing Rose. He's very lovely as he explains he just wants to take Rose back home.

Promise you won't hit her again, dream Mickey says.

Kevin nods. He won't. He'll be good.

But then Mickey hears a scream.

In her dream, Mickey tries to find where the scream came from. She knows she's asleep and she's telling herself to wake up but her body won't comply. She keeps thinking she is awake, but then she realises, no – this is still the dream.

And it's filled with bangs and thuds and cries of *stop*.

The nightmare fades as quickly as it began, leaving Mickey in a deep, disturbed sleep.

Morning comes and Mickey wakes, staring at the wall beside her bed. Her bladder is bursting and the smells of the Caribbean fill her nostrils: flowers blooming in the morning sun in the courtyard, fresh pastries baking, coffee brewing.

She frowns, unused to how her body feels. Mickey always wakes in the night to go to the bathroom. She has a set body clock that drives her mad sometimes. Five a.m., and she's up, then back to bed for two hours hoping she'll be able to go back to sleep.

Mickey reaches for her phone on the floor and sees the time on the screen.

Nine a.m.

That can't be right, she thinks.

She turns and sees Rose's bed beside her, empty.

Mickey sits up. She feels sluggish, not herself.

She gets out of bed and goes to the bathroom.

Rose is not in there.

Don't tell me she's gone to breakfast alone, Mickey thinks. Her brain feels foggy but one thought is clear: she needs to wee.

Mickey sits down on the toilet.

And while she's sitting there, feeling disturbed and restless and unlike herself, a thought hits her.

The dream from last night seeps back in.

And the haze is lifting from her mind.

Mickey pees faster than she ever has, splashes her hands with water, and rushes outside.

The chain she put across the room door last night is still on it.

The locks are still turned.

Inside.

Rose didn't leave by the door.

Mickey turns around and surveys the empty room.

Then she looks at the window, the smell of outside fresh in her nose.

It's open.

Not smashed. Not broken. Open.

It's been opened from the inside.

Rose opened the window.

'Oh, fuck,' Mickey says.

She thinks of the wine last night. She thinks of the waiter she saw near her table and how he'd looked familiar. She thinks of Rose saying she had to go to the bathroom, just before that waiter appeared, and how on edge she'd seemed when she returned.

Was it the waiter or Rose who did it?

Mickey's wine was drugged.

She should have gone with her first instinct.

Rose is in on it.

Rose has scammed Luke Miller.

Donegal

It's late September. Elliot reminds himself of that fact as he drives the road that circles Glenveagh Park. He's heading towards Errigal, in the direction of the remote fishing village where the Davidson family hold sway.

But with the rain beating down on the car, combined with the dullness of the day, it feels more like mid-December.

He keeps a keen eye out for sheep on the deserted road. The man he rented the car from warned him to drive safe. Apparently, the length of the drive, the absence of other cars and the flat, surrounding wilderness of the bog tends to lure drivers into a false sense of security.

Several cars a year go off the road thanks to wandering sheep and Elliot doesn't fancy lying in a ditch and waiting for help in this isolated part of the world.

He tries to digest what he's learned about the Davidson family and balance it with what he's seeing on this trip.

Elliot doesn't have a whole lot of contacts in the criminal world but he does know how to access the Dark Web, and it's incredible what you can find out there when you ask the right people the right questions.

The Davidson family – fishermen, wealthy, powerful – appear to be channelling a decent proportion of Europe's drugs through the North Sea, using their small home village as a base.

Now he's physically here, he can see how the geography works to this private, anonymous family's advantage.

More specifically, Elliot thinks, who the hell would ever think to look up here for proper criminality?

He's only been in Ireland since yesterday but he's already reached out to Mickey's contacts and made a few of his own through his networks. His destination is a pub in the fishing village, where he's meeting a woman who used to work in the Davidsons' shipping business. She's anxious, apparently, but Elliot has judged her price correctly. The woman, like so many before her, wants to emigrate to the United States. She doesn't just need money. She needs help with an impossible-to-get visa.

By the time he gets to the village, Elliot is already calculating how long it's going to take to drive back to Letterkenny, Donegal's main town and the location of his hotel. He doesn't fancy the return journey in darkness. Elliot is used to driving in cities with lots of lights. He already has a headache from concentrating on these lonely, completely unlit roads – from that, and Nana ringing him every hour because she doesn't like the idea of him driving through, as she calls it, cowboy land.

To be fair, as far as Nana is concerned, everything outside London fits that description.

A quick lunch in the pub and a chat with this woman, then he's out of here.

The rain is still falling in sheets and the village's main street is deserted. It's perched at the top of a hill that slopes down to the

Atlantic Ocean and he can see the harbour at its foot. It's bereft of vessels right now but, he imagines, they'll return shortly.

Beside the harbour stands a large warehouse. The name Davidson Fisheries is painted across it in large lettering.

Elliot is glad of the inclement weather, now. Fewer people about, fewer people to see him.

It's not like he can move about unnoticed – he's seen barely a handful of black men since he landed in the county – but it's better he doesn't have too large an audience.

At the pub, he realises as soon as he opens the door that this is where *all* the people are.

On cue, everybody turns to stare at him and his heart sinks.

Cheesy nachos. Not much chance of getting in and out of here incognito.

He sits at the counter, presuming his contact will come to him.

And she does, in the form of a waitress. Her name tag says Bronagh.

'Are you planning to have lunch?' she asks.

'Yes.'

'You'll be more comfortable at one of the smaller tables over here, so.'

He follows her to a small snug at the end of the bar, beside a roaring turf fire.

'There's the menu; what do you want to know about the family?' she says, so fast and in such a thick accent, he struggles to understand her for a moment. She looks at him expectantly and he translates quickly. He glances at the menu, and says:

'Shepherd's pie. You know Kevin Davidson?'

'An attention-seeker in a family that prides itself on not seeking attention. You want a drink to start?'

'What do you recommend? How long has he been gone?'

'Two years now. I'll get you a Guinness. The guards are checking more these days so you have to be careful driving but you'll be grand with just the one pint.'

She leaves and returns after a few minutes with his stout.

'Thank you,' Elliot says. 'There's a bit of a rumour his family weren't happy with him?'

'Aye. Think he fell out with them. Or them with him. How long are you staying in Donegal? You just visiting?'

'That's right. Just wanted to see the Wild Atlantic Way.' He'd read about that in a magazine on the plane. 'Any rumours about why they fell out?'

'You should try cycling it. You look nice and fit. I can only tell you what the gossip is – the only way somebody in that clan would be cast out is if they started working against the family.'

'Working against, how?'

'With another organisation . . . or with the police. One moment, please.'

She leaves and Elliot waits. An old man passes on his way to the toilets. He slows his walk and stares openly at Elliot. Elliot can distinguish innocent curiosity from an actual recce, and he believes this is the former. The guy is just interested in what a stranger is doing in his village.

Bronagh returns with his pie.

'You'll enjoy that. Shall I get you ketchup? His body is probably lying in one of those bogs out there. He'll never be found.'

Elliot swallows. The casual way she dropped that sentence has made his blood run cold.

'Have you got any HP sauce? Would they really *kill* one of their own?'

'You don't turn on family. If I was him, I'd have scarpered before they could deal with me. No HP. Just ketchup.'

She leaves and returns with a box of condiments.

'Did he have a girlfriend?'

The woman ponders this. Elliot observes her closely.

'Maybe. Not from around here, if he did.'

'He wasn't with a local girl?'

The woman frowns.

'Not that I know of. But he liked to go down to Letterkenny. Maybe he met a girl down there? I have to go serve some other people now. Will that be all?'

Elliot nods, his mind running overtime.

When she brings him his bill after lunch, he leaves a tip to make any waitress's eyes water and a number for the man who's going to help her get to America.

Outside, he notices the harbour is now full of returned fishing vessels; an assembly line of men, carrying boxes to and fro between the ships and the factory, is up and running.

He gets in his car and puts his phone on Bluetooth. As he leaves the village, he gets a call. It's a number he doesn't recognise but it's an English mobile so he answers it.

'Hello?' a woman says.

'Yeah?'

'Um, is this Elliot?'

'Who's asking?'

The woman on the other end of the phone takes a breath.

'My name is Rachel. I'm a friend of Richard Cosgrove's and I recently met Mickey Sheils. She said she was away and I had to ring you if I found out anything about Kevin Davidson.'

'Go ahead,' Elliot says.

And as he listens, his frown grows deeper.

When Rachel is finished, Elliot thanks her. They agree Rachel will send him on photos.

Then he phones Mickey. It goes straight to voicemail.

'Mickey, we have a problem,' Elliot says. 'A big one. Stuff your girl is saying doesn't make sense. Ring me as soon as you get this.'

Saint-Thérèse

Mickey sits on the end of her bed in the hotel room as Inspector Alleyne's man dusts down the windowsill.

The policeman himself is looking through Rose's suitcase, her clothes and belongings, which are all still sitting there.

Where she left them.

Except her passport. That's gone.

Every now and again, the inspector glances at Mickey and she at him.

They're both thinking the same thing but neither of them have said it.

Mickey keeps placing her hand in her pocket, checking the chip is still there, taped in place so it's extra safe. The presence of that bloody thing is driving up her blood pressure, she's sure of it. She'd hoped Rose would take it and now she's praying she can put it in Luke's hands. From what she's learned about the cryptocurrency, the chip alone is of no use, not without ID and the correct code, but no matter how many times Mickey tells herself that, the thought of losing it makes her heart stop.

She suspects she knows what Rose has done, but she still can't make sense of it.

Inspector Alleyne's man finishes up and leaves, nodding to his boss before he goes.

The policeman sits down on the side of Rose's bed so he's looking at Mickey.

'You've figured it out,' he says.

Mickey inches her body around so she's looking at him, too.

'Yes,' she says. 'But, also no.'

'Tell me what you think,' he says.

Mickey takes a deep breath.

'Rose opened that window herself,' she says. 'She let herself out. Or somebody else in.'

Inspector Alleyne nods.

'Yes.'

'Did she unlock the French doors in the villa, too?' Mickey asks.

He nods again.

'Yes,' he says. 'It struck me as odd at the time. Luke Miller insisted he'd locked everything, but the deck door and the French doors were open. It was just something to keep note of. He could have got confused operating some of the locks. Rose might have done it half asleep to let some air in, or maybe she'd thought she locked them and had actually unlocked them . . . a strange detail but maybe an innocent one. But for it to happen twice, at the villa and now here. . .'

'I checked the window and the door several times before I went to sleep,' Mickey says. 'And there's more. I didn't sleep properly. I normally wake during the night. But I slept heavily, too heavily for me. And I thought I saw somebody at our table last night, when neither of us were there. I presume now it was Kevin Davidson. I drank a glass of wine . . .'

'Hmm. We can get your bloods taken. See if you were drugged. But a lot of these substances—'

'It will be well gone,' Mickey agrees. 'I know. It's just, it makes sense and it doesn't. All the parts don't fit into place.'

'What has you perplexed?'

'Luke is very wealthy. He offered Rose his money. She wouldn't take it.'

'How do you know she hasn't taken it now?'

Mickey again fingers the shape of the chip.

'I can't tell you, but I just know.'

'That is strange,' the inspector agrees. 'A set-up normally involves a financial motive. I was starting to question if *Kevin Davidson* even exists, or if she's just hired somebody to create this monster that allows her to be the victim.'

'He is real,' Mickey says. 'But if they're in it together, he can hardly be an abusive ex. They made that part up so Luke would feel sorry for Rose. That's what I'd guess. Luke's father was abusive. It's the sort of thing that would suck him in.'

Inspector Alleyne nods, thoughtfully.

'Clever,' he says. 'And terrifying.'

Mickey hears her phone buzz. She leans across the bed and picks it up. It's a voicemail; it hasn't even rung.

She listens to the message, brow furrowed.

'Do you mind if I make a quick call?' she asks the inspector.

He shrugs.

He stands and wanders over to the window while Mickey dials Elliot.

When he answers, she can hear that he's got her on loudspeaker.

'Where are you?' she asks.

'Driving through Donegal,' he answers.

Mickey is surprised. That's a real development for Elliot. Actually going out to meet people.

'I couldn't get any more online, I had to come here,' Elliot says, and Mickey almost smiles.

'Okay,' Mickey says. 'Your message sounded urgent. What have you learned?'

'I have a few concerns about Rose,' Elliot says. 'Her backstory doesn't add up. She told Luke she was from the same town as Davidson, right? Which was why she had to do a runner? But she's not. She might be from the county but not the town.'

'Donegal is not exactly overpopulated. That's a minor detail. But I have questions of my own now, too.'

'You and me both,' Elliot says. 'You know your pal, Richard? Nathan's boss?'

'Yes.'

'That woman he found for you in Heathrow, Rachel.'

'What about her?'

'She was trying to get in contact with me but she'd lost your text with my details so she got it from your pal Richard. She found something.'

'What?'

'The day Rose and Luke flew out of Heathrow, Rose went to the toilets when they arrived at the airport.'

'And?'

There's a moment's silence down the phone. Then Elliot speaks again.

'Rachel said something was irritating her. I'm going to send you a photo. It was taken from CCTV outside the toilets in Heathrow.

The day Luke and Rose flew out to Saint-Thérèse. I know we have Kevin Davidson flying out the following day but . . . Well, look at the photo.'

'Okay. Thanks, Elliot. And mind yourself. You're a fish out of water.'

'What are you talking about? I'm a black man in the middle of what seems to be the last town on earth populated solely by white people. I'm practically anonymous.'

Mickey smiles and hangs up. She waits, as Inspector Alleyne watches her. He knows something is coming.

The text message arrives. Mickey opens it.

The camera still is grainy but clear enough to see everybody's faces.

There are lots of people in the corridor outside the toilets but her eyes are drawn to two in particular.

Rose Miller and Kevin Davidson.

Mickey's blood runs cold.

'Look,' she says to the inspector. She hands him her phone.

He stares at the photo and nods, slowly.

'Rose and Kevin,' she says. 'That's them, meeting in the airport the day Rose and Luke flew out here. Kevin was on a flight the following day . . . but he went to the airport and met her the day she flew out.'

Alleyne frowns.

'If they're not after his money,' he says, 'what the hell *are* they after?'

Mickey is sitting in the passenger seat of Inspector Alleyne's car when the call comes in.

He pulls over to take it and Mickey stares out at the beach, watching a couple walking hand in hand by the water's edge.

She and the inspector are on their way to see Luke.

Mickey doesn't know how to break it to him. She knows he loves Rose. She knows it because when he talks about her, he has the same look on his face he used to have when he was in love with Mickey.

There's a little part of her that feels like this is karma.

Even though what happened between them is so long ago, she can summon with ease how hurt she felt.

The worst part had been the shame. She had lain in bed in an anonymous hotel room, staring at the door, willing to hear him knocking on the other side. Which was impossible because he didn't even know where she'd gone, no more than she knew where the hell he was.

All she could think was, I've blown up my whole life for a man who feels nothing for me. Luke hadn't even had anything to lose. He'd been single. She was the one who'd walked out on her marriage and her future, thinking she was taking another path. Thinking she meant as much to Luke as he did to her.

She had been humiliated. Heartbroken, but mainly humiliated.

And now she's going to tell Luke that the woman he actually loves is not who he thinks she is.

Inspector Alleyne is nodding and murmuring assent to whatever he's being told on the other end of the phone. When he hangs up, he looks troubled.

'I have bad news,' he says.

Mickey braces. What now? she wonders.

'They got the first flight out this morning. Rose Miller and Kevin Davidson.'

Mickey's face contorts in anger.

'Didn't you have Davidson's name flagged at the airport? How the hell did he leave?'

'It was a clerical error. We only decided to alert the airport yesterday when I believed he had become a significant factor. The officer charged with doing so went home last night before he sent Davidson's name through. It was a mistake.'

'A mistake?' Mickey glares at him. 'I'd say it's a little more, wouldn't you? Utter incompetence would be closer to the mark.'

Inspector Alleyne glares back.

'Let's be clear, Miss Sheils, I am dealing with a crime where there is a victim in the morgue and there is a perpetrator, currently detained in custody. Everything else – all of this situation with Rose Miller and Davidson – is speculation and theory. Maybe there is something there, maybe they have questions to answer, but neither of them shot Jeremiah Williams to death.'

Mickey is about to retort but stops herself. Alleyne is angry, embarrassed. He's lashing out at her, just as she did at him. He knows he's fucked up and she knows that she has, too.

She'd believed Rose.

'Is there footage of them at the airport?' she asks.

'Minimal. She appeared to be leaving of her own accord. She wasn't resisting being with Davidson; she didn't leave his side the whole time they were there.'

Mickey stares out the front windscreen.

'There was something not clicking for me,' she says, sighing.

'Excuse me?'

'With Rose. I've worked with abused women for years. When it's that bad, their fear is consistent. When they run, they keep running.

Luke offered Rose a lot of money, the means to get off the island and go into hiding because Davidson was still here, and . . . she didn't take it. I thought she was being brave but—'

Mickey shakes her head.

'She *should* have wanted to run.'

Alleyne is looking at her.

'Sounds like she fooled a lot of people.'

He turns the key in the ignition.

When they arrive at the jail, the inspector lets Mickey go in alone.

Luke is brought down and sits in front of her, his face expectant.

'Any update?' he asks. 'I'm going out of my mind in here, Mickey. How's Rose?'

Mickey rubs the tips of her fingers on the table between them, then balls her hands into tight fists, trying to send all the tension in her body to her hands.

'Luke, I don't know how to say this—'

Luke's features tighten.

'Jesus. Is she okay? Mickey?'

She looks up at him, then down again. She can't bear to witness his panic, to see how much he cares for his wife. The woman he doesn't even know.

'She's gone,' Mickey says.

'Gone? Gone where? Did she . . . has she gone into hiding?'

'She hasn't run again. Not like last time. She's left. Luke, she left with Kevin Davidson.'

Luke says nothing. Mickey looks up at him. He's shaking his head.

'What are you talking about?'

'Rose and Kevin. They've set you up.'

'Mickey, don't be so fucking stupid.'

Luke stands up, abruptly. The guard in the corner of the room glances over, on alert.

'Is she really gone?'

'Yes.'

'Then he's taken her,' Luke snaps. 'I asked you to take care of her. How the fuck? What happened? Who's looking for her?'

'Luke, you need to calm down. He didn't take her. She left the hotel room with him last night. She went willingly.'

Luke freezes.

'You saw this? You saw her go? She walked out the door with him?'

'No. She went through the window—'

'What?!'

Luke makes a strangled sound, somewhere between rage and a snort.

'Luke, the inspector confirmed it. Her fingerprints were on the inside of that window and there were no fingerprints on the outside. And she opened the French doors in your villa that night—'

'She opened a window and you've jumped from there to her willingly leaving with a man who abused her for years? Have you lost your mind, Mickey? You, of all people!'

Luke is pacing now, looking over Mickey's head at the door, back at the guard, who's standing up now, sensing where this might go.

'You need to calm down,' Mickey says. 'Luke, they'll take you back to your cell and I can't talk to you then.'

This seems to register with Luke. He looks over at the guard then sits down, his body language reluctant.

'She's in danger,' Luke says. 'I have to get out of here, Mickey. I have to find her.'

'You won't find her. She and Davidson left the island this morning.' Mickey pauses momentarily as Luke absorbs this. 'Luke, it wasn't just the window. There's footage of her meeting Davidson in London the day you two flew out. At the airport.'

'Met him how? I was with her the whole time.'

'When she went to the toilet, they talked in the corridor outside.'

'She was gone five minutes! He must have been following her; that's what you saw.'

'No, Luke. You need to listen to me. I doubt Kevin Davidson was abusing her at all. It was all fabricated. They planned this from the start.'

'Planned what?' Luke cries, and Mickey can see from his expression that he can't even begin to grasp how his world has been torn from under him. 'I don't understand. What are you saying?'

'They *set you up*.'

'Set me up to do what? To kill a man? For what end? She couldn't have known I'd do that. She begged me not to shoot him. None of this makes sense.'

'I know,' Mickey says. 'And I'll get to the bottom of it—'

'Did she take the money?'

Mickey looks up at Luke sharply.

'No.'

He stares at her.

'She had access to twenty million and she didn't take it?'

Mickey opens and closes her mouth. She has no answer for that. She knows it doesn't fit and she can't make sense of it.

'I have to get out of here,' Luke says. 'Mickey, you need to get me out.'

Mickey's stomach knots.

She has never felt more useless.

Donegal

Elliot's hotel in Letterkenny is a strange mishmash of traditional Irish charm and modern international hotel.

The bar beside the lobby has a large open fire which is burning turf, and the shelves surrounding it are adorned with various kitschy items and knick-knacks from eras past.

At the same time, the table Elliot and his guest are sitting at has a socket beside it for a USB cable and the sharply dressed barman has just brought Elliot a sparkling Evian and a menu for bar snacks that reads like Michelin-star quality.

Elliot is surprised at the size and shape of the man sitting in front of him. Mickey's guard friend Stephen is in uniform and he fills it . . . horizontally. He's average height and touching on obese and nothing like what Elliot is accustomed to seeing in policemen. He wonders if they just don't have size requirements in the Irish police force, or if this guy was slimmer once but nobody has checked in with him lately.

And he's drinking a Guinness. Elliot has never had a drink with a policeman before. Especially not one who plans to drive home after the meeting.

'You working long with Mickey?' Stephen asks.

'Few years.'

'She's a good woman. She tell you we were in college together?'

'Yep.'

'She was head and shoulders above the rest of us. If she'd stayed in Ireland, she'd have ended up in chambers.'

'Where?'

'She'd have been appointed as a judge. Real shame to lose her to England.'

'You didn't just lose her to England. She left the law.'

'That's a shame, too. But I understand it. You nail some of these little bastards and next thing, they're walking down the street, giving you the finger and laughing at you. A pal of mine in Dublin, he left the force and took up taxi driving. Picked up a fella one night by mistake. He didn't take a good look at him, you see. But your man in the back realised that my pal had nicked him a few years previous. He'd been done for grievous bodily harm, got out two years later. Gave my pal sixteen stitches that night and his next sentence was only a year long. Disgusting.'

Elliot winces.

'Sometimes, I think you're better off just driving somebody up to the mountains and having done with them,' Stephen says, and Elliot nearly chokes on the sip of water he's just taken.

'So, our lad Davidson,' the policeman continues, unperturbed. 'I've done a little more digging and I think I've found out why the family may have got rid of him.'

Elliot puts his drink down and leans forward.

Stephen picks up his pint, takes a long gulp and puts it back down.

Elliot is impatient but recognises that this is a man who likes to tell a story in his own time.

'There was a complaint made against Davidson and then it was withdrawn,' Stephen says.

'What sort of complaint?'

'He was accused of rape.'

'By who?'

Stephen picks up his pint again. Elliot tries not to let his irritation show.

'By a lass called Róisín Gallagher.'

Elliot mulls on this.

'Could Róisín Gallagher be Rose Miller?' Elliot asks. 'She was Rose Gillespie when Luke Miller met her, but she told him she'd changed her name when she came to England.'

'Well, Róisín is the Gaelic version of Rose, so very possibly. And I can't track Róisín Gallagher down. She grew up over in Inishowen. You would have driven through a part of that peninsula on the way over from Derry airport.'

'Where could she have met Davidson?'

'Probably here. I don't mean this hotel, I mean in one of the local bars or discos around about the town. Most young people in the county would head down here of a weekend.'

'What exactly was the complaint?' Elliot asks. 'And why was it withdrawn?'

'Why it was withdrawn, I can't tell you. Only she can tell you that. But I believe he raped her and beat her very badly.'

Elliot can feel himself tensing up. Every story is different and yet all of them remind him of what happened to his sister.

'She spent a few days in hospital,' Stephen continues. 'And if I hear right, some of his family may have visited her there. So, maybe she was intimidated into dropping the complaint. I've got a summary of her hospital report for you and we can get more medical records if I speak with the right people.'

Elliot ponders what he's heard. He still has a lot of questions.

'What's your theory?' he asks. 'Did Davidson go on the run after the complaint?'

'I don't know. But here's the thing: Davidson would have been on the police's radar because of that rape complaint. He could have been turned, you see, made into a CI – confidential informant. But if she'd already dropped the complaint, we wouldn't have had a hold on him. So, maybe he was encouraged by his family to get his arse out of town before he caused any more trouble.'

Stephen shrugs.

Elliot studies him. The policeman has no more information.

Elliot looks out the bar's window at the rain-sodden streets. The headlights of the passing cars illuminate the locals, rushing home from work and shopping, umbrellas up, bags clasped close to their chests.

He's more confused with each passing minute.

If Davidson actually *was* abusive to Rose, why would she be working with him now?

Is she in thrall to him?

What part of Rose's story is true and what part is lies?

Elliot knows what he must do.

He has to contact the Davidson family to get to the truth. So far, they only have Rose's version of Kevin to work off.

Elliot needs to know what the man is really like.

Saint-Thérèse

Luke has never felt more helpless and frustrated than he does right now.

He tries pacing the length of his custody cell while he thinks, then sits on the hard bed, looking at the wall, looking out the tiny window, unable to keep his body or brain still.

He's trying to put everything together. He understands why Mickey, and now Inspector Alleyne, think what they do. From what the policeman has told him, there are no witness accounts of Rose struggling at the island's airport. She didn't cry for help, or ask anybody to intervene. To all intents and purposes, it looks like she was happy to leave Saint-Thérèse with Kevin Davidson.

But then there are the anomalies.

If Rose had set Luke up, why didn't she take his money when he offered it to her? He was handing her twenty million; she didn't even need to ask for it.

And what was the set-up? How could Rose have known Luke would buy a gun, shoot a man dead and end up facing a prison sentence?

Luke shakes his head.

That's not his Rose. It's not the woman he knows. And sure,

people might argue he couldn't know her that well, they've only been together for nine months, but Luke understands something those people don't.

Everyone has secrets, things they're not telling the world.

But you know, you just *know* if somebody is fundamentally good or bad. That can't be kept hidden. You can ignore the red flags if you want, but Luke has never encountered anybody who's turned out to be a bad person without seeing some hint it was there to begin with.

He remembers the first time he saw Rose, in that pub at her work Christmas party. That weird teacher colleague of hers had been trying it on with her.

She had been nervous around him, around every man in the place. She had no idea she was the focal point of the room for most of those men. Two of Luke's workmates had already spotted her before Luke and considered making a move, but Rose's body language, *I'm not available*, had put them off.

Then Luke had caught her looking at him.

Luke had been intrigued and he'd chased and chased and chased. Always him. Never her.

She never made him feel like he wasn't the one making the choices.

No, he knows his wife. He knows that she's a good person. He knows that every time she said the name Kevin Davidson, she was legitimately scared.

She doesn't want anything from him. He was the one who had to convince her to love him, to marry him.

There's only one rational answer: Davidson has threatened Rose with something that made her go with him. The only thing that would make Rose act like this would be to protect somebody she loved.

Had Davidson threatened to do something to Luke in prison? He'd been clever, finding Jeremiah Williams to do his dirty work. Who knows what else Davidson had in mind?

If that's what has happened, Rose is in danger and Luke needs to get to her.

He has to get out of jail and back to London. Inspector Alleyne said that's where the flight Rose boarded was heading. And if she's not in London, Luke will go to Donegal, or wherever she is.

But always, always, Luke comes back to the same thought.

The CCTV footage of Rose meeting Davidson in the airport on the day Rose and Luke left.

Luke gets up and starts to pace again.

How can he explain that? He can't.

He remembers her going to the toilet that day when they arrived at the airport. She'd seemed nervous, jittery, which he'd put down to the adrenaline of organising the surprise holiday. It felt like she was gone minutes.

Luke hasn't seen the footage from the airport. Is it possible the people who watched it misread the situation? Davidson passed Rose but Rose didn't see him?

She wouldn't be expecting to, if she thought he was lying dead in their apartment.

But Mickey insists that they spoke. That the footage showed Rose and Kevin exchanging words.

Luke can't figure it out and it's driving him absolutely crazy.

If Rose knew Davidson was alive, why keep up the pretence that she'd killed him? Why bring Luke to such a point of anxiety that he was ready to do something rash?

And then . . .

An idea starts to take seed.

No.

No, he can't even entertain that thought.

There's no way.

Luke shakes his head angrily. The cell, his inability to do anything, it's making him insane. Paranoid.

I know her, he tells himself. I know my wife. I've slept beside her. I've been inside her. I've seen her at her most vulnerable and scared, and at her happiest.

She's never lied to me.

There's something Luke is missing. That's all. He doesn't want to imagine anything else.

Rose told him once that when Davidson started hitting her, her friends didn't believe her. He'd been so nice to begin with that they struggled to match their image of him with what she was telling them.

And then he slowly manoeuvred her away from them so she didn't have anybody to tell, anyway.

He's a master manipulator. Luke knows this. Mickey, Inspector Alleyne – they don't understand Rose and what's happened to her like he does.

Davidson has taken Rose.

And Luke is going to get her back.

London

September 2022

The flower market is a blast of colours and smells, but most of the buckets are filled with Rose's namesake – bunches of red, white and yellow roses – and she's never been a fan of her own flower. Rose has always preferred more exotic blooms. Unusual varieties. And if she needs to go bog-standard, she likes the look and the scent of stocks or freesias.

She wanders through the market looking for something that stands out. She knows no matter what she picks, it will barely make a dent at disguising that bloody ugly unit in their bedroom. She smiles. Luke's one concession: stick a vase of flowers on it. She shouldn't complain. He handed over the entire apartment to her to decorate and didn't mind the various soft shades she chose.

She settles for a bunch of stargazer lilies and pays the stall owner.

As Rose walks home – home, she still can't get her head around Luke's apartment being home – she wonders about what to make for dinner. Luke doesn't want her to cook every night, but the fact she finishes so much earlier than him means she's always there first, and she passes dozens of shops en route. It makes sense to call into the butcher or the fruit and veg shop and pick something up. She likes to cook, she keeps telling him. She doesn't feel like a little housewife. Luke's kitchen is huge; he has everything she needs to feel like a pro chef and when she puts music on and prepares a meal with a glass of wine, it's actually Rose at her happiest.

She picks up scallops at the fish market and then walks back to the apartment.

Rose lets herself in and immediately senses something is different.

Is Luke home?

She sets down the flowers, puts the scallops in the fridge and calls out his name.

There's no answer.

Her first thought is that he's come home sick and is asleep. She hasn't seen Luke sick yet but he's told her that when he does fall ill, it tends to hit him fast and hard and never lasts long.

Rose walks down the corridor towards their bedroom.

She's trying to quash the rising paranoia but she can't.

And it feels even stronger when she places her hand on the bedroom door handle.

It couldn't be anybody but Luke here, right?

Rose braces herself and opens the door.

Kevin is sitting there, on the bed, looking through Rose and Luke's wedding album. He has the page open on a photograph of the couple, smiling. Rose is gazing up at Luke and there's no disguising that she's in love with that man.

'Hello, Rose,' he says, in his soft Donegal accent. 'Anything you'd like to tell me?'

Rose's knees buckle.

PART III

Saint-Thérèse

Mickey misses Elliot's call when it comes in. She's on the phone to Nathan.

And he's not happy.

'I don't see what more you can do out there,' he says. 'The wife is not there to protect. You don't practise law any more. You've sorted him a legal team. Come home.'

Mickey glances inside the restaurant window. Inspector Alleyne has brought her to one of the less touristy districts. It's quiet on these streets; the little bars and eateries are populated mainly by locals and the more adventurous island visitors. It's also better. The cuisine is simpler and tastier, the prices are cheaper. Mickey handed over ordering to Inspector Alleyne – or Marcel, as he's insisted she call him – and there's some delicious rice dish making its way to her table right now.

But she's out here talking to her increasingly irritated husband.

'I know, Nate,' she says, trying to placate him. 'But this has stopped being about him. I need to get to the bottom of what's happened. My curiosity is piqued. You know what I'm like.'

Nathan falls silent. He does know what she's like and he knows she's lying. Of course she's still there for Luke.

Mickey clenches her jaw. He has every right to demand she come home, right this instant.

But a tacit agreement has underpinned their marriage ever since he took her back.

He could take his revenge and she'd say nothing, so long as he did it discreetly.

She has swallowed a lot over the years and she's been able to because she knows that for him, his dalliances are just about sex, whereas she had been madly in love with somebody else. She loved Luke more than she loved Nathan. And that's been harder for him to swallow.

They've never talked about it. Not properly. When she told Nathan she was leaving him, he asked her if there was anything he could say to change her mind. She'd told him there wasn't. And he'd said he loved her but there was no point in trying to make her stay if she didn't want to.

That had filled her with more guilt than anything else he could have said. And all Mickey could do was apologise. It wasn't that she didn't love her husband. She just wasn't as in love with him as she was with another man. She couldn't even explain why or how she felt the way she did about Luke. It just . . . was.

So, when she came back, Nathan had to live with the knowledge that he was second choice and, sure, they'd made a life, but it had never been filled with passion or romance or the things Mickey would have wanted for herself.

She's starting to question if she can go on like this.

Ten years is a long time to pay for a mistake. It's a long time to carry guilt.

She could just be on her own. She'd get by. It would be fine.

What if she met somebody new? She's not so old she should rule that out.

This thought surfaces again just before Nathan says:

'I miss you.'

It throws Mickey.

She turns away from the restaurant window and faces the street. A guy is cycling an old bike that's dragging a now empty passenger carriage, his face and body exhausted after a long day's work.

Mickey wants to say, how can you miss me? We're like ships in the night. She wants to say, I'm sure you can find some way to entertain yourself, or some person to keep you busy.

She wants to say, did you miss me when you were out with that blonde the other night, pretending you were with Richard?

But she doesn't say those things.

She says, 'I miss you, too.'

Maybe it's seeing how Luke feels about Rose. Maybe it's that the last few days have been a little traumatic and Mickey is grateful that there is somebody on the other end of the phone who cares enough to miss her.

She hears Nathan take a breath.

'I'm sorry,' he says.

'For what?'

Now they're on really strange ground.

'I don't know. For . . . everything.'

Mickey feels a lump in her throat.

'I know it was my fault,' Nathan adds. 'I didn't see you. I didn't see you until you were telling me you wouldn't be there any longer. I took you for granted.'

'I . . .' Mickey doesn't know what to say. Could they really be doing this? Having a conversation they should have had ten years ago, because now Luke is back in her life again?

She blinks back tears.

'That doesn't excuse me,' she says. 'I made choices that weren't fair.'

'You made choices that were fair for you and you don't need to apologise or punish yourself for that. If you'd known how much I loved you, you wouldn't have been looking anywhere else. I promise you. And that *was* my fault.'

The lump in Mickey's throat is so big, she can barely swallow.

'It was very long ago, Nathan. I hope you know that I don't feel that way any more. There is a part of me that wants to help him, because of the past, but mainly, I just want to know what's going on. It's nothing more. I haven't forgiven him for what he did. I never will. There's no chance I'd ever feel anything for him again, if that's what you're worried about. Even if he wasn't a married man now.'

She listens to Nathan's breathing for a few seconds.

'Okay,' he says. 'Maybe we should talk more when you're home. I think we need to talk.'

'I . . . yes. We should.'

'Is there anything I can do in the meantime? Do you need resources?'

'I have everything I need. I think.'

'Well, if you find you don't, call me. I know a banker from Saint-Thérèse. A banker who's no longer welcome on the island. Tax evasion, among other nefarious activities. But he still has a lot of contacts.'

'That could be useful,' Mickey says. 'The only person I've met here so far is a straight-as-a-die police inspector.'

'They can be useful too. Mickey . . . I love you.'

'I love you, too.'

She stays surprised at the exchange even after she's hung up.

She turns to go back into the restaurant before realising she's missed a call. She checks the phone. Elliot, again.

That man has become doubly resourceful in her absence.

He's sent her a text: *read your emails.*

Mickey opens the email as she re-enters the restaurant. She's approaching the table when she sees the line about a Róisín Gallagher being raped by Kevin Davidson. She stops, does a double take and reads it again. Then she quickly scans the rest of the email.

When she sits at her table, she barely notices the plate of food in front of her. Inspector Alleyne – Marcel, she reminds herself – is looking at her with curiosity.

'What is it?' he asks.

'I don't know how to say this,' she replies. 'My colleague has done some research. Rose Miller changed her name before she met Luke and I think we may have her true identity now. A woman named Róisín – that's the Irish version of Rose – reported Kevin Davidson for rape and her hospital file shows she was very severely assaulted. My colleague has spoken to a few people and the physical description for this Róisín Gallagher certainly fits with Rose Miller.'

Marcel frowns.

'So, he *was* abusive to her?'

Mickey nods uncertainly. She can't wrap her head around it, but she knows Elliot wouldn't have passed this information on to her if he wasn't sure of it.

'But, if that were true, why would she leave with Davidson of her own accord?' the inspector asks.

'I don't know.' Mickey shakes her head. 'But she did, right? Meeting him in the airport the day she flew out from London, then letting herself out of my hotel room after I'd been drugged . . . it puts to bed any suspicion that she wasn't working with him. But it doesn't add up. There's so much here that doesn't add up.'

'Is it possible he is making her do these things? You have more experience with abused women than I do—'

Mickey blinks. Is it possible?

'Yes,' she says. 'I've seen abused women do the most unncharacteristic things out of fear, or because they're being controlled. I've seen them turn a blind eye when their children are being hurt, I've seen them prostitute themselves because they've been told to, I've seen . . . well, Jesus, everything. But if he is making her do this, what reason could it be for other than money? And I keep coming back to the fact she didn't take the money.'

Marcel lifts a forkful of rice to his mouth and indicates to Mickey she should do the same. Mickey chews distractedly but she still notices how tasty the food is. There's a saffron flavour to the rice and the seafood is among the freshest she's ever had.

'Mr Miller is looking for bail,' Marcel says.

'Will he get it?' Mickey asks.

'He has a good lawyer, but the judge will ask me if he's a flight risk. Is he a flight risk, Miss Sheils?'

'You can't keep telling me to call you Marcel and then refer to me as Miss Sheils.'

'My apologies. Mickey.'

She nods her approval.

'You have his passport,' she says. 'And I'm staying here, too. He's not a danger to society. You know that.'

Marcel chews another forkful of food.

'It is a possibility, with him being a British citizen, that I could get a judge to agree to house arrest in a temporary location – at your hotel, perhaps – if we keep his passport and he agrees to present at our station daily. Our authorities like to be seen to be cooperative when it comes to other jurisdictions' citizens. For tourism reasons.'

Mickey feels a flicker of hope.

'He will agree to that,' she says. 'I'll keep an eye on him. I need his help, Marcel. He knows Rose – or at least more about her than I do. There's more to this. You know it and so do I.'

Marcel nods.

'I am taking you at your word,' he says.

Mickey puts down her fork and cocks her head.

'Why are you choosing to trust me?' she asks.

'I have good instincts.' He shrugs. 'I can tell if somebody is good or bad. Every time, without fail.'

'And you know Luke is good?'

'That is not what I said.'

Marcel lifts his glass of water, takes a sip and places it back down, then pats his lip with his napkin. All his movements are precise and considered.

'You are good,' Marcel says. 'Luke Miller is very definitely not good.'

Mickey frowns.

'What does that mean?' she asks.

Marcel studies her. Mickey starts to feel uncomfortable under his gaze. She can feel her cheeks colouring.

'I don't know,' he says. 'Something I can't put my finger on. I agree — there is more to this situation than we know. I do not think Luke Miller intended to kill Jeremiah Williams. He is genuinely remorseful. And I believe his story. But there is something about him that's just a little off. He is capable of things. He has hurt people.'

Mickey flinches. She regrets it, immediately. The all-seeing Marcel notices, of course he does.

'Ah,' he says. 'Even you. He has hurt you.'

'Yes,' she says, because there's no point denying it. 'But he was young and stupid and it wasn't a crime. Just a love affair gone sour. People make mistakes. He is a good man.'

Marcel shakes his head. He looks sad and, Mickey realises with horror, his sadness is for her.

'Luke Miller might be trying to be a good man now,' he says, 'but he has a darkness in him.'

Mickey stares at him. He meets her eye, unblinking.

She looks away first, down at the table and her food.

She's lost her appetite.

The inspector has secured Luke a room next to Mickey's at the hotel. Luke is so happy to feel part of the real world again, it could have been a tent on the beach and he'd have been grateful.

But to have this feels indecent somehow.

He stands in the shower, the water a notch below scalding, and lets the shampoo he's rubbed into his scalp run down his shoulders and back as he faces the taps.

He's having a hot shower in a luxury hotel room and a man is lying dead in the morgue because of him.

It's not the first time Luke has thought of it, but it's the first time it's been to the fore of his brain. While he was imprisoned, his primary thought was, how do I get out of here? Is Rose okay? Where is Kevin Davidson?

But as worried as Luke is about Rose, the realisation that he is enjoying something that Jeremiah Williams never will again still hits Luke like a steam train.

He asked the inspector about Williams. The dead man was known to the police as a petty criminal. He arrived on the island a few years ago and fell quickly into a life of recreational drugs and law-breaking.

Luke knows Davidson paid Williams to break in. He might have told him Luke needed a scare, that Luke had money – he probably sold Luke as a bit of an English idiot, who would cower in the face of an intruder.

Williams has no family – thank God – and was a bit of a loner, according to the inspector. Luke wanted to know how Williams became a loner, how he ended up with no family. The inspector had shrugged. How does it ever happen that way? Shit parents, shit life, addictions.

It made Luke feel marginally better that there was nobody immediate to mourn the man he'd killed, but not a whole lot. Jeremiah's life was not Luke's to take.

Luke wonders if he'll ever stop fucking up other people's lives.

He hears a noise outside the bathroom and then there's a tap on the bathroom door. He knocks off the shower.

'It's just me,' he hears Mickey call.

Luke steps out of the shower and puts a towel around his waist. He wipes the steam from the bathroom mirror. He needs a shave but he can't be arsed. Instead, he opens the bathroom door.

'Why are you in my room?' he says to Mickey.

'To check on you.' She shrugs.

She's pointedly ignoring the fact he's in a towel and Luke knows it. The last time he was in a hotel room with Mickey, he'd spent most of the time naked or in a towel. It had been a weekend in Bath and they'd barely left the hotel bed. That was the weekend Mickey said she couldn't live a lie any more and that she needed to be with Luke. He'd asked her if she was sure, she'd said she was and then he'd told her his world would be complete with her in it.

And then he'd gone and fucked up her life, too.

'What do you think I'm going to do?' Luke says. 'Make a run for it? To where? I have no passport.'

Mickey doesn't say anything. Luke looks at her. That's not what she's thinking.

'I'm not going to hurt myself,' he says. 'Why the hell would I do that?'

'Because you're traumatised?' she responds. 'Because something terrible has happened to you and you don't know how to handle it? You wouldn't be the first. But no, I don't think you're going to kill yourself. I'm just worried about you. I want to make sure you eat and get some rest.'

'I've had lots of time to rest. Do you mind?'

Luke is at the bed, where his suitcase is lying open. He doesn't have anything Mickey hasn't seen before but he's a married man now. Even if his wife is missing.

Mickey turns around and faces the window.

'Have you eaten since you got here?' she asks.

'I'm here an hour, Mickey.'

He dresses while she dials reception.

'Room service? Can I order for room 248? Yes. The steak, please. Rare. And a glass of Jameson's Irish whiskey. Neat. Thank you.'

Luke has pulled on his boxers and jeans and now grabs a T-shirt.

'I don't eat much steak these days,' he says.

'I don't know what you do these days but a good steak and a stiff drink is the best medicine for shock.'

Luke sits down on the edge of the bed.

'I need to talk to you about Rose,' Mickey says.

'And I need to find Rose,' he replies.

'Yes, you do. I want to help, but I need to know more about her. A colleague of mine has been looking into her background. He's found out a few things that don't add up.'

'Let me guess. Her real name isn't Rose? In fact, she's not even a woman. She's not even human.'

Mickey says nothing. Luke rests his head in his hands.

'I'm sorry,' he says. 'I'm lashing out because my head is . . .'

'I know.'

They look at each other and Luke can see Mickey's expression soften. She still cares about him. After all this time, after what he did.

His throat constricts.

'What was her name before she met you?' Mickey asks.

'I don't know,' Luke mumbles. 'She said she wanted to leave that part of her life behind. She'd come to London as Rose Gillespie.'

'We've found some information on a woman named Róisín from Donegal,' Mickey says.

'Aren't there hundreds of women named Róisín in Donegal?'

'Sure. But this one accused Kevin Davidson of rape. He left her in a bad state. And there are rumours some of his family visited her in hospital and, subsequent to that, she dropped the charges. Now, nobody knows where she is.'

Luke looks up sharply.

'Are you serious?'

Suddenly, he's standing and he didn't even realise his legs had moved.

She nods.

'My partner, Elliot, got hold of her medical records. She was in and out of doctors' surgeries with minor injuries before he raped her. It went on for years.'

Luke sits in the chair at the room's small table. He's filled with relief. He didn't even realise he'd begun to doubt Rose until Mickey said what she just did.

A memory assaults him. The first time he thought he and Rose were going to make love, her being into it and then seizing up. She was paralysed with fear and he'd realised in that moment that her ex had probably sexually assaulted her on top of everything else. It was the only thing he could think of that could cause fear like that.

He has never seen Rose around Davidson. He can't even imagine how terrified she must be in his presence.

If Davidson had approached her, threatened her, would she have told Luke or would she have just run? If he'd found her in this hotel, would she have gone with him because she was too frightened not to?

'Mickey, I need your help,' he says.

'I've already agreed to help you,' she says.

'No. I mean I need your help with something else.'

Mickey waits for him to tell her what it is, her expression wary.

'I need to get home,' Luke says.

'The authorities have promised a quick hearing. If your lawyers manage to break precedent and get you a manslaughter charge, it will be a short sentence and it might even be commuted. I've spoken to the lead attorney and he thinks the judge will accept current island practice is out of step with international best practice, so they're confident. Meanwhile, I will look for Rose—'

'No, I have to find her, Mickey. I can't wait for a trial. I have to get off this island and back to London.'

'Luke, that's impossible.'

'Mickey, I think Rose is in real danger. I've seen her and how she is when she even thinks of Davidson. I know you think you know what's happened here but I'm telling you, don't make assumptions based on how it looks. Please, trust me. I need to break bail.'

Mickey is looking at Luke as if he's lost his mind.

'I understand you're worried,' she says. 'But I will find her, Luke. If she's been telling the truth and she's in danger, I'll find her.'

'I'm desperate, Mickey. Just see it from my perspective, please. I offered Rose all that money. She wouldn't take it. You know how strangely abused women can act. And she's with him right now. We have no idea what he'll do to her. I'm begging you. I can't leave this to anybody else. This is my job. Help me get home so I can look for her.'

'If you break your bail, Luke, your sentence will be even worse. Even if I could help you get out of here—'

'You can. Mickey, I just need you to do one thing for me. I won't even tell you what it is so you're not complicit. All you have to do is collect an envelope from an address and give it to me.'

He watches Mickey as she processes this. Her face starts to pale.

'Oh, Luke. If you got stopped at the airport – God, if you made it to Britain, even . . . I don't know what the extradition laws are between England and here.'

'Mickey, if you do this for me, I swear, I will never ask you for another thing.'

'What you're asking for is too much.'

Luke stares at her, beseechingly. He racks his brains for what he can say to convince her.

'If you do this for me, I'll tell you the real reason I never turned up when we were supposed to leave together.'

Mickey looks at him like she's been slapped.

Luke bites the inside of his cheek so hard he can feel blood.

He knows he's hurting her. He hurt her before, too, and it was necessary then as well.

But this time, it's even more necessary.

He's hurting her so he can save Rose.

He can't let Rose down. If he can do this one thing . . . it will make up for all the other things he's failed to do in his life.

Mickey turns away. She stands with her back to him, looking out the window. Her shoulders are tense and when she lifts a hand to her face, he knows she's wiping away tears.

He waits, his heart in his mouth.

He's being an absolute dickhead. He knows that. There was a time when she was the woman he'd break every rule for.

I'm a bad person, Luke thinks. He can only hope she'll forgive him. For this and for . . . everything.

'I'll collect your envelope,' she says.

Luke's heart surges with hope.

'Mickey, I can't thank you enough. You're an angel. You're so much better than I could ever be. I . . . I don't know how to say this—'

'Stop. Don't say anything.'

She turns again and looks at him. He doesn't recognise the expression on her face.

She hates him. Even before, when she was angry at him, she never looked at him like this. Hurt, betrayed, disappointed – never contempt. But now . . .

'When this is over, I never want to speak to you again,' she says. 'I don't want to know why you didn't come through for me all those years ago. I don't want to hear your reasons or excuses. I don't want to see you, ever. Inspector Alleyne is right. There's something wrong with you, Luke.'

Luke receives her words like a punch to the gut.

She's correct, of course. He doesn't know why or how the inspector has reached that conclusion, but he's not wrong, either.

There's nothing Luke can say to redeem himself. This is the final time he'll let Mickey down.

He prays it will be worth it. He prays Rose is worth it.

There's a knock on the door followed by a call of room service. Mickey moves to answer it.

Luke frowns, remembering something.

'What was her full name?' Luke asks. 'Before she moved to London? Róisín what?'

It might be information he needs if Rose is currently in Donegal.

'Róisín Gallagher,' Mickey says, her voice low.

Luke hangs his head.

Oh, God.

Gallagher.

It can't be.

How could he have been so stupid?

But he hadn't been, not at first. He'd wondered, hadn't he? And then he'd buried it, way down. Because it couldn't be true.

She couldn't be that good an actress.

Gallagher.

'And she didn't ask for the money?' he repeats, but he barely recognises his own voice. It's like he's speaking from outside himself.

Gallagher.

Mickey pauses at the door.

'No,' she says. 'I've already told you. But I've been thinking about it and the only reason I can fathom is that the two of them, when they planned this, didn't expect you to kill somebody. Maybe it's gotten more serious than they wanted and she's just run. Or maybe she didn't realise you had that much and figured it was too big a con, that you'd come after her for that amount. I don't know. Perhaps you're right and she's actually in danger. Maybe she was never after your money at all. I hope you're right, considering what you're about to do for her.'

Luke doesn't respond.

All he can think is that he's the blindest, most idiotic man alive.

Nathan didn't ask Mickey why she rang to give him yet another update.

Something has changed between them. Mickey feels softer towards her husband. And she thinks he feels the same way towards her.

She's looking forward to going home, Mickey realises. She wants to see him. It's so long since they were intimate, properly intimate.

She misses it. Maybe this was what she needed, to see Luke again, to remember how flawed he is.

To make herself realise she had a lucky escape.

Mickey is making her way to the part of the island Luke visited when he went looking for the gun.

She thinks about why she's doing this.

Part of it is to simply conclude her story with Luke Miller. By doing this for him, she's ending their relationship with him in her debt. And there's a smug justice to that, somehow.

But it's not really for Luke, she realises.

It's for Rose.

Mickey doesn't know why Rose is doing what she's doing now.

But she knows Rose wasn't lying about being abused by Kevin Davidson. And Mickey liked Rose. It's what Inspector Alleyne said, about knowing if somebody is good or bad. Mickey didn't spend very long in Rose's company but, even with her doubts, she still felt that Rose was a virtuous individual.

If Rose is in danger, even the slightest bit, Mickey wants her found.

Then Mickey will have discharged her duty.

The sun is still strong overhead, but there's a cool breeze today drifting in from the sea and the island's temperature is starting to adjust, now it's almost October.

It's pleasant. The perfect place for a late honeymoon.

It's what Luke must have thought when Rose surprised him with flight tickets and brought him here.

Luke.

Mickey winces again.

She can't even think of him now without feeling anger.

She'd known all those years ago that there had been more to him not turning up to collect her when she was leaving Nathan. Luke wasn't unreliable. He wasn't a flake.

But she'd come to terms with the past, as much as she could, and for him to dangle the truth in front of her like that, to use it like a weapon . . . It had been cruel.

She thought less of him for it.

For a moment. And then, she was glad he'd done it. It was far better to feel anger towards the man than to constantly see him as a missed opportunity, to believe he was the path she could have taken, the alternate life.

Mickey has the cab pull up at the house she's been given the address for.

She asks him to wait ten minutes and ten minutes is all she needs. She imagines she's collecting two passports. Luke would have ordered one for Rose and one for himself when he came here to get the gun. She assumes his fake one will work, too.

As long as Luke looks a little different passing through the airport, he should be fine. Saint-Thérèse airport security aren't known for their high-level attention to detail and the photograph of the man on the fake passport would be a close approximation of the actual Luke Miller.

Mickey left Luke at the hotel dying his flecked hair fully black. Between that and the beard he is cultivating, he certainly won't resemble the police photofit.

Mickey leaves the house clutching a small envelope.

She's just back inside the taxi when she sees a police car go by.

She ducks the second she sees who's driving it. Marcel Alleyne.

When she sits up, the taxi driver has put the car in gear and is taking off in the same direction as the police car.

'No, not that way,' Mickey says.

'That's the way back to town,' the taxi driver says.

'I don't care. Just drive up the hill for a bit and then take me back.'

The taxi driver looks pointedly at the meter, then shrugs. If the Irish lady wants to act crazy and pay him extra, who is he to question it?

Mickey sits back and looks out the window as the taxi climbs the hill. The island is more lush up here, a hint at what it would be without tourism and progress. It's a tropical paradise.

She has a fake passport in her lap and is about to help a man she doesn't even know any more become even more of a criminal than he already is.

If she gets through this and gets home, she's taking a holiday.

Back at the hotel, she finds Luke cleaning the bathroom sink of hair dye. He joins her in the main room.

She doesn't look at him as she slaps the envelope down on the table.

'There's a flight leaving at 8 p.m.,' he tells her. 'A taxi will come for me at the back of the hotel.'

'I told the inspector he could trust us,' Mickey retorts. 'And he trusts me.'

She says this last sentence with the bitterness she feels.

'I'm sorry, Mickey,' Luke replies. 'I'm not trying to avoid facing up to what I did with Williams. I just have to find Rose and make sure she's safe. I'll come back, I'll take whatever sentence they hand me. You can tell them that.'

'I don't care. When you're gone, this has nothing more to do with me.'

'Are you . . . are you sure you don't want me to tell you the truth about all those years ago?'

Mickey glares at him.

'I am sure,' she says. 'I know the truth. You were a coward. I don't care what reason you have; what it boils down to is: you were a coward.'

He visibly flinches at her words but, she notes, he doesn't deny the accusation.

She hesitates.

'What happened to you, Luke? When we met, I know you weren't exactly a saint. Nor was I. But you were . . . you were kind. I thought you were a kind man. I thought I was the one doing the corrupting. What made you like this?'

Luke looks like he wants to say something but can't find the words. Mickey, now she's properly watching him, notices something.

Since she's arrived on the island, he's had this lost, confused, terrified look to him. But now, all of a sudden, Luke looks broken. Devastated.

She wonders what has brought that on. Just earlier, he was passionately defending Rose. Now he looked like a man who's been told he has a terminal disease.

'What is it?' she asks, and even though she's furious with him, she can't keep the concern from her voice.

'I did a terrible thing,' he says. 'A long time ago, but it was terrible. And I think this is my karma.'

'Is this to do with . . . ?' Mickey trails off. She wants to ask if whatever he did is the reason he abandoned her all those years ago, but she can't. She's already said she doesn't want to know any more.

'Has it to do with Rose?' she asks, instead. 'And that money?'

'I don't know for sure,' he says. 'I think so, but I hope not. I have to find out. I have to speak to her.'

Mickey crosses her arms.

'Where are you going to look for her?'

'In London, I guess.'

'London is a big city.'

Luke's shoulders slump.

Mickey sighs.

'I'll see if Elliot can find out anything. She might go home. Back to Donegal, I mean.'

'I've thought of that.'

'Luke, I'm really fucking angry at you, but I'd rather be angry at you with you still alive. If Rose is with Kevin Davidson, you might not be safe.'

Luke is facing away from her when he speaks again but Mickey can still hear what he says.

'Maybe I don't deserve to be.'

Donegal

When Elliot was a kid, he liked to spend every free minute he had on his computer. He wasn't into sport. He wasn't considered smart in school – at least, not beyond computer studies. He wasn't into girls.

He was into gaming. And then, coding.

His mother never minded. As far as she was concerned, Elliot sitting in his room and not mixing with other lads was the safest option for a working-class teenage black boy.

It drove his father nuts. His dad wanted a son who was a football player, or at the very least . . . popular.

Elliot didn't have friends, or at least none who called to the door. He did have plenty of online friends but his father dismissed them as if they were imaginary.

Nana was always the popular one. Nana was the one they all called around for. Especially the boys. His father wasn't too happy about that, either, but at least Nana was out living in her life, not hunched over the artificial light of a monitor playing Call of Duty for six hours a day in a tiny box room.

Everyone called for Nana.

Including the man who would father her two children, isolate her from the rest of her family, rape her, and beat her so badly that she almost died.

Elliot preferred computers. But he made a decision, after what happened to Nana, that he would interact with the world a bit more. He'd interact with it in the way that gave him the greatest satisfaction.

Helping women get away from scumbags like his sister's ex.

Elliot tried to explain to his father at one point that it wasn't just nerds who hung out in gaming chat rooms. It was all sorts — teachers, lawyers, bankers . . . prison guards. They, in particular, were very active. Elliot supposed it was having very little else to do when you were monitoring cell doors on a screen or security hatches at the end of wards most of your waking hours.

To reach inside the Davidson family, Elliot has jumped through a series of bizarre hoops. Via a prison guard friend of his called Betty960, he's found a reformed prisoner who once ran drugs across the channel. The former drug dealer has confirmed that the Davidson family are indeed high up the ladder in terms of Irish trafficking. And he has a contact.

Elliot has made it clear he's not interested in buying drugs or anything illegal. That's not how these kind of meetings work. He's let it be known he merely wants to talk about somebody connected with the family who may be causing hassle.

But no doubt about it, Elliot is absolutely crapping himself. This is not the sort of thing he does. He can find out information about anyone and anything. He can sort tickets, temporary IDs, bank accounts.

Reaching inside criminal families . . . very far from his comfort zone.

Elliot is sitting now in a car park by an isolated beach, waiting for his contact to arrive. The beach looks so undisturbed and beautiful. If it wasn't lashing rain sideways, with a wind that could cut a man, he could imagine this being a top tourist destination.

As Elliot looks through his windscreen at the couple of dog walkers in the distance, evidently the owners of the other cars parked here, he thinks: that's commitment to your animal. There's no way on earth Elliot would walk that beach on a day like today.

It's only the end of September, he reminds himself again. He left England in the warm embrace of an Indian summer.

How the hell do they stay warm around these parts?

He hears a car approaching on the lonely road that leads to the beach. He gets out of his own vehicle when it comes into view.

Elliot is aware there's trust required here and he knows he's the one who needs to appear non-threatening. Which he is. Elliot is shaking with fear. He's just trying not to look that way.

The black BMW pulls into the car park, its full headlights on, mitigating the gloom of the day.

Elliot is caught in their glare and raises a hand to shield his eyes.

The car rolls to a stop. A man gets out. He's smaller than Elliot and Elliot immediately relaxes. The guy is on his own. If this goes to hell, at least Elliot can get away from him and hotfoot it back to the safety of London.

'Elliot Ibekwe?' the man asks in a thick Donegal accent.

'That's me,' Elliot says.

'You've been looking to talk to the Davidson family?'

'Yes. I don't want to cause any trouble. I just have some questions about one of the family. It's to do with a client of mine.'

The man smiles. Elliot relaxes.

In the same moment, he catches movement in the corner of his eye.

As the gun is raised to the back of his head, Elliot does the split-second calculation.

Two dog walkers on the beach.

Three cars parked besides his own.

They were already waiting for him when he arrived.

'I'm not a problem for you,' he says, weakly.

He feels a sudden, searing pain in the back of his head.

And then the ground is rising to meet him very fast.

Elliot wakes in pain. He's in a dark, confined space. That much is obvious. His limbs ache, he can't move in any direction and he's being bumped around.

He smells petrol.

His eyes adjust.

He's in the boot of a car.

Elliot is able to feel the back of his head. There's a large bump and something wet and sticky. But he's alive. And they're bringing him somewhere. If they'd wanted to kill him, he'd already be dead.

Elliot has time to consider two things before he loses consciousness again.

He might never see Nana and his family again.

And the Davidson family are more dangerous than he or Mickey had realised.

Saint-Thérèse

Mickey is alone in the hotel bar when Marcel calls by that evening. She's wearing a short black dress and is relieved that the only thing she has to worry about in it is her lumps and bumps, and not a twenty-million-pound financial chip.

She has already knocked back half of her rum cocktail.

The meeting is at her invitation. She wants to tell him herself what's happened; it's the least she can do. But when she sees him walking into the bar, as slick and cool as ever, she has the very juvenile reaction of wanting to run upstairs and hide under her bed sheets.

'Mickey,' he says in greeting. He joins her at the bar and checks out her drink, before raising a hand to the barman.

'Mojito and same again for the lady,' he says.

'Thank you,' Mickey says, trying to quell the butterflies in her stomach.

He seems relaxed. Not like somebody who's just apprehended a fleeing parolee at the airport and now wants answers.

She looks up at the clock. It's 10.30 p.m.

She's heard nothing so assumes everything went fine with the flight.

Luke should be over the ocean by now, en route to London.

'And thank you for meeting me so late,' she says. 'Is there a Mrs Inspector you've had to placate?'

Mickey wants to play for time, even though it's not necessary. She's not looking forward to being diminished in this man's eyes.

Marcel laughs.

'Is that a, how do you say it, come-on line?'

They both laugh this time. There's nothing remotely sexual between them. Mickey respects this man's professionalism and he hers . . . up until now, she thinks.

'More a "am I keeping you away from your family" line,' she says.

'Ah. Yes, there is a Mrs Inspector. And three mini inspectors. But they are used to me working late. And early. And all the hours in between.'

'You should watch that,' Mickey says, with feeling. 'A wife will always say she has no problem with her husband being busy in work but she'll resent it. Deep down. She'll think he's choosing work over her.'

She can tell by Marcel's lack of reaction that he's studying her and wondering if she speaks from personal experience.

She is.

'Well, this sounded important,' he says. 'So she will forgive me this evening. Plus . . . I love my wife. With all my being and heart. She is the sun around which I revolve. But she is a really, really terrible cook. Awful. She can burn an egg. Every night I work late is a night when I eat out and save myself from a premature death caused by food poisoning.'

'You could always learn to cook yourself,' Mickey says, with a snort.

'I cannot, because she thinks she is a wonderful cook, so I have to let her feed me. It pleases her. It does not please me, but that is love, no? To sacrifice.'

Mickey smiles. She's never heard a truer declaration of what love is.

It's a nice, friendly moment between them and she's about to shit all over it.

'I'm really sorry,' she blurts out.

'Sorry for what?'

Mickey can't look at Marcel, now. She looks at the barman, who's still making the mojito. She should have let the inspector get a drink into him before she landed the bombshell.

'Luke Miller is gone,' she says, before she can talk herself out of it.

The inspector gets off his stool, immediately in work mode.

'Gone where?'

'He has left the island.'

'He has no passport.'

Mickey doesn't meet Marcel's eye.

When she'd spoken to Nathan earlier, he had told her to leave at the same time.

You're aiding and abetting, he'd said. *They could arrest you.*

Mickey knew he was right but a sense of honour meant she felt she had to stay and explain. And take the consequences if they came.

'Did you help him?' Marcel says, and his voice is laden with disappointment.

'I can't answer that,' Mickey says, because it's one thing to be honourable but quite another to walk yourself into a jail sentence. 'But . . . I didn't stop him.'

Marcel glares at her. The barman puts the two drinks on the counter.

'What time was the flight?' Marcel asks.

'8 p.m.,' she answers.

He considers this, then sits back down, heavily. He picks up his drink and takes a gulp.

'I could charge you,' he says. 'If I find evidence you helped him.'

'I'm aware of that.'

The inspector looks angry for a moment, but then he shakes his head.

'I hope he's worth it,' he says. 'This faith you have placed in him.'

Mickey looks down at the counter.

'He's not,' she says, her voice small. 'But I think he will try to redeem himself. He's promised me he will come back.'

'Ha! You help women who have been hurt, Mickey, yes?'

Mickey nods.

'Don't *they* always believe their men, when they say they will do better?'

Mickey is feeling smaller by the minute. She takes a deep breath. She's tougher than this. And while he's right that she's shown weakness, she doesn't think he's right about Luke.

'I know you have no reason to believe or trust me or him, but I think he was genuine. He needs to find his wife. He's beside himself with worry. Everybody is capable of rash acts when they're in that place. And when he finds her, he will return here and face the consequences of what he did. He is filled with remorse for killing that man. That's not a lie.'

'Are you telling me this so I'll let you leave, too?'

Mickey takes a deep breath.

'I would like to leave. But if you want to charge me, I understand that, too.'

They meet each other's eyes.

'I will face disciplinary action for this,' he says.

Mickey tries to meet his eye.

'You don't deserve that,' she says. 'And I assure you, anything I can do to help, I will. If charging me helps to bring some balance, do it.'

It's Marcel who looks away this time and Mickey's stomach knots.

He's not ashamed to look at her, he just doesn't want to. She barely knows him but she knows enough to be aware she wants to be held in his high esteem.

Thank you, Luke fucking Miller.

'You had best leave first thing,' he says.

He drains his drink, gets up and walks out of the bar.

Mickey watches him go.

She wishes she could be as helpful to good men as she seems to be to bad ones.

Donegal

When Elliot next regains consciousness, he's tied to a chair.

He opens his eyes and stares at the soft carpet beneath his feet. He raises his gaze and he's looking at a desk, a small TV sitting on top of it.

It's a hotel room.

How did they get him into a hotel room in this state?

Elliot tries to turn his head left and right, wincing with the pain.

'Stop. Stay still.'

The male voice comes from behind him. It's the same voice as earlier, the guy in the car park.

'Listen, man,' Elliot says. 'I don't know what's happening here but—'

'You can stop talking now.'

Elliot shuts up. He's not going to be antagonising anybody. He wants to get out of here alive, whatever that takes.

But he's starting to wonder if that's going to happen.

He's messed up. He assumed that because he wasn't a threat, they wouldn't see him as one. But these people are clearly not the sort to take chances.

God, he's been naïve. Thinking he could come here and ask

questions about Kevin right inside his family's heartland. For all he knows, Kevin is doing what he's doing with the full knowledge of the Davidsons. Their support, even.

I'm going to die inside an anonymous hotel room at the hands of somebody I don't know and I can't even see, Elliot thinks.

He'd shoot himself for stupidity if they weren't going to kill him first.

'How's the head?' the voice asks.

That throws Elliot.

'Not great,' he says, with trepidation.

'Sorry about that. Had to incapacitate you for a while. You're a bit bigger than me. You work out?'

'A bit,' Elliot says. 'Sorry.'

The man behind him laughs.

Elliot wonders if this is a sick game. Lure him into relaxing before they shoot him. It's not unheard of. But another part of him realises this is going somewhere else and, honestly, he could almost cry with relief.

Elliot wants to live. He wants to go home to London and be in his house again. He wants to see Nana and Mickey and his niece and nephew. He wants to cook his favourite food and watch reruns of *Only Fools and Horses* and go online to tell people the crazy stuff that happened to him here. He wants to finally chat up that girl who works in the phone shop on the corner and see if he can talk her into a date. She has pretty black hair and he's had dreams where he imagines it spread out on his pillow after he's made love to her all night.

He wants to get out of this freezing, wet country and return to what he knows.

And he wants to tell Mickey he's thinking about a new career. Something a little less likely to get him killed.

'If I untie you, you're not going to lose the head, are you?' the voice asks.

'I won't lose my head,' Elliot promises.

'Good. There's a minibar in the corner and a nice rainfall shower in the bathroom. I suggest a stiff one, a wash and then the boss will meet you downstairs. Your jacket's a bit scruffy and this is a nice place, so maybe go down in your shirt. The room is paid for. You can sleep here later if you want. Lovely springy mattress.'

Elliot is still trying to process this when two things happen. His wrists are loosened and he hears the hotel door click closed.

He stands up and turns around fast, ready to defend himself. There's nobody there.

Well, he thinks. That was odd.

When he's ready, Elliot goes downstairs to the bar.

He doesn't know who the boss of the family is. He only knows he'll do whatever the man says, because Elliot is scared to death.

He suspects they knocked him out so they could investigate him and have him to hand should he need to be disposed of.

He's made it over the first hurdle, that's obvious.

He orders a sparkling water and sits facing the door. He had followed his assailant's advice and had a whiskey upstairs to steady his nerves, but now he wants to have a clear, albeit still throbbing, head.

He looks up when a lone, dark-haired woman enters the bar. He's about to look away again when he does a double take.

Elliot hasn't seen a single person in this county dressed with the sort of money this woman is wearing. Dior, perhaps. He's guessing from what he's gleaned from all those overpriced magazines Nana leaves around the place.

Is this the boss?

Or one of the bosses?

She's mid-forties; she hardly looks old or experienced enough to be in charge of a family drug empire.

Whoever she is, she makes a beeline for him.

He's surprised she hasn't come flanked with bodyguards, but when she exchanges pleasantries with the concierge, and then the waitress, Elliot realises that this woman and her family run this town and she doesn't need to bring protection with her. Everywhere she goes, she's protected.

And that also explains how he ended up being carried inside the hotel, clearly bleeding and certainly not willing.

'Mr Ibekwe,' she says, in a musical accent. 'I'm Máire Davidson. It's nice to meet you.'

'And you,' he lies, though maybe it's the truth, because he's so relieved to not be dead he's happy to meet anybody.

'I apologise for our precautionary measures,' she says. She glances at his head, purses her lips then nods, satisfied he's got no lasting damage.

'They weren't necessary,' Elliot says.

'I'm afraid they were. We're a very private family. We're not used to people demanding an audience. Especially people we've never heard of.' She shrugs. It's all water under the bridge, the gesture says.

Elliot bites down his bitterness.

'I reached out to you through the appropriate channels,' Elliot points out.

'Through your associate in London, yes. He seems to have had a bit of a turnaround since his time in jail. Last I checked, he was a reformed man. Prison changed him. He's not interested in anything illicit – and yet, he put you in touch with us.'

'My mother used to say everybody can be Tina Turner.'

'Excuse me?'

'She was obsessed with 1980s musical icons. She meant everyone can reinvent themselves, even their own careers.'

Máire smiles. She's a pleasant-looking woman but Elliot is already starting to get a read on her and he suspects that, for the second time, he's made an error of assumption.

This woman is the powerhouse in the Davidson family. She hasn't been sent here as an emissary to check him out. She's checking him out for herself because she's the one the family trusts to gauge people.

'I was telling the truth,' he says. 'I'm only here to ask questions. Not to cause any trouble.'

'Asking questions is trouble,' she retorts.

'I promise, if you don't want to talk to me, I'll be on the first flight out of here and you'll never see me again.'

Máire sits back and studies him.

'Did you enjoy your pie in the pub? I believe they've started to stock HP sauce now. In case any black guys from London call back in.'

Elliot winces.

She gives him a half-smile.

'I've looked into you,' she says. 'You're a man who operates on the edge of society. But I don't believe you're working for anybody I need to worry about. I'm intrigued.'

Elliot considers how to frame his question. Máire is smarter than he could have imagined.

'I work with a woman who helps people in difficult situations,' Elliot says. 'Women, mainly. Ones who've been abused or hurt by their partners.'

'Noble.'

Elliot doesn't think he imagines seeing a slight flinch.

'Sure,' he says. 'It's a rewarding job.'

'And what does that have to do with me? Wait . . .' A smile tugs on her lips. 'You don't want us to become a patron of your little cause? Davidson Fisheries sponsors a shelter?'

This time Elliot smiles.

'Perhaps that can be second on the agenda. First, let me tell you about our current client. We believe she's an ex of your brother, Kevin.'

A shadow crosses Máire's features. Elliot fears she's shutting down, that he's about to lose her.

'She goes by a different name now but we believe she may have been Róisín Gallagher when she lived here.'

Máire has picked up her tea but now she brings the cup down with a clatter. One or two of the other patrons in the hotel bar look across, alarmed. Máire ignores everyone.

She sits back and studies Elliot.

'I like you,' she says. 'I like what you do. I already knew what you did before I came here. Not the full extent of your job, but enough. And I enjoy the fact there are some men out there willing to still be gentlemen. You strike me as a gentleman.'

'I like to think so.'

'You know my world, Mr Ibekwe, even if you don't move in it. That is the world of fishing, in case you misunderstand me.'

'I understand.'

'Fishing can be dangerous and competitive but also very lucrative. My family has worked very hard to become good at fishing, and sometimes, we've had to do things that aren't very pleasant. You got a taste of that earlier. But for the most part, we keep our business professional. That's how it works these days. All very . . . professional.'

Elliot nods. He's following.

'Sometimes a little charter boat comes into your waters and tries to fish. And you can suggest they leave or you can deal with them another way, to send out a message. It can get heated.'

'Yes,' Elliot says. His knee has started to shake. He might be agreeing with this woman, he might know what she means, but this stuff is completely foreign to him.

'That is a sort of violence I can live with,' Máire says. 'Unfortunate but necessary. I cannot live with violence for violence's sake. There are some who can.'

Elliot cocks his head.

'Like your brother?'

She winces again and he hopes he hasn't overstepped the mark. But after a moment or two, she's as calm as ever.

'Like my brother,' she agrees. 'You cannot choose your family, you understand.'

'Or who your family chooses to be with,' Elliot answers. 'I speak from experience.'

Máire cocks her head. There's a moment between them, some mutual understanding. Máire is evidently starting to get an insight into why he does what he does.

'Indeed. Well, my brother always had, let's call it, a "vicious streak", to him. As children, sometimes you do cruel things just because you can. And then you learn empathy. Kevin never learned empathy.'

She takes a breath.

'He treated a girl very badly. Her name was Róisín Gallagher. He abused her for years and then he raped her because she had the audacity to try to run from him. He left her in a very bad way. He deserved to be punished for it. She deserved justice. But if he had been prosecuted for that crime, it would have opened a can of worms. If he was convicted, we couldn't be guaranteed of his discretion in relation to our business affairs.'

'Of course.'

'So, Róisín was taken care of. I haven't a clue where she is now, or what she's doing, but I know she was left in a position to make a fresh start.'

'And Kevin?'

'Kevin isn't hurting any more women.'

'Are you sure of that?'

'I'm very sure.'

Elliot sits forward.

'You see, I think he *is* hurting somebody,' he says. 'I think he's hurting Róisín again. He's found her.'

Maire grows pale.

'And how do you know this?' she asks.

'Ways and means. Passenger lists, sightings. What I'm trying to establish is whether he's a danger to her or whether she's come around to forgiving him and is now working with him on something.'

Máire blinks.

She sits back and indicates to the waitress that she wants to be served.

Elliot waits.

'I'm going to need a vodka and tonic,' she tells the waitress. 'And my friend here – what's your tipple?'

'I'm okay with water.'

'He'll have the same as me.'

The waitress leaves and Máire looks at Elliot.

'You're going to need alcohol for this,' she says.

Elliot frowns.

London

1 October

Mickey comes through Heathrow feeling more relieved than she ever has in her life.

Nathan has organised a car to pick her up and he's in the back.

She knows Elliot is waiting for her at their home. He has something to tell her, he messaged, something he needs to explain in person.

Mickey is exhausted. She's spent the last eight hours on a plane reading about the extradition process between Britain and Saint-Thérèse, all via material Elliot sent on.

Mickey's conclusion, even after having left the law some time ago, is that any extradition process between the two jurisdictions is non-existent.

Inspector Alleyne can lodge an application for Luke to be arrested by British police and handed over, but Luke can fight any extradition request while remaining a free man and the strong probability is that the British courts will refuse the Saint-Thérèse authorities. Luke's case of self-defence is strong and will be understood in a British court of law. If his team can convince a judge that Luke won't be given a fair trial under foreign law, he won't be sent back.

Knowing all this, Mickey struggles to see how she can convince Luke to go back of his own volition.

And if she can't, she doesn't like to think of the fallout.

She'll have let down Inspector Alleyne.

But then, she already has.

Nathan gets out of the car as she approaches and walks towards her, his arms open wide.

Mickey almost collapses into them.

He smells so good. So . . . familiar.

He's her home.

'You must be exhausted,' he says.

'Shattered,' she agrees. 'But I still have a lot to do.'

'I could send Elliot home, get you comfortable in bed and let you sleep for a day.'

'Much as I would love that . . .'

Nathan smiles. He knows his wife and Mickey is starting to appreciate that.

She squeezes his hand and gets into the car.

All through the journey, Mickey rests her head on his shoulder.

This is my husband, she tells herself. I can love him. I do love him.

Back at the house, Elliot is waiting in the kitchen, drinking a coffee.

'She's tired, so let's make this quick,' Nathan says.

Elliot nods.

'You read the extradition material?' he asks Mickey.

'Yes,' she says. 'On the plane. The chances of Luke Miller being returned to Saint-Thérèse are slim to none.'

'Yep. And he's not at his apartment. My intel – via your new friend Rachel – is that he flew to Derry a couple of days ago.'

Mickey purses her lips. She knows Derry is just a stop en route to Donegal.

Nathan touches Mickey's arm.

'If he keeps his head down and gets a good barrister, he'll be fine,' he says. 'I've spoken to some police contacts. They say he defended himself in a terrifying situation. It's manageable. And as long as you weren't involved in helping him break bail, you'll be fine, too. Nobody imagines you were, but, you know, if you had even thought he might consider skipping, it's best you don't mention that to anybody.'

Mickey and Nathan maintain eye contact. An unspoken agreement passes between them. He won't ask, she won't tell, but they both know he no longer sees Luke Miller as a threat.

'I'll leave you to it,' he says. Mickey kisses his cheek, then Nathan leaves the kitchen.

She sits down heavily beside Elliot.

'You want something strong to drink?' he asks.

'I need coffee to stay awake,' she tells him.

He pours from the jug and she takes a sip of her fourth cup in as many hours.

'Are you okay?' she asks. Up close, she can see Elliot looks a little different. She can't put her finger on it. He's holding his head stiffly, like he has an injury . . .

Mickey leans back in her chair and sees the cut and large bump on the back of his head, visible through his tightly cut hair.

'What happened to you?'

'I had an accidental encounter with the butt of a gun.'

'Jesus. Is this to do with the bombshell you said you have for me?'

'Yep,' Elliot says. 'I met Máire Davidson.'

'Kevin's mother?'

'Sister. And more or less head of the family.'

'She did this to you?'

'No, Mickey. Máire Davidson did not hit me with a gun. Seriously? One of her gang did. Massive lad, twice the size of me. There might have been five of them. Anyway, they wanted to make sure I wasn't a threat.'

'By knocking you out?'

Mickey is shocked he was in danger and she didn't know it.

Yet another casualty of the Luke Miller head-fuck situation.

'What's done is done,' Elliot says. 'And I have something to show you.'

He takes an envelope out of his pocket and opens it.

He places a photograph down in front of Mickey.

'What am I looking at?' she asks.

'That's Kevin Davidson.'

Mickey stares at the picture then back at Elliot.

By the time Nathan returns to the kitchen, Elliot is on the phone booking the tickets.

'What's going on?' he asks Mickey.

'I'm going to Donegal,' she says.

'When?'

'Tonight.'

Nathan frowns.

'Mickey, you've only just got here.'

Mickey takes both his hands.

'I know. And I'm very much looking forward to being home. I mean home, *properly*. But I have to do this one last thing.'

343

She leans forward and kisses him on the lips. Nathan, after a moment's hesitation, kisses her back.

He pulls her close and whispers into her ear.

'I've grown up, Mickey. I'm very much looking forward to you being home, too.'

He turns and walks towards the door.

'What are you doing?' she asks.

'I'm getting my driver back for you!' he calls, still walking.

Mickey smiles.

Donegal

Luke checks into the Airbnb with an email to say he's arrived, and immediately receives a number for the lockbox.

The house is remote, just outside a small town called Malin on the peninsula of Inishowen, in Donegal.

The anonymity of an Airbnb suits him. He didn't want to check in at any of the hotels. The county is underpopulated, and he imagines even more so after tourist season. The children have gone back to school, so there are no visiting families here to avail of the long sandy beaches and the plentiful restaurants and pubs. Somebody told him once that poor transport infrastructure connecting it to the rest of Ireland had left Donegal blissfully isolated and that was why it possessed some of the most beautiful, undisturbed landscape in Europe.

But that means locals always know who's there and it wouldn't be long before somebody mentioned the Englishman staying in such and such hotel.

Luke had made a brief stop at his and Rose's apartment in London on the way here. He'd gone through everything she'd left there, which wasn't much. The apartment had been cleared of most of her belongings. He presumed she'd stopped off there too, before going home. To Donegal.

There was no rush for her. As far as she was concerned, he was incarcerated on Saint-Thérèse and that's where he'd be staying.

While he was in the apartment, he'd lain on their bed on Rose's side, his head on her pillow.

And he'd acknowledged, properly, that he'd suspected from the start.

Of course, he'd suspected.

You don't have that much money to your name and not think one day somebody will come after it.

And when she said she was from Donegal . . .

But he'd told himself not to be paranoid. There were more people in Donegal than the man he had known. He'd found Rose, not the other way round. He'd chased her.

He'd believed that.

Something had changed, though.

He knows whatever she'd planned for him, something changed at one point.

She'd loved him. He's sure of it.

The Airbnb in Donegal is a far cry from the private villa he'd got for them on Saint-Thérèse. Inside smells of damp and old people, and while it's surface-clean, the décor clearly hasn't been updated since the 1970s; the whole place is like the set of an old horror movie. He notices in the bedroom that the whitewashed wall is chipped with dozens of tiny dots behind the bed. He suspects he knows what they're from.

Something else somebody had told him once – the winters in Donegal are long and lonely and farming the land is hard. Plenty of men have taken a shotgun to their mouths late at night in bed.

Luke takes the bed in the spare room.

Over the next two days, he moves about the peninsula, trying to stay unseen. He drives to Derry to buy food so he doesn't need to eat in restaurants.

He doesn't think Rose will stay at her family home. He doesn't think the family home still exists. He imagines she's living somewhere else these days, but he's hoping it's close to where she grew up.

In Malin.

The man Luke had known had children. Luke remembers that. He remembers it every day of his life. But Rose said she was an only child.

Something else she'd fabricated to trap him.

Donegal might be sparsely populated but it's still big, geographically, and it takes Luke a full two days before he spots her. They're driving towards each other when he does.

She doesn't notice him and he guesses that his new beard and artificially darker hair are doing their job, but he also knows she's distracted and not expecting to see him.

When he's travelled up the road a little, he does a U-turn – not easy on such a narrow stretch, the car almost ends up in a ditch, but when he gets it back on the road, she's easy to follow.

She drives to a small cottage with undisturbed views of the Atlantic Ocean. He pulls up at the hedgerows outside it and watches her take bags of shopping from the boot.

She looks thin. Fragile. Unhappy. Not like a woman who's had her revenge and is now content.

Luke hopes that means something. He hopes it means she misses him as much as he misses her.

He hopes it means that she regrets what's happened.

He's standing at the foot of the drive when she comes back out to get the final shopping bag.

She senses him before she sees him and stops.

'Luke?'

She looks like she wants to run.

'You don't have to be scared of me,' he says. He feels a pang just standing there, just looking at her.

This is his Rose.

He can see, even though he's a good twenty feet away, that she's trembling.

They look at each other.

Rose seems to be frozen on the spot.

'I think we need to talk,' Luke says.

London

September 2022

Rose stares at the picture in the wedding album that Kevin is holding. She knows now that this life she's built with Luke, this apartment, everything in it – she's about to lose it all. And she's frightened. She's suddenly really frightened. Because this was never part of the plan, for her to fall in love.

But she has – and she doesn't want it to all end.

'This wasn't supposed to happen,' he says. 'You need to leave him, now.'

Rose scrunches her eyes closed. When she opens them, Kevin is still there, staring at her. Accusing her.

'This is exactly what was supposed to happen,' she says.

Kevin gives her a look, then he slams the wedding album on the floor with such force it bounces on the soft pile carpet.

'No!' he shouts. 'You were supposed to get him to fall in love with you. To get him to ask you to move in. You weren't supposed to fucking love him back.'

Rose looks away.

She's filled with both anger and guilt.

She didn't want to love Luke. She hadn't meant to.

The first moment he touched her, her skin had been crawling.

She'd watched him for months. Learned where he worked. Where he played football. Where he drank, where he ate, where he shopped.

She'd suggested the pub for the Christmas party. It hadn't been the first time she'd been in the same place as him. But it had been the first time he'd noticed her.

She'd gone after him as part of the plan.

But something had changed over the weeks and months, as she got to know him.

He wasn't the person she'd always assumed he was.

He was a good man. That's what she'd come to believe.

He'd done something wrong in the past, but he had changed. And she couldn't square that circle and she couldn't stop herself feeling for him.

'Get your things,' Kevin says. He gets up and walks towards her.

She's still standing in the door frame.

'No,' Rose says, her voice small.

'What do you mean, no? Pack a fucking bag, Róisín.'

Rose pushes past Kevin. She picks up the wedding album and opens it on the first page to slip one of the photographs back inside its sleeve.

'You're kidding me,' Kevin says. 'You're worried I've torn a photo or something? You're bloody besotted, aren't you?'

Rose can't look at him.

'We were meant to do this weeks ago,' Kevin says. 'Did you forget, Ro? You were to move in and then do a runner because I'd come after you and he'd join you and bring the money and you'd

talk him into giving you the money so you could get away properly . . . why am I even reminding you of this? What happened?
What's gotten into you?'

She turns to face him. There's nothing but fury in his expression.

'Have you forgotten?' he says. 'Have you forgotten what he is?'

'He's not that man any more,' she protests. 'He's not who we
think he is.'

'Jesus Christ. You stupid, stupid girl.'

Kevin pokes her in the shoulder as he talks. Rose takes a step
back.

'Stop touching me.'

'Oh. Why? Is only Luke allowed to touch you now? Get your
bag and then you do what we agreed. You need to make it look
like you ran in a hurry.'

'I'm not doing it.'

'You *are* doing it. This is the set-up, Ro. Pack a bag, book a
flight and run.'

He pokes her again but this time it's more of a shove. He's angry
with her, angrier than Rose has ever seen Kevin and she's seen him
get pretty mad.

'Stop touching me! I'm not going through with it!' she yells.

'There was a plan,' he shouts back. 'You had one job.'

He shoves her again.

'Stop!' she cries.

But he's not listening to her. She can tell he's lost it.

There's nothing she can say that will make him understand why
she's done what she's done.

Kevin doesn't know him. He doesn't know Luke like she does.

He shoves her again. But this time, all the frustration and

confusion and rage that Rose has been keeping a lid on for the last nine months – no, the last nine years – comes out.

She shoves him back. She pushes him with every ounce of hate in her body and sends Kevin flying backwards, towards the unit by the door, the big bloody awkward thing with the sharp corners.

She hears the crack as his head hits it, and then Kevin is on his knees, absolutely stunned.

Rose stares at him, shocked.

He places his hand to his head, then brings it in front of his face to look at it. It's dripping with blood.

'Oh my God,' Rose cries.

Kevin's face drains of colour.

'It's okay,' he says.

Rose walks behind him. She gasps; the wound is spurting blood. The back of Kevin's T-shirt is already soaked through.

'Kevin, there's so much blood,' she cries.

He's shaking but he takes her hand.

'It's a head wound,' he says. 'It's okay. They bleed like this. It hurts but I'm okay. We need to staunch it.'

He pulls off his T-shirt. Rose feels like she's going to vomit. His blood is spraying, actually spraying.

Kevin clamps the T-shirt, already soaked, against the back of his head.

'Ro, we need ice.'

His teeth are chattering as the adrenaline courses through his body.

'I'm sorry,' Rose sobs. 'I'm so sorry.'

'Ro! Ice.'

Rose blinks.

She's a teacher. She knows injuries, she knows what she needs to do.

She has to pull herself together.

She runs and grabs an ice bag from the freezer, then races back to the bedroom and holds it to the wound.

All the while, she's praying she hasn't done proper damage. She prays Kevin is okay.

When they've got the bleeding under control and cleaned up in the bathroom, Rose makes them both cups of sugary tea.

They sit on the edge of the bed drinking it and Rose looks around.

Her choice of pastel colours has never looked so incongruous.

The room looks like an abattoir.

'I didn't mean to do that,' she tells him, her voice a whisper.

'I deserved it,' he says. 'I shouldn't have pushed you. I know you can't handle being touched. I shouldn't have made you do any of this. I'm sorry, Rose. Can you forgive me?'

She rests her head against his shoulder.

'Of course I can forgive you,' she says. 'Can you forgive me?'

'I love you,' he says.

Rose swallows the lump in her throat.

'Kevin, please. Let's forget this ever happened. I'll get my stuff. We'll just leave. I promise, I'll go with you and I won't come back. But I can't do the rest of it. I can't go through with it.'

She feels Kevin tense.

'Are you crazy?' he says. 'This is better, Ro. Look at this place.'

'I'll clean it up.'

Kevin turns and looks at her.

'Don't you see what this looks like?'

Rose feels the knot tighten in her stomach.

'It looks like somebody was killed in here,' Kevin says. 'We wanted to make it look like I'd attacked you, Ro. But what if . . .'

Kevin drifts off and looks around the room again. Rose watches him, her mouth dry with fear.

She doesn't know what he's thinking but she knows his brain works differently to hers and she's terrified what he's going to suggest, even before he says it.

'What if we change the plan?' he says. 'What if I attacked you and you fought back? What if you thought you'd killed me?'

'But I haven't killed you!' Rose can't keep the bewilderment from her voice. 'There's no dead body here. What are you going on about?'

Kevin's not looking at her now. His eyes have a manic glaze to them. Rose feels herself shrinking inside. She's seen him like this before.

'What if you took him with you when you ran?' Kevin says. 'Because you thought I was here, dead.'

'Then why would I need his money? You'd be dead, we'd be gone . . . Kevin, you're not making any sense. The point was I'd need his money to get *away* from you. That was how I'd get it.'

Rose grabs Kevin's hands, hoping she can bring him back to sanity, but he ignores her.

'He'd come back, Ro. He'd come back to get his money. You could send him back. And he'd see all this, but no dead body, and he'd know – he'd *know* I was coming for you. He'd be petrified and rush back to save you. Then I could attack him—'

'And get yourself killed? You've lost your mind.'

Rose is despairing now.

'Okay, I'd hire somebody else to go at him. He'd get into a fight, get himself arrested – and you'd be on your own. He'd beg you to take the money then. He'd want you to be safe.'

Rose stands up and starts to pace.

It's crazy. It's beyond crazy.

And it's exactly something Kevin would think up.

'What if he came back here, saw you weren't dead and just left me on my own in another country?' she says, her voice small.

'Ha! You really think he married you to abandon you? He's your saviour, Ro. He'll do anything for you. Won't he?'

Rose sighs.

'This is so much better,' Kevin says. 'He'll be climbing the walls. When he sees this, it'll tip him over the edge.'

'No, Kevin,' Rose groans. 'It will never work.'

But Kevin isn't listening to her.

He's always been like this. Ready to use every opportunity to his advantage.

He doesn't care what Rose thinks or wants.

Kevin, realising she's not as enthused as he is, pauses. He's trying to get the manic look off his face, Rose realises. He wants to reassure her that he's thought this through, that he's calm. That she can rely on him.

'I know you've started to have feelings for him,' he says. 'I should have considered that. I should have factored it in. It can't be easy living with somebody, making them love you, convincing them you love them back. It was bound to have an effect. Fake it until you make it, eh? And after everything you've been through. It's not like you've a great history with men, eh?'

Rose stares at the floor.

'You were vulnerable,' he says. 'I wish I'd known how much. I'm sorry.'

'Forget it,' Rose says. 'But please, let's just go.'

'Not before you tell me.'

'Tell you what?'

Kevin takes her hand.

She looks at him, this man she's loved for most of her life, despite his flaws.

'Who do you love more? Me or him?'

Rose flinches.

'What? How can you even ask that?'

'I'm asking because I know you've fallen for him. But it's only been nine months, Ro. Who do you love more? Me or him?'

Rose tries to cover the moment of hesitation.

'You,' she says. 'Obviously.'

'Then you need to listen to everything I'm about to say. I can fix this.'

Rose nods, slowly. She tries to quell the bad feeling in her stomach.

This wasn't the plan.

Kevin is scaring her.

And she, of all people, knows that going off-plan never ends well.

Donegal

They're sitting across from each other like they're strangers, which, Luke supposes, they are. She offered to make tea, and even though he declined, she's made it anyway and now there are two cups on the table, both untouched.

'Róisín Gallagher,' Luke says, sounding out the vowels in the surname like it's foreign to him. When, in reality, Gallagher is a name he hasn't stopped thinking about in a long time.

'How did you figure it out?' Rose asks.

'I didn't,' Luke says. 'I'm still trying to put it together. I think part of me wondered. Rose from Donegal? It felt like too much of a coincidence. But he had two kids, not one, and you were an only child. And then I got to know you and I thought, nobody is that good an actress.' He snorts. 'What did I know?'

She blushes.

'If you suspected something, why didn't you say at the start? You were the one who kept chasing me.'

Luke shrugs.

'I've thought about that a lot over the last few days. I think, deep down, I always thought karma would come for me. But, as time wore on with you, I convinced myself I was seeing ghosts.

You were . . . you. And even if I was wrong, I could see you were falling in love with me. I can't believe it was all a lie, Rose. Was it?'

She averts her eyes. He knows she won't admit it but he's sure of the answer, nonetheless.

'Everything else – the abusive ex, all of that . . .'

'Not a lie,' she says. 'The things I told you – they happened to me. I used the truth. Kevin Davidson was real. And my pain was useful in convincing you I was somebody who needed to be looked after. It was useful to get you to where I needed you to be. But I don't want to talk about me, Luke. You don't deserve to know anything about me bar what I want to tell you. Why don't we talk about you? Why don't we talk about what you did?'

Luke flinches at the anger and accusation in her voice.

He looks down at the cup of tea, hot steam still rising from the rim.

'Let me tell you a story,' he says. 'Will you let me do that?'

She shrugs in return. Her facial expression says, *Why not? It will change nothing.*

'It took me a while to get to where I was when you met me,' Luke says. 'I didn't have a great start. I've told you my father used to beat my mother. I didn't tell you that we were poor as hell and most of that was down to my dad thinking he could keep his family afloat with dodgy dealings. Which never panned out. He used to use me sometimes. Bring me shoplifting, send me running somewhere with stolen gear. He brought me to that shooting range because he and his mates were planning an armed robbery. Which, luckily for them, they fucked up before it even got off the ground. Imagine, getting your own kid to do that sort of stuff. I'd like to think if we'd had kids . . .'

Luke looks up at Rose. She looks away, quickly, but he can see her eyes are wet. For him or for herself, he doesn't know.

'I was a really clever child, Rose. But I wasn't given a good grounding and I knew I had to get away. I also think that how I was reared, who my dad was, it left a mark. When I finished school, I took something I was brilliant at – maths – and decided to use it in the way that would make me the most money. You know what hedge fund managing is like? It's brutal. Everything you've ever seen. *Wolf of Wall Street*, *The Big Short*, it really is as bad as they make it look. Greed is everything. But you don't make the big money straight away. At the start, you're a lackey, and you're looking at all these shirts around you making tonnes of cash and you want some of it.'

'You would have got there, anyway,' Rose says.

'Yes,' Luke admits. 'But I wanted to get there quicker. Because, and this is completely true, I fell in love. It wasn't for greed, just love. I worked for a guy, Nathan Sheils, and I had fallen really fucking badly for his wife. Mickey. I wanted to offer her something. So . . . that's where I was when I met Pádraig Gallagher.'

Rose looks at him sharply. Luke takes a deep breath. He doesn't know how to present this story in any way that makes him look less lousy. And he knows she won't believe him, anyway, if he tries to excuse his actions.

He has to be honest.

'Pádraig had a lot of money to invest,' Luke says. 'Four million. He'd sold his family cement quarry and he didn't want to open a new business and build it up again; he just wanted to set himself and his kids up for life. We met in a bar in London when he was over on business and we became friends – he didn't even know I was a trader at the start, did you know that?'

Rose nods.

'But when he found out, I was the obvious guy to invest for him. Even though I was young and inexperienced and who the hell would trust me? Pádraig did. Your father trusted me. He thought I was a decent sort and he wanted a nice, safe investment – all his money in one good pot.'

Rose wipes tears from her eyes.

'You know how I did it?' he asks her.

'Yes,' she says, meeting his gaze. 'My dad figured it out. He told me, the week before he died. The week before he sat in his bed and put his shotgun in his mouth. On Christmas Eve.'

Luke winces and swallows, hard.

'It was only half a lie at the start,' he says. 'I didn't tell him the truth because I thought I could make him so much money, he'd be thrilled. I had split his investment without telling him, you see. He wanted it all invested in one place and I thought he was an idiot. I put three million into a portfolio that looked set to perform, a portfolio that he agreed to. And I figured I'd play with the rest and make him proper money. Then something came across my desk and I realised there was a way of making more than even I'd imagined. The portfolio I'd invested in for your father was with a company making a new type of plastic. A compostable one, well ahead of its time. Lots of interest in it, all very ethical, all very profitable. But there was a move against it from within the traditional plastics industry and a rumour started about the research underpinning the new plastic.'

Luke takes another deep breath. His chest feels tight. Every fibre of his being is ashamed of who he was back then.

'I shouldn't have done what I did. Nathan and his boss had loose rules, even as cutthroat as they were, about shorting our own clients' stocks. But I shorted the plastic company and bet on the traditional rivals. I did it so much, it worked.'

'You collapsed the new plastic company's shares.'

'Yes. Without my bosses knowing.'

'And you did it using my father's money. You made him bet against himself.'

'Yes. It shouldn't have worked. It was only a million. But every day it increased and then I had so much to play with – I destroyed that company. But I hadn't told Pádraig and when he saw the new plastic company collapse, he thought he'd lost it all. He presumed that was where all his money was. I was planning to tell him that actually, I'd done something very clever. And he was going to be a rich man because I'd used his money to make an absolute fortune with the rival company. But I didn't. I can't explain how or why I made that decision. It just . . . happened.'

'He found out,' Rose says. 'He wasn't stupid. Over the following year, he read the trade papers every day and researched everything he could. He saw what had happened to the plastic company, how it had been traded against. They held it up as a case example of a hedge fund attack. He started to put two and two together. At first, he thought he was being paranoid. He knew you. He liked you. I think you could have convinced him he was being delusional but you wouldn't take his calls. That's when he knew you were hiding something.'

'I always thought he'd figure it out,' Luke says. 'So I was afraid to speak to him. And by that stage, I was in trouble. I was panicking that I would be found out and I didn't know if your dad would be the one to rat me out. He was a good man. Much better than I could ever be. But he would have wanted justice. I had ten million in the bank. I wanted to keep it. I figured your dad would be fine. He was a brilliant man. He'd start up a new company . . . he'd be fine.'

Luke looks down at his hands. He can't justify what he did or who he was back then. But he can remember the shock he felt when he saw the news. He'd been keeping an eye, of course, on Pádraig. From afar. Hoping one day he'd see that the man had recovered or, if not, that maybe Luke could make it up to him somehow.

But he never got the chance to make amends, because Pádraig took his own life.

'I kept investing the money,' Luke says. 'I couldn't spend it. I thought, one day, something will come along and I can do some good with it.'

Rose stares at him, shaking her head.

'You killed my father,' she says.

'I know.'

'He couldn't start up a business again. He felt he'd let everybody down. He'd never so much as gambled on the Grand National before then. We weren't destitute, not by any means, but that money was meant to be for our future. And you took it away and left him feeling like the idiot who'd blown it all, the stupid idiot who'd trusted somebody he liked and got completely conned. He got more and more depressed and there was nothing any of us could do to help him. He killed himself, Luke, and my mother died heartbroken because of it. Even the doctors said it. It was cancer, but she could have fought it. She just didn't want to. You destroyed their lives and you destroyed mine. I had nobody keeping me on the rails after that, do you understand? I had no anchor. That's how I met Kevin Davidson. That's what you did.'

'Rose, if I could turn back the clock, if I could feel every bit of that pain for you, I would. I swear on my life.'

They can't look away from each other. He knows that as much as she hates him for what he did then, she is still utterly torn about how she feels about him now.

'Rose, will you tell me how you did it?' he asks. 'Will you tell me how it was for you?'

They don't hear the door open.

Luke turns his head and finds himself looking down the barrel of a shotgun.

'Kevin!' Rose yells.

Luke's eyes widen.

Luke looks at Rose. He still can't figure it out.

Why is she still with Kevin, if he was so abusive to her?

'This is my brother,' Rose says, looking at Luke. 'Kevin Gallagher.'

Donegal

2013

Rose doesn't want to ask her father for the laptop she so desperately needs but she's also stymied as to how she's going to get it.

Things have been tight around the house. Not that her parents would ever burden her with it, but she can see it in their faces, hear it in the whispered conversations late at night out on the porch patio.

She shouldn't still be living at home. She should be contributing. But continuing with her master's in education has made her father so happy. He doesn't want her to work. He wants her to study and end up in a job she and he can be proud of. It's the only thing he's ever wanted from her. And he's so depressed right now, it's all she can do for him to try to make him happy.

So she can't earn, and she can't ask for money.

She wishes she had Kevin's natural tendency towards oblivious-ness. He'd wandered into the sitting room the week previous and announced he needed money to replace his car tyres.

Their father gave it to him, of course. And Rose watched as their mother mentally subtracted the amount from their bills fund.

It's been like this since the Loss. That's what they call it. The Loss, with a capital L. Not the bad investment, not the risky choice, not the . . . trusting a man who never should have been trusted with their money.

The Loss.

The strain of it is permanently etched on to Rose's father's face.

It's breaking him. He can't come back from it. Maybe twenty years ago, when he was younger and fitter and had it in him to start again. But he can't. Not this time.

And she's worried what it will do to him, what it will do to their family.

Rose is out in the garden, her mother is in Letterkenny shopping for the meagre Christmas they can afford to have, when she hears it.

She knows what it is, even while she tells herself that's not what it is.

Her feet refuse to move, her hands refuse to drop the shovel she's been using to clear some snow from the hilly drive.

She just stands there and thinks, life insurance. He knows how much he's worth in life insurance.

But while she's thinking that, she can hear movement and then she realises. Kevin. Kevin is in the house.

Rose finds her younger brother cradling their dead father, half his brains blown out, the gun on the floor.

Donegal

2017

The nightclub in Letterkenny is heaving. The drink is overpriced, more Dublin than Donegal. And the whole place could do with a few windows being opened to let some air cool down the hot, sweating bodies packed on to the dance floor.

Rose doesn't care about any of that. She loves it. She loves losing herself in the crowd, the sense of being one of many, not the one, not Rose Gallagher of, yes, those Gallaghers. The one with the father who . . .

She throws her hands up in the air as the bass thrums and then takes the shot offered to her.

Kevin Davidson has been buying her drinks all night. Kevin Davidson, who every woman in here would like to go home with.

Rose knows the score. Kevin is no angel. She thinks this as she looks into his big, brown, angelic eyes; he has that puppy-dog look down pat.

His family have a lot of money and rumour is, they didn't come into it from hard graft alone. And Kevin is known to get into the odd scrape, to be a bit handy in a fight.

Rose doesn't care about that, either. Lads get into scraps. Her brother Kevin can't be kept away from them. Ever since their mother died, he's been venting his grief through violence. He's filled with rage but he's not big enough to be the guy inflicting the most damage. He mostly sustains it.

Rose hopes he'll grow out of it. She wants to stop worrying about him. She wants somebody to worry about her, for a change.

Kevin leans in and licks the sambuca that's dribbled on to her chin, then stands back and grins at her, his dimples on show.

Rose is weak at the knees for him.

He'll take care of her.

Donegal

2020

Her brother has barely left her bedside since they admitted her. Rose was aware of him when she came to, feeling like every inch of her was broken, but she hasn't been able to speak for a few days and she doesn't know what to say to him now.

They had fallen out of touch for a while. She imagines it was the hospital that rang him. He's still down as her next of kin. But they haven't spoken in over a year. Partly because Kevin Davidson didn't want her talking to anybody. Partly because her brother needed too much from Rose. He's never got over what happened to their parents. He's never grown up. He has aggressive, manic mood swings and Rose can't deal with them, even if they're not directed at her the way Kevin Davidson's are. They're still too much.

She can't talk, but he can. He holds her hand like it's glass and that's about right because Rose feels like glass. The hospital has glued her back together but she'll never be the same. She'll always be cracked from what he did to her. Kevin Davidson made sure that even if she did leave him, she'd always bear the scars of what he did to her. Not on the outside. On the inside.

'If I'd known,' her brother says, fervently, with tears in his eyes. 'If I'd known, I'd have killed him.'

Rose nods. Her brother couldn't kill anybody. But she understands what he means.

He tells her Máire Davidson is sitting downstairs in the hospital waiting room. She wants permission to come up, from Rose herself. She won't force her way in.

'She's angry,' her brother tells her. 'Furious. At him, not you. I can see it in her. But Rose, you know whose fault this is? Davidson, sure, but it's not only his. It's Luke Miller's. This all started with him. Every shit thing that's happened to us. Do you think Dad would have let you spend time with Kevin fucking Davidson?'

Rose sighs. She hates Luke Miller – as much, if not more than, her brother does – but what can they do about it? How can they get revenge?

'He still has Dad's money, you know,' Kevin says. 'Rose, I've been thinking.'

Rose can barely turn her head to look at her brother.

'Máire Davidson will offer you money or something. It's what her sort do. But . . . there might be something else you can ask her for.'

At this, Rose croaks a 'What?'

She's half expecting her brother to suggest they ask the Davidsons to take care of Luke Miller.

Maybe it's not a bad idea.

But when her brother tells her what he's thinking, Rose can't even respond.

A set-up. Shame him and get their money back.

It's too crazy to consider.

And yet . . .

'You want to get out of here, don't you?' he says. 'Do you want to stay in Donegal with that animal still here? You could easily move to London.'

Rose doesn't want to stay in Donegal.

And later, after she's spoken to Máire Davidson and she knows what's going to happen to Kevin, Rose starts to add to the plan on her own.

London

2020

London is so much bigger and busier than Rose could ever have imagined. It terrifies her but she's also adjusting to it well. Máire helped her get a job and an apartment and Rose has taken the opportunity presented to her to carve out a whole new life.

And that life, as well as the teaching career and being the new, improved Rose Gillespie, also involves following Luke Miller wherever he goes.

Once Rose found where he worked, it wasn't long before she was able to track down his gym, his local pub, where he played football.

She's been studying every aspect of his life, learning everything she can about him. She knows he doesn't come from money. A conversation with an old neighbour has given Rose her biggest piece of help so far. Things weren't perfect in the Miller household. Luke's father used to beat his mother, and possibly Luke the odd time, too.

When Rose tells Kevin this, they both know what it means.

'You can use what happened to you,' Kevin says. 'With Davidson. Miller is bound to be sympathetic. And that way, you're not always lying. It's easier, when there's some truth.'

'Isn't it a bit clichéd?' Rose asks. 'To want to save a woman because your mother was abused?'

'Absolutely,' Kevin says. 'Clichéd and very common. You just play up to it and he'll be putty in your hands. Make him think Kevin's coming after you.'

Rose flinches. Play up to it. As if she has to pretend to be haunted by her ex.

Then she tells her brother what's happened to the real Kevin Davidson and how they can now pretend he's still after her. But it won't be her ex . . . it will be her brother, playing a role.

They plan it for months. What they'll do, how they'll do it.

And then Kevin promises to back off. He understands Rose can't do this with him breathing down her neck.

'I mean it,' Rose says. 'He has to believe you're a ghost and I'm on the run from you. And he can't know I have a brother. He probably knows Dad had two kids so I'm going in with the story I'm an only child. There's no point hiding that I'm from Donegal, Kevin, but I can change my back story.'

'You know what you're doing; I'll leave you to it until it's time,' Kevin says.

Rose doesn't believe him. Kevin has no willpower. He'll want updates. He'll pretend it's because he's worried but it will really be because he can't think of anything else to do. And she can't deal with him while she's trying to lie her way into Luke Miller's heart.

She's not even sure she can do it. She almost pulls out, in fact. But then, a few weeks before Christmas, she's walking through an old cemetery and there it is. A random grave, but with her father's name on it. Pádraig Gallagher.

She hasn't been home in years. And she misses having somewhere to go to remind herself that she was happy once, that her family was happy once.

It's the grave that convinces her to do it.

The next day, she suggests to her colleagues a nice pub where they could have their Christmas party.

They all agree. It sounds like a great place to have a drink.

And it's Luke Miller's local.

Donegal

Mickey has never met Máire Davidson but she has a feeling that, despite their different life paths, Máire might be a woman after Mickey's own heart.

Máire is the one who has found out where Rose and Kevin Gallagher are currently living, and Mickey and Elliot are almost there.

Elliot has told Mickey about the conversation he had with Máire after his bruising ordeal. Máire had been frank with Elliot. She knew he wasn't police or a threat, and she also knew he was the sort to keep digging, so she'd decided to help him out.

Máire had never been fond of Kevin, she explained. She knew what he was.

When she found out he was seeing Róisín Gallagher, a girl he'd met in Letterkenny, she'd warned him to watch himself. Máire, a strong woman herself, looked into the Gallagher family and could see Róisín had had it hard over the years. A father who'd taken his own life after losing the family's money, a mother who died from cancer shortly afterwards. Róisín was fragile, vulnerable, and susceptible to Kevin's bullshit.

The first time Máire heard Kevin had gotten handy with Róisín, she'd spoken to the girl herself and told her to steer clear of her brother.

But Róisín thought she was in love and, to be fair to her, Kevin could be a right charmer when he wanted to be.

Kevin obviously warned Róisín after that not to speak to his family.

And things went quiet.

Through hearsay, Máire knew the slaps were becoming beatings.

And then Róisín did try to get away . . . but Kevin taught her a lesson.

Rape.

Máire had had it happen to her once, and she had done to that man what she was determined to do to her brother.

She put him in the ground.

Kevin had always been a liability. He would be more so in prison.

The Davidson family met. It was a difficult decision but the course of action was accepted and agreed. Family came first but, in this instance, the wider family was at risk from somebody within.

Róisín was taken care of. All the girl had wanted was a new identity and money to go to London.

Kevin was taken care of.

His body would never be found.

When Elliot showed Máire Davidson the still taken from airport CCTV of Kevin Davidson, she'd immediately realised who it was.

It wasn't her brother. It could never have been.

It was Róisín Gallagher's brother, also named Kevin.

It had only taken a little more detective work by Elliot to get to the bottom of what had happened.

Rose and Kevin had leaned into the truth when they made their plan to get Luke Miller.

Rose had an abusive ex named Kevin Davidson. Kevin Gallagher just had to set up a fake online life in the name of Davidson for anybody to search, organise some forged documents, and he became Kevin Davidson. Kevin Gallagher was the one who'd met the former prisoner in Derry and learned how to establish a fake identity for himself. Rose's had been sorted by the Davidsons, but her brother couldn't exactly approach them when he intended to falsify being one of their clan.

Mickey doesn't know everything yet. She can only guess that the money Luke possesses must have been obtained by doing something very wrong, most likely to do with the Gallagher family.

But now she wants to know the truth.

She hadn't lied to Nathan.

Her curiosity really is piqued.

They turn on to a lonely road that runs alongside the Atlantic Ocean.

Up ahead, there's a single dwelling.

'We're here,' Elliot says.

Kevin hasn't lowered the shotgun.

Rose looks between her brother and her husband. Because that's who he is now, Luke Miller. Her husband.

'Kevin, don't do this,' she says.

'He's meant to be in jail,' Kevin says. 'That was the plan.'

'It wasn't the plan,' Rose cries, exasperated.

'It became the plan and it worked, didn't it!' Kevin shouts. 'Except, now he's sitting here. How do you keep getting away with it, Miller? How do you keep destroying people's lives then walking free?'

'I'm not free,' Luke says. 'I broke bail. The cops will be after me and I've promised to go back to Saint-Thérèse. I'll serve my time.'

He's holding his hands up, defensively, but Rose notes that Luke is not scared. He's resigned.

'Was that the plan?' Luke asks, and now he's looking at Rose. 'To have me kill somebody? It's poetic but . . . Jesus. Pretty fucking dark. How did you know I'd do it? I saw your face that day. You didn't expect me to buy that gun. You'd no idea I was doing that.'

Rose shakes her head.

'Of course I didn't want that,' she says. 'The original plan was to wind you up so you were on edge in Saint-Thérèse. I wanted to make you believe Kevin was coming for me and that he was a psychopath. Kevin had the idea of hiring somebody to scare you into doing something stupid. If you didn't attack him, I was supposed to stab him. I knew you'd take the blame for me. Williams was only meant to be injured, but you would be in trouble and probably in custody and Kevin said you'd give me the money and tell me to get off the island. When I'd left, we'd tell you that I'd been lying to you all that time. That was the plan. It was to get revenge. Not to kill someone.'

'The new plan was better,' Kevin says, staring at Rose, his voice pleading.

'It was fucking stupid!' Rose snaps.

'You took the bullet out of the first chamber,' Luke says.

Rose drags her eyes away from Kevin.

'I should have taken them all but the gun felt too light unloaded and I thought, he'll only fire once. And then Williams will come at him and I'll cut him. Kevin said he'd get a big guy, capable of defending himself but not dangerous enough to cause us any real harm. It got out of hand. It was an insane thing to do. I'll never forgive myself for it.'

'I don't understand,' Luke says, looking between them. 'The body in the apartment, all the drama . . . Mickey said there was blood everywhere. How did you get all that blood?'

'An accident,' Rose says. 'We fought and I pushed Kevin and hurt him.'

Luke is staring at Rose, pain and confusion on his face.

'But I sent Mickey to the apartment. She was the one who told me there was no body there. How did you know I'd do that?'

'I didn't,' Rose says, honestly. 'I thought you'd go back yourself. I begged you to go back. I knew you'd left the money there. I'd seen your bank accounts so I knew you had the money somewhere else. You had a safe – it had to be something in there, and I found the chip one day. But I couldn't use that chip without you.'

Luke places his head in his hands. Rose knows he can't make sense of it because she knows how utterly insane it all is.

She shouldn't have listened to Kevin. She shouldn't have indulged him. Losing their parents like that, then seeing what happened to his sister afterwards, did something to him.

And for a while, Rose had thought he was right. She'd wanted revenge as much as he did. It seemed fair and just, that Luke would end up being punished and betrayed.

The last thing Kevin had said to her in the apartment that day was a reminder that Rose's favourite book was *Rebecca*.

We can do a Mrs Danvers on Luke, he'd said. *Make him paranoid and scared and panicky. It will be easy.*

That was what had made up Rose's mind, because wasn't that what Luke had done to their father?

He'd driven him mad.

But Rose wasn't mad and in the cold light of day . . .

'I wasn't acting all the time,' Rose says. 'But I do hate you, Luke. I hate you for what you did.'

'And now what?' Luke asks. 'Are you going to let him shoot me?'

Luke looks at Kevin at the same time as Rose does. Rose fears Kevin is now capable of it. He's not right. Not any more. Even hiring Jeremiah Williams, who looked so much like the real Kevin Davidson. What had he been thinking? Rose had nearly wet herself with fear that night when Williams came through the French doors.

'I deserve it,' Luke says, defeat in his voice. 'Nobody knows I'm here. But I suggest you don't do it in your fucking kitchen. Take me somewhere. Get it done.'

'I don't think so.'

Rose's head whips around in shock.

Mickey and a black man have just come into the kitchen behind Kevin. The black man is holding a gun to Kevin's head, but his hand is shaking, like he's not used to brandishing a weapon. Not that Kevin is aware of that. He just feels the muzzle against his skin and he looks at Rose, scared.

'What are *you* doing here?' Luke gasps.

'We just called in for a cuppa,' Mickey says.

She eyes Rose. Rose can't look at her.

'What do you want to happen here?' Mickey says. She's addressing Luke but her gaze is still on Rose. 'If I ring the police, these two will be arrested and it will help your case in Saint-Thérèse. But you'll be arrested too, Luke. I've checked. Ireland has an extradition treaty with the island as part of a European Union deal. The Irish police will most likely take you into custody.'

Rose looks to Luke and then to her brother.

Kevin has reluctantly lowered his weapon.

He'll never get over this, Rose thinks, and she's not sure if she's thinking of Luke or Kevin or both of them.

'Call them,' she says, at the same time as Luke says, 'Don't call them.'

Luke and Rose look at each other.

'Don't,' Luke says, softly. 'They don't deserve any more pain from me.'

Mickey is frowning at Luke now.

'I'm going to leave with Mickey,' Luke says. 'Unless you want me to stay?'

He aims this question at Rose.

Rose feels a lump in her throat.

This man, somebody she had made into a monster in her head . . . she is looking at him now and she can't put a name on what she feels. She's afraid to.

'No,' she says.

Luke looks at her for a few seconds more, then nods, tears in his eyes.

'I understand,' he says.

He stands up.

'I can never apologise enough to you both,' he says.

He places a small silver chip on the table, and a piece of paper.

'But I can give you this. It's your father's money and what I made from it. And the access codes. It's for both of you.'

'I don't want it,' Rose says.

'It's our money,' Kevin snaps. 'You should have let me take it from her in that hotel room.'

He nods at Mickey. Rose flinches. She'd practically had to drag Kevin out of the room to stop him from searching Mickey for the chip. Everything had gotten out of hand. It wasn't about the money any more.

'You take it, then, if it means so much to you,' Rose retorts.

She wonders now if that's all Kevin ever wanted, if that's all that mattered to him.

She turns and looks out the window.

She hears Luke, Mickey and the guy with the gun leave.

She hears her brother take the chip from the kitchen table.

And then she shuts out all the noise and everything around her and the memory of her father lying dead in his bed, and she lets herself feel something other than sadness and pain and anger.

She feels regret. She feels a terrible regret because she knows she truly loved Luke Miller and now it's over.

London

Luke has barely spoken since they left Donegal.

They're in his apartment now and Elliot has judiciously decided to wait downstairs while Luke and Mickey talk. Mickey just wants to get it over with. She wants to go home. She wants to see Nathan. She wants her husband and normality.

But she also wants to know what Luke is going to do next.

'I'll book a flight for Saint-Thérèse in the next couple of days,' he tells her.

'Are you sure?' Mickey asks. 'You will get away with it. If you want. They gaslighted you, Luke. You can prove it. Not from over there, but you can from here.'

Luke shakes his head.

'You don't get it, Mickey. Rose and Kevin need to see me in jail so they can move on. And I deserve it. I cost their father his life. I took Williams' life. I need to take responsibility for what I did.'

Mickey sighs. She will speak to Inspector Alleyne. She knows the sentence will be harsher for Luke because he fled the jurisdiction. But she's hoping his voluntary return will be taken into account. It's like she told Luke when all this started: sometimes the law allows for a shocked reaction. As long as people own up eventually.

'Well, I can only wish you luck with it,' Mickey says. 'I can't do any more to help. But I'm sorry it came to this. I don't know how or why you took their father's money but . . . if you feel you need to answer for it, so be it.'

Mickey stands and prepares to leave.

'It was when I was working for Nathan,' Luke says.

Mickey hesitates.

'I traded from the inside. I bet against a company portfolio the firm had clients invested in. Nathan and Richard found out. I hadn't done anything illegal, technically, but I had bent their rules and I had cheated Pádraig Gallagher. Nathan gave me a choice. He'd contact Pádraig and report me for fraud and have me arrested. Or I could walk away from you and never tell you why. I chose to walk away.'

Mickey stares at Luke, her insides doing somersaults.

'I didn't want to,' Luke says. 'I agreed in a panic. I said I'd do what Nathan wanted and then I changed my mind. I told him I had to tell you the truth and he could have me arrested, I didn't care. I loved you. I want you to know that. I was scared but I loved you and I was willing to take the consequences and try to convince you I was worth taking a second chance on. But you'd gone home then. You'd gone back to him. And I couldn't put you through any more pain.'

Mickey is trembling.

She wishes he hadn't told her what he just has.

She stares down at the handbag in her hands.

She's spent her life trying to help people, women mainly, get away from controlling men.

And she'd had no idea that ten years ago she was the pawn in a battle between two of them.

'Goodbye, Luke,' she says.

Downstairs, Elliot opens the passenger door for her.

'Home?' he asks.

'No,' she answers. 'Let's go to the office. I'm sure we have cases piling up.'

'Your hubby has been calling.'

Mickey looks out the windscreen.

'Let him,' she says.

Epilogue

Saint-Thérèse

The jail cell in Saint-Thérèse is rougher than the custody cell that Luke had been held in when he was first detained.

It gets tough at times but he's promised himself that he will get through this, his purgatory. But it's not as bad as it could have been. He has two years to serve. His lawyers managed to get the charge reduced to manslaughter, and his character references, the fact he's a foreign citizen, and a psychological evaluation explaining his fear on the night of the shooting all contributed to a lighter sentence.

But he still has to serve his time.

Luke follows the prison guard towards the visitors' room. He doesn't know who's there to see him. He speaks regularly to his friends but none of them have said they'll be flying out yet. Xander is keeping an eye on the apartment but even he's in shock at what happened. Luke hasn't even told them the whole truth. Not because he doesn't want to, but because he wants to keep Rose out of it as much as he can.

All they know is that somebody broke into their villa and Luke shot him fatally and Rose isn't able to deal with her new husband being a convicted criminal.

He's hoping his visitor is Mickey. That last day in his apartment, he realised, immediately, that telling her the truth had been a fucking terrible idea. It had been for his benefit, not hers. He'd needed her to know he wasn't as bad as she thought he was. He needed her to forgive him.

He'd seen the look in her eyes as she absorbed the news and it struck him – she still blamed Luke.

And then he realised that she'd fallen back in love with Nathan and Luke's revelation had destroyed all that.

He's written to her repeatedly to apologise but she never answers. He knows she's moved, though. His last letter came back with a 'not at this address' scrawled across the envelope.

Luke follows the prison guard through the door to the visitors' room. It's busy; all the other inmates are meeting family and friends.

The guard points at a desk down the end.

It takes Luke a moment to realise who's sitting there.

Her hair is shorter but she looks more like herself.

She looks like the woman he fell in love with.

It's Rose.

He sits across from her, his heart beating hard.

'Hi,' he says.

'Hi,' she says.

'I – What are you doing here?'

'You handed yourself in.'

'Yeah.'

Luke is shaking his head in amazement, puzzled.

'Mickey told me.'

'She won't speak to me. Understandably. I can't believe . . . what are you doing here?'

'Luke, do you forgive me?'

Rose's voice is small, scared. He wants to take her hand. He wants to hold her.

'Are you serious?' he says. 'Of course I do. There is nothing to forgive. I deserved everything I got. I'm a terrible person, Rose. I really am.'

Rose looks down at the table. When she looks up, Luke realises she's reaching across to him. He sees the guard is distracted and takes her hands and every part of his body tingles with relief.

'I forgive you,' she says.

Luke closes his eyes. It feels like an indescribable weight has lifted from his chest.

'And I'm sorry,' she adds.

'Don't be,' he replies. 'I can never stop begging your forgiveness for what I did. I'll never let myself off the hook. You got your revenge. I had it coming. I started this. Is your brother okay?'

'He seems happier. With the money. He's travelling. I haven't talked to him in a while.'

'I'm sorry about that. But I'm glad he's in a better place.'

They sit in silence for a few moments.

'I don't know where we go from here,' she says. 'But I'd like us to be friends.'

Luke looks at their entwined hands.

'I'll prove myself to you,' he says.

She doesn't respond. But she squeezes his hands.

And it's enough.

London

The woman Mickey is driving to the airport reminds her of Petra. She's small and looks like a strong gust would blow her sideways but she's also starting to regain her feistiness.

'Mona-gan?' she says, bewildered.

'Monaghan,' Mickey corrects. 'The G is silent. Think of it spelled as Mona-han with just a H.'

'Right. And where the fuck is it?'

Mickey laughs.

'It's just north of the middle of Ireland. But you don't have to stay there. My friend, he's a guard, will meet you in Dublin and drive you up. He'll get you a safe place for a couple of months. If you want to move on, move on. I'll let you know when you're good to leave.'

'Okay. I always liked travelling. Before he stopped me from doing it. I wouldn't mind going somewhere warm.'

'You'll appreciate somewhere warm after Monaghan, let me tell you.' Mickey smiles.

Her smile dies when her phone starts to ring on the hands-free and she sees the caller ID.

Nathan, again. He just won't let up. He's phoned her every day since she's moved out.

She still can't forgive him.

To have left her suffering such heartbreak after Luke, and never to have told her the truth . . .

A tiny part of her understands. Another part of her is furious at him for controlling the situation, for never letting her know she'd had a choice.

She knocks the phone off.

She thinks one day, if he keeps this up for long enough, she'll phone him back. When she's ready. If he gets tired before that or gives up, then she'll have her answer.

They pull up at Heathrow.

Her client gets out. Rachel is waiting at the front door. She waves at Mickey. It's handy for Mickey now that she has a second contact at the airport.

'Are you going home now?' her client asks.

'No, I'm actually picking somebody up from here,' Mickey says.

'Another broken butterfly?' the woman asks.

Mickey smiles.

'A friend. And his family.'

Marcel, his wife and their three children should be almost through baggage and passport control. Mickey is going to park up. And when she collects them, she's going to drive them to their hotel and then show them around London. Her London. Marcel will then understand why she moved here. Then they'll meet Elliot and Nana and go for dinner, and Mickey is really looking forward to that, being surrounded by people whose company she enjoys and who enjoy being with her.

'Hey,' Mickey calls, before her client walks away. 'You said somewhere warm . . . have you ever thought about the Caribbean?'

Acknowledgements

As always, thank you to my publishing team, to everybody in Quercus and Hachette, and especially my editor Stef Bierwerth and agent Nicola Barr. Each book brings us a little closer to the yacht. Or rowboat. One or the other.

Thank you to my family and friends, particularly Martin and my children for letting me disappear into my criminal headspace for days at a time. I hope I've done you proud.

Thank you to my TV writing partner David Logan for reading a first draft of this and cheerleading it all the way. Who's the better writer again, Dave?

And to you, the person who's reading this now. I'm going to presume you read the book before you got here. I hope you enjoyed it and thank you for choosing my story to keep you company. It's an honour. Also, I have eleven more books if you fancy checking out my back catalogue.